THIS IS
HAPPINESS

THIS IS HAPPINESS

NIALL WILLIAMS

BLOOMSBURY PUBLISHING
LONDON · OXFORD · NEW YORK · NEW DELHI · SYDNEY

BLOOMSBURY PUBLISHING
Bloomsbury Publishing Plc
50 Bedford Square, London, WC1B 3DP, UK

BLOOMSBURY, BLOOMSBURY PUBLISHING and the Diana logo are trademarks of
Bloomsbury Publishing Plc

First published in Great Britain 2019

A catalogue record for this book is available from the British Library

Library of Congress Cataloguing-in-Publication data has been applied for

ISBN: HB: 978-1-5266-0933-5; TPB: 978-1-5266-0936-6; EBOOK: 978-1-5266-0934-2

2 4 6 8 10 9 7 5 3 1

Typeset by Integra Software Services Pvt. Ltd.
Printed and bound in Great Britain by CPI Group (UK) Ltd, Croydon CR0 4YY

To find out more about our authors and books visit www.bloomsbury.com
and sign up for our newsletters

To the memory of
P. J. Brown (1956–2018)

All these squalls to which we have been subjected are signs that the weather will soon improve and things will go well for us, because it is not possible for the bad or the good to endure forever, and from this it follows that since the bad has lasted so long, the good is close at hand.

Miguel de Cervantes, *Don Quixote*

I

It had stopped raining.

Nobody in Faha could remember when it started. Rain there on the western seaboard was a condition of living. It came straight-down and sideways, frontwards, backwards and any other wards God could think of. It came in sweeps, in waves, sometimes in veils. It came dressed as drizzle, as mizzle, as mist, as showers, frequent and widespread, as a wet fog, as a damp day, a drop, a dreeping, and an out-and-out downpour. It came the fine day, the bright day, and the day promised dry. It came at any time of the day and night, and in all seasons, regardless of calendar and forecast, until in Faha your clothes were rain and your skin was rain and your house was rain with a fireplace. It came off the grey vastness of an Atlantic that threw itself against the land like a lover once spurned and resolved not to be so again. It came accompanied by seagulls and smells of salt and seaweed. It came with cold air and curtained light. It came like a judgement, or, in benign version, like a blessing God had forgotten he had left on. It came for a handkerchief of blue sky, came on westerlies, sometimes – why not? – on easterlies, came in clouds that broke their backs on the mountains in Kerry and fell into Clare, making mud the ground and blind the air. It came disguised as hail, as sleet, but never as snow. It came softly sometimes, tenderly sometimes, its spears turned to kisses, in rain that pretended it was not rain, that had come down to be closer to the fields whose green it loved and fostered, until it drowned them.

All of which, to attest to the one truth: in Faha, it rained.

But now, it had stopped.

Not that anyone in Faha noticed. First, because it happened just after three o'clock on Spy Wednesday and the parish was concertina'd inside the Men's Aisle, the Women's Aisle and the Long Aisle of the sinking church which at that time was still called St Cecelia's. Second, when the parishioners came outside their minds had been exalted by the Latin, and the suffering of Christ the Redeemer made inconsequential thoughts of anything else. And third, they and the rain had been married so long they no longer took notice of each other.

I myself am seventy-eight years and telling here of a time over six decades ago. I know it seems unlikely that Faha then might have been the place to learn how to live, but in my experience the likely is not in God's lexicon.

Now, that world, the one whose front doors were never closed in the daytime, whose back doors were never locked but unlatched and entered on an evening, where you stepped down, God bless, on to a flag floor into a cloud of turf and tobacco smoke, that one has perished. And though some of its people, like Michael Donnelly, Delia Considine, Mary Egan and Marty Brogan, have postponed the graveyard and are in lonely old houses out the country that are home to rheumatism and damp and the battle of the long afternoons, its doors are shielded by caution and fear of the corrosive nature of nostalgia. And because I'm antique myself now, aware that by the mercy of creation the soonest thing to evaporate in memory is hardship and rain, I understand that between then

3

and now, as between mystery and meaning, there's maybe too great a gap, and in the world you're living, this one, the one where it stopped raining in Faha on the Wednesday of Holy Week, might be too far, too remote in time and manner for you to enter.

Bear with me awhile; grandfathers have few privileges and the knowledge of your own redundancy has a keen tooth.

A hundred books could not capture a single village. That's not a denigration, that's a testament. Faha was no more nor less than any other like place. If you could find it, you'd be on your way somewhere else. The country is filled with places of more blatant beauty. Good luck to them. Faha doesn't care. It long since accepted that by dint of personality and geography its destiny was to be a place passed over, and gently, wholly forgotten.

To the Fahaeans, the rain then, both implausible and prehistoric in that valley where the fields were in love with the river, was a thing largely ignored. That it had once started was already a fable, as too now would become the stopping.

The known world was not so circumscribed then nor knowledge equated with facts. Story was a kind of human binding. I can't explain it any better than that. There was telling everywhere. Because there were fewer sources of where to find out anything, there was more listening. A few did still speak of the rain, stood at gates in a drizzle, looked into the sky, made predictions inexact and individual, as if they were still versed in bird, berry or water language, and for the most part people indulged them, listened as if to a story, nodded, said *Is that so?* and went away believing not a word, but to pass the story like a human currency to someone else.

The church at that time was not what it is or where it is now. Once Tom Joyce, sacristan, crossed the street in suit and waistcoat, climbed the twenty-seven steps of the belfry to ring what was still an actual bell, a bell blessed by the Bishop and heard in the seven townlands of the parish, people just walked out of their houses and went, the sinners as well as the saints. All routes into the village ran busy with bicycles, horses, carts, tractors and walkers. The roads out the country were not tarred yet, some not even gravelled. The one outside my grandparents' house was mud, tramped hard and soft and hard and soft again, it was foot- and wheel- and hoof-made and bowed upwards in its centre like a spine along which pulsed the townland, passing the open doors, and in that passing picking up and dropping off those pieces of news by which a place is made vital.

And so, for an hour before Mass, there was human traffic of all kinds. You stood outside the door and looked west and what you saw were heads, scarfed, capped or hatted, floating like hosts above the hedgerows. In the fields the cattle, made slow-witted by the rain, lifted their rapt and empty faces, heavy loops of spittle hanging, as though they ate watery light. The human procession, on foot, bicycle and cart, would gradually dwindle – the clack of horseshoes outliving the actual horse by several minutes – but finally it too was swallowed into the green hush. By the time Sam Cregg, whose clock ran slow, in fact and metaphor, passed in the long commandant coat and jodhpurs his brother the General had sent from Burma, the introit would have begun. All roads into the parish fell into an absolute quiet.

Faha then had more to it too than it does now. The shops were small but there were more of them, grocers, butchers, hardware, draper, chemist and undertakers, each implacably marked by the character of their owners. You shopped by blood and tribe. If you were related, however thinly, to Clohessy, or

Bourke, who both sold the same tea, flour and sugar, the same three vegetables and tins of imperishable foodstuffs, that's where you did your business. You didn't darken the door of the other. One of the privileges of living in a place forgotten is the preservation of individuality. In Faha, because the centre was distant and largely unknown, eccentric was the norm.

As decreed by mulishness, recalcitrance and tradition, the men gathered before Mass along the two windowsills of Prendergast's post office across from the church gates, with latecomers settling for the sloping one of Gaffney's Chemist. Faha's version of the Praetorian Guard, the men wore suits of brown and grey and hats or caps but no raincoats though the rain would have already saddled their shoulders and made necessary the stratagem of smoking their cigarettes backwards, inside the cup of the hand. They were men from out the townlands whose character was made crystalline by solitude. That they were going to attend church was not in doubt, but because of the thorny relation of religion to the masculine they would show no eagerness and shielded off any sense of the spiritual with a studied casualness and a mastery of the essential art of saying nothing.

People in Faha hadn't got the hang of parking yet. That Holy Week it was still five years before the introduction of the driving test, and another three before anyone in Faha would attempt to pass it. There were only ten cars in the parish. The drivers didn't mind if they just landed in the general vicinity of where they were headed, let out the children and the old people and the neighbours who had God-blessed the car when they got in and God-blessed the driver when they got out. If, like Pat Healy's, the car stuck halfway out and nothing could pass up or down where the street turned with hopeless yearning towards the grey tongue of the river, what matter, they were going to church, let the heathens be damned.

———————

Like those in the Ark, there was an unwritten order to how the parishioners came into St Cecelia's and where they sat. Because they were the same people who came each week, strangers and foreigners being then virtually unknown, you could close your eyes and know that Matthew Leary, first in and last out, was prostrate in the front pew, pate lowered, prayer-hands clasped out in front of him, the weight of his sins imponderable and awesome; that Mick Madigan didn't enter but for reasons unknown stood just outside the church doors in the rain; that though she had come that morning from a house you'd see in a famine museum the small upright pillar of Mary Falsey was at the very front of the Women's Aisle, her husband Pat sniffling with permanent headcold at the back of the Men's. You knew that Mrs Pender, who kept the cleanest house in the parish (her Sean now dust), sat with seven dangling Penders beside Kathleen Connor who was already thrice anointed, but would not depart for Heaven, it was said, until she knew her husband Tom was in the other place; that midway up the Long Aisle were the Cotter family, beautiful people, behind them the Murrihys, who all took the road to ruin and made few stops along the way, long-side or near enough them the Fureys, Sean the scholar who would die for love, overside, one proud pew (God bless the work) worth of McInerneys, one huddled abashed but no less seedful one of Morrisseys, each born in April nine months after the hay-making and each with something of summer in their natures. Some ways down the Long Aisle on the left the Liddys, Bridget and Jerome, with ten children who spent

7

their nights in three beds trying to kill each other, and in the daytime had the look of it. Near enough them, any number of Clancys, whose childhoods tasted of tears. Across from them, the Laceys, the four girls disguising their lameness from wearing hand-me-down shoes they had outgrown but which would not be replaced until Christmas. Behind them, Mick Boylan, who suffered from an incurable affliction called Maureen. Two pews from the front, Mona Clohessy, who, when he needed extra help in the shop, Tom had brought back as his wife from some prosperous farm up the country. Tom was no fool. Mona could sell toys to China. Behind Mona, Mina, a gaud. The Collinses, the Kings, Devitts, Davitts and Dooleys, Johnny Mac who had the kind of ugliness irresistible to Hegartys, Thomas Dineen a fine fiddle-player, and in fact the Dineens were that mystical thing, a musical family, and any of them could pick up an instrument and draw a tune from it.

Midways back, not too close to the saints at the front, or the sinners at the back, sat Doctor Troy and his three swans of daughters, looking as if they hadn't come in the door but had *landed* from another dimension where human beings got closer to beauty than they did in Faha. Perhaps by virtue of distant-breeding, dress, deportment, or the mystical numerology that decreed three the number of the divine, their presence alone was enough to trigger the silent ripples of a natural disturbance. Attraction is opaque and puzzling as an onion, but it's fair to say that in the parish of Faha the beauty of those girls provoked a torment, to which I was not alone in being defenceless.

I will say nothing more of the Troy sisters here, you'll meet them soon enough, but I'm gladdened to say that even now, inside this ancient chest, my heart still stirs at the mention of their name.

The Women's Aisle I can picture less easily. But bear with me. While all the men were unhatted, all the women had their heads covered, a throwback maybe to Bathsheba. Some women took the head-covering rule as an invitation to display, most notably Mrs Sexton who had a line in outlandish hats, one creation a kind of exotic wonderland with a hill of artificial flowers that were an Indies atop her, complete with tiny green hummingbird, and required significant mastery of equipoise as she came to the altar-rail.

———

Someone has said religion lasted longer in Ireland because we were an imaginative people, and so could most vividly picture the fires of Hell. And perhaps that's true. But despite all that would in time transpire and need to be rewritten in the record of the Church, it was part of the order of the world then and in ceremony and ritual had its own loveliness too. That Holy Week, St Cecelia's was dressed with flowers. The four-foot, more-or-less matching statues of Saints Peter and Paul, along with the hooded one of Saint Senan, and the one that was dubbed Saint Cecelia, had each had their faces painted for Easter and their chips mended. A fine musician on the concertina, Mrs Reidy put aside the jigs and reels, furrowed her brows and played the organ with a graven solemnity.

Father Coffey, the curate, was young then, and in vocational love with his new parish. Pale and thin as a Communion wafer, he was addicted to the Wilkinson Sword and shaved to the blood vessels. He had the raw look of a trainee saint and the glossy eyes of those in combat with their own blood. But he lived within the inviolate privacies of the priesthood then, so no one in Faha ever questioned or considered his welfare. Empurpled with the primacy of Easter, he was alone on the altar that afternoon. Father Tom, the PP, who had succeeded the Devil when he went by the name Canon Sully, was a man beloved in the parish. He had heard the confessions of every soul for forty years and was exhausted from absolution. From storing inside himself the sins of the congregation, he was suffering one of his regular chest infections.

To give young Father Coffey his due, that man would serve in the parish fifty-one years, confound the common narrative by doing more than one man's share of good, twice refusing edicts to be transferred, silently suffering what sanctions came from the Palace so that he could stay faithful to Faha, where in later years, unretired long after retirement age, white wires growing out his ears, a congregation of four souls for daily Mass that he'd say in his socks, two unresolved Morton's neuromae making shoes intolerable, he'd be robbed so often he'd take to leaving the key in the front door of the Parochial House, some coins and food on the table, until they took that table too.

That Spy Wednesday then, Father Coffey, his back to the congregation, closed his eyes and chinned the air. From the base of his throat he urged a plangent *Te Deum* to ascend, not yet knowing that as he did the heavens above cleared.

3

I was not in St Cecelia's that afternoon. I was seventeen. I had come down from Dublin on the train, not exactly in disgrace – my grandparents, Doady and Ganga, were too contrary and crafty for that – but certainly distant from grace, if grace is the condition of living your time at ease on the earth.

What I was like then is hard to capture, the Crowe-ness in me manifest mostly in self-contradiction, my character an uneven construct that swung between flashes of fixedness and rashness, immovability and leap. One such had landed me in a briary boarding school in Tipperary. Another had put me down in the thorny austerity of a seminary, and another out of there when I woke one night with a fear I couldn't name, but later came to think of as the fear I might not discover what it meant to live a fully human life.

I'm not sure what I thought that was at the time, but I had enough sense to know there was a lack, and somehow that was to be feared. If it is true that each of us is born with a natural love of the world, then the action of my childhood and schooling had been to vanquish it. I was too afraid of the world to love it.

It turned out that it was easier to enter the Church than to leave it. Father Walsh was my Spiritual Director. He had the pink, unmade lips of a baby, but the ice-blood of the county coroner. To ensure the seminarians remained single-minded, he was schooled in stratagems, gambits, wiles. His wavy hair, tamed by a gelatinous pomade, was jet-black; his skin had never seen the sun. In a room, weighty with the mahogany furniture favoured by the religious, his first tactic when I told him I was leaving was to say nothing at all. He tented his long fingers and tapped them, like a small church coming asunder and being pressed together. He didn't take his eyes off mine. Silently he ran through some inner arguments, the little lips tightening, his glasses glinting, until he reached a satisfactory conclusion. He nodded, as if in agreement with a Senior Counsel. Then he explained to me that I was *not* in fact leaving, that he would consider me on leave, in retreat, for a time. There were many examples from the lives of the saints. He was confident, he said, that when I saw what was 'out there' I would return, with deepened vocation. He stood, pressed the tip of his tongue between his lips, offered me his cold hand and a copy of Augustine's *Confessions*.

'May God go with you.'

I lived in a profound loneliness at the time. I am not sure why or how it happens that a person finds themselves on the margin of life, but there I was. I was the opposite of sure-footed. I couldn't get any purchase on the ground and was unable to see how to belong anywhere.

I came home from the seminary to Dublin, all rawness and intensity. My father, in deliberate revolt against his Crowe blood, was very careful in everything. He had few words, short dense eyebrows like dashes of Morse that lent him a look indecipherable. Your father is a mystery it takes your whole life to unravel. After my mother died, he had taken the required three days off, performed the public business of grief, and then gone back into his preferred purgatory of the Department where a legion of men in grey suits were busy inventing the State in their own likeness. It was a common stupidity then to think of your father as unreachable. I did not try to reach him until twenty years later, the year he was dying, and the first time I ever called him by his name. I'm older now than he was when he died and appreciate something of what it must have taken for him to stay living. It's a thing you can't quite grasp, I think, until you wake up an old man or woman and have to negotiate the way. At that time, we never embraced our fathers enough. I don't know about now. I embrace him and say his name, Jack, now that he's dead, which is the kind of foolishness old men allow. I'm not sure it does him any good. It helps me a bit sometimes.

For a few weeks then I had stayed at home, and he went to work. But there's something undoing about the dying light of mid-afternoon. In that empty old house on Marlborough Road all that had stitched me into this life came undone and I couldn't escape the feeling that folded against my back were wings that had failed to open.

I sometimes think the worst thing a young person can feel is when you can find no answer to the question of what you are supposed to do with this life you've been given. At moments you're aware of it balanced on your tongue, but not what comes next. Something like that. I can now say that another version of that happens in old age, when it occurs to you that since you've lived this long you must have learned something, so you open your eyes before dawn and think: *What is it that I've learned, what is it I want to say?*

Unable to stay at home any longer, with no money and nowhere else to go, I had come down to Clare that April, to my grandparents', to their long low farmhouse, that had originally been three rooms, then four, and four-and-a-half, and then five-ish, as seed overtook sagacity and the twelve Crowe brothers burst forth, my tearaway uncles whose first propulsion into the world did not stop when they had sacked Faha of all cups, medals, plaques and trophies, but continued until all but my careful father had rampaged into what Ganga said were the twelve corners of the world. There they would be rough-shod plasterers, happy-go-lucky layers of pipe, throwers-up of blocks, splintery off-square carpenters, speeding bus drivers, and in one unlikely case a Chicago policeman, but never be together again until back in Faha the famous day of Ganga's funeral, when it was discovered he had so many friends.

From that funeral, this memory: Ganga had a dog he loved called Joe, and, with that facility innate in dogs to recognise human goodness, Joe loved Ganga in equal measure. Joe was a small-sized crossbred black-and-white sheepdog of about a hundred in dog years, but it's fair to say he knew the lineaments of Ganga's spirit better than any living. On the day of the funeral, Joe was left inside the house, lying on the crocheted cushion he had long since learned to pull down from Ganga's chair, and which Doady had long since given up complaining about. The black cloud of uncles, cousins, near and distant, neighbours, and the two of the Conefreys who had been sworn in as staff of Carty's Undertakers, had finally floated out into the yard. The last, Uncle Peter, told Joe to mind the house, then he locked the door with the dog inside, and lifted his chin to follow his father to the church.

At the end of the Mass the brothers bore the coffin by turns out of St Cecelia's and down the hapless slope of Church Street. The entirety of west Clare was there. And, as the cortège reached the turn by Mangan's, there was Joe sitting waiting for it. 'There's Joe Crowe,' Mary Breen said, and without by-your-leave or beckon the dog rose from where he was sitting and joined the funeral procession and followed on to the graveside, from which he did not move the rest of that day. True as God.

———

Although it is a fact that each time I came to Faha I found it smaller and poorer than my boyhood had made it, the sense of it as a place of escape endured.

Doady and Ganga's house was built on a slope a field back from the river. The house was built in haste, Ganga said, because his ancestors had stolen the stones from the walls of the agent, Blackall, when he was above in Leinster.

Built in a puddle, Doady said, because his ancestors were frogs.

A short and almost perfectly round man with eyes always near to laughter and tufted hair that sat like a small wig on a football, Ganga had the large ears that God puts on old men as evidence of the humour necessary for creation. Perhaps following the prompting of his physiognomy, he had the philosophy that life was a comedy. Like one of those rubber figures that cannot be toppled, in him this philosophy was irrefutable, and despite the weighty evidence of life he insisted on a blithe insouciance which, for the most part, kept the acid of disillusionment at bay. (This may not have come entirely naturally; in time I discovered the ditches around the house were a graveyard for blue bottles of Milk of Magnesia.)

Doady, who was once a girl called Aine O Siochru, had come across river and mountain from the Iveragh peninsula in Kerry. *Why, I can never understand.*

'Ganga' I understood was what my infant tongue made of Grandfather, and he loved it and for his entire life I called him nothing else, but Doady, which came I think from Doodie, the name of my soother, sat less easily on her. Though she was the mother of twelve, succour was not apparent in her nature. But women are deeper than men, so it's unfair to say. What is true is that to survive she had pared away any surface softness, was as practical as her husband impractical, appeared to have small tolerance for the whimsy, dreaming, and grand designs of men in general, and Ganga in particular.

Doady had a narrow whiskered chin and a brownish complexion – her mother was a pipe-smoker in Kerry and had puffed out seven umber babies no bigger than smoke rings. She had a fierce attachment to fresh air. Fresh air was the cure for most things. She walked. Her shoes were shoes out of old times, square-heeled hooked-and-eyed with black laces running neatly crossways. The shoes of all grandparents are inestimable mysteries, hold them in your hand and they are strange and tender somehow, and hers were particularly so, polished and worn, mucked and puddled and polished again with that kind of human resolve that to me is inexplicably moving. She'd walk those shoes until the roads came through them and two dark welts would appear on her soles, then the shoes would go to Jack the cobbler below the village and for three days she'd wear a pair of Ganga's stompy boots and head out evenings to walk by the river all the same.

There was a world of saints then and people knew the Saints' Days and whose feast fell when, and from the full gallery they chose favourites. Doady's missal bulged with all the regulars,

Anthony, Jude, Joseph and Francis, but also some of the lesser known, Saint Rita, Saint Dymphna and Saint Peregrine, as well as a personal selection of Saints of Last Resort. And I'll admit that some vestige of that remains, not taken by the tide, inside me. Saint Anthony has often found my glasses, wallet and keys. Why he keeps taking them in the first place, harder to say.

Doady gathered saints as insurances but backed them up with more ancient advocates including the moon and stars. She had an iron cauldron of remedies and pishogues inside her: a cough could be cured by a frog, a headache by a chew of hawthorn bark; the rowan tree brings luck; a leek in the kitchen saves a house from burning.

Secretly, she fretted about her vanished children, lost to unknown stories in what was then a very distant else-where. She also had the sorrow all Kerry people have when they're not in Kerry, but this she countered with copious letter-writing. Letters took several days to write, the lost art of composition then a tenet of civility, and sheets of blotting paper with traceries of script indicative of the hand-pressed, my-hand-to-your-hand nature of the thing. She'd write those letters until the day she died, her forefinger inked and with a permanent pen-welt. She had many correspondents. One was Aunt Nollaig, who went to America, and defeated the phys-ics of space by writing ever smaller on the single page of the aerogramme, her character apparent the moment Doady ran the knife carefully along the dotted line and held to the light the script that with Ganga's loupe would take days to fully decipher. Doady's own missives went across the river and over the mountains and brought replies that were read over several times, then folded back into their envelopes and stored inside a foil-lined tea chest stamped CEYLON, where in ink, paper and penmanship a kind of inner Kerry endured, and could be visited easier than the real thing.

In recent times, in a gesture, partly of love, because he knew she was lonely for the voices of her home place, and partly of self-interest, because he himself could not resist the newfangled, Ganga had sold a cow and secretly ordered the installation of a telephone. It was the first telephone that was not in the village, had the number FAHA 4, and was delivered and installed by two big-booted line engineers from Miltown Malbay who made the first call, to Mrs Prendergast on the switch in the village, one of them giving the thumbs-up to Ganga once she answered and shouting down the line the kind of wooden conversation they may one day use on Mars. The telephone had a winder on the side and, like the cartoon bombs in comics, a large battery on the floor with wires coming out of it.

Ganga's plan misfired. Doady hated it. First, she asked, how were they to pay for it. To which Ganga gave his common response to all uncertainty: 'We'll figure it,' which infuriated her more than Cork people. Second, she hated how the receiver sat silently on the wall, as if it were a black ear listening; in response she covered it with a doily and for the first weeks whispered when next to it. The telephone, it was decreed, would only be used for absolute necessities, which in her language meant funerals. Father Tom came on his rounds and before he left was asked to bless it. Unwilling to concede that science had answers where religion had mysteries, he improvised a blessing that was a prayer to Gabriel the Archangel, the patron saint of messengers, who was now, he said, in charge of telephones. Doady sent the number in a letter to Kerry and when the phone rang with a throttled pulse for the first time she knew before she lifted the doily that her ailing Auntie Ei had passed. The ring of the telephone retained that sinister aspect until word circulated around the hinterland, after which neighbours and people out the country gradually started to arrive at the door to make a call. The house became a kind of unofficial outer post office without opening or closing hours, and it was not unusual to have someone sitting on the stool inside the front window shouting the news of a death, or a sick cow, down the line while a game of cards or draughts was going on the pine table alongside. The first few times, it was Muireann Morrissey or Noirin Furey maybe, they offered the few pence for the call, Ganga shrugged off the offer and said how could you pay for talk. But by the second week Doady had placed a large jamjar on the sill with a few of her own threepenny bits inside it, and callers took the hint and the bill when it came was paid.

What I can say about my grandmother is that she was testament to the opacity of human beings. She was small but wiry, had iron-grey hair that I never saw out of a bun until it was combed out and gave her back thirty years the day she finally lost her heroic battle with gravity. She was laid out in the parlour with a faint but noticeable smile, perhaps because, sitting alongside the casket in one of Bourke's mourning suits, shoes shining and silver hair near enough to combed, Ganga looked like Spencer Tracy, and she realised that after forty years of marriage she almost had him trained. She had large but nimble hands, thin legs amplified by thick tights. She wore a wrap-around sleeveless apron, the blue one or the red one, and round glasses that made huge her eyes and at times lent her a look of fairy tale. As a shield against despair she had decided early on to live with the expectation of doom, an inspired tactic, because, by expecting it, it never fully arrived. She was equal parts Christian and pagan, never said the Good Lord without just a hint of irony, made no distinction between giving me my first set of scapulars and telling me that if I didn't wear them the *púca* would get me.

In her speech were bits of Irish and words that were half-way between two languages, accommodated into the mixture but strange as sloe berries, so that not only did she speak of a *gabháil* of turf or a *beart* of hay, a sky that was somehow more than just cloudy when it was called *scamallach*, but she had a whole range of descriptive words so onomatopoeic and exact that though I did not know their translation I somehow understood that Hanley the *bodachán* was a horrible small man, the brocky face of Gerry Colgan was pocked, shad-owed like a badger's, that big slow Liam O Leary was a right *liúdramán*, Marian Boylan a snooty *smuilceachán*, and that Sheila Sullivan had a little wet *prislín* of a son who couldn't stop dribbling.

My grandparents' marriage was less than idyllic, for many reasons, one of which was Ganga had an incomplete under-standing of money. That is, he did not believe in its existence, because, as he told me, his life thus far had provided no solid proof otherwise.

'Another man would be ashamed to say that,' Doady said, 'but not your grandfather. Your grandfather has no principles.'

'O Jeez, I do, Noe,' he smiled a pained smile, the round face of him turned to me and his hands holding on to his braces. 'But my principles have a small p. That way I can keep on loving my fellow man.' He winked at me; Doady blew out in exasperation and with the venerable duster of a goose's wing went at the dresser.

They lived by dispute, and as there were often several running concurrently you had to be alert to keep up, to under-stand that when Doady shouted 'Water!' it meant Ganga had let his hands drip instead of turning them in the cloth, that 'Boots!' meant he hadn't used the mat, 'Press!' that he had forgotten to close a cupboard door – 'Should nothing have a door on it? Is that what you're telling me? Open the doors, come dirt, come dust, come mice, and Welcome. That man won't be happy till our clothes are crawling with *sciatháns.*'

But in all Ganga maintained the equilibrium of the just and could not be risen or riled. And in this was the theatre of their marriage, which in Faha was also a spectator sport, and many evenings Bat or Martin or Jimmy might lift the latch and come calling, sitting hunkered over impenetrably strong mugs of tea to watch it play, flicking their ash in the general direction of the fire when the intermission was called.

Ganga, being a complete world unto himself, had no politics. With a silver loupe, at a seat by the window, pages tilted down to catch the daylight, he read one book a year, *Old Moore's Almanac*, and in that found all the explanation the universe required.

He was, Doady would say, an impossible man. And although I believe she meant it, although often she would tell him to get out from under her feet before she took the broom to him, and other times say he had broken the heart of her, I'm not sure I ever saw a more married man and woman. As image of their marriage: first thing every morning Ganga riddled out the fire from the embers and reset some sods on the grate of the big hearth. Half an hour later, once he had gone outside to see to the animals, Doady took the tongs and repositioned all the sods, the way they should be. She said nothing about it, he said nothing about it. The fire survived it all.

Of course, I didn't understand the economies of their life then, realise that four cows was not an income, that a

vegetable garden and hens were not just country pastimes, or that there was a reason why Ganga had made and hung all the crooked doors and windows himself. Why everything was repaired after a fashion neither textbook nor expedient, why, although all of Ganga's solutions gave birth to unforeseen problems, he continued to pursue them. Why the now lost art of darning was in their world essential, as if life was all the time undoing and holing their enterprise, and so Doady with glasses off, then on, then off again worked by paraffin lamplight with wools and threads of unmatched and often garish colours at elbows, knees, seats and cuffs, every angle of him that needed to be thatched back in against the exuberance of his leaking out.

The fact is, I did not appreciate until much later in my own life what subterfuge and sacrifice it took to be independent and undefeated by the pressures of reality.

4

It is true for Doady that the house may have suited frogs. Except for an apron around the open fire much of it was permanently damp. Pale mushrooms could rise at the base of the dresser, the sills of windows wept, and after midnight when the fire in the big open hearth went low, when the spun cotton of cobwebs began to enshroud the upper rafters, there was a sense that all five-ish rooms were longing for the river just a field away.

I had come down frequently in early childhood, first, accompanied by my parents, when what I remember are long chaotic dinners in the middle of the afternoon, a goose *and* a ham, a great bowl of rough-looking floury potatoes that sat in split jackets – in Dublin potatoes had no skins – milk that came not in bottles but thick and off-white and foaming at the edges of what Doady called a can but was an enamel jug kept cold inside the amateur refrigerator of a tiled but never-lit fireplace in the parlour. The carrots, the parsnips – there were no parsnips in Marlborough Road – the butter that bore no resemblance to what we called butter, a kind of all-out feast packed on to every inch of the table and along the dresser, and Doady running back and forth for things Ganga had forgotten and never seeming to sit down herself. The meal was made savoury by the addition of the indomitable mint that grew like an old man's beard between the broken flagstones out the back, or the class of perpetual onion that, by mercy or message, God had made flourish in Faha. But perhaps because she tried too hard, because her own mother had passed on no skill, or because life enjoys confounding effort, Doady was a terrible cook, a fact that Ganga not only never mentioned, but flouted by praising as just beautiful the cremated pork chops, stringy bacon and desiccated chicken.

Still, whenever we arrived down there was no possibility of going elsewhere for a meal. Generosity to visitors was a helpless affliction in west Clare, and though this was a time of desolation in the west when houses were emptying and on roads lingered the sorrow of a departing people, Making the Welcome remained a kind of constitutional imperative. My grandparents, like all the old people in Faha then, preserved intact ancient courtesies. The cost of it, the way they would be living in the days after we left, was not hinted at, nor did it once occur to me.

———————

Then, when my mother fell in Dublin for the first time, I was sent for the first of many times like a parcel down to the old people. It was not unusual. There was significant traffic of children in the country then, infants born to exhausted mothers or young girls, sent to be raised by maiden aunts, others, to escape ravages of poverty or alcohol, transited to temporary guardians, some of whom they took to be their parents and became enmeshed in the secretive and coiled history of the time. People aspired to adhere to the teachings of the Church, but, for human beings, abstinence proved unequal to desire, and more and more children kept coming.

I was seven years old. A white card with NOEL CROWE and my address was safety-pinned on to my jacket. I was accompanied by Mother Acquin, a large black-and-white albatross who smelled of bull's eyes. Mother Acquin was a relation on my mother's side. On that side there were several priests, nuns, and missionaries vanished into Africa who we were to pray for, because they were all praying for us, my mother said, and, with the softness of her eyes and the lamb in her voice, the boy I was did not doubt it.

There was nothing of the lamb in Mother Acquin. She could have been second choice to command the Allied Forces. She was on her way to take the sea air with the Sisters of Mercy. She'd take all they had, I'd say. As though a significant peril lay ahead, she set up a prayer-shield over us in the carriage, black rosary beads harnessing the horns of her fingers. The ticket collector looked in and backed immediately out.

The journey from Dublin took a full day and several rattling trains, each one smaller than the one before, with the result that arrival seemed uncertain and the country enormous. Always you were heading west, and always, in defiance of science and geography, there was further to go. All boys were schooled on cowboy stories then. Cap guns are gone now, but in my cardboard suitcase I had a small silver Colt 45 and a black-barrelled Mustang. The Winchester rifle I had to leave behind. So, when Mother Acquin left the carriage to see what inefficiency was delaying the tea service, I pressed my forehead to the glass and considered how fast the Apaches would have to ride before a Brave would slip his horse, clamber up into the carriage and come with raised tomahawk for Mother Acquin.

In Ennis there was a long delay. We were to transfer to the narrow-gauge West Clare Railway. The engine and carriage were there, the driver was not.

We boarded the carriage and sat. There were five other passengers, one of them a hen.

I think the flat black eye of the hen put Mother Acquin off starting the Glorious Mysteries.

Outside, rain was falling and not falling. It meant the coalsmoke did not rise but curled into the carriage where to the other passengers it seemed a familiar. Mother Acquin pushed up the window, but the air was already acrid and on sitting back down her fingertips were black.

'Touch nothing.'

Our fellow passengers, all quite smudged, took on the natural timidity of those in the company of a religious habit.

We sat on the train going nowhere.

It continued going there for some time.

At last, Mother Acquin, who considered patience an over-rated virtue, pulled me up by the arm and we got off the train and marched down the platform.

'You,' she said, to a low-sized porter in the uniform of a man two feet taller. The uniform was black, or black now, the trousers bagging at the knees and concertinaing down over his boots. Although the suit was shabby, the cap was firm and had a strap that gleamed. He was inordinately proud of the cap.

'What is the delay?'

'We're waiting on the driver, Ma'am,' the porter said, and touched the cap to assert its authority.

'Is he a figment?' Mother Acquin asked.

The porter had known the latitude of public enquiries and considered that possibility for a moment. 'No, no he's not,' he said.

'Well, where is he?'

'That's just it,' he said, and gave another little touch to the cap. 'That's just it, Sister.'

'Mother,' she said, and gave him the albatross glare. He lowered his head so we were only looking at the cap. 'Is there another driver?'

The head came up. '*Another* driver?'

'Because this one is clearly not available.'

'Oh he is,' he said. 'He's available all right.'

Mother Acquin looked at him. He put his cap a touch straighter. 'What time is it now?' she asked, pointing to the watch chain that looped like a smile across his jacket.

He was pleased to be able to provide an answer. 'Quarter past four.'

'And what time was the train scheduled to depart?'

'New Time, or Old Time?' he asked.

Mother Acquin just looked. The porter may have been about to explain to her, as Ganga did me one time, that during the Second World War Ireland fell out of synch with the world. The British, with breathtaking command, introduced some-thing called Double Summertime, putting the clocks *two* hours forward to enable a longer working day. The Irish did not, and in fact Dublin was, is, and will always be twenty-five minutes and twenty-one seconds behind Greenwich, and as west Clare had to be further behind that, Ganga said, it stood to reason that clocks were not a true measure of time there.

The porter looked like he might be about to attempt to explain the perplexity, but at that point the driver appeared.

He was leading a white pony on a length of rope.

'Isn't she some beauty?' he said, coming past where Mother Acquin had extended an arm to guard me back against the station wall.

She was a fine pony, but as skittish as my Great-Auntie Tossie. In any case, the driver took not one bit of notice of her little kicks and jumps and general spasm but opened the door to the carriage and *hup hup* with a clatter of hoof she was inside and tied, her head coming out the dropped window like any other curious passenger.

'We'll be off now, Sister, if you're ready,' the driver said as he went past us and swung up on to the locomotive.

An instant passed in which my guardian was lost for words.

'Mother,' said the porter softly, by way of correction and apology, touching the cap and marching away to perform his official duty of raising the signal.

Two Sisters under mournful black blooms of umbrellas met Mother Acquin off the train at Moyasta Junction, a station without village or town where at the end of the world's most meandering railway you stepped off into a wetter Wyoming. Rain was falling, though not exactly. Rain in Clare chose intercourse with wind, all kinds, without discrimination, and came any way it could, wantonly.

The Sisters must at first have been alarmed by the small package of the boy at the Mother's side. But mercy was their speciality. They parked me on a sack of meal and left.

Ganga was to meet me. He thought it would be fun to hide from me when the train pulled in.

The train, with pony as only remaining passenger, at last laboured away. From his cockpit the driver saluted a soldier's salute to me and called out, 'Pony Express,' and then was gone with the same unperturbable air of the world's gaiety.

Once the train had left, I got off the crate and marched down the platform into what we'll call soft rain. Short pants, white socks and sandals, a quiff, and my blue cardboard case containing my guns and six weeks of the *Hotspur*, I walked out on to the Kilkee road. I'm not sure where I thought I was going, but I was definitely going there.

My grandfather delighted that, despite my father's carefulness, here was the latest demonstration of the waywardness of the family genetic.

I suppose in all childhoods there are pockets where you discover freedom. I kept walking towards the grey sea of the sky. I don't remember having the slightest anxiety.

I had walked a long way it seemed when a bicycle bell jingled behind me.

'Young gentleman, could I offer you a lift?'

As though it were the open door of a Rolls-Royce, Ganga gestured the bar of his bicycle. Joe was standing beside him.

Ganga had no carrier and so took my case in his left hand and I climbed on to the bar. For balance I leaned back into the brown smells of his chest and there I left the world, not only because my feet were no longer on the ground but because when you're a boy your grandfather's chest has a peculiar and profound allure, like a spawn pool for salmon, wherein mysteries are resolved.

His yellow-laced boot pushed us off. The bicycle ticked minutely, like a hundred tiny clocks, and with the weave and waver of one-handed cycling we sailed not back along the estuary road towards Faha, but west to the coast, because, with heart-wisdom, Ganga understood that the ageless remedy for a boy whose mother was ill was to bring him to see the ocean.

———

From boyhood, in a high place where sentimental old men keep what sustains them, a hatful of Faha memories:

Faha was where an innocent grandfather would sit with a boy and play endless games of draughts, 'King me, Bucko,'

29

his eyes glittering and his smile soft and genial because he had left most of his teeth after him in Plunkett's, the pulling dentist in town. It was where I would go with him and Joe on intrepid missions to get Hector, Downes's bull, leading the beast back along the road by a ravelled twine tethered in its nose ring, the bull's pace slow and his gait that of a world-weary and well-travelled gentleman, holding no apparent interest in proceedings until he reached the gate and saw the heifers kick their hind legs and run.

It was where, though the rain was a constant veil, there was never any water, and buckets had to be carried to the well (which was not the well you see with stone wall and pulley in English picture books, but a glassy green eye in rushy ground two fields over, which was 'cleaned' in summertime by the antique practice of slipping into that eye an eel), and carried back again, slopping until you found that pace, old as time, by which a man or woman walks with water.

It was where Doady, watching the sky, would call 'Drying!' and we'd run out with the basket, hens darting after us in hen-brained forgetfulness that they'd already been fed, and get the white sheets pegged and flapping maybe a full ten minutes before the rain, bad luck to it, would sweep in behind a herald of gulls. Those sheets would never dry completely. Evenings they'd hang on two chairs across from the fire and be turf-smoked in downpuffs every time someone opened the back door to come for a *cuaird*. Still they wouldn't be dry, but what-of-it, you'd sleep in them all the same, the heat of humanity the last stage of drying, smoke and rain making other-worldly your dreams.

It was the smell of bread always baking, the smell of turf-smoke, the smell of onions, of boiling, the green tongue of boiled cabbage, the pink one of bacon with grey scum like sins rising, the smell of rhubarb that grew monstrous at the edge of the dung-heap, the smell of rain in all its iterations, the smell of distant rain, of being about to rain, of recent rain, of long-ago rain, the insipid smell of drizzle, the sweet one of downpour, the living smell of wool, the dead smell of stone, the metallic ghost stench of mackerel that disobeyed the laws of matter and like Jesus outlived itself by three days.

It was where you were left to your own devices, where a child with the diminished name of Noe was let off, out the door and into the soft damp wonder of the world, a piece of piping or stick his sword, and pools and drains and ditches his country, a country which yielded uncertain treasures, a half-buried boot, a verdigris coin, or the oyster gloup of tadpoles. It was where a boy of no more than eight could come clopping past on a horse, bareback, eyes wild as he clutched the mane, exulting in a speed he was not in control of as he raced past you and on into storytime, where a man might come along the road after, carrying a hames and asking: *Have you seen a horse at all?* It was where you lived by the clock of your stomach, came back to the house only when you were hungry, ate whatever was put before you, and ran out again, only partly aware of the privilege of solitude and the gift of time.

It was where every field had a name, where *Gairdín na scoile* was once a hedge school, and *Páirc na mónaigh* the field of the monks, monks you all but saw with your boyhood eyes when you heard that.

It was also where, notwithstanding your age, there was work to be done, up on the bog there was turf to be turned – 'You're the perfect size for this job' – lifted and turned and footed again, and again, because with turf the rain defeated all ploys amateur and ingenious to make believe it didn't exist, where the skin of your fingers quickly calloused from contact with a more real world and your fingernails became black-rimmed, where you lost all sense of yourself in the brown narcotic of the bog, which summoned antiquity or pre-antiquity, whenever that was, and where you only real-ised you were close to starvation when at noontime Joe cocked his ears because Doady was coming, *There she is, look!* with tea in a bottle and wedges of griddle bread that wore intricate black prints of the fire, like most of her cooking burnt, but in kindness called smoked.

Whether in recompense for the hard work, or native alchemy, tea on the bog tasted better than any tea before or since. Ganga took off his jacket and laid it over the heather for sprung seating that would scratch your calves but not dampen your trousers. 'Whist now, Noe, listen for the cuckoo.'

It was where, seventy-eight years after the first arc lamp was lit outside the offices of the *Freeman's Journal* in Princes Street in Dublin, and seventy since public electric lighting was switched on while Charles Stewart Parnell, addressing a large crowd, used the light as a symbol of a free Ireland, Faha still had no electricity. It was always on the way, rumoured to be coming, with accompanying stories of catastrophe and wonder, but as yet always elsewhere.

It was where bathtime was a Saturday-night production, a general tantara of buckets and pots as a holy halo of steam rose, a prelude to the carbolic-and-Rinso-ed air in St Cecelia's on Sundays.

It was where there was always a cat called Sibby, the name, to conquer mortality, being both individual and general, so the cat was the Sibby and also Sibby, could be called at the back door with a vowel-less sibilant hissing of *ssssbbs*, and at different times be a black or black-and-white or ginger, large, middling or small cat, but like a soul in transition always remain Sibby.

It was where flies came in to escape the weather and lived unremarked in the middle air or attached to looping honey-coloured fly cemeteries that were never full, where you sat on a three-legged stool made out of bog deal in Doady's milking parlour, a stool constructed by Ganga and so without equilibrium, a stool with an air of advancement just beyond the Stone Age, and under your grandmother's instruction you pressed your head hard into Gerty's flank – 'a cow so milky you could bring her home to your mother' – and you felt blindly for her teat which was a thing unimaginable, large as your boy-hand, pink and coarse and somehow *worn* too as you coaxed down and not just squeezed out a fierce jet of milk that came hot and greyish and shot alarmingly sideways against the enamel of the bucket with an urgent milk-music.

It was where, when darkness fell, it fell absolutely, and when you went outside the wind sometimes drew apart the clouds and you stood in the revelation of so many stars you could not credit the wonder and felt smaller in body as your soul felt enormous.

When you came back in you went up the steep steps of the Captain's Ladder to sleep on a mattress too thin to deserve the softness implied in that name, sleeping in the garret room up under the thatch that was like being inside a coarse brush and under which all the smells of the day were trapped. You knew the thatch was alive with life and so you resolved to stay awake and stare at it until that life would appear, but it never did. You fell brownly asleep and into another dimension where a ragged version of yourself plunged through a world vivid but infirm until you woke to unseen light and a bat asleep upside down just above your bed.

It was where once, in town, I watched my grandfather come out of Brews, take a big copper penny from his pocket, place it on the path, and walk away. When I asked him why, he smiled an iceberg smile whose depths were unknown, and said, 'The man, woman or child that finds that will think it's their lucky day.' He delivered a large wink, added: 'And it will be.'

It was where I sat inside on the back step of Blake's, Keane's, Cotter's and O Shea's kitchens on the nights of house dances, where after an eternity the adults pushed back the table and various chairs and forms to clear the flagstones for the sets, leaving stools for the musicians, where cigarettes were served on saucers and where, like a benevolent spirit, smoke hung permanently along the ceiling, where the music would take another age to start up, but when it did, Ganga and Doady would put away their disputes and lose forty years, springing into improbable steps, like figures in fables, dancing without looking at each other, her hand inside the mitt of his, faraway looks on their faces as their bodies spun and their feet kept perfect time.

Faha was where, one day when I was ten, Ganga, his own fingers crook-shaped from the handles of shovels, had gone into the room down and rooted about and come back bearing a case and said: 'Now, Noe, here, try my fiddle.'

It was where I had learned the music.

5

I'm not sure how much of that helps bring you there. It brings me, and I suppose that's a start.

———

You don't see rain stop, but you sense it. You sense something has changed in the frequency you've been living and you hear the quietness you thought was silence get quieter still, and you raise your head so your eyes can make sense of what your ears have already told you, which at first is only: *something has changed*. Because, in Faha, you won't believe it yet. Because in that place the gap between not-raining and raining-again was usually so short you only had time to shake the drops off your cap before it started once more. You won't believe it until you look at the sky and hold out your palm.

That Spy Wednesday, I got up from the table and went to the threshold. In my knowledge of it, the sky in Faha was mostly the colour of distillate, a grey luminousness you might imagine was on the point of becoming other, revealing a brighter reality that lay all the time just above. The problem was, it never did. I had not at that time been up in an aeroplane. I'm not sure anyone in Faha had, or those that had had not returned to tell about it. Shannon airport was still in its infancy. I had not yet experienced the spirit-shock of that moment when the plane pierces the canopy and you discover what was for me the unimaginable immaculacy of blue above. I realise this is common now and many don't remark it. But the memory remains for me and in dark days it helps somehow to think of that all the while above us. In any case, the point is that for enough of the time to make time itself irrelevant, the sky over Faha remained unchanged. You couldn't conceive of it changing.

But now, the veil of weather lifting, I could see across to Miniter's, down to Considine's where Delia lived with her brother Paud, an innocent, see the gleaming back of the river where it turned the bend near the house that was Talty's and later became the poet Swain's. The world dripped and glistened. The ash trees on the bounds of the bog garden were unleafed yet but flickered now because birds were about and in the first moments of after-rain there was an undeniable newness.

There was no actual sunshine yet. Nothing of what was to come. Just a lightening, a lifting, that in St Cecelia's was in concert with the *Te Deum* and sent a flood of coloured light in through the stained glass above the Men's Aisle as Father Coffey delivered a sermon binding together Church and State by announcing the coming of the electricity and the resurrection of the Lord.

Joe lay on Ganga's cushion in the snaffling of a dog dream. I went to the threshold and was stood in the first instants of the departed rain when a man's voice called out, 'Hello.'

When you're young everyone is old. I remember that. This man was old, I thought then, but now know he wasn't out of his sixties.

Whether he was passing or had been waiting below at the gate I couldn't say but he came in the yard now with a brisk gait, a small case at his side. He was full-bearded, a man who had probably been slight when young but the world had muscled and beer had bulked him, so although of mid-height he was strong and square and full, but he carried the weight of himself with a look of bemusement, as if it was he who told the world the joke of himself.

He came in the yard with the strange nimbleness of a large man. When he smiled he had what Frances Shea calls Atlantic-eyes, which I think means deep and blue and distant. They were extraordinary. I think I got that right away. I would never see eyes quite like them again.

'There you are,' he said, as though I was the one who had just appeared.

His hair once fair was now that colour between blond and silver. It had a small scattering of hedge-confetti.

Because this was sixty years ago some details are imagined. Nobody who's lived an anyway decent amount of life remembers everything.

He put down his case, sat on the sill, looked down at the smallness of his boots and extended towards me a strong hand.

'Christy,' he said.

6

And for moments, nothing more.

Some people understand the privilege of stillness and can sit and breathe and look and hear and smell the world turning and let what's next wait the while. He sat and looked down towards the river and I sat beside him, both of us looking I suppose thirteen different ways at the river but saying not a single word.

I thought he must be a travelling man, there were many at the time, not just the whitesmiths and pot-menders but people adrift in the country generally, for all the reasons known to man unmoored from family or home and making a kind of living from wares carried in cases and opened like miniature theatres to display whatever was newest in the larger world. They were generally talkers, with a line of patter that although worn thin from repetition was still indulged and acknowledged for the craft and craftiness in it. There was little threat and only a measured distrust of them. The planet was not yet so full that another human being coming to the door was not cause for curiosity and interest, and because the ordinary orbit of one life then was smaller the stranger brought a sense of a curtain drawn aside. Their manner and stories, phrasing, the cut of their clothes, a travelled quality in the very creases of their skin, all carried an air of elsewhere to those who would not venture out of the county in their lifetime. The travellers came out of storytime, you felt, and although some were notorious and some had the guards in plodding pursuit, for the most part they were harmless, understood to be a stray thread stitched into the fabric of the countryside, and on different visits I had seen sellers of brushes, knives, pots, ointments, oils, carpets, spectacles, and once, teeth, lay out their wares in the kitchen before Ganga, who always wanted to buy everything, and Doady who wanted none, bar the set of Saints & Martyrs cards that it might be unlucky to refuse.

Encyclopaedias, of course, were a speciality, offered by gentlemen scholars in shabby tweed who came with their own diploma qualifying them to handle the sum of human knowledge, that had been condensed down to *Only twenty-four volumes, sir,* and was continually revised so it was accurate of what was known in the world up to yesterday afternoon. The full set of encyclopaedias, the scholars knew, were beyond the purses of Faha but, not wanting to concede to the disadvantages of geography or to cut the Fahaeans off from the prime desire of mankind since Adam, they announced that the Board had decreed that the volumes could be purchased on an instalment plan, and, for signing up today, there was authorisation to make a one-time special offer of a free atlas with three hundred colour plates wherein you could visit everywhere from Acapulco to Zanzibar. Furthermore, to house the sum of human knowledge, you could also purchase this display case, this handsome set of shelving, or the deluxe glass-fronted facsimile library. And under the spell of *That's India paper, sir, now just feel the quality,* many were sold, and in houses out the townlands where there wasn't enough money for shirt collars or socks it was not unusual to see sets of encyclopaedias, but with gaps, Light to Metaphysics say, or Pre-Columbian to Sacred, where reality had overtaken noble sentiment and left some sections of alphabetised knowledge unavailable, but with people none the worse for that.

Despite the certainty that everything new cost more than was at hand, no salesman was ever driven from the door and many were temporarily accommodated in haybarns or outbuildings, or given *just the mug of tea, Mam, and a cut of bread* before they passed along the road and into the twilight. Like swallows then, some came back the next year, and recalled the welcome in such a house and what such a one had told them about a sick child or a son or daughter gone to Boston or New York, and by some secret skill of binding place to people they remembered the story of each household and forgot that no wares had been bought here. But what matter, they had the necessary optimism of all traders and this year they had these colourful mixing bowls and, *Look here, tap on that, Missus, go on, you can't break them, because see! They're made of plastic.*

Christy, I thought, was one of these. Or maybe like Hartigan, the bug-eyed, whey-faced and toothy piano-tuner from Limerick, who had an untrustworthy air Doady said because he could not be fattened, who was stitched into the narrowest pinstriped suit and always came through Faha after, as he put it, *tuning the nuns* in town. Though pianos were something grand and mostly only notional in Faha, Hartigan would stop at a few houses along his way in case he could spark an interest in a second-hand one or just some sheet music that would *suit the accordion too, Missus*, if there was one in the house at all. He smoked while he stood in the doorways, eyeing up the sale. 'Virginia blend,' he'd say, looking at the cigarette burning in his fingers. 'Smooth as cream.'

Perhaps because of some primitive but profound allure attached to the tuning or because of the mysterious attractiveness of those even tangential to music, he had a long train of rumoured paramours and illicit relations, all of which were in defiance of his actual looks and testament to the unknown depths of females.

So, because I didn't want this stranger to begin whatever presentation he had prepared when Ganga and Doady were not yet back from Mass, because of the binds of my own shyness then, and because he seemed perfectly at ease sitting on the damp sill, to Christy I said nothing more than: 'They're not here. They're gone to church.' And, I'm not sure why, after a moment added: 'It's Spy Wednesday.'

To which he made no reply but nodded and smiled out at the river and the road he had come.

The cat came out the window of the cow cabin to investigate by back-rubbing the leg of his trouser. He rubbed her head. 'Hello, Sibby,' he said.

You live a decent length you get an appreciation for the individuality of creation. You understand there's no such thing as the common man, and certainly not woman. But even then, in those first moments beside him on the windowsill, I think I knew there was something arresting about him. Everybody carries a world. But certain people change the air about them. That's the best I can say. It can't be explained, only felt. He was easy in himself. Maybe that was the first thing. He didn't feel the need to fill the quiet and had the confidence of the storyteller when the story is still unpacked, its snaps not yet released. His hair had not been barbered in some time, his beard rose into his cheeks and descended inside the collar of his shirt, around the top-button of which was grey with finger-grease. The flesh of his face had the same travelled quality as his clothes and belongings, as if cured by hot suns and cold winds. He was deep-wrinkled, like a chamois. His life was written all over him. His eyes I've mentioned. I can see them still. It seems to me the true and individual nature of a human being's eyes defy description, or at least my capabilities. They're not like anything else, or anyone else's, and may be the most perfect proof of the existence of a Creator. Maybe that old thing about eyes and the soul is true, I can't say, but I did wonder the first time I saw him what gave a person eyes like that.

'You're?'

'Noe, I'm called.'

Somehow the name Noel had never quite fitted me. As was common in towns, perhaps to combat the numerousness of people and the blurring of individuality, people were given nicknames, or had their own abbreviated. In the schoolyard in Synge Street I was first Know-All, but soon enough became Noe, to rhyme with Crowe, which, by the genius of chance, was both No and Know, and pretty accurately captured the polarities of my person.

We sat there, a mismatched pair. He looked away at the river, I looked sidelong at him.

His suit too was blue, a startling blue now, and from travel and time creased not just at knees and elbows but in every inch of it, a sense not so much of uncared as comfort. The material was not the coarser durable cloth of suits sold in Bourke's then but maybe linen I think and as unsuited to the weather in Faha as anything he could have worn. It could have been tailored in Egypt, or, I had heard of a panama hat, maybe this was a panama suit. There was a button missing at the cuff of his left sleeve. The centre one on the jacket where it crossed his belly had under pressure shattered, but a heroic remnant still held it closed. Along the hem of both trouser legs were brown exclamations of dirt thrown up from travelling a puddled road. The suitcase, on the ground in front of him, was a kind popular then when journeys were few and one or two transits were all the lifetime expected of them. It was a little more than cardboard, a lot less than leather, of what had once been a tan colour but from sunlight or rain was now a paling mustard. It was small enough, maybe for no more than a single change of clothes, and like all the rest of him it had mileage put on.

We sat watching the river.

'Is that a pheasant?' he asked, nodding towards one down at the foot of the ditch thirty feet away. I was surprised he couldn't see it.

He was unperturbed. 'I used up most of my eyesight on the wonders of the world and the beauty of women,' he said.

I'm not sure why exactly, but that knocked me an inch off myself, an inch I could not seem easily to recover. He angled over to one side, fished out and offered a crushed pack of cigarettes.

'No. No, thanks. I won't,' I said, as though I sometimes smoked.

He took one out for himself, rolled it gently between his palms to return it to tubular, put it in his mouth and began what would become familiar, the fruitless search about his pockets for a match. As long as I would know him he would never find one, but each time search and each time arrive at the same mystification at the devil taking all his matches.

'There's some inside.'

I went in, looked in both sets of places that by continuing marital dispute the matches were supposed to be, until I gave up and took a taper from the fire.

When I came out carrying it he was gone. His case was there, but he was not.

7

In the same way that order of entrance into St Cecelia's was preordained, so too it was a given that men lost interest once the service climaxed. Mossie Pender was always the first to leave. Mossie had reached the age when he no longer held dominion over his bladder, and in the last moments of Mass, host unmelted on his tongue, rushed from St Cecelia's into Ryan's next door, where the small back window of the urinal released the splash of his waterworks as the general congregation emptied out. Most of the men, as if they had no religious dimension and had in fact not been to Mass, were already back on the post-office windowsill.

The church was the biggest draw at the time, and in the hour before and after Mass, Mission or Devotion, the shops did brisk business. People availed of the opportunity offered by being in the village, and the shopkeepers profited from the lightened spirit of man and womankind fresh from church and optimistic that the Lord was looking after them. I don't know what the equivalent is now, or if there is such a thing.

That they came outside that Spy Wednesday into the cleansed light after the rain can only have bettered business. Of course, no one considered that the rain had actually stopped, only paused, miracles being unknown in Faha.

While the women went into the shops the men waited, lighting up. To a man they were all skilled in the essential but unsung art of passing the time of day. On Sundays, they would be next to the open boot of Conlon the newspaperman's Volkswagen, wisps of white smoke rising off them like minor Pentecostals.

A small butt of a man, Conlon came from Ennis and traded on the insecurities of the far-flung. He used the Ennis greeting, 'Well?', to which the correct reply was, 'Well.' He had the slit eyes of a Norseman and an out-and-out mastery of eyebrow-throwing: 'Could you credit Sputnik?' or 'The Minister for Posts and Telegraphs!' or 'United!' he'd say, throw the eyebrows and extend towards you an inverted newspaper, folded even as a tablecloth, inside which was what you didn't yet know about Sputnik, what the Minister for Posts and Telegraphs had promised now, and the news of Manchester United, to which, with the native affinity for tragedy, the sensate half of the country now supported after the Munich crash.

Ganga didn't take a paper, but his neighbour Bat Considine did, and on Sundays, out of an avid craving to secure himself more thoroughly on to the spinning planet, Bat took all the papers, one of each from Conlon, who sold them with an approving nod. 'You're a gentleman.' Bat was a bachelor and until late in life would take no lift but tramped home the four miles with the papers tucked under his oxters and sticking out of both the inside and outside pockets of a greatcoat, and he didn't mind at all that when Ganga came calling he took an old paper or two back with him and in that way kept up to date with what was new in the world last week.

Now, it is not my intention to paint the parish in an overly rosy light. It had its full share of villains, in due course some of which were found out, and some of which were not, as is true everywhere. There were many wrong things thought then, as no doubt in

45

time we'll find out there are now too. Time has unpeeled a history of infamy for the country's institutions, and failures of compassion, tolerance and what was once called common decency were not hard to come upon. Faha was no different; cruelty, meanness and ignorance all had a place then, but as I've grown older the instances and stories of them seem less compelling, as if God has inbuilt in me a spirit of clemency I wasn't aware of when younger. It may be, of course, that I'm just grateful to be above ground and what seems more significant to note is human goodness. I'm at an age now when in the early mornings I'm often revisited by all my own mistakes, stupidities and unintended cruelties. They sit around the edge of the bed and look at me and say nothing. But I see them well enough.

That Spy Wednesday, in the absence of Conlon, the men stood around and talked and didn't talk. Most of them lived in a green isolation, found solace in company without needing it to be scintillating.

Doady reappeared from the throng in Clohessy's, avoided getting snared in the veil mantilla of Kathleen Connor, whose head was full of funerals, and nodded a single nod down the street in the direction of her husband. Ganga said, 'O now,' and left the men and joined her. They went into Clohessy's yard, untethered Thomas and mounted what they called the car, but was in fact a flatbed cart pulled by a horse already older than me, who knew the time of horses was ending and had the melancholy and manner of an ancient. Many had a pony and trap they brought out on Sundays. But Ganga and Doady had little vanity and thought Christ would appreciate the savings and overlook the plainness of the transport. In 1958 my father in Dublin drove a black Ford, had been driving a car since he was twenty-five years old, washed it every Saturday morning and picked from the floormat any pebble or dirt so it retained an air of dark chariot, but in Faha his father drove the horse and car no different to his father or his before that and probably all Crowes back across the thresholds of ages since Faha had come out of the sea. Ganga neither wished for a motor car nor thought less of those who did. In her secret heart Doady may have yearned for the luxury and grandeur, but, if so, she had early quenched that girlish dream, pinched it out so that the chill and damp, the rattle and shake of the horse and car on the Faha road did not make her regret her life.

The church bells had rung and I knew they were on their way out of Faha as I stood outside like a lesser disciple with the burning taper. The man, Christy, was gone. I tossed the taper, and then noticed the small blue heap of his suit on the grass across by the riverbank and perhaps in the same moment saw the off-gold crown of his head in the river.

For an island people, at that time we were appalling swimmers. Whether from an overdeveloped respect for the power of nature, a shame of undress, or breathtaking stupidity, no one learned how to swim then. Most went into the water only occasionally and a good deal of these were trouser-rolled-to-the-knee men who stepped into the low waves at Kilkee with hats on and heads down, their whiter-than-white feet under the surface a source of some astonishment and their big toes digging into the sand like an experiment in worms. As always, the women were more daring and the sight of girls shrieking in the icy waters, holding high their skirts and running bare legs back out of the foam was not uncommon, and one of the principal reasons for men going to the seaside. But none of this was actual swimming. For those who did strip off, swimming was achieved by a sort of head-up back-and-over tossing accompanied by wild arm and leg thrashing in the belief that you could outrun drowning if you thrashed fast enough.

When you saw someone in the river your first thought was not swimming, it was drowning.

In a lifetime there's more than one doorway. Even as I was running I think I knew this was one.

It's not so easy to run across a field in springtime, and in my memory a field like Ganga's, pock and lump, dung and rushes and slick April grass, was treachery. And because an old man has only the story of his own life I am running across it still, a lanky seventeen-year-old from Dublin, shy and obdurate both, running with a premonition that I thought was doom but was maybe fate if you're a party to that. I was running believing I was going to save him, when of course it was he who would save me.

At the edge of the field I clambered over the stone wall and crossed the road that came alongside the estuary. I may have been calling to him. I was probably waving. I'm still not sure how I intended to save him. Maybe by shouting. He was a good ways into the flow of the river, and that river was cold, there was nothing clement or forgiving about it, it was a dark tongue and each year swallowed some more of the despairing.

I was stopped next to his clothes. I called his name again, and this time Christy turned his head and yelled out. So compelling is the evidence of our own eyes and ears, so swift is your mind to assemble your own version of the story, that one of the hardest things in this world is to understand there's another way of seeing things. It was a yell ripped out of his chest, a head-back and full-mouthed howl. But his arm came up through the water then, his palm flagged, and, with a great slow rolling, he swam towards me.

Out on the road came Doady and Ganga on the horse and car. They slowed when they saw me standing next the river and were stopped when, with significant difficulty, a leg thrown up and sliding back, a hand grabbing rushes, Christy

48

eventually clambered out on to the bank, pale, slimed, smiling, and altogether naked.

———

At the time you're living it you can sometimes think your life is nothing much. It's ordinary and everyday and should be and could be in this or that way better. It is without the perspective by which any meaning can be derived because it's too sensual and urgent and immediate, which is the way life is to be lived. We're all, all the time, striving, and though that means there's a more-or-less constant supply of failure, it's not such a terrible thing if you think that we keep on trying. There's something to consider in that.

———

When Christy came up to the house he was dressed in the wrinkled suit and smelled like the river. His hair and beard were darkened and he'd lost ten years. He knuckled the jamb of the open door and Ganga shot out of his chair to greet him. 'O now,' he said, and although he had not the slightest idea what this man was doing there, his big face beamed.

'Christy,' Christy said.

'Christy,' said Ganga, as though that was wonderful altogether.

I was sitting in the nook by the hearth, the darkest place in that room, and looking at the silhouette on the threshold against the daylight that was not yet actual sunshine just the glow of after-rain. There was the motion of light behind him, raindrops pulsing on the far thorn bushes so they seemed pearled or Christmas-lit in April. What I was thinking was: this is what Faha is like. What I was thinking was: this man had not the slightest scintilla of abashment at having been seen naked, and, although I could not have explained it in words: *something has happened.* Then, Doady, in testament to the unprescribed character of Kerry people, or her own impenetrable nature, wiped her hands in the teacloth, left it by the basin, and, with arms folded across herself, said, 'You're early.'

In that instant of perplex and delight both, Ganga realised she was expecting this Christy, and that forty years of marriage had not mummified the wonder of Aine O Siochru.

A key thing to understand about Ganga was that he loved a story. He believed that human beings were inside a story that had no ending because its teller had started it without conceiving of one, and that after ten thousand tales was no nearer to finding the resolution of the last page. Story was the stuff of life, and to realise you were inside one allowed you to sometimes surrender to the plot, to bear a little easier the griefs and sufferings and to enjoy more fully the twists that came along the way. He stepped aside as Doady eyeballed the visitor and shot out: 'After Easter, they said.'

The man shrugged. 'I came early,' he said, as though he himself was not in charge of his own arrival.

'The room is above in the garret. You'll have to share with our grandson who we weren't expecting but is here now,' Doady said. 'We don't know for how long.'

I caught the inference, took no offence. Christy was not bothered.

'The bed is … plain,' she said.

'Any bed at all is fine.'

'We've not had a lodger.' She looked at him blank and big-eyed through the roundrims. 'I don't know the rates.'

His face crinkled. It passed as a smile when you saw his eyes. 'I paid three pounds a week in the County Meath.'

'You were robbed.'

'Jeez, you were,' Ganga said, and pushed a palm across the top of his head.

'We have no toilet. No electric. Fifty shillings a week.' Doady was getting the hang of bargaining against herself. 'If you go home weekends, thirty-five shillings a week. We have our own eggs and brownbread so my only cost will be the meat.'

'No meat for me,' Christy said. 'You'll be spared that.'

It was unclear to Doady whether he was forgoing the meat to seek a lower rent or simplify the cooking. 'After Saturday, there'll be meat.'

'Not for me,' he said.

Now, at that time, perhaps because stomachs recalled the privations of war, or in folk memory the famine, for a man not to eat meat was almost against God. In Faha there were no vegetarians until Arthur and Agnes Philpot arrived in a faded-to-pink Volkswagen van from Bristol in the 1970s, moved into a plot of muck and rushes behind John Joe the whistle player's, began slashing brambles and digging drills and were overcome with the generosity of John Joe who by way of welcome said *Go ahead, take all my cow dung*.

To not eat meat was penitential, which, outside of a season of penance, suggested an inner turmoil. Doady was still blinking at this when Ganga offered 'Fish?' and Christy said, 'A fish is beautiful.' He offered Doady a large hand. 'Shall we settle on a pound a week?'

So, it was transacted. I showed him up the steep Captain's Ladder to the garret room. For a big man, he was fairly *souple*, as they say in Faha. He put down his case, toed off his boots, laid out on the bed whose mattress was as giving as a cream cracker, and promptly fell asleep.

8

When I came downstairs, Ganga whispered, 'He's an electric man,' and nodded one good nod which translated as *Now for you.*

His lodging had been arranged by telephone, Doady taking the call when Ganga was out and agreeing to house the lodger for the duration while the electric was being installed in the parish. The fact that the house had a telephone had signalled it as eminent and would facilitate reports back to headquarters.

Twelve years after it was first proposed in Dublin, two years after the adept and wily politicians across the river had lit the north of Kerry like a fairground, Faha was now moving into the last stage of electrification. The policy at the time was to connect what were considered the most profitable areas first, and so the parish had remained in ignoble darkness years after towns and villages east of it. Three years earlier, an official canvass had taken place. An Area Organiser called Harry Rushe had come door-to-door extolling the virtues of various appliances that would banish hardship, transform mundane chores into pleasures. Rushe, a scientist pressed into being a salesman, was a blunt individual from the cosmos of Limerick. He aimed to secure the signatures and be gone. He had little appreciation for the subtleties of the situation or the complex nature of the Fahaeans. He knew that he was advocating for the single greatest change in the way of life there but didn't have the acuity to understand why anyone might object. This was a country that through the ministry of the Church and other interested parties was encouraged to think of change not only with suspicion but outright fear, a country where most of the politicians were elected on the familiarity of their surnames, and when they died were replaced by their sons whose principal qualification was they were the same as what went before. The President was in office until he was ninety. Rushe, a ginger block with short arms, came in the doors of the parish, stood in dim kitchens, a dog sniffing at his trouser legs, and by rote listed marvels – a pump which would make water come out of taps, boil at the touch of a switch, a room bright enough to see across.

I'm aware here that it may be hard to imagine the enormity of this moment, the threshold that once crossed would leave behind a world that had endured for centuries, and that this moment was only sixty years ago. Consider this: when the electricity did finally come, it was discovered that the 100-watt bulb was too bright for Faha. The instant garishness was too shocking. Dust and cobwebs were discovered to have been thickening on every surface since the sixteenth century. Reality was appalling. It turned out Siney Dunne's fine head of hair was a wig, not even close in colour to the scruff of his neck, Mick King was an out-and-out and fairly unsubtle cheater at Forty-Five, and Marian McGlynn's healthy allure was in fact a caked make-up the colour of red turf ash. In the week following the switch-on, Tom Clohessy couldn't keep mirrors in stock, had a run on hand-, oval-, round- and even full-length as people came in from out the country and bought looking glasses of all variety, went home, and in merciless illumination endured the chastening of all flesh when they saw what they looked like for the first time.

Rushe brought with him testimonials from householders in the east of the country. '"O what a Boon and Solace is the electric,"' he read aloud in a dead voice, unaware that in Faha theatre was esteemed. He also had a memorial to be signed if the householder agreed in principle to take the electric when it would come. On his first round, he used the oldest tactic, the names of neighbours who had already signed up, but then realised he had underestimated because that was the very reason some people refused to sign. On a second round, he deployed the second oldest tactic. He brought Father Coffey with him. The young curate was an advocate of modernity. (Father Tom was not, either because he no longer believed the world capable of improvement, or because he knew the electricity bills would leave nothing for church dues.) Father Coffey was energetic and intense. His eyes were lit. His cheeks burned plum. Inflamed with zeal, he spoke more quickly than he intended and found himself employing the stratagem of the Gaelic Athletic Association, which, in the cause of football and hurling, had turned the Second Commandant on its head by instilling a fierce parochial rivalry to the point of hatred of your neighbouring parish. Father Coffey conflated this with freedom from slavery in Egypt, confusing the biblical reading by adding that if everyone in Faha didn't sign the Electricity Board would pass over, and switch on the parish of Boola instead. Faha would be left in a mean and shameful dark while the Boolaeans would be illumed, he said, like seraphim.

These arguments won over a majority. In truth, the priest hadn't needed to speak at all. His presence was enough.

Showing a keen understanding of the national character, the Electricity Board had secured a concluding masterstroke. By special arrangement, and the goodness of His Grace the Archbishop, each house that took the electricity would get a free Sacred Heart Lamp. The small red bulb with the illumined crucifix would be set up near the ceiling and show all callers that this was a house where the Lord was always present. (In due course, a sanctimonious salesman called Finn Clerkin would come in the wake of the electricity men with a framed print of Jesus exposing his red heart. That print was a bestseller. In time, it would be hard to find a house that didn't have one. It was put up behind the lamp, and even in those houses where in fear of the bill the electric light was not turned on, the Lord maintained a ruddy glow.)

As I've said, I am keenly aware I am dealing in antiquities. When you are born in one century and find yourself walking around in another there's a certain infirmity to your footing. May we all be so lucky to live long enough to see our time turn to fable.

Following the collection of signatures, Rushe disappeared, and nothing happened. Some were certain the entire exercise had been a fiction, or that the unschooled penmanship of people's signatures had failed to assert the reality of their persons. In the following three years stories of the electric would find their way to the church gates: at the National Wholemeal Breadmaking Championships which were held in Tramore, and where the electrical sponsor's intention was to conclude once and for all the argument of the best method for baking bread, the billing being 'Pot Oven versus Electric Oven', a gale had blown up and twisted the back half of the tent towards the sea. Unwilling to surrender to nature, the adjudicators had urged *Keep Baking! Keep Baking!* But the rain made the electricity short out, the electric bakers stood idle, and the Pot Oven bake of Mrs Fidelma Healy carried the prize home to Cork. That's a fact.

In these stories the future of modernity was uncertain and people were consoled to backwardness. Nothing happened and continued to happen. Then, one Sunday from the altar, Father Coffey stirred the congregation from their Latinate sleep by announcing a meeting in the hall to establish a Rural Electrification Committee for Faha. 'The notional is to be made actual,' he said, and in the instant after, realising his register had gone over the heads of the parishioners, added: 'The electricity is coming.'

On the night, the hall was packed, not least because it was rumoured the Deputy might be there, and people wanted to see what their public representative looked like. The building itself belonged to Eustace, wasn't yet the community centre. It was a long narrow shed that by an act of communal dreaming converted once a month into a dance hall, except during Lent, when it converted into a theatre. Old Dan was the caretaker then, as Young Dan would be later, and Younger Dan after him, and Old Dan knew that human animation would offset the absence of heating. There was a table and six chairs set on the stage. By prearrangement, the two priests took their places, then Doctor Troy, hands pressed deep into the pockets of his tweed jacket, that same air of wound and wisdom that had settled on him since the death of his wife. The doctor kept his foreignness to Faha intact by being punctual, a thing unique in the parish, and establishing the phrase Troy-Time, which meant exact and the opposite of Tom-Time, which meant any time other than when Tom Keane said. Mrs Reidy, powdered and pursed, hair curled to within an inch of its life, sat in next to Father Tom, and finally, on the very point when it seemed he must not be coming, Master Quinn strode in, climbed the steps at the front of the stage in a manner befitting a headmaster of the national school and his annual role as leading man in the amateur productions. From paucity of entertainments or respect for a discipline old as the Greeks, the ability to stand and deliver a speech was still venerated, and the hall fell into a hush the moment Master Quinn stood. And a moment after, as ordained by Rushe's directive that every tactic be employed to remind people these were matters of State, the one of the Kellys whose nose was never dry appeared from the wings. With the same freckled bemusement with which he would tell of it thirty years later in Melbourne, Australia, he laid a tin whistle against his lower lip and delivered the first notes of the National Anthem.

The congregation rose as one, or the Fahean version. The simple act of standing, like that which precedes the paternoster, made grave the evening. Though breathy and thin, the music performed the magic of all anthems whereby people feel united and find the spirit of Nation rising in their gorge.

Doady and Ganga were both there. From them I had the story.

Before the last note had faded, the Master dismissed Kelly with his master's look and called the meeting to order. The Deputy sent his apologies, he said, with a curtness that cut the legs from the notion that he might actually have appeared. The Master proposed Father Coffey as Chairman and, when he was elected by a show of hands, Father Coffey proposed Father Tom as Honorary President, and when he was elected by a show of hands, he proposed Master Quinn as Secretary. The Master was a bachelor on whom Father Tom leaned not only for local intelligence but everything else, including anything that actually needed to be done in the parish. Master Quinn proposed Mrs Reidy as minute-keeper and, though already doing so, she observed the niceties by feigning surprise and honour and agreeing with a single nod of the immovable curls while dipping the nib in the ink to note her own appointment. The election completed as rehearsed the night before in the Parochial House, Master Quinn launched the meeting by announcing the unlikeliest point first: Faha had been chosen over Boola to be the Rural District Headquarters.

For many, nothing more needed to be said, and for the remainder of the meeting the details of what this entailed floated like the vapoury formulae when they had all been prisoners of the Master's classroom.

Now, because this decision was to affect my life so profoundly, I dwell a little on it, and sometimes wonder what's the nature of chance. I wonder what my life becomes if that decision is not made and Christy doesn't appear in Ganga's garden on the afternoon of Spy Wednesday just as the rain stopped.

The Master drove on, detailing what Faha could expect in the weeks ahead. Firstly, a suitable premises for the Area Office had to be found – Tom Clohessy had one. Then, a stores were needed, an outdoor storage compound for every kind of— Tom got in just ahead of Bourke, volunteering the late Mrs McGrath's, who, for reasons unclear, was the third pensioner to leave Tom her house in a will.

Warming to his role, the Master read aloud the list of necessities for which the electrical people would require storage: ironwork, struts, ties for headgear, insulator pins, suspension clamps, shackles, earth rods, stay rods, nuts and bolts all sizes, connectors, dead-end thimbles, fuses, air-break switches, and insulators for HT and LT fuses, he concluded, having no iota what they were but understanding the potency of language, employing every ounce of his stagecraft and thirty years' familiarity with those floorboards. Aluminium conductors, from the Aluminium Union of Canada, he said, were on the sea and would arrive in due course. The work was expected to take a few months. Digs would be required for the travelling members of the crews, which included the Rural Area Engineer, assisted by the Rural Area Clerk, the Rural Area Organiser, and the Rural Area Supervisor, along with a number of linesmen. In addition, the Master announced, between forty and fifty general workmen had to be hired locally. That stirred the crowd. 'One million poles have had to be erected across the country,' he said. Because inconceivable, the number was breathtaking, and the visionary audacity of the whole enterprise landed in the mind of Faha and swept along many of the unconverted. *One million poles.*

9

The electricity poles, it turned out, would not be Irish. Irish forests, we had learned in school, were felled to make Lord Nelson's fleet and were now fathoms deep with the rest of the Admiralty. Instead, after extensive research, which in those days meant sending a man, the Board learned that the best place to purchase the poles was the country of Finland. To Finland they dispatched a forester, Dermot Mangan. Mangan had never been north of Dundalk. He tramped through the snow directly to the Helsinki offices of Mr Onni Salovarra, stood melting alarmingly beside the ferocious stove and said he was there to negotiate for poles on behalf of the Irish State.

Mr Salovarra thought him a novelty. He considered the comedy of the clothes the Irish thought adequate to the Finnish winter. The shoes, the shoes were little more than cardboard, a detail that inexplicably moved him, conjuring a country poor and valiantly endeavouring to overcome its circumstances. Still, business was business. Like all who had to outwit savage climate, Mr Salovarra eschewed sentiment and offered an inflated price of £4 a pole.

Mangan furrowed his brows and melted some more. He was not a businessman, his prime negotiation was with saws, but he had been told to drive for £3 and 10 shillings per pole, and if things did not progress, the Department Secretary had told him, drop in a mention of Norway, they won't like that.

Mangan sat down. He said he was sorry he had travelled so far in vain. He said he had been hoping to see the glory of the Finnish forests, which he believed the finest in the world, but now would have to travel on to Norway.

Mr Salovarra said £3 and 10 shillings per pole.

Mangan said he would send word back to the Government and asked for the nearest telegram office.

Right here is the only one, said Mr Salovarra and smiled. He had the kind of teeth that suggested the tearing of fish-flesh.

Mangan wrote out the words of the telegram. Please send this, he said, and passed the wording across the desk to Mr Salovarra. The message was written in Irish.

Mangan crossed the frozen street and into the tropic of a wooden hotel where three stoves were kept going and the floor of the lobby wore a permanent stain of male thaw. His room was spartan but it was overhead Reception and the heat fairly cooked him. The floorboards up there had been shrinking and creaked like the bones of old men, but they dried his shoes in jig-time. In the same jig-time the stitching of them gave up the ghost and he could hear the tiny snaps of the cobbler's thread as the soles came loose. The fish he ate for dinner was larger than the plate. He had no idea what kind it was, but with enough salt you could eat timber was Mangan's thought.

He went back to Mr Salovarra the next day and received the telegram of the Government's response, which was also written in Irish. Translated, it read: *Delighted with offer. Accept on behalf of State.*

Mangan looked across at Mr Salovarra, whose teeth were smiling. 'Offer refused,' he said.

Mr Salovarra could not believe it.

'Look, here,' said Mangan, and read aloud the impenetrably harsh sounds of the Irish. He finished with a flourish the sign-off, *An tUasal O Dála*.

Mr Salovarra asked him what *An tUasal* meant and Mangan explained that in Irish we remembered we were noblemen and greeted ourselves as such.

Mr Salovarra said £3 a pole.

In all, ten telegrams went back and forth from Helsinki to Dublin, all of them in Irish, and, because in Irish and incapable of being translated in Finland, they were able to take on whatever degree of intransigence Mangan thought apt. Ultimately, because of the unnegotiable severity of the Gaelic, Mr Salovarra was bargained down to £2 a pole, and on that the two men shook. A fact.

But that was not the end of it. Now fearful that their inexperience might be taken advantage of, the Electricity Board insisted that each individual pole be inspected, calipered and approved by Mangan himself before being shipped to Ireland.

Mangan told Mr Salovarra he would have to stay in Finland for some months. He was to visit the northern forests in person.

Mr Salovarra lifted on to his desk the gift of a pair of fleece-lined lace-up boots and made a small respectful bow. '*An tUasal*,' he said.

Dermot Mangan travelled by sleigh into the snowbound forests of Finland. He didn't take the suggestion of using preventative fatty oil on his lips and they cracked off like flakes of pink paint, making of his mouth a glossy sore until he learned respect of where he was and daubed his whole face. It was too late to save his eyelashes. In the deep woods was a preternatural silence and a sense of the beginnings of time, and Mangan was not surprised to learn of the Finnish epic poetry of the Kalewala in which the earth is created from pieces of duck egg, and the first man, whose name is not Adam but Väinämöinen, starts by bringing trees to barren ground.

Mangan took to the woods. They were his dream habitat. He wore furs, Mr Salovarra's boots, and went from pole to pole and made his mark, selecting the ones that in time would criss-cross the green spaces of Ireland. He became a story, and that story was well-known by the electric crews that came into Faha and told and retold it with greater or lesser detail depending. But the fact is that for the next thirty years, May to December, there was always a ship bringing poles from Finland to port depots in Dublin, Cork or Limerick. In the interests of story, sometime you could do worse than go out into the country, find one of those quiet roads where time is dissolved by rain, look out across ghost fields that were once farmed and you'll still see some of those poles An tUasal Mangan first laid a frozen hand on in the forests of Finland.

———

I drifted a bit.

It's licensed by time on the planet.

The bones of it are fact.

When Master Quinn mentioned the jobs, like a human concertina, every woman in the hall in Faha elbowed her man. Although she knew the intention was to hire young farmers, and Ganga was not young, Doady did the same. The prospect of his getting a job would float through the following weeks. Sometimes, with rehearsed casualness, she would land it Kerry-cute in conversation – 'Young Carty, they say, has a job got with the poles' – and always Ganga showed genuine interest, 'Is that right?'

'So I hear.'

'Good man, Carty.'

'You could ask.'

'Jeez, I will.'

'They might need experience.'

'That's true.'

He'd carry on diligently buttering his bread and somehow, by the magic of intention, it would be as though he now had the job, so there was no need to apply.

A wife knows with some exactitude the limits of her husband, and so in her heart Doady already knew that Ganga would not sign up for the work, but it's human nature to dream, and in the vexed nature of marriage to hope time will harmonise the irreconcilable. When she finally conceded to reality, Doady took a different road and decided to take in one of the electric lodgers.

And now that he's slept enough, here he is, coming backwards down the Captain's Ladder in his socks, his large figure in untucked shirt, forked hair, and sleep-eyes, stepping on to the flag floor and to the audience of the three of us says: 'That bed's heaven.'

Perhaps from unfamiliarity, Doady met compliment with brusqueness. 'There's food,' she said, and turned away.

We sat to the table for a Lenten meal. Eggs were plentiful but being saved for Easter Sunday, so what was served was a black seaweed of imperishable salt and fried cakes of onion-seasoned mashed potato that since the nineteenth century Ganga had been calling Pandy. Doady brought a pot of tea from the hearth, tea that brewed beyond time and became so strong it defeated sugar. Christy acted as though the tea's bitterness was imperceptible and the meal a feast. Although I couldn't have put it in words yet I think I was already struck by what I'll call the generosity of his spirit.

Ganga and I pretended not to be watching him. I noticed he was a *citog*, and there were few enough of them then, left-handedness having been almost entirely purged by Sisters, Brothers and Masters who were all of one conviction: the world spun right-handed off the fingers of God. He ate with appetite and relish, a thing approved by all mothers then, but caused me to wonder when he had last sat to a meal.

'It's a difficult job, the electricity,' Ganga announced, with blithe knowingness.

'Ah no, it's not really,' said Christy.

To uphold the masculine charade of appearing informed, or in combat with the Faha feeling of inadequacy, my grandfather surprised all by disagreeing. 'It is, though.'

Over by the basin Doady turned and looked at the perplexity she had married.

'The insulator pins, the suspension clamps sure,' Ganga said.

There was an astonished pause when my grandmother and I were not sure if we were hallucinating.

'All the earth rods, stay rods, *and* the connectors,' Ganga added, as though he knew these last were particularly troublesome. The performance of Master Quinn had made the list indelible, and by magic of theatre and a man's need for fantasy it was as if Ganga believed he had signed up for the job when Doady urged him, was in fact an electricity worker, and had been for some time.

Sparked with the novelty of speaking technology, Ganga drove on: 'The dead-end thimbles. The dead-end ones. And the air-break switches.' He gave a slow shake of his big head to acknowledge vexatious encounters with air-break switches, then stopped short. It was all he could remember. He had come to the end of his lines. He knew there was more, but no prompt was offered from the wings. He looked blankly at his audience, air leaking out of his performance, then some switch inside his memory was thrown, he blinked twice, tapped his forefinger on the table, and added: 'Of course, there can be trouble with the insulators for the HT and the LT fuses too.'

It was an instance of triumph and display worthy of Conway's cock. *Now for you*, was his look back at Doady, as though the whole speech had been an articulation of love, all the more eloquent for being in the argot of electricity. Speech over, he tugged once on his braces and returned to carving his tomato.

But the triumph was instantly confounded when Christy, whether impressed by the listing or partial to the comedy, turned to Ganga and asked, 'Would you like a job?'

I didn't have the feather to knock Ganga off his chair.

Knowing he was under the round-glassed scrutiny of Doady, he showed no sign of it. With the composure of a life-long draughts-player, Ganga took the breath you take before a leap. He put down his knife. He swallowed a crescent of the thick-skinned tomato along with the indigestible truth that the fate he had managed to evade for so long had come in the door and was sat beside him.

'I would, of course,' he said. There was always on his person a great-sized handkerchief, it was common enough at the time, and he drew it out now and covered his expression by trumpeting into it like the nineteenth century.

Prayers were never answered in Faha, so it was Doady's turn with the feather. She stayed standing by the basin twisting the teacloth.

My grandfather pocketed the white flag of the hanky, sipped and swallowed sour tea.

'But, do you know,' he said, 'I know a man who would be ahead of me in the queue.' His round face assumed a look of resigned acceptance, and then, masterfully slipping impossible binds, he slowly extended his hand, like a living signpost, and pointed at me.

10

Although she had the rigour and meticulousness of all realists, my grandmother had not considered what she would do with her lodger in the evenings. The entertainments on offer were few and the natural decline of evening was towards the rosary, at the approach of which now, Ganga recalled that Bat Considine had asked him to take a look at an ailing calf and reached for his cap. As most of the world then, he was amateur in all things but offered a veterinary counsel firmly founded on both the full and near failures of his own farming. He headed to the back door, but before he lifted the latch, said, 'Noe, take our visitor into the village.'

Now, as I've said, I was on unsure footing then, and as both failed priest and Dubliner the last person to take Christy into Faha, but Ganga had the shrewdness of seven foxes.

Christy was considerably shorter than me, but in deference to his bulk or age took Ganga's taller bicycle and I the smaller one of Doady. There were bicycle clips somewhere, if only they could be found. Your right sock did emergency duty and was the better for being black and taking the streaks of oil without comment. See us then, a mismatched little and large, pedalling uncertainly out the yard.

The lamps on the bicycles had long since conked out. The small ambit in which my grandparents lived made them redundant, but less so for us, and we met each bump and pothole and progressed into the falling night by jolt and glide.

'My God,' said Christy, 'the stars.'

The rain having departed, the evening sky was million-flecked. It felt opened, as though previous ones you just now realised had been closed. Because there was no electric light, because we were at one of the edges of the universe, and because they were usually shielded with an impenetrable cloud, the stars hung with naked wonder. You could hardly credit it was the same world you were in yesterday.

Christy cycled in slow meander, head tilted upward. The weight of him on the bicycle, sporadic pedalling, and general absence of effort made reaching any destination indefinite. The village may have been ten, twenty miles away, he had no urgency and seemed content to be in minimal motion along the small rises and falls of a road in west Clare. If I looked over at him I'd say he was near enough to smiling, and I was maybe thinking he had something of poor Matthew Poole, who thought life too funny for words and could be seen sometimes giving a little quiet chuckle to himself. There was no harm in it.

Occasional silent figures came up out of the dark like bats, walkers, cyclists, or some standing for unknowable reasons by the ditch looking out into a blind field. In Faha you passed no one without a nod or a wave, and I did, knowing that, even as we passed, Christy and I were being stitched into the fabric of the townland: *Do you know who I saw this evening?*

'The last time I was on a bicycle I was getting away from a man wanted to shoot me,' Christy said, whether to himself or me I couldn't say.

Either way I didn't know what you reply to that. I didn't understand yet my part as audience and hadn't the skill of returns by which a story is moved. He glanced at me, but in the half-dark I concentrated on the potholes. We cycled on.

'That was in Bogotá,' he said.

He was behind me, trying vainly to catch up. I said nothing. It was too fantastical for commentary. After a time, heard: 'Colombia.'

On the winding fall of the road by Furey's we freewheeled, I nursed the brakes a bit and he came near enough alongside. 'A bicycle is not faster than a bullet,' he said, a little breathlessly. Again, I was found wanting.

We left the bikes above by the forge and considered the village ahead of us. He seemed nervous of it. I think I noticed that. He peered down the crooked street but was not inclined to go further.

Pubs in Faha were almost never lively, most were deathly, at their natural best after a funeral. Craven's was nearest to the forge. It was not in the village proper, but on the fringe, as though to accommodate those coming from the west whose thirst could not endure another thirty yards. Its origins in desperation, its fixtures and furnishings were according.

Christy was in the door before me.

Dimness, dampness, an odour acrid and brown, through which was tangled the purple tongue of paraffin and a pall of smoke. The proprietor, a triple widow, was a woman whose name had evolved by general and her consent to Bubs, perhaps because of what Mick Roughan called her boozums, which were enormous, and had grown a counter to support them.

From Bubs's three marriages nothing had sprung but for Roo, a fawn three-legged dog that hopped, lived off scraps and spillage, and in whose hectic eyes, Bubs thought, the ghosts of the three husbands seemed to wrangle.

The Parochial House had a housekeeper, Mrs Divine, and as was universal then, this was a risen station. Mrs Divine revealed nothing of the inside workings of the domain of her employers but by the clockwork of her nature it was known that once she left the Parochial House in the evening, the priests were abed, the strictures of Holy Week were relaxed and the pubs could reopen. Like shades then, hollow-eyed customers, who by day had adhered to the laws of fasting and abstinence, and had nominally given up the drink for Lent, now appeared and, with the constituent shyness of men exposing vulnerability, came sheepish to the counter and ordered with their eyes.

When Christy and I came in, from helpless curiosity, customers drew minutely forward an instant, saw us, then drew further back than originally, interest in others perhaps the first of the many things extinguished by alcohol. Craven's had glasses, they filled a shelf behind the bar and may have been washed once, but customers preferred bottles, and sat along the wall silently sucking, at bladder-intervals staggering out the back door where, licensed by nature, they urinated loose loops in the general direction of the river. As the evening drew on, some only got as far as the door, came back with trouser legs painted.

'Missus,' Christy greeted Bubs brightly.

Bubs's eyelashes lowered to half and came up again.

'Two bottles of stout.'

Bubs didn't move. 'You're the electrics,' she said.

'That's right.'

She had the smallest eyes. They were bedded into a lumpen head, and not it nor any other part of her had moved an inch as she considered him. 'I'm not wanting it,' she said. Then she smiled. There are better smiles on deflated footballs. 'I signed but I'm not wanting it now.'

Christy nodded.

'Why would I want it?' she asked Salty Pepper, who had the gift of counter-apparition. Salty was an intelligent customer; by Aristotelian and Jesuitical reasoning he had ascertained that though Lent was prescribed as forty days and nights, the true measure between Ash Wednesday and Easter Sunday was forty-six, which showed Our Lord wanted human beings to have wriggle room.

'Do I look like I could afford it?' Bubs asked. 'I'm a single lady, do you see?' She rolled her head to one side, and, employing the antic that had ensnared the three husbands, raised the eyelashes to full and fluttered them.

Christy escaped to a bench with two bottles of stout.

After which, a blur.

I know I did not drink the first bottle. His was gone in instants and, leaving me looking at mine, he went to the counter and came back with two more. There were certainly two more after that. I now had three waiting, and before the two after that I probably started not sucking, mind, just barely kissing my lips to the mouth of the bottle and sipping what seemed spewage, but by the tricks of acids and enzymes my stomach accommodated, and the two bottles after that were not so terrible.

With the two after that, Christy started singing.

Now, Craven's was not that class of venue and the moment he stood and raised his voice the singing was already going past telling, past gossip, beyond that evening and right through the doors into Faha lore, not just because it generally went against Church teachings and practice during Holy Week, not just because it broke what passed for decorum (all places had their own propriety, and Craven's was that it was a place of despair, it was where there was no further to fall, where you could hunker down and linger in the dark and because your company was like-minded and likewise afflicted you would not have to face the fact of how far you had descended); no, not just because it broke with a long-standing unwritten rule, *you don't sing in here*, but because of the manner of the singing. Not only was Christy singing, he was singing with screwed-up eyes and fists by his side a ballad about love. He was singing it full-throated and full-hearted and before he had reached the second verse it was clear even to Roo the dog that a passionate truth was present in that place. It wasn't only that this didn't happen in Craven's, it was that there was something raw in it, something deeply felt, that was, even to those who had descended blinking into the umbrae and penumbrae of numberless bottles of stout, immediately apparent and made those who first looked now look away.

Christy sang. I cannot tell you how startling it was. If you believe in a soul, as I do, then my soul stirred. The song was not composed by Christy, but by the alchemy of performance, you felt it was.

It seems to me the quality that makes any book, music, painting worthwhile is life, just that. Books, music, painting are not life, can never be as full, rich, complex, surprising or beautiful, but the best of them can catch an echo of that, can turn you back to look out the window, go out the door aware that you've been enriched, that you have been in the company of something alive that has caused you to realise once again how astonishing life is, and you leave the book, gallery or concert hall with that illumination, which feels I'm going to say holy, by which I mean human raptness.

So here it was, that quality, that life, in a man singing.

Now, I'm not saying Christy was a great singer, or even a good singer. The world has enough critics, and technique, tone, pitch, and the rest were all rendered irrelevant by the fact that the singing stopped your heart. It reached in and seized it and didn't let go. It said *Listen, here's a human being who has suffered for love*. It said *Here's a heart aching*, and that ache was large enough, urgent and familiar enough, for you all to feel it and by feeling participate in something you yourself were either too timid, closed or unlucky to have known personally, or had known in the long ago of your own innocence over which you had since grown the skin necessary to tolerate the loss and stay living.

He sang. After the first few lines I couldn't look at him. Nobody could look at him. It felt like an intimacy you weren't entitled to, but knew it privileged you and you didn't dare move in case you broke whatever had made it happen. He sang the love-song in a way that made you realise a reality that existed not outside but alongside and even inside the one you were accustomed to. It woke you up. And you thought that, by whatever contingency or circumstance, here was a man who had managed to escape the easy contempt for songs and stories of courtship and love that others used as a measure of maturity, as though these were toys of youth. In that place that was doggedly, darkly masculine he made the air tender. I can't say it any clearer.

When the song ended, Christy sat down. There was no applause, not a sound from the dozen or so souls along the wall in the dark. He sat across from me. Like a man in the throes, his forehead was beaded with sweat. He pulled the back of his hand in a wipe across his lips. I didn't say anything. I had no idea what to do. It was as if he was naked beside me. In the aftermath of the intimacy words seemed unwieldy, and so to close over the moment I did the only thing I could do. I went to the counter and got two bottles of stout.

The two after that were probably the culprits.

The two beyond them certainly, no question, no question at all now, because at that stage some of the shades started shuffling past, feet leaden and crêpe-like by turns, hands feeling for invisible handrails as they progressed from dark to dark out the door and intrepidly homeward. The last was Greavy the guard, who turned out to have been there since Mrs Divine left the Parochial House across from the barracks. In refutation of clocks, calendars, and what laws were passed in the distant capital, Guard Greavy preserved inside his person the authority of Closing Time, and when he arrived ponderously at the door and cast a sergeant look back at us Christy and I knew we had to get up and leave.

Then we knew we couldn't.

Getting up proved aspirational. There was the idea of it, quite clear. Unmistakably clear now. There were hands placed on knees for push-off. There was a *Right now.* There was another when that failed to produce action. A *Right so* following. And still nothing. Between thought and verb a vacancy, not intended, but not grievous, just gently perplexed, and in that perplex the realisation that Craven's was not in fact such a bad place at all, was downright comfortable in fact, in fact there were few places on this earth as agreeable. True? Too true. A person could stay here, could stay right here and be quite happy now, quite, for a very long time. What's your rush? There's no rush. All the problems of the world could be settled right here.

Right.

Will we go so?

We would.

At last, a gentle little rock back to assist propulsion upward, and then a crash as I came up and found the dimensions of the world awry and a table full of bottles in my way. The shatter opened Bubs's bead eyes momentarily. Propped on the counter she was in the dream of the three husbands, found it the more compelling and closed her eyes again. Christy steadied me. Which is like saying I leaned on a wave.

I believe I considered picking up the bottles and the glass. I certainly looked down at them, but the distance was enormous, and Christy had his arm hooked in mine and now sailed we gallants out the door.

The night air was syrup. I gulped, gagged. As though air was a new element, or I was not in mine. My head was a cannonball, and now a balloon.

The stars slid down the velvet sky. You could put them back in place by locking them in your gaze and lifting your head slowly, slowly up. *Stay, stars*. But look, between the buildings the river is rolling. It rides up the banks. Turn your head sideways to see and now the stars are sliding down again. *Stars, get back up*.

Faha fast and not so fast asleep was a thing tender and serene, the twist of the village street like a child's drawing, innocent of history and stain, every shop suspended, every house shut-eyed and blind and huddled to its near neighbour, the church august and grey and grave like a watchman.

If only it would stay upright.

The only moving things in the stilled scene, Christy and I sailed along. In the unstable of blood and brain, a galleon the image that came to me. The short and tall masts of us, the old man and the young, swaying. For reasons too profound or obvious, liquid flowing to loquacious, say, lines, that in

76

school had been learned by heart and by rhythm fastened on to it, now flowed out of me: "'O up and spak an eldern knight, sat at the king's right knee: 'Sir Patrick Spens is the best sailor, that ever sail'd the sea.'"'

And like a chorus, Christy: "'That ever sail'd the sea.'"

Felix Pilkington was Faha's Shakespeare. He looked like Shakespeare and spoke like Shakespeare, as Faha imagined him. You could find these people then, remarkable originals, men and women who thrived on remoteness and kept alive the individuality of human genius. I can't speak of now. A phenomenon, Felix was uncorrupted by success, or fame outside the parish, but could compose on the spot, in rhyme or iambic pentameter what's your fancy, improvise poems for all occasions, do tragedy, comedy, history, pastoral, pastoral-comical, historical-pastoral, tragical-historical, tragical-comical-historical. O Jephthah, judge of Israel, what a treasure, but even Felix Pilkington would have been challenged by the fluency of what flowed out of me, avid and a-sway then in Church Street, Faha.

"'O my dark Rosaleen donotsigh donotweep thepriestsareontheoceangreen theymarchalongthedeep.'"

"'Along the deep.'"

What else I declaimed I am not sure. The poetry anthologies of two State examinations had been nicely grilled on to my brain. Most, happily, are there still. I am sure only that we were in the small hours of tomorrow, that Christy had my arm and by the north-less compass of the blind-drunk led us circuitously at last back to the bicycles.

Coming from who knows what house dance, there ghosted past us two of the Donnellan sisters. A giggle bubbled out of one of them and the other hooked her arm and hurried them past.

Christy shook his large head slowly and then said the thing that had not dawned on any Faha native: 'This is a parish of magnificent women.'

We stood, momentarily immobilised by this declaration. Then Christy put his arm on my shoulder and steered us onward.

That we set off, that after attempts doughty and determined to mount the abstruse contraptions that were bicycles we finally rode off into the deep dark, was testament to the valour of the euphoric and the reasoning of brains banjaxed. But we went beautifully, mind. O beautifully. Smooth sailing. Christy and I, small and tall, old and young knights riding out the gentle fall the road takes out of Faha, so it seems the road itself encourages you to leave, and with no effort at all you're moving away. The river on one side, rumpled fields the other. In them, statues of horses with starlit eyes, cattle still as cattle in toy farms. The immemorial scent of grass growing, the coconut of gorse, and the profound, moving, if momentary sense of absolute well-being.

It is a freeing thing to flow into the dark. Now that I am entering my Fourth Age, the Age of Completion they call it, I think of that cycle ride and take courage from it. We could barely see the road we raced down. We came round the bend at Furey's and past Considine's discovering that blind cycling is its own art and into each instant compresses the knowledge of how to master it.

'O ho now!' Christy shouted.

'O ho now!' I shouted, both of us happy as heathens beneath the warm breath of the night sky and pedalling now in the boy hectic of blind momentum and nocturnal velocity so we missed the turn at Crossan's went straight and straight on and straight in through Crossan's open gate and across the wild bump-bump-bump and sudden su-su-su suck of their bog meadow where my front wheel sank in a rushy rut and I and a cry and a jet of brown vomit were projected out over the handlebars and flew glorious for one long and sublime instant before landing face-first in the cold puddle and muck of reality.

By the grace of new chapters, it was morning.

God loves donkeys, and reserves for them a special clemency, so we awoke in the garret bedroom, face down and fully dressed on our beds, but without the memory of how we got there. I lay blinking in the chastened light as the world condensed to two certainties, one, the jelly of my brain had swollen too large for my skull, the other, I would never again drink alcohol.

There is a universal recipe to the reaction on waking after such a night. It is one-part shame, two-parts rebuke, three-parts disbelief, and the rest is just pure astonishment. The inside of my mouth was sandpaper, my eyes on stalks. I felt as far from myself as I ever had, but not without an element of thrill.

Sometime maybe you've had the sense that something has arrived in your life, and what it is you can't tell, but it's as though a gate you haven't checked in a while must have blown open, and without even going to look you know it has. You've no proof, nothing you can point to, but you know: something has blown open.

Thatch has the density of a fairytale forest. Through its dark weave and wove there's not a glimmer of light, but still you can tell when the sun is overhead. The roof is minutely alive and feels forgiving, as though it has lifted like an eyebrow towards the sky with surprise and welcomes back the all-but-forgotten. As I lay on the bed trying to improvise stratagems for raising my head without hurting my brain, I knew I had woken to a day of sunshine.

I know now that, when you get to a grandfather's age, life takes on the qualities of comedy, with aches. That morning Christy must have been feeling them, but he was up before me. He went to fully awake in an instant and showed no wear, nor any acknowledgement of the night past other than a wink at me as he went downstairs.

Befogged and smarting, I lay in the bed and tried to recover some of what I had learned the night before. He was not an electric man as such, in that he had not joined the company as a young man and worked his way along the ferried ranks. I got that. Had he come from Munster? Did he say his father was a strong farmer? I may have misremembered that. He employed a throwaway style that I hadn't understood yet was bait. His history was all gaps. He had taken to the road and then the sea, the theatre of that phrasing still with me, so he must have used it. While the greater world was at war, he was slipping through its sequestered quarters, travelling the North, Central and South Americas where he had been variously a cook, barber, carpenter, apprentice cobbler, merchant sailor, lumberjack, boat-builder, a bookstall man, and a hodgepodge collector of the earth's idiosyncrasies – *In Peru they eat a purple potato. In Valparaíso the ocean smells of flowers. They wear a hat on top of a hat in La Paz, Bolivia, I nearly left a toe there.* Interspersed through them had been the names of women, of which, mid-alphabet alone, I think I could remember a Marie, a Magda, and a Monique.

In the early part of the evening I hadn't the guile to draw the stories, and in the latter the brown bottles had, as Siney O Shea would say, separated me from my wits. I cannot be sure what I heard that night, what I heard later and added to the fog-memory, and what invented, a perplex that deepens after sixty years, but with less consequence. The truth turns into a story when it grows old. We all become stories in the end. So, though the narrative was flawed, the sense was of a life so lived it was epic. I grew aware that night in Craven's that Christy carried with him the prodigious mythology of himself, but not yet that he wanted to tell it, or needed someone to tell it to.

Disproving the wisdom common then that fortune was to be found overseas, he had returned to Ireland owning nothing but the linen suit on his back and what he held in the small suitcase. Unperturbed by arriving home and in his Third Age, with less than he had set out, he had answered an advertisement by the Electricity Supply Board for able-bodied men to work on establishing the rural network. The interviews were held in headquarters, Merrion Square, Dublin, but, aware of the bifurcated nature of the nation and the challenges of integrating into rural communities, the preference was for men from the country.

'I told them to send me to Kerry,' he said. 'They did. I went to Sneem. Do you know Sneem?'

I didn't. In Craven's he had let Sneem have its moment, but I hadn't known why.

'Then I knew I had to come to Clare.' He had tapped that out on my knee, my knee now remembered. But why, what Clare meant to him, what purpose he had here, and whether he had told me, were all vanished in the aches of morning.

When at last I came downstairs, the house was in disorder, and Christy was helping Doady carry her mattress out the front door. Sunlight was flooding in. Like a blessing, the sunshine had come in time for Easter and that springtime remedy which in Faha was called airing, and which since Noah had been part of the clockwork of mankind, and since Christ part of the preparation for Resurrection, was already in full swing. (I don't reference Noah casually here. Once, in boyhood, footing turf up on Breen's bog, I had asked Ganga about the whitened bones of giant trees the cutaway of the bog had exposed. 'This was an oak forest, Noe, the time of Noah,' he had said, as if that history was almost recent, pausing to look with happy amaze at the memory of the flood waters departing.) Now, every window was open. Curtains, by pyjama cord, trouser belt, braces, frayed lengths of sugan, were tied up, not only to let the fresh air in and the dust out, but also to let go of the wintering, because God, whose mercy was never in doubt, had finally forgiven what sins the parish had amassed, and turned off the rain.

Not that it was a magnificent day now. I don't mean that. Just that there was light and a lightening, a lifting, and when I stepped outside the air had the slender, quickened and hopeful spirit that is in the word *April*. Since early morning Doady and Ganga had been emptying the house of all clothes and soft furnishings. As though parked there by flying Persians, mats and carpets were lying about the yard. Blankets, pillows and cushions were scattered along form-benches. Across every bush were spread not only sheets, towels, teacloths, but, with an absence of restraint and even an air of display, knickers and underpants, slips, tights and other sundries. Drawers had been emptied. Things hitherto unseen were disporting themselves like sunbathers, the entire garden colourfully draped and looking as though partaking in a pagan custom, like the hanging of lights on trees.

I stepped in to relieve Doady and help with the mattress, and Christy and I set it, their marriage bed of forty years, with distinct Ganga and Doady hollows, at a slope, unabashedly facing south to Kerry and the full sun.

With a little swill of guilt, I saw the two bicycles from the night before were leaning to at the gable of the cow cabin, evidence of the debauch cleaned without comment by Ganga who, with the dispensation of the fine weather, had gone to the bog with Joe.

Charged by the sun, but certain that its appearance would have the short-lived character of all novelties, Doady was all business. While Christy and I breakfasted on tea in the hand and a burnt scone, she whirled around the kitchen with the briskness of those butterflies that must condense a lifetime into a few days. Where they angled inside the house, the lowered lances of God's sunlight showed no mercy. Like the 100-watt bulbs, they revealed the coating of time on all surfaces and the air thick with the tiny motes of a travelling dust. The windows were discovered to be opaque, screened with smoke and printed with thumbs, palms and smears that had escaped the forensic of the Christmas clean undertaken in December dark. Now, the sunshine more than redoubled the urgencies of Easter. Since the first telling of the story of Calvary every house in the country was rendered spotless for the Resurrection of the Christ, but in Faha that morning there was spirit added to industry, the sun made actual all metaphors and, if not quite the pallid brightness of Jerusalem, to those with the deep and untroubled well of Doady's conviction, it must have seemed as though this year the Father Himself was setting the scene for the drama of the Son.

I'll say this too. It seems to me, there was little culture of complaint then. I may be wrong here, but in my thinking hardship had been part of history for so long it had become a condition of life. There was no expectation things could, or would, be otherwise. You got on with it, and through faith, family and character accommodated as best you could whatever suffering and misfortune was yours. And so, it was only gradually, over the days to come, when they lifted their eyes and saw the improbable plane of blue overhead, that people began to acknowledge to themselves that up to now they had been living under a fall of watery pitchforks.

At that time, there endured in Faha an antique belief common in all rainy places, that sunlight was curative. Down the road the Miniters put their white, blind, hairnetted grandmother outside in her armchair where she sat in a citrus dream of Spain. By noontime the mouse-coloured mustiness that was in every house in the parish, and which people thought was the smell of mankind, had begun to resolve and vanish. Some clothes carried into the garden let escape brown flights of moths whose larvae dated to the days of Parnell and who now transitioned to powder in mid-air. I saw them but did not remember for fifty years until I saw a figure pixelate on a screen. The moths of Easter, I said aloud, and they flew in memory and dissolved again the way the smallest things of your life do. Many garments, which had been living on borrowed time, were discovered decrepit and began to fray in the firm fingers of the sun. Set outside, big-jointed furniture creaked an asymptotic series of aches that soon went unremarked because it was understood to be the bone-music of resurrection. Some items, invulnerable to time and decay, and prized accordingly, were borne outside for no reason other than the personified one that the air would do them good, and the shelves that were home to them could be dusted. So Doady carried out her two pieces of Limoges china – a

85

wedding gift from a hotel owner in Kenmare where she had been a scullery maid – a pink Staffordshire dish that was part of a collection that was never collected, two brass candlesticks that saw service only at Christmas and funerals, where like formal courtiers they would stand at the head and foot of the laid-out, and finally, any number of those blue willow-patterned plates and platters that for reasons lost in time had been ordained the good ware and were in every house in the parish then.

It was the finest airing in memory. When everything was outside and garden and yard had the appearance of a blithely hurricanoed bazaar, Doady stood in the midst of all they owned. The broad light of day was only growing broader. It was already certain to be a remarkable day. But that was inseparable from the temporality of it: it won't last, fortune never did.

Doady surveyed the accumulation of a lifetime without the slightest emotion. 'These things happen,' she concluded at last, and went inside to begin scouring.

Christy did not need an assistant. Although I didn't realise it at the time, he was not empowered to employ one. Why he said he did has remained a mystery to me, except for the fact that he enjoyed an audience.

In what was the first enduring change to the landscape since the human desire to be elsewhere had drawn the roads, the line for the electricity, devised in the high-ceilinged Georgian rooms of headquarters in Dublin, had now been pegged out across the unforgiving fields of west Clare. Dermot Mangan's poles had begun to arrive and were stockpiled in various locations on the edges of the parish where they were playground mountains to children whose mothers were soon to discover the fun of cleaning creosote. Wayleave notices had already been

served for each pole. But, with the casual imperiousness of officialdom, the authorities had failed fully to appreciate what it
meant to impose something as radical as posts and wires over
ground that had remained unchanged since creation, what,
with the perplex of our particular history, it meant to let someone or something into your land. They had fallen prey to a
classic trap of conceit and the very condition that at least since
the Pale had resulted in one side of the country distrusting the
other. They had also overlooked the soul-stubbornness that
was an essential for survival in the porous west. An amount of
what Harry Rushe, the Area Organiser, called backsliding had
taken place, and now some of these yahoos are starting to dig
in, he had told the field crews.

The long delay had had something to do with it. Between
the heady night of the hall meeting and the appearance of
any crewmen, the reality of an electrified future for Faha had
faded. Many who had been swayed by the rhetoric found that
resolves born of fine speeches did not endure, and in the deep
privacies of their person men felt foolish and chastened for
having envisioned wonders.

But Rushe had small time for subtlety, and particularly for
the people in the furthermost corners. Betraying a caustic he
had absorbed from the Brothers in Limerick, he had told the
crews the best way to solve any disputes was shame. 'So, ye
want to be behind the times, is that it? That's what you tell 'em.'

This was a tricky one, on three grounds. First, being behind
the times was not the spur it might have been to a townie,
who maybe lived within the illusion that they were not in a
backwater on a salted rock in the middle of the Atlantic. Faha
knew it was not only behind the times, but much further
back than that, it was outside the times altogether, *And what
of it?* Second, there was the question of unworthiness. This

had been ingrained by the Church from birth. With recourse to a pure Aristotelian logic, the bishops understood that making people feel lesser was a way of making the Almighty mightier, and with native extremism Faha took that to new lows. If there was something good out there, we probably didn't deserve it, was the basic position. Cormac Tansey, of course, went further: if there was something bad out there, he deserved that. The whole notion of unworthiness began to disappear, coincidental with the Church, by the approach of the millennium. But then it was absolute. And finally, farmers, with the natural caution of those who lived within the uncertainties of season and the brevity of life cycles, understood that of the land they were custodians only, and so change was always to be resisted.

As was traditional, but contrary to the clockwork of Rushe's nature, the roll-out was behind schedule. On every front there were impediments, setbacks, delays, the trials of which inflamed his gums and glossed his eyes. Addressing the field crews he was het up, face flushing into his ginger hair and short arms out stiff like a tweed penguin. 'If any farmer says he won't allow a pole, if he bars any gate, make no bones about telling him he will face the might of the Law. Tell him he will be taking on the State, and all her agencies, officers and Justices, and will not only incur and visit upon himself the expenses thereof but relegate his parish to the bottom-most rung.'

Christy was there to hear him, and told me now as we set out, judiciously walking the bicycles, to call on farmers, affirm their signatures on the memorial, and let them know the construction crews would be arriving immediately after Easter. 'Today we are the agencies of the State, Noe,' he said grandly and patted the State-issued leather satchel which bore the names of the signatories.

The State, in truth, was moidered with a headache.

The morning continued to lift, a last flotilla of clouds just then departing out the estuary. There was one of those mild breezes that in April can seem eloquent. What I remember are the birds, sudden quickened flights of them, ten, twenty taking flight together, with a magician's flourish, leaving bare one tree and finding another.

From a lifetime, how do you recall such a thing? The truth is you don't exactly. But you think you do, and you might have. At this stage that's good enough. Main point is, it seems to me every life has a few gleaming times, times when things were brighter, more intense and urgent, had more *life* in them I suppose. In mine, this was one.

We came up the hill by the fort, stopped at Matt Cleary's, a contrarian. We left the bicycles by the cow cabins. Matt was out in the haggard and came warily, followed by a little inquisitorial committee of hens. He had the wan face of a farmer in calving season, eyes small from lack of sleep and close encounters with viscera. He knew who I was, he said, but this man?

'With the Electricity Board,' I told him.

Christy was looking at Matt's way of pursing up his mouth and holding his head back a few inches, as though all in front of him was untrustworthy. Matt was looking at the blue suit. So were the hens. 'That right?' Matt said. He was fifty, singular in the parish because of his relation with the Doherty family, where he had courted the mother but married the daughter. Both lived with him, along with the hens.

'We're just visiting those whose land is to be crossed. The poles are here and the crews will be coming. You signed the waiver,' Christy said, rummaging in the satchel.

'Did I, though?'

This was a surprise. Christy checked the form, showed Matt his signature. 'Is this not your signature?'

Matt peered at it, pulled back his head, shrugged. 'Who could say?'

Straightforwardness was not in Faha's nature. There were reasons, historic, geographic, politic, civic, linguistic, possibly biologic, and all of them were operating behind Matt Cleary's dull grey eyes. Like many another in the parish, he was a privacy specialist and scrupulous with personal information. It'd be unchristian to call him a fanatic. Faced with the impasse, Christy was neither hasty nor confrontational.

'Right,' he said, nodded, and looked down at the signed memorial. He studied the form some, then held it out to Matt. 'Whose signature do you think it might be? Do you see there, where it says Matt Cleary?'

Matt looked at his own handwriting. He shooed a hen from pecking the cuff of his trouser, stood in a random of flies.

'Is that your hand, do you think?' Christy asked.

'I don't know. Give me your pen,' Matt said, and Christy gave him one and Matt made three clean strikes right through his signature. 'No, I'd say.' He handed back the memorial.

We walked out the yard after, silent until we got to the bicycles. The hens didn't come out past the gate. Down in the village Tom Joyce was tolling the angelus bell, the sound like silver rings thrown one after the other across the sky.

'Human beings are creations more profound than human beings can fathom.' Christy mounted his bicycle. 'That's one of the proofs of God,' he said, 'there's no other explanation.' And he smiled and pushed off and freewheeled ahead of me down the hill, the blue jacket winging out and the bulk of him flying past the hedgerows like a class of contented bird, only bigger.

With respect to his girth and his years, Christy did not cycle up hills, slopes, or the most gradual inclines. We walked mostly.

We went to Tom Pyne's, a low little lump of a house with faulty chimney; in bad weather the smoke came out the window, in good it came out the front door, but either way went unremarked.

Many were the houses of a people who lived outdoors at the time, a thing I didn't consider, nor how the electricity would change the habits of centuries. We went to Marty Mac's, to Marrinan's and Collins's, and met with a range of response from open enthusiasm to closed refusal. At most houses, there was an enlivened air of Eastering, and in the novel sunshine something *extra* about it. Outside, clothes were flapping on lines. Inside, paint pots, polishes, pastes of soda, of vinegar were being employed in urgencies of renewal. The same way it happened at Christmas, there was a personal sense of the coming feast day, as though, once he rose on Sunday, Jesus himself might drop by. A mirror of what confession was for the soul, surfaces had to be made spotless. I'm probably not the only one who, going from house to house and witnessing this, would have thought: what soaps and abrasives it might take to launder my spirit. To which you'll say: *You were only seventeen*, or maybe, *That's because you were only seventeen.*

Delineated I'm not sure how, in Faha whitewashing was a job for the women. Clouds of lime were mixed up in buckets and daubed on the cabins with elder sweeping brushes whose bristles were combed one way by wear and which had been retired to this last job. The wash went up grey, streaked and maculate, but, like old men, blanched as it dried. A thing to behold, the townland turning white.

We walked the bicycles along by Griffin's, took a scowly look from Griffin, whose blood was curdled by the fact that the electric line was not going to cross his land, and so, not only would there be no compensation, but his neighbour Carthy would profit. Neighbours, as Jesus knew, can be a not insignificant challenge to anyone's Christianity.

After a time, we came past the big house of Mrs Dinah Blackall, a Faha notable, now of great age, whose judgement had decayed, and who survived I'm not sure how. Her mind was like a bookcase whose shelves had been pulled away, leaving the books pell-mell. All the stories of her life were in there, only confounded one into the other. Christy stopped by the rusted gate to Blackall's avenue, or rather, with only nominal brakes, stuck his boot-heel into the ground and by juddering intervals came to a halt. He laid the bicycle in the ditch.

'This isn't on the list,' I said. But Christy was already walking up the avenue.

Mrs Blackall was in the courtyard. She was a tiny woman, really, but redoubtable. Beneath false eyelashes of flawless construction, her eyes had the triumphant spark of those who have eluded death. By something radiant in her nature, or excess of creams, her face appeared Vaselined, its features perfect but about to slide off unless she kept her head at a slight tilt towards the sky. Her hair floated in a wispy cloud of white, was thin in several places where the pink of her scalp showed like an egg, tender and vulnerable. She was wearing a fine dress of long ago, it was saffron, taffeta I think they call it, loops of several different necklaces that gave the appearance of a pale coil come apart, and satin slippers that had once been silver but the patina had cracked like porcelain and the soles made decrepit by the dirt of living. Her hands were cruel to consider, swollen, knobbed and knuckled out of proportion, but each of her fingers was ringed.

'You've beautiful rings,' said Christy.

She beamed and then pitched slightly forward. 'They can't be taken off,' she whispered. 'To rob them you will have to take my fingers.' And she smiled quite happily at the ingenuity, then sang a little clutch of words in Italian, whether about robbers or rings hard to say.

Perhaps the clockwork of the Church calendar was intact inside her, or a childhood memory of an Easter ritual had resurfaced, when one of the groomsmen would whiten the stables and outhouses, for she had a bucket of lime poorly mixed and had been about the business of it when we approached. Splashes of whitewash had been daubed here and there at a height of four feet in an application a Junior Infant would have improved upon.

'We're not robbers at all,' Christy said. 'We'll help you with that,' and he had the suit jacket off and laid across the gate and was rolling up his sleeves.

'O thank you, Frederick,' said Mrs Blackall.

I wanted to say: *but the memorial?* This was not among the houses we were supposed to be calling to, but Christy took the sweeping brush and held it out to me. 'You do the high, I'll the low,' he said.

Mrs Blackall was delighted. She clasped her ringed hands together. 'Mr Choppin keeps white doves,' she said, watching Christy stir the limewash. 'Beautiful white doves.'

'Is that right?'

'O yes.' She tilted her head to look up at where they were flying then, I suppose.

Christy looked up too. 'Beautiful,' he said.

Women enjoy watching men work, the same way men enjoy watching women dance. There's otherness and mystery in it. Mrs Blackall stood and watched us working, or rather me working and Christy directing – 'You might as well do all the way down', 'No harm to go over that bit again' – a role natural to him. He knew encouragement dissolved resistance: 'You're a gift at this, Noe. Top class.' And while I was slopping up the limewash, flecking face, clothes, hair and etcetera, he was standing back and surveying. 'That's her. Lovely job, wouldn't you say, Mam?'

'Father will be home before dark. We'll hear his carriage. Jason says he won't leave us. He never will.'

'Of course he won't,' Christy said.

By a trick of time Mrs Blackall was a small girl then, a net curtain drawn aside and her face against the cool glass of the bedroom window.

Pieces of story she would discover intact in her. She would draw them into the air with a single phrase and be elsewhere for a moment, eyes distant and eyelashes winging as an image fleeted past. Christy would gently try and bring forth more, but like a fallen chandelier inside her the whole was shattered and beyond repair and there were only exquisite shards.

'Shall we have tea, Thomas? We shall,' she said after a while and went into the house and did not return.

I finished all the limewash there was, coaxed the pasty last of it on. There remained an unpainted fringe, two feet from the ground, but there was no more.

'A Christian act,' Christy said, admiringly. 'Don't you feel better?'

I couldn't say I did. My hands were already calcifying.

'We'll see she's all right and tell her it's done.'

'Yes, Thomas,' I said.

Christy looked at me and smiled, as though I had come through a test.

We went up the porch steps and into Blackall's. The one-time land agent's house, it was infamous in the parish, its history leaving a stain that had endured the way it might at a plague site despite the passing of a hundred years and the balm of generation. Horace, his sons George and James, George's son Victor, were alien threads stitched into the story of the place. The people of Faha did not despise the Blackalls, they took a higher position and ignored them. So, when, through debt, drunkenness and the despair of solitude, the house and grounds went to wrack and the family disintegrated, Faha was looking the other way. I didn't know anyone who had been inside Blackall's.

The interior was dark and darker for coming in from the blaze of daylight. There was a front foyer of fine flagstones with a tall wicker basket for walking sticks, canes and umbrellas that had neither walked nor umbrellaed in decades and a hat rack with the hats of ghosts.

'Mrs Blackall?' Christy called, but didn't wait for reply and headed on through into the reception room where two cats were lying by the windowsill in a lemon bath of sunlight. We didn't attract their interest. Tearing to threads the Turkish rug had exhausted them. The room was grand in proportion but desperate in appearance, the walls once cream now skinned with a green mildew that was the living coat of the rain, a chaos of oddments, a credenza covered with cat-food tins, a long, narrow table that bowed under a yellow mountain of newspaper, a flittery straw hat on a tilted globe, an elegant wicker cage that made me think of India, its door open and bird flown, a wheelbarrow filled with men's shoes I remember, all in general abandon overseen by oil portraits glowering and darkening like Hell's gallery and six of those cartoon drawings of hunting scenes to which Siney O Shea said the gentry were partial.

'Mrs Blackall?'

We went along the corridor past rooms colder than a cold day and mummified by neglect and heard the singing of the same phrase in Italian ascending the stairwell. Christy pointed a finger and followed it down the stairs. The kitchen was partly below ground and as you descended you felt you were visiting the buried. There, gaily, Mrs Blackall was between forgetting and remembering that she had come down to make tea. She had taken out a tarnished silver teapot, and into it she had spooned three heaps of tea leaves, and, when she forgot this, she had spooned three more, and when she forgot those, three more still.

'Job's done, Mrs Blackall,' said Christy. 'You're all set.'

'Most kind, Frederick,' she said. A fine hairnet of cobwebs on one side of her head, she looked at us as if we were benign apparitions, which I suppose we were, and smiled a kind of small-girl smile, and I forgot the chore it had been, and that I was million-speckled with white.

She poured the tea. It came out in glops, lumpish and black.

'There's eating and drinking in that tea, Mrs Blackall,' Christy said.

'You don't take milk, do you?' Clutching on to her necklaces, she looked vaguely at the shelves and presses.

'We prefer it black. Don't we, Noe?'

'Yes.'

He lifted the teacup and performed an impeccable demonstration of how you deny reality.

Tea parties no longer part of her days, Mrs Blackall was charmed. I cleared a space and she sat at the oak table with us, her ringed hand going to her necklaces and running gently down them, as though confirming all the pearls within her were still strung. Prompted by who knows what, she began to say the names of women. A Mrs Bainbridge, a Mrs Pilkington, a Doris, a Dorothy, I don't rightly recall them now, but I understood they were the company she had kept, bridge-players, wives of captains, doctors, lawyers, I'm guessing, a little congregation of Church of Ireland gentry whose ghosts came downstairs now and briefly populated the gloom of that basement kitchen while Christy and I negotiated the tea. When she had finished summoning the ladies and had fallen into one of those reveries that are the prerogative of age, Christy leaned towards her. 'Mrs Blackall, you don't know me, at all? Do you?'

The question stunned me, but upset her, like a test she didn't want to fail. Her face clouded.

'Christy,' he said. 'In Sneem. Years ago. Before you were married.'

The clouds didn't lift.

'Annie Mooney,' he said.

Mrs Blackall went around in the past. I looked at Christy, he looked at her. And, in the suspended moments while Mrs Blackall walked the question around to each corner of her mind, I knew he had not asked it idly and I felt the same charge of the personal I had felt the night before when he had stood to sing.

Mrs Blackall blinked her eyelashes, twice, thrice, and returned to us.

'No, dear, I don't think so,' she said. But she stayed in the realm of that question for a time, and then her entire face had a kind of light come to it, and she looked at Christy the way you look when something that was always right in front of you has just come apparent. 'O now,' she said, 'I know you now,' and she reached across and touched his knee, and from that seemed in some way gladdened or consoled. But she said no more and Christy didn't press further on the thinness of her memory.

Before long we were back in the sunlight and crossing the courtyard to the bicycles.

'Her tea tasted like blackbirds,' Christy said with a small chuckle, taking his jacket from the wall and putting it on.

The sky was as blue as earlier, the stables and what was finished of the outhouses whitening by the moment.

'Who is Annie Mooney?'

Christy didn't change his expression, he just paused, a count of one, two, three, in which he turned the back pages of his history, then he said, 'She was my greatest mistake.'

For a moment, he didn't take his eyes off mine. Then he gave a little toss of his head, as though motioning back a swarm of regrets, and with that he mounted the bicycle, pushed off into the centre of the road and let the hill take him.

That evening, by the grace of God, we did not go to Craven's. I was exhausted and Christy was quiet in himself. At twilight, when it was time to bring the furniture back inside, Doady, with the percipience of Kerry people, said, 'Leave them. It won't rain tomorrow either.'

The aired sheets, towels and clothing she had already restored to their presses. Christy and I carried in the mattress, and on Doady's instruction set it upside down and back-to-front on the bedframe, an age-old recipe for renewal about which I chose not to think closely.

Ganga, who was enthused by all novelty, loved the idea of the furniture in the garden. He went out and sat in an armchair and discovered the thrill of a room of air. 'You feel like the King of Munster,' he said. Joe lay like a wolfhound at his feet.

The evening was balmy. Lidded by a night haze, the heat of the day did not escape. The midges had gone to Boola.

Whether Ganga recognised that Christy was folded up inside himself, whether he thought it an obligation to entertain lodgers, or he himself wanted entertainment, he took from his jacket pocket the pack of cards, removed the two jokers, turned over the top card, the ace of hearts, and said, 'I'll deal.'

We played Forty-Five, outside in the April garden, in the slur of the river-sounds until night fell. We played after that too, shadow-bats like fragments of dark dipping and swooping, and all but the company become insubstantial. We played the way all card games were played in Faha, not to make money, but to pass the time, provide a way to escape reality and by the happenstance of chance allow someone to believe good fortune existed. We played until Doady said she couldn't tell the knave from the king and Ganga said no word of a lie in that.

Certified by the blurred divisions of the gloaming, Doady told the news she had in a letter from Kerry.

'Mrs O Dea is on her way out.'

Not knowing who Mrs O Dea was, we were sparing in our sympathy, but nodded a nod and the phrase *on her way out* hung there and the image of a doorway through which Mrs O Dea was to pass was carpentered into reality.

Gadge Gallagher, a widow, had gone a step further and died, Lord have mercy on her. She had lived in some mountainy townland far from the church. Fearing that she would go to her Creator without receiving Communion on her deathbed, one Sunday Gadge had secretly saved a host before it melted on her tongue, brought it home in a linen handkerchief she had from Quills in Kenmare and preserved it in the ciborium of a purple hatbox beside her bed, a china plate next to it as paten. It was not a theft because Father Fahy had put the host in her mouth himself, Doady said, lest our minds be gone that way. In any case, Gadge Gallagher's strategy had proved effective, she said, up to a point. The poor woman had taken a turn in her bed, blessed herself and reached for the hatbox.

No one played a card. Gadge Gallagher's salvation hung in the balance. Doady had the cuteness to hold her whist.

'And?' said Ganga, laying his cards face down till he heard.

'And,' said Doady.

Savouring the turn in the story, she said no more. She looked above us into the immensity of the firmament. 'And,' she said again, forefingering the bridge of her glasses and with the unbounded theatrics of all the O Siochrus milking all the udders of the pause.

'And?' Ganga opened his two hands to receive the ending.

Doady leaned in over the table. Across from her, in mute manifestation of the married, Ganga leaned forward too. She lowered her voice. 'Didn't Sullivan the undertaker find the host after, stuck to the roof of her mouth.'

Doady sat back, made a little nod, her glasses flashing.

The conundrum landed, we were silently all Sullivan then, trying to decide which way to send the host.

Gadge Gallagher's soul lay suspended in the air.

To resolve the impasse, Doady played a trump and left the story there, leaving the finer points, physic, metaphysic and ecclesiastic, to private debate.

As was customary, the card game made elastic the time and assured the playing of another hand after *This will be last hand so*, and another after that. Dissolving the grit of reality, it left us to float free as the stars appeared. Christy drank a dozen cups of tea, played inexpertly, losing to Ganga who took victory each time with a little doubled-up kink of laughter. Christy relished it, I think, enjoying the company and privacy accorded by the cards. As the river sang on, soft and blind in the distance, not for the first nor last time was there the sense that Faha had slipped its moorings and slid away from the country, which sped on, without noticing the lack.

In the end Doady concluded the game by a tactic cunning and adroit. She took the pack for a shuffle, pocketed it in her housecoat, and began the rosary. That put the kibosh on it.

The rosary was said in most houses then, but in few midnight gardens. The version that night was murmured and swift. By native decree, and the proven truth that no nation spoke faster, punctuation in prayer had been long ago dispensed with, breathless delivery was acceptable to the Lord who could pause, parse and separate the string of prayers in His own time.

Our prayers said, we went inside and left the furniture. On the bottom step of the Captain's Ladder, Christy paused. 'Ye're great people,' he said, nodded towards Ganga who swelled a little with the compliment, and climbed to his bed.

I carried the cups to the basin.

'Doady, do you know an Annie Mooney?'

She turned and looked in a way that made me feel I had just become interesting.

In the dark of the attic bedroom later, I crept under the blankets. Christy was laid out straight, hands folded on his chest. I couldn't tell if he was asleep.

I lay like him, face to the thatch, but after a while, because human beings are helpless when seeded with story, I turned towards his bed and said, 'Annie Mooney is Mrs Gaffney, the chemist's wife.'

Whether he heard or not, he made no sound or movement.

13

Good Friday was not only sunny, it was warm. Actual tempera-
tures had an anaemic unreality then, nobody in Faha knew
them, or if they did would not have paid them one whit of attention. Numbers were displaced by something more tangible. A
ball, a bundle, an armful and a fistful were measures. People
knew what a perch was, and a rood, and could show you by
walking in a field. So, what the mercury rose to in the weather
station at Birr, County Offaly, was irrelevant to Fahaeans. But
once you walked outside, the flesh of your body told you you
were out of your element. It was like arrival in, if not quite
Mexico, maybe Marseilles. By eight in the morning the haze
that hung over the near bank of the river was lifting. By nine
the grass was drying, and by ten the air was thickening with
heat, and many were relieved to discover that the houses they
lived in, unbeknownst to their architects, could not have been
better constructed to keep the cold inside. The depth of the
stone walls and the small deep windows defeated the angle
of the sun. While in Faha the dictionary of rain ran to many
volumes, it was quickly apparent that for sunshine there was
only a single phrase: it was *roasting*.

In keeping with the local phenomenon of rain-denying,
whereby whole parishes refuted claims that it ever rained

in them – *Was it raining over in Faha? Really? We only had a drop* – now an equal competition for the sun had begun. It was hotter in Boola than in Faha, which was nothing to the heat in Labasheeda, mind, over in Kilmurry the sun was fierce, in Kildysart the skin would burn off you in about three minutes flat. In Cahercon, two. With an acuity that was both pagan and inside the origins of the Church calendar, it was understood that to be favoured by the sun at Easter was to be favoured by the Son, and in this heat and light you couldn't speak against that.

The favour brought with it its own challenges. Farmers, who only now realised they had been waiting a lifetime for dry weather, were spirit-quickened, wanted to profit from the fine day, but were bound by adherence to the regimens of Good Friday.

Good Friday was then a day of almost universal quiet. Consider it. Some beautiful things have perished. A hush was laid like an altar linen over the green townlands, and not just during the three hours of the Agony and the veneration of the Cross. The pubs were closed. Only work that was absolutely necessary was done, there was no construction, no horse was shod, because no nail could be driven, a commandment that endured in Faha until the boom, when the Church had collapsed and electric nail-guns turned to a fable the visceral realities of Calvary.

Faha being Faha, there were exceptions. Poaching, already widespread, was on Good Friday licensed by Christ, and lads young and old dug worms and took off for the river with rods actual or improvised. In acknowledgement that Easter Sunday required you to look your best, barbers and drapers were allowed to stay open. A haircut on Good Friday, Doady said, kept headaches away for a year. By some uncertain logic, Jack, the cobbler, was also the village barber. Short back and sides was the omni-cut, the common appraisal after was *scalped*, the cropped lines and the white skin at the back of men's necks making them look boyish and prepped for the guillotine. In Boylan's drapery, the fine weather provided a double boon, first because in Faha the proverb was reversed, you saved for a sunny day, and second, no woman had an outfit thin enough for this heat.

In the morning, Christy was not in his bed. The blankets were folded at the foot of it, and he and his suitcase and all sign of him were gone.

'He went out early,' Ganga said. 'Joe heard him.' He patted the dog under the table in the garden.

'Did he say where he was going?'

'Did he, Joe?'

Was he coming back? I didn't ask. On a seventeen-year-old, indifference is both common mask and shield, and remoteness was a native trait then.

I did feel the loss of him. Why had he gone? Why had he said nothing? At the cards, he had said the electricity work was suspended until after Easter, but not that he was going anywhere.

Briskly tidying the breakfast back into the house, Doady announced that after confession she might take a look into Boylan's.

'Be no harm find a hat,' she said. If fishing for compliment, she caught none. She would also visit the graveyard. They were Ganga's not her dead that were there, but he was allergic to cemeteries and guarded against the grief that arose from too much reality.

'Say hello for me,' he said, hunting for a fishing rod.

'You'll be in the church at three,' she called, but all that was left of him was his whistling.

She looked at me, a vexed look. The forthrightness that was natural in her wanted to say: *You'll be in the church too*, but the pact she had made with my grandfather forbade it, and instead that imperative flew in a wordless glint across her glasses. She clutched the war-chest of her huge handbag and headed out.

When they were both gone, I sat in the kitchen. The front door open, a ladder of sunlight footed on the threshold, a hectic of birdsong. There was every reason to feel natural joy in the world, but for the one that makes it accessible. When your spirit is uneasy, stillness can be a kind of suffering. And when you're young, the unlived life in you, all that future, urgent and unreachable, can be unbearable.

When I was young, I meant.

I write this now, having spent a lifetime trying to be, by which I mean the best version, a thing dreamed by those stricken with imagination. Not that you ever quite know what that is, still there he is, that better man, who remains always just ahead of you. I write this now, having come to realise it's a lifelong pursuit, that once begun will not end this side of the graveyard. With this I have made an old man's accommodation and am reconciled to the fruits of a fruitless endeavour. I don't torture myself with my failures, but when I was seventeen I did little else.

That Good Friday I was in four minds, maybe five. What was I doing there? What exactly was I hoping for? Where would I go now? Should I not just return to the seminary?

I sat inside the door, stewing on the edge of the splendid day.

After a time, Brendan Bugler came to make a call for the vet. A shambles of a man, dogged with ill fortune, he had the slit eyes and tobaccoed teeth of a desperado. Waiting to be put through, he told me a calf born on Good Friday was lucky. When he was done, he apologised for the fact he hadn't the coins for the call. He'd make good again, he said.

Eventually Joe returned, and, a breathless minute or two after, Ganga, with an eel alive in a bucket. 'Supper, Noe.'

Whistling, he changed his clothes, tying his bootlaces, and betraying no hint that his grandson not going to church was an embarrassment.

We could hear the church bell ringing. Sam Cregg marched past the front door.

'Joe, you stay with Noe.'

Joe was exhausted from the excitements of the fishing and lay on the cool flags.

When you've been raised inside a religion, it's not a small thing to step outside it. Even if you no longer believe in it, you can feel its absence. There's a spirit-wound to a Sunday. You can patch it, but it's there, whether natural or invented not for me to say.

When Ganga was gone, I couldn't bear the quiet, or the company of the eel slithering in the bucket. I went outside. I looked left to the village and the spire of St Cecelia's, right to the slow flow of the sparkling river. The countryside had an emptiness that felt utter, and it was not impossible to imagine complicity between heaven and earth. The church bell tolled a final time.

All of the small decisions of my life have been led by reason, but none of the important ones, so there's no reason I can offer now why I crossed the yard then and went inside the lower cabin. A dim once-cowshed, it was packed with old tools, buckets, broken pieces of harness, busted hair-sprouted ass collars, leathers, handles, handleless heads of shovels, hammers, forks, two-, three- and four-pronged, bent out of line by close encounters with the unforgiving, retired bronze-winged sleans, rusted cans of oil, open jars of grease with raisin flies, lamps oranged with rust, old boots, some singular, some in pairs, planks, boards holed and unholed, rods of osier, balls of hairy twine, loops of rope, forged flanges, a metal badge embossed *P. Daly, Kilmihil,* and multiple other pieces of iron, to what end impossible to say, the entire cabin a catch-all of a hundred years of country living and a more-or-less exact replica of the inside of Ganga's mind.

Twenty minutes later, having found what I was looking for, I was back at Blackall's yard, working the loose and clanking arm of the pump until it seemed the earth could not have such depth, when suddenly the water glugged and shot out. From the bucket of Ganga's lime, it made puff up a pale cloud that burned the back of my throat. Work was not permitted, I knew, but there is a natural wilfulness in youth that is consummate, damnation be damned. That Good Friday afternoon, in the trapped sunlight of an unvisited court-yard, I worked as hard and fast as I could, whitewashing the moment into my memory where it would remain the rest of my life, painting the unfinished ends of Blackall's outhouses until they gleamed.

Mrs Blackall did not appear. Whether she noticed or ever knew, I don't know. She knows now, I suppose.

14

Christy did not return. Although in Ganga's mind, where all stories worked out for the best, he was probably gone visiting family or relations for the holiday and would be back soon, I knew this was not the case. He had come because of Annie Mooney, and now he was gone for the same reason. I knew it was true.

After the hiatus of Good Friday, as if a switch was thrown, Faha woke up thrumming. Light-headedness from the fasting combined with the imminence of the feast day to provoke an emergency of preparation. It was discovered that nothing was ready, and soon people were on the roads, by horse, cart, bicycle and boot, under an imperative to secure the last essentials. These were as various and unaccountable as human nature. Each family had its own best ware, and small peculiarities that they thought of as normal. This being Faha, normal ranged from the simple to the baroque, and had direct or tangential connection to the seasonal theme of eggs – lemon placemats, napkins the colour of egg-yolks, small salt-and-pepper hens that only came out for Easter, *but weren't they just the perfect job?* More obscurely paschal, a brass menorah bought in Kilrush market from a Limerick trader who sold it as antique Easter ware, an ornamental plate showing sheep grazing, and a silver salver, preserved who knows how, hidden from thieves in a tea chest and taken out twice a year for the goose or the lamb. Everywhere, a world of tokens, individual and abstruse, but none pass-remarkable, because all were in silent accord on the primacy of the Church holiday and that you had to go all-out for something as unearthly as Resurrection.

To this end, now were needed: ladles, linen tablecloths, lidded tureens, gravy boats, cake stands, candlesticks, egg cups, doilies, napkins and a small viscid ocean of mint jelly. It was understood that upon these finishing touches hung the substance of glorification, so none were disregarded and a brisk commercial holy hysteria had its heyday.

By Fahaean good fortune, in cardboard boxes on the deep, top shelves in Bourke's and Clohessy's was an absolute every-thing, or a compromised version. No one went without.

Both butcher shops had a line out the door, and in tight bundles of brown paper expertly trussed with white twine came not a small herd's worth of spring lamb. It was an hour before the blood would start seeping, and men who had stopped into pubs for more than just the one could be told by the brown stain of the lamb's leg under their arm. Across the street from the two butchers' shops, in McCarthy's Hardware, bashful men in raw new haircuts stood waiting to get carving knives edged.

You were inside the engine of Easter. With the enduring magic by which a people, on budgets thin as air, not only survive but celebrate, the feast was everywhere being readied. Breads, sweet loaves and cakes of all kinds were underway. Come early from Africa, heralds or harbingers of the summer, twists of swallows dipped and swooped with bird delight over gardens Barbadian with the black scent of molasses or the golden one of caramelised sugar.

To Doady a handful of neighbours called – 'You don't have a fist of cloves for the ham, Aine, I suppose?' 'There isn't, by any chance, a spare saucepan in the house?' All were accommodated.

There were telephone callers too, a troop of handle-crankers, waiting to be put through, and then, in a foreshadowing of technologies yet undreamt, looking into the big black Bakelite receiver to see down the line the face on the other side, shout their Happy Easter and tell who had died.

As well as callers, we had a visit from Mrs Moore. Nominally, Mrs Moore was my grandmother's occasional housekeeper. A humped widow of Methuselah, Mrs Moore could recall the origins of the village when the tide withdrew and the fish were flapping on the grass. If she had the time she could relate the whole of the parish history. She knew first-hand the thousand days of rain, the fur time of the midges, and the *ciúnas mhór*, the Big Quiet, when the women in Faha stopped talking to the men. It was one of the wonders of Faha that Mrs Moore remained above ground. She retained a flawless internal roll call of the dead and their relations, could outdo the Annals of the Masters and was better than the forty dusty volumes of the parochial records that existed up to the time of the fire, the rescued fourteen that existed up to the time of the flood. She knew who was in which grave, and who in the one below that one (and the ones below those too, who were working their way back to the surface through the self-raising agent of a colloquy of worms fat and contented from passing through life, until chosen by Simon of the Kellys as best bait for the smirking salmon passing in the river). Mrs Moore lived long enough to become an unofficial consultant on the dead when the time for seeking ancestors came. In her habitual tricolour of green gaberdine, orange headscarf and off-white judge's wig, Mrs Moore landed, clutching a large bag from which, with great seriousness, she emptied tins, jars and bottles of various cleansing solutions, two of her 'clean' rags, a ball of wire wool, and Flo, the world's saddest feather duster.

Mrs Moore made Doady look young, which may have been a subterranean reason for her employment. Another may have been that she was a smoker. No sooner had she landed than she had to have the one, a Wild Woodbine, and Doady always joined her. Though Mrs Moore wheezed and sputtered and was prone to the bad chest, though her skin looked like linoleum, the features of her face scrunching together to escape the smoke, it was the weather was the culprit. She held the record for ash-balancing. She would work with a burning cigarette held out ballerina-style in one hand, a tower of ash she didn't need to look at building nicely while she dusted, or performed a slow-motion version of same, the dust in no danger, until the tower was certain to fall, and at the last moment, as though it were a smoking extension of herself, she would bring the cigarette to her small mouth and suck like the damned. She would draw on the cigarette and the smoke-coloured dashes of her eyebrows would float up and leave no doubt that from ashes to ashes was her destiny, and not such a bad one at that.

At cleaning she was not expert. She had her system, always did the same jobs in the same order, she had a great fondness for wax-papering the top of the stove, but often lost her way mid-task leaving a trail of opened bottles, tins and rags, that Doady followed, topping and capping, adopting a tone less stern than herself to call, 'O Mrs Moore?'

'Is that where it got to?'

There was pantomime to it. But like everything in Faha, something more too. Eventually I learned that it was Ganga who had first hired her, when the last of his sons had left and his wife had fallen into a silent suffering that in those days was not called depression and did not exist in any discourse but devastated just as many. On remote houses in the rain a spirit-conquering loneliness fell, and entered, and, though front doors were kept open, it would not easily leave. I learned that Mrs Moore was my grandfather's surprise and under-stood that she was the least likely emissary of love, his way of acknowledging to Doady that he knew she was afflicted, and company would be a balm. Knowing that Doady would refuse any such, he had presented it as charity. Knowing that Mrs Moore would not accept charity, he had presented it to her as an act of kindness to his wife. The few pence Ganga paid Mrs Moore I expect were her only income.

As was the way these things were transacted in Faha, the arrangement operated on one level, while being truly another. So as not to hurt her feelings, Ganga and Doady preserved the pretence that Mrs Moore was still an excellent house-cleaner. And not to hurt Doady's, Mrs Moore preserved the pretence she was there to clean. She was a fixture for many years. On the stormy night of the census in 1956, Mrs Moore was under my grandparents' roof, took three years off her age to list it as seventy-five and in the comedy of statistics was categorised as Serving Girl.

All peoples disadvantaged by the chance of geography devise ploys to outfox circumstance. Among the virtues of being a forgotten elsewhere is the fact that everything has to be invented first-hand, and all needs met locally. Faha was no different. It had one of everything. You just had to know where to look. In the cleared centre of Maureen Mungovan's parlour there operated a hair salon, which, in the days before electricity, meant pots of water simmering on the hearth,

buckets for head-dipping, and a mirror framed by two smoking paraffin lamps. Maureen herself was a Mona Lisa, that
is, she was not classically beautiful but had conquered time
and preserved forever the face she had at thirty. As the ashen
look of Lent came to an end, a legion of women filed in to
Mungovan's for a do. Hair-colouring was still in its infancy
then, there was nothing of what the next ten years would
bring, but a foresighted frontiersman, a salesman by the
exotic name of Oscar Sloane, had come through Faha with
a range of bottles and a Tint Card 'for all known hues of
human hair', he said. 'Plus some in Excel shades,' he added,
knowing womankind the more adventurous sex and novelty
a better sauce than chocolate, with the result that several new
blonde, brunette, red- not to say orange-headed women came
out of Mungovan's that afternoon.

Some women, living the hard-edged adventure of the penni-
less, resorted to home-styling. Because it was mostly through
newspapers that people caught glimpses of the greater world,
styles were inspired by the pictures in the picture houses and
the illustrations in the ads in the *Clare Champion*, which
showed the latest look of ten years ago. In an unfair feminine
paradox, it turned out that those women with straight hair
wanted curls, those with curls wanted straight. In half the
houses of Easter Saturday afternoon, curlers were critical. In
the other half, makeshift prototype straighteners, flatteners,
calmers, anti-wave, anti-bounce and -flounce potions of all
sorts, concocted from what I could tell out of the ingredients
of cake – oil, milk, sugar and eggs – lent an air of experimen-
tal baking.

Doady was in the former. Although in normal times I never
knew her to have an ounce of vanity, all her pride reserved
for Kerry people and Kerry things, after a stray comment

from Mrs Moore when she was leaving, the idea took hold in Doady that for the Feast of the Resurrection her hair should have 'a bit of a lift'. She owned no curlers and did not wish to borrow on two counts, first because she wanted the privacy of reversing the styling in case of a disaster, and second, if successful, the reveal as she walked in and up the Long Aisle would provide one of those redeeming moments that all women who have married into hardship crave. Undeterred by the absence of curlers, she began rooting around in drawers to improvise some.

'I'll make 'em,' Ganga said.

'Out of what?'

'Pegs.'

'Pegs?'

Whether vexed by the lack, or the greater gall that her husband thought everything could be resolved in a trice, Doady threw both hands out as if shooing her hens. 'Go away. Go away and leave me in peace.'

Momentarily, Ganga forgot his wife's intransigence. 'I'll have 'em made in jig-time.'

'Pegs in my hair! A nice look that'll make for Easter.'

With the placid air of a hexed husband, Ganga said precisely the wrong thing: 'You don't need them at all, sure. Aren't you grand?'

If there was a cup to hand it might have flown. Doady made do with a dart of her eyes. Ganga felt it land and stick into the flat of his forehead. He opened and then closed his mouth and retreated to the obscurely Easter business of washing all the wellingtons.

Doady was left to her own devices, which in the end consisted of twists of letter-paper soaked in a saccharine concoction of sugar and egg-whites which, when twined about wet hair, gave an appearance of small Swiss rolls or a gateau-ed experiment of the French aristocracy. Trying the small reserve of her patience, she sat in the garden, her wet head inside the giant cylindric hairdryer of the blue sky. While the sun cooked her hair, I was posted as lookout. Later, when it was time to leave for the Vigil and the lighting of the *Lumen Christi*, Doady undid the twists to reveal a hairstyle so sprung that Ganga beamed like a boy with a candied toy, not for the first nor last time forced to concede an undeniable truth: women are always right.

The styling had an underlying urgency I wouldn't be aware of until the following day. It was wrapped in a headscarf for the journey to the village.

When they were gone I fell again into that place of lost faith. My grandparents went to the church without thinking, it seemed to me, without question, and I envied them that. That year's Easter Vigil could be threaded on to all the others they had attended down the years and, though they would not have thought of it in these terms, these things were footholds and, to the man I was then, seemed both to belong to them and give them belonging.

These things are no more, and the feeling I am telling here, of the entire parish gone to church to await the lighting of the Easter candle, and what it felt like to know that and not be going, may have perished too. It felt like a tide had gone out and taken all the ships with it, and you were left on a shore, a debris.

The quiet of the country can sit on your heart like a stone. To lift it, to escape the boundaries of myself awhile, I took down the fiddle.

One of the things about Irish music is how one tune can enter another. You can begin with one reel, and with no clear intention of where you will be going after that, but half-way through it will sort of call up the next so that one reel becomes another and another after that, and unlike the clear-edged definitions of songs, the music keeps linking, making this sound-map even as it travels it, so player and listener are taken away and time and space are defeated. You're in an else-where. Something like that.

Which, I suppose, is both my method and aim in telling this story too.

Anyway, I was playing, not well, not wonderful, but for myself and inside the solace of it, playing at the table outside in the garden when Christy returned.

I wasn't aware of him at first. He stood at the small gate listening. Because I was playing to escape myself it was some time before he found a gap and clapped.

'You're a fine player.'

'I'm not.'

'Have you heard Junior Crehan play?'

'No.'

He looked at me a moment and the look said I had been cycling past the Pyramids and never seen them.

'Neither have I. We'll go hear him next week,' he said, as though it was already decided.

Because he had gone away, and without saying, and because I only then realised I had the stupid bruise of it, I was cool with him.

He put down his case. He pulled a palm down his beard, which like all of him had been barbered. I knew he was wait-ing for me to ask where he had been, and because I knew I said nothing.

He paced some, not far, he was large and unswift, a few steps over and back. He hunted in the pockets of his blue suit, found a foiled mint he had not been seeking, picked it free of pocket fur, popped it in his mouth. He stood, eyes glittering. The haircut had made him not younger exactly, but *edged*.

'She buried the chemist,' he said, snap, like that.

I found the fiddle strings needed tuning.

'Three years ago. Annie Mooney. She's a widow.'

The river behind him, he waited for my response. I had known and not said. I ran my finger across the strings. He drew his lips tight together. He put back his shoulders and let the solid block of himself roseate in the sunlight. In moments his face ran a riot of freckles. He had resolved to say no more, I am sure of it, but he couldn't help himself, he had the affliction of the infatuate for which the only salve was to say her name again. 'Annie Mooney.'

It was inexplicably tender, the slightly abashed boyishness of a big man in his sixties.

'For her I once ate a dozen purple tulips,' Christy said, and in the blueness of his eyes you could see he was amazed by and not a little admiring of his younger self, who entered the garden on that statement and strode through, all innocence and earnestness, a wildly impetuous boy with small boots, glitter eyes and tufted hair, in love with Annie Mooney.

He was as present as I am here. Maybe you've seen that sometime sitting with an older person, the youth they were passes through their eyes, and is in silence acknowledged, hopefully acquitted. The Christy who ate the tulips would knock you down if you tried to stop him, I got that. His adamancy, certainty, his belief in what the poet called the holiness of the heart's affections, these I'd like to think I understood then without the vocabulary or experience, but maybe I only understand them rightly now. He was a boy with heart blown open in the amaze of the world and the largeness of his own feelings, that I can say, and for long moments he was there amongst us until Christy lost sight of him again and shook his head slightly and said, 'To what end exactly I can't remember.'

To counter the airiness of sentiment he sat heavily on the windowsill. I offered the box of matches and he smoked a cigarette. 'Play a tune for us.'

'I'm not good enough, I only play for myself.'

'Play for yourself and I won't be here.'

But you are there, I probably said, but will absolve myself of that stupidity here.

He smoked. The sun parcelled us in dazzlement. Licensed – I use that word too often, but can think of no better – by the light, Eastertime, and perhaps the word April, the river ran like a child-river, free, and for a time talk vanished into the place where all the world's conversations have gone.

I knew where Christy's mind was, or thought I did, until he held the second cigarette out from him and said, 'The morning I turned sixty I was in a boarding house in Boston. I was lying in the bed and was gifted one clear, cold realisation, like a glass of spring water.'

I didn't ask what it was.

'*You've still time, Christy. You've still time to go back and right all the mistakes you've made. That's what it was.*' He looked at me, his face lit as if he had won a prize.

On that morning he had become possessed by a single idea, simple and fantastical both, and he had set out on a personal crusade, to make what amends he could, and this was what had brought him to Faha.

I didn't know what to say. My first thought was: he is a simpleton. Or, in Doady's vocabulary, a *dudaire*. It was absurd, naïve, childish, and sentimental. You can't correct the mistakes of a lifetime. You are your own past. These things happened, you did them, you have to accommodate them inside your skin and go forward. Even if you could – and you couldn't, can't – there was no going back. Something like this was running through my mind.

Christy watched the smoke, there, and not there. 'I am resolved on a career of reparation,' he said.

'And have you? Made amends?'

'It is one of the tragedies of life, that life keeps getting in the way of good intentions. I've made some. I'll make more.'

I looked away and left him eating the purple tulips of memory.

'Annie Mooney,' he said after a time.

Because words failed me, and because the air was angular and awkward with emotion, I lifted the fiddle.

I can't remember what I played. I wasn't good, I'm fairly certain, but I suppose it was not a thing of nothing.

15

That evening, above in the room, Christy began preparations in earnest for his approach to Annie Mooney. Whistling softly, he took off his blue suit, hung it off the rafter, appraised it as though it were a suit of armour. With cursory flicks, he backhanded dust from both lapels, brought over his glass of water from the bedside and, dipping three fingers, towards the thousand wrinkles shot a general dousing. It had an air of benediction. With the palm of his hand he ironed the more grievous of the rumples, finding some stubborn, flicking more water at them, pressing harder, flicking and pressing, flicking and pressing until at last the suit reached an assessment of Pass, and for a moment he considered it and saw himself in it in Annie Mooney's eyes and the whistling slowed just for a tick and I knew his heart had bumped against the idea of what she would see after so long a time. Just for a tick there was a broken-off lump of his heart in his throat, then he swallowed and the whistling came on again.

I was in the bed over, reading the amber pages of Augustine by the lamp, noting the passages about his mother's death and thinking maybe Father Walsh had method in him when he gave me the book. I was watching and not watching as Christy stood sidelong in vest and underpants and improvised a calisthenics, informed both by an absolute non-acquaintance of exercise and the vexed attrition of a long-lived-in body. Softly whistling all the while, he held in both hands the bulk of his belly and tried in vain to push it inside him. When this failed, by pressing from the top he tried to send it south below his beltline. He pulled up the underpants to try and arrange a meeting. Abandoning this, he sucked in his breath and stood to his full height and with both hands again pressed his belly in and upward, as if its rightful place was in his chest cavity. It remained there for five seconds, and for five seconds he was delighted at the figure he cut, the vanquishing of time, gravity and human sinkage.

'What do you think?' he hissed, chin up, shoulders back and chest out like Conway's cock.

He tightened his everything another touch and occupied that illusion until it exploded in a gasp.

He was not defeated. 'I am a loose-strung fiddle, but she'll know the head of me.'

'How long is it since you saw her?'

'In the flesh? Near enough fifty years.'

I nearly laughed.

'But in every other way, some time every day since.'

And that stopped me. That was one of the things about him. He walked this line between the comic and the poignant, between the certainly doomed and the hopelessly hopeful. In time I came to think it the common ground of all humanity.

A thing I didn't consider then was that he was over sixty years, that getting up, getting down, twisting, bending, flex-ing, in all the moving bits of him, could no longer be taken for granted, and twinges, pulls and strains in the elasticated parts were matched by aches, clunks and creaks in the skeletal. I pardon my ignorance by the fact that no one then spoke of their ailments, there was a now depreciated philosophy of offering it up and half the people of Faha were dead before they thought to complain of a pain.

In his vest and underpants, Christy took a position and did a push-up that did not push anything up, except neck and head. His body remained magnetised to the floor. He was not dismayed, but carried on, raising and lowering his head and perhaps imagining the rest of him in lift-off. He counted ten of these, rolled over and did the reverse, straining to get his head off the ground, but nothing else, in his version of a sit-up. He stood then, pushed out and back both fists, as though pressing an iron bar with weights. To flesh out the impression, he puffed with each effort, went directly into an exercise of arm propellers whose force was such his face went bright red, and I worried what Ganga and Doady must have thought.

Despite the dubious value of this programme, once he had finished, Christy had the lustre of well-being and the added gleam of the virtuous. He drank back in a gulp the rest of his water. 'If we go to all three Masses tomorrow we'll catch her,' he said.

'What?'

'She'll be there. Probably at the ten o'clock, but to be sure we'll go to the eight first, and if she fails the first and second, she'll be at the noon. When I go up to Communion, you'll come behind me and watch her, you'll see if she knows me. I won't embarrass her by stopping and looking. I'll just pause and you'll see her reaction, you'll watch for any sign, and we'll know where I'm starting from.'

He'd considered it closely and in telling it now his face was alive.

'I'm not going.'

'It's Easter Sunday.'

'I'm not going.'

'Even the thieves go Easter Sunday.'

'How will you even know her? Mrs Gaffney,' I said, obscurely knowing that the name would hurt him. 'After fifty years, how will you know her?'

'I'll know her.'

'Well, I can't help. I'm not going to church. I don't believe in God.'

'Sshhh.' He patted down the thought with both hands like it was a small fire. He came closer, whispered: 'Don't say that. He could lame or blind you. Just to prove Himself.'

How do you answer that? I put down the book and extinguished the lamp. Christy got into his bed, crossed his hands on his chest. 'For both of us, wonders are coming.'

I couldn't let that go. I leaned up on an elbow. 'How can you say that? It's nonsense. How do you know?'

'Only God knows. But He is old and needs reminding.' He raised his voice and to the thatch said: 'Wonders coming for Noe and Christy.'

16

In Faha, the three Masses of Easter Sunday would all be full. For any number of reasons, family tradition, habit of sleep or sleeplessness, urgency to worship or be done worshipping, different congregations chose different Mass times and generally stuck to them.

Christy and I took the bicycles while Doady was milking Gerty and Ganga polishing his polished boots. My grandfather was too much a gentleman to pass comment, but just as I knew his spirit was wounded by my staying away from the church on Good Friday, so too I knew that it was in some ways healed that I was going with Christy. This life is full of hurts and heals, we bruise off each other just by living, but the hope is some days we realise it. Ganga and Doady would hitch Thomas to the car for the ten o'clock.

The early morning of Easter Sunday in Faha was a serene and flawless creation. Absurd as it might seem, the sun over the fields, the sky in slow but irrefutable bluing, it was impossible not to feel the countryside concordant in the feast day. And although back then I'd have mocked myself for thinking that, that morning you'd have been a stone not to have felt it. Stillness, like a thing laid out.

We cycled slow and silent out of the townland, Christy, scrubbed and Imperially scented, charged with the gravity of his quest and employing a wide pedal to guard his trouser legs from the capricious chain. What he was thinking, how exactly he expected it to go, was unknown to me, but I was now aware that he had orchestrated everything, the job with the electrics, coming to Clare, to Faha, and to Doady and Ganga's, so as to be at the altar-rails of St Cecelia's on Easter Sunday to see Annie Mooney.

It was too big an idea for me to digest at the time. People's lives were small and everyday, I thought, the last great gestures of heart probably vanishing with Yeats.

In the fields, cattle, memories dissolved by so many liquid mornings, noons and nights, had forgotten they dreamed of April grass and, by a clemency reserved for those who live placid in a perpetual now, standing in a green sweetness forgot the cold muck-grazing of February. On the roads, on foot, bicycle, cart and car, the small but steady traffic of the early Eastering, complete with a passing of the nods, near- and full-, the looks, half-and quarter-looks, smallest of head-lifts, shoulder-lifts, full-hand, half-hand, or just forefinger-raises that among passers were, in mute eloquence, all translated the same, *'Tis Easter.*

We parked the bicycles by the forge. With two short tugs, one front one back, Christy righted his suit, palmed flat his beard. 'How do I look?'

'What?'

'How do I look?'

'Tired. Flushed. In the face, red.'

It was small encouragement for a valentine, but he sidestepped reality by sucking in his stomach. 'It's the sun. A glow is healthy.'

He marched off down Church Street and I hurried after, aware that that morning I was as much a novelty as he, and that to the Christians already planted on the post-office windowsill I was the first story of the day. If I stayed for all three Masses, what Faha would think, God only knows.

Because she could be stationed either in the Women's or the Main Aisle, Christy chose a pew halfway up the church. We settled in on to the outermost edge and were at once engulfed in a white floral ambrosia.

As decreed by a Church authority supremely oblivious to the reality of climates beyond Rome, for Easter lilies were paramount. Throughout Holy Week, Mrs Queally, small woman, one large coat button, had been on her fraught annual mission to secure the best of the 'white-robed apostles', a mission vexed by the fact that Mrs King, large woman, three small coat buttons, over in Boola, was on the same hunt, and that nowhere was an actual lily in bloom. Expeditions were undertaken, promises made a year ago called in, as Mrs Queally attempted to find an absolute minimum of twelve of the white trumpets. But there is a hierarchy inbuilt even in geography; the florists in Ennis preserved the best blooms for their cathedral, the second best for St Joseph's, third for the friary, and the fourth best, with only a small white lie, Mrs King had been assured were the finest altogether when she secured them for Boola. *What about some nice daisies, dear?* With a slightly lesser view of humanity but an undiminished zeal, Mrs Queally unearthed a cousin of a cousin of her husband's who worked in the Buttermarket in Limerick, took the bone-shaker two hours to the city, from the personal abundance set aside for the Bishop's Palace purloined a portion, and came back on the bus with an archangel's look of victory, the front four seats bedecked with lilies.

In normal weather, the church river-cold and the cruciform three-door draughts mortifying the flesh, the scent of the blooms would have been contained inside the altar-rails. But this year the sun amplified their perfume and men, women and children were not only bombarded by Doreen O Dea's douse of French toilet water that gave the lilies a run for their money but encompassed inside a white sweltry bouquet that made thin their breathing and took their thoughts elsewhere. Christy was already sweating. I had a sense, perhaps incorrect, that he had not been in a church for some time. He seemed in some inner negotiation, eyes slipping up to the crucifix and head dipping after. There were already plenty of parishioners in place, but as far as I could tell Annie Mooney was not among them.

First Mass drew an older congregation. By apparition almost, and with an accompanying cloud of inexpensive florals, the Women's Aisle filled with an antique collection of females, in hats and bonnets of all colours, styles and engineering. As I've said, there was an unwritten but understood placement in the pews, in the front directly across from Matthew Leary in the Men's, Mrs Frawley, who had one day decided to go on living and had now reached the folkloric age of a hundred, by which time life had pared away all sentiment and bestowed on her the fierce and forbidding eye of an ancient crow. Among the seniors, seniority counted, in Faha survival the only victory that mattered, and due deference was granted anyone who had been left on the planet that long. Next to Mrs Frawley, Mrs O Donnell, a spring chicken of ninety on far-sighted lookout for a potential husband across the way. Eyes straight ahead, the women prayed that kind of timeless praying that rises murmurous and general the way you imagine the land might pray, dangles of rosary beads moving through fingers like some circular riverworks of soul.

The Men's Aisle didn't fill until after the Women's. What became apparent was that, by whoever in a distant elsewhere had calipered the Standard Size, the feet of Faha were not that. Because of inadequacies of measurement, a weakness for the modish, or because they didn't want to admit that from tramping out the land their feet had grown outlandish, women wore an astonishment of ill-fitting footwear. The men were no better, out of wellingtons and boots, in black shoes that might have passed for boats, for the early Mass there were some dragging a foot, some favouring the left, some the right, some who had been lamed by a beast, who had caught a foot in a wheel, under a wheel, who had lost a toe, lost two toes, who had heel-spurs, hammer-toes, ankles ballooned and in all manner bocketty, who had been foot-mangled by farm machinery one way or the other (that is, in all the ways that farming could figure out to do it), had gaits fouled in small or large measure, and on top of this (both in the tradition of and an advancement on their great-grandfathers and -grandmothers who had come barefoot to the village carrying the shoes they only put on once they arrived at one of the four crosses, coming new-shod into church), they wore the good shoes that, though laced and shining, from small use and foot disorder were pure murder.

So, the general sigh when all sat down. And my feeling that I was in the company of the heroic or the needing to be healed.

Father Tom said the first Mass. He said it swift and without sermon, a kind of no-nonsense service that went down the tracks of the iron faith of all parishioners. You were witnesses more than participants then, you watched the Mass pass by and later when you were asked *Did you catch Mass?* there was just that instant of uncertainty that in fact you had.

The Latin rose and hung above the candled altar like air carvings, intricate and ornamental, and other, which was how

God was supposed to be at the time. Christy kept his eyes out for Annie Mooney, and only when at Communion he was certain she was not there did he push back into the pew and his whole body relaxed. We alone, I think, did not go to receive Communion. Mrs Frawley received first, the gravity of her person and century of living causing Father Tom to wait at the rails for her, in the pause one of the Kellys dandling the paten and earning the cuff he'd get later.

There was time to pass before the next Mass. We filed out with everyone else, and because Christy had set in his mind how and where he wanted to see Mrs Gaffney for the first time, we strode out of the village and went down by the river. 'She'll be at the ten,' he said, drew out his cigarettes, patted in vain for matches, and, once I had struck one for him, released some of what had been inside him in a ladder of smoke.

When I think of it now, I think how improbable it was that after six decades a man could retain in himself the derided, outmoded, naïve, but still-alive dream of a happy ending, of meeting again a woman he had loved decades earlier and imagining that the result could be anything other than catastrophe.

If we spoke by the river, I forget what we said. Nothing pertinent, most likely.

St Cecelia's was full half an hour before ten o'clock Mass began. *This is the big one*, the church seemed to say, and an entirely different congregation assembled, one notable for brightness of colour and a quiet if unexpressed joy that once again Christ had risen. We met Ganga and Doady as they came down Church Street, and accompanied them in the Long Aisle, Doady, wearing the triumph of her bouncing do, and walking an inch taller with the risen station of having a lodger, the electricity man, Ganga in thrall to the splendour of occasion. 'O now.'

All the pews were filled as we came in past Mick Madigan standing by the door. This made no earthly difference to Ganga, who chose a midways pew and waited while its outer occupant pushed in a bit, then Doady sat and sidled in, then Ganga sat and did the same, then Christy did, and I did. I didn't dare look in along the line crushed to the wall. But the same thing was happening all over the church as the latest Christians hurried in, genuflected and, without looking, sat themselves into a space that to that moment had not existed. The pew sucked in its breath, concertina-ed closer, and the church became one living sea of the washed, the ironed, the shampooed and the shone.

In the time before Mass the congregation participated in one of the characteristic joys of all mankind, looking at itself. Easter being a time for bonnets, Maura Sexton had outdone herself with a hat that this year came not only with feathers but fruit. Maureen Mungovan had taken licence from the weather and wore a sundrop dress of lemon linen. There was Greavy the guard, over here, Bubs in a daylight version, and Sheila Sullivan wiping her son's mouth in a halved-nappy hanky. There was the world of children, twisting, turning, being sat, leg-dangling, *Stop that*, turning, staring fresh-faced and wide-eyed at the mystery of an adult on their knees behind them, being pulled back, being sat again but soon sliding off, finding the pews to be perfect pirate gangways, castle ramparts, and if you slipped past the knees of just one you could walk along the kneelers, and by an unwritten statute of Church law be beyond the reach of reprimand, until you remembered there was chocolate at stake.

The next of the Kellys jingled the bell and Father Coffey came from the vestry. The primacy of the feast day had come to the surface in the phosphor of his cheeks, and, against the white of his vestments, lent him a paschal look. He said the Mass with high seriousness, as if he'd never said one before, and it touched me, the way something you've lost can. In his saying of them, the Kyrie and the Confiteor were like stone tablets, ancient and indisputable. He lifted his face and upturned his palms, as though through the stained glass above the Long Aisle he could catch the sunbeams reflecting right then off the risen Christ.

For his sermon, Father Coffey chose the simplest of arguments: by the fine weather we were all being blessed, and, with clerical sidestep, did not draw the corollary: that up to now we had been cursed. He was midways through his delivery when Christy pinched my arm, his face was in thrall, and when I turned he nodded across the aisle and there I saw Mrs Gaffney.

I had seen her once before, I now realised.

In Faha, at that time, people who in the normal course of life never gambled made an exception for the Aintree Grand National. Because town was distant, and fortune craved, unofficial bookies sprung up where they could. In Faha, one such operated out of Arnold Gaffney's chemist, and one April Saturday when I had been sent down for the Easter holidays, Ganga had brought me in there. I was to say nothing to Doady. We'd surprise her with the winnings later, he said, and I think it was that surprise more than the money he was looking forward to. Mr Gaffney was a short man with the quick, blinking eyes of a man married to someone too beautiful. The fact of that had made him a natural cousin to good fortune and, by the way these things come about, given birth to a sideline as a bookmaker. He was not handsome, but he was lucky, his soft smile said. Some time back, in a gesture perhaps to increase his allure, he had purchased a pair of the large black-framed glasses of Cary Grant, but to small effect, his three crossing strands of hair attached by Brylcreem, his well-worn white shirt and shirt garters lending him the look of a cowboy saloon-keep.

Luck, like justice, love, and maybe everything else of worth, being blind, Ganga selected his horse by flying a forefinger on to the runners and then seeing who he'd chosen. His wager was in coins, it can't have been much, but just the placing of it made him boyish and I remembered that his only song, sung in the small hours after a funeral feed of porter, was *Bet my money on the bobtail nag. Somebody bet on the grey.*

Mr Gaffney was noting the wager in a ledger when his wife came through the strips of hanging rainbow that divided the shop from the house. What did she look like? The truth is, I didn't really take notice. I didn't take much notice of anyone until I was seventeen and began to realise there were more people living than myself, but she did have an extraordinary long thick wave of brown hair and the kind, sad eyes some women have looking at a small child when they've had none. She gave me a twisted stick of crystallised ginger.

Now, here she was in St Cecelia's. I saw her and felt an involuntary fall in my heart because, though still extraordinarily long, her hair was a weave of almost-white. In profile her face had a graven look, but also something of what, I would only come to understand years later, time did to great beauty, refine it, as though after coming through a fire. The bones of her cheeks were prominent. She kept her head erect and tilted slightly back. I couldn't speak to beauty then, but I could to dignity and bearing and deep quietude in her. Sorrow, I thought, had given her a look classical and apart. I'm not sure what I was expecting. But what I felt was sadness. I might have turned to Christy to see his reaction, but there was no time because the whole church was moving. Communion was beginning.

'I'm not going,' I whispered. 'I'll watch from here.'

He looked but didn't argue. There was no time.

It turned out that those who had originally been sitting on the outer pew were the ones most desperate to be first to receive. It was why they had sat on the edge, but meekness and charity had forced them to slide in. Now, they stood the moment the *Domine non sum dignus* had ended and a general shuffling happened as they tried to come out past those whose consciences were larger and were still kneeling. The Long Aisle filled in a bumping instant. Two lines were formed, both heading to the altar-rails, but, because those in the pews nearer the front kept joining, for a time the line went backwards and Christy was nearly out the back door.

He had sight of Annie Mooney. Then he didn't.

What he thought of her, what impact the sight of her had on him was unknown. Whether he had worked out the detail of his meeting her again after so many years, whether he had thought the thing to do would be to arrive on his knees at the altar-rail alongside her, I can't say. But if so he had underestimated the imperative of Communion at Easter, and the chaotic nature of how things happened in Faha. There was a crush, a slow rush, a small push and pull back as the whole line shuffled backwards when someone returning from the rails had to be readmitted to their pew. In the host-traffic I lost sight of Annie Mooney, not least because of the dazzlement of the three Troy sisters. Christy craned his head. For a moment I thought he would say 'Excuse me now' and start pushing his way up through a parting sea. I thought:

Here comes pandemonium. But he held off. She was above at the rails now, now Father Coffey was before her. Christy's moment had passed, he was still some ways down the aisle of St Cecelia's whose windows had never been opened and whose airless atmosphere was made unreal by Mrs Reidy's organ music, incense, and the actual sun outside approaching noon.

He resolved on a new strategy. Annie Mooney would be back in her pew by the time he passed, so in the slow procession of souls he would be able to pause before her. He would pause alongside her, his prayer-hands would hold in and press upward the loose-strung girth of him, he would throw back his shoulders and angle his chin just so to defeat the years and allow her to recognise the Christy he had once been.

The line shuffled forward, stopped, backed up, shuffled on again, stopped again.

At last, he was alongside her. The line surged and a gap opened but Christy delayed and offered her his profile, and from my place I watched her make just the slightest turn of her face in which she had to have seen him.

But she showed no sign of it. She turned away almost at once.

There was not the slightest change in her expression that I could see.

Nor was there when Christy did the same on the way back. 'Well?'

We had come out in the flow and press of the congregation, both lighted and lightened in the sloping churchyard. Mrs Gaffney had gone out ahead of us, for the third time been three feet from Christy and for the third time not taken notice of him. She was gone into the chemist's, *Closed* hanging in the door. The post-office windowsill was already full, there was a cluster around Conlon the newspaperman, and over everything this far-fetched and foreign sunlight turning Church Street a pale lemon colour I believed I would never forget, until I did, but remembered years later in a gallery where I found out it was called Naples Yellow, and that name would take me back to the magnanimous feeling that was a Naples light falling in Faha that Easter morning.

Christy tugged at my sleeve. 'Well? Did she show any sign? Anything of a smile?'

I blame the sunlight. I blame the eagerness and hope in his eyes. I blame the Easter morning and the bestowed innocence that blanches the soul after Mass when you are returned to your child self and can believe the plots turn out all right.

'Yes,' I lied. 'There was.'

17

What does it matter? What does it matter what one old man was hoping one time? I haven't the wit to argue it now. All I can say is I know it did matter and knew it then too. We're more than bones and flesh. That underlies it. And a man in his sixth decade trying to make amends for the mistakes in his life, that speaks to me. Spoke to me then too, although less deeply than it does now. I'll say nothing of his carrying a torch for that long.

Easter Sunday dinner, it was decided, would be served outdoors. The decision was not Doady's. 'Bring in the table, let ye,' she had said, getting down off the horse car, unbuttoning her coat and heading into the scullery with the valorous look of Napoleon's marshal. She kept the headscarf on the while and the curls contained.

'No need,' Ganga told Christy and I when we set about the table. 'We'll eat outside, like the Lord.'

By the time Doady discovered, the argument had passed. All that existed of it was a look in my grandmother's eye with which it was clear my grandfather would have to negotiate later.

But all argument was postponed under the imperative of the Easter feast. There was a general to-do again in all houses in the parish, pots boiling, lids clattering, roasting trays checked, fingers burned and final touches applied, and all under the scrutiny of astute generals in wrap-around house-coats and floral aprons. The thing for you to get, I suppose, was that it felt *personal*. The religion wasn't abstracted, historic or chosen. The Lord had risen, it was fact. To Ganga and Doady, Easter was an inarguable actuality same as the rain or the river, and with as little call for debate. I wasn't wise enough to envy them then. Christy and I went in and out of the house following orders that, under the pressure of engagements on multiple fronts, Doady abbreviated to single words, 'Napkins!', 'Salt!', 'Mint!' Christy was three inches off the ground now. My lie about Mrs Gaffney had gladdened him beyond words, and beyond words was a dangerous place. He had achieved the next stage of his plan. He had found Annie Mooney, he had come to Faha, and now she had seen him. More, she had recognised him, and had, it seemed, smiled. He let the thought of that feed him, the way lovers do, and he fed it in turn with an Easter optimism and the time-worn fantasy of things turning out according to plan.

I of course was bound up with an indigestible guilt, and the feeling of transgression you didn't escape just by turning your back on the Church, but there wasn't time to adjudicate between sins venial and mortal. A leg of lamb appeared, I don't know what paid for it. Then, moments before the dinner was to be called, Ganga set a fifth place at the table, and moments after that, a car drove up and, again like a great black-and-white bird, Mother Acquin landed.

I had not seen her since my mother's funeral, when she had presided from a front pew with a pale, august solemnity that let all know she was a close cousin to Death. Nuns at that time were a kind of aristocracy and a Mother Abbess was up there, as they say. She changed the air around her and, whether intentional or not, had the effect of making most people smaller in her company. After removing the headscarf and the housecoat and giving a little up-push to both sides of her curls, Doady came outside with a girlish timidity just as Ganga was pumping Mother's hand like a well. 'Now,' he kept saying. 'O now.'

Doady did a small genuflect with her face. 'Welcome, Mother.'

'We're dining in the garden?' Mother Acquin asked. There was a skill in how much she could fit into a single question.

'Like the Lord,' Ganga said. He had the kind of smile you couldn't get around. I couldn't anyway.

By the world in general, Mother Acquin was unimpressed. Nuns lived outside the normal calendar of time, many it seemed were of an indeterminate age and, as if by covenant, endured undiminished year after year, but by consequence had witnessed every failing humanity had to offer. By a soul-telegraph employed by the religious, Mother Acquin knew that my vocation had faltered, and, a pale nuncio, she had come now with the intention of stiffening it. Her dark eye sought me out. 'There you are.'

'Mother Acquin.' I escaped the scrutiny by turning sideways and saying, 'This is Christy.'

'Happy Easter, Sister.'

'Mother. And you are?'

'I'm the lodger.'

'The electricity man,' Ganga said.

'I'm bringing the light,' Christy said, light-hearted, a tone that was snapped off sharpish as Mother sat in the chair planted

139

in the garden, at once sliding sideways and clutching on to the table as she came face-to-face with Columbus's incontrovertible truth: not one foot of the parish of Faha was flat.

With magnified mortification, Doady retreated inside, throwing two beckoning hooks to Ganga at the door before heading in to administer last rites to the lamb.

I hovered by the table.

'Sit!'

I sat. Christy sat too.

Mother Acquin looked me in the eye. 'Your mother in Heaven sent me,' she said.

'How is she doing?' Christy asked.

———

It is a dolorous fact that a meal, months in the dreaming, weeks in the planning and days in the preparation, is eaten in minutes. Neither niceties of manners, Mother Acquin's lengthy Grace Before Meals, nor Ganga's theatrics with the novelty of a napkin – placing it on one knee so it showed the stitched insignia that suggested the English Admiralty, then on the other knee because the gravy chose that one, before finally wearing it, a stained flag under his chin – delayed the inevitable. Under the full flush of a Floridian sun, the leg of lamb disappeared, along with the roast potatoes, the mashed potatoes, the peas, the carrots, the onions, turnips, God help us parsnips, and a gravy the sun made phosphorescent in its boat, the rainbow dissolving when it met the meat. Because no one actually liked it, its place at the table vouched only by tradition, the exodus of the Israelites and the genteel custom of the eighteenth century, the mint jelly survived.

Eschewing the native custom of eating in silence, Christy employed a cuisine commentary. Though he ate no lamb he gave out a continuous host of compliments to which Ganga and I added our tuppence, mostly in a form outside vocabulary. There was too much awe for small talk. Perhaps because of the foreignness of Fahaean dining al fresco, because the meal was so outside the usual, there was a sense the feast was a further extension of the Holy Day. Mother Acquin had the signs of it. She ate straight-backed and silent, as though performing a devotion. There was no savour in it. Thankfully, she didn't begin the lecture I presumed was coming. Eventually I realised she supposed her presence alone would, as they used say, speak volumes. Those volumes were stacking up inside me.

The sun beat down like the best day of a remembered summer.

As befitted the occasion, Christy ate with deep relish and high manners, his only lapse using his fork as a spoon when pursuing peas, pushing the last of them on with his finger. Ganga, whose habit was to open his trouser belt after eating, made it halfway before he caught Doady's glare and turned the unbuckling into a patting.

The meal was not done yet. We would match the gentry and have a sweet, and call it 'dessert' too, according to Ganga. '*Two* desserts,' he whispered when Doady was gone.

From the multitude preserved during Lent, an egg custard landed, and, a French inspiration, the planet-like surface of Faha's only Easter meringue, with a coating of heavy cream and the well-spaced segments of a single orange.

'It's supposed to look like that,' Doady said.

Ganga beamed at his wife as if she was the Eighth Wonder of the World.

'None for me, thank you,' Mother Acquin said.

'Both, please.' Christy passed her his plate to pass along.

Soon enough some of the Clancy children appeared, short-trousered or -skirted, each with the same home-barbering and the crusty badges of skinned knees. From infancy, it seemed, they had learned the tactic of rushing from their own house after dinner and showing up at my grandparents', a tactic born of the fact that there were twelve of them on two benches, some with longer arms than others, and the time-worn truth that the stomachs of growing children can never be full. Doady had learned this first-hand in Kerry, and although Ganga and Clancy were not on speaking terms since the time years earlier when, in an antic both schoolboy and Greek, Ganga and Bat had kidnapped Clancy's cock, Doady fed the Clancy children whenever they appeared.

The sight of them settling in to our Easter leftovers discommoded Mother Acquin, whose driver had been told to return in two hours exactly. But, as had been true since her girlhood, men never materialised, and she sat, high, beaked, and brewing him a scalding. It brewed some more I think when, the Clancys leaving for a third dinner up at Dooley's, with a hedonist happiness unavailable to humans, Joe made a beast of himself with the lamb bone at the bottom of the garden.

As though she was a figure inflexibly carved, Mother Acquin adjusted herself squarely to face me. I didn't hear the bell ring but somehow Ganga and Doady knew a round had been called. Ganga excused himself to attend to the cattle. He pumped her hand and thanked her for joining us. Doady interrupted the pumping by giving him some of the ware to carry in, and more for Christy, all of them withdrawing like figures in a garden play to leave me to my fate.

'You will go back of course.'

It was a statement, there was to be no disputing.

'You will stay for a time. That is perfectly fine. You will work out of yourself whatever it is that has come into it. But then you will go back and follow your calling and be the person your mother thought you were.'

Her eyes. Her eyes were Old Testament eyes, grave and grey and allowing not the slightest room for manoeuvre.

'I think my mother would want me—'

'She wants you to devote yourself to God.'

I don't believe I came up with any response. I believe some part of me was knocked down unable to speak or think or do anything at all, only hear that phrase boom in my ears.

That wouldn't be the only time it would boom.

I'm not sure anyone speaks this way any more. I'm not sure the idea itself endures, without the association of fanatic, or that, if it does, it can ever emerge out loud into the air, sort of vast and winged and breathtaking.

Mother Acquin's driver coughed. He was Heaney, a hackney man. After a liquid lunch in Craven's, he had found the margins of the roads badly drawn. The motor was one-side mucked. Heaney did the hackney for years and years, continued driving long after his cataracts made imaginary the roads when he drove craned forward to the windscreen, always throwing up a hand in salute moments after he had narrowly missed killing you.

'Time, Mr Heaney,' Mother Acquin said, giving me a last dose of the eye and sweeping from the table. 'Time!'

Heaney had a white puff of Einstein hair. He employed it like a prop that signalled the mystery of things, scratching at it by way of reply. 'I know, Mother,' he said ruefully. 'I was early, until I was late.'

Heaney gave Einstein a scratch.

Mother Acquin boarded the motor. The engine roughed the quiet and scattered the hens. Then she was gone.

In dribs and drabs, people came to make and take prearranged phone calls. One shouted into the receiver while another sat waiting on the stool. There was no privacy in it. Tidying up the table we could hear all, but telephones were not for the private then, letters were, the spoken word still somewhere below the written. Mostly it was voices people wanted to hear. Centuries of storytelling had instilled the knowledge that any story of worth took longer than the three minutes the philistines of the Department of Posts and Telegraphs allotted for a phone call, and because to overshoot three minutes incurred an exorbitant expense, callers with something important to tell delivered just the headline and said: *I'll tell you all about it in a letter.*

Waiting to be put through, there was time to pass, but the technology was still recent enough to be a marvel, and it was not resented. Distance was still humanly dimensioned, the country still large, and the miles and miles of wires everyone had seen looping, drooping, across fields and bogs, made visual the miracle of speaking to the invisible.

Tommy Two Boots Halpin came, walking up the garden with that peculiar high-step of his, that recalled the time when Faha was three-fourths underwater.

I wasn't expecting him to get in here, but there he is. He thought his son in Queens might call. He sat waiting, big hands hanging between his legs. He wouldn't take a bit of the meringue thanks all the same. He didn't eat much since Mary, he said. He waited an hour, then went home.

Soon enough I slipped away and went walking by the river. There were some boats on it, the pilots who worked the estuary were off for Easter Sunday and instead, because spring had been skipped and summer had arrived in April, there were a handful of pleasure boats and fine-weather sailors flirting with the wind and the current and the ageless allure of the coast of Kerry. There was freedom in it and some gaiety, I suppose, in the holiday of the sunshine, but I could feel neither.

It was some time later when Christy came and found me. He didn't choose an avuncular or advisory approach. He didn't say *You've been thinking of your mother*, or *None of us can escape loss*, nor even *That nun was a right one*. He just appeared in front of me on the riverbank in the wrinkles of his white cotton shirt and blue trousers, pushed flat the jut of his beard, glistened his eyes, and said, 'Junior Crehan?'

18

Now, you may not be able to credit what the music meant in Clare, means still, and what the name Junior Crehan stood for.

The origins of it are in storytime. They're in the dust of the roads and the memories of birds. They're in the bars of the rain, in the floods and the tides, in the salt of the air and the thorns of the ditches.

Like all stories of music, there are various strings to it.

Once, there was this child blind from birth, or near enough, and what they did in that time was give the child a set of pipes to play, believing that one sense dead the others awoke, and if he played the pipes he'd have a trade and make his way in the world. And this blind child became a man, Garrett Barry, and he was small, and when grown black-bearded, and by the senses of feeling and hearing travelled the country in and around Miltown and Mullagh and Inagh and south of there too down into Kilmihil, into Kilmurry, and on down into Faha, playing airs and making a living and becoming in his time a small sensation so that his playing stopped what work was being done and made the mark of a different world on that day so that any who heard him recalled it even on to the nodding of their dotage.

Now this was back in old God's time. And in that time Garrett visited Casey's house in Annagh where Tom the Master lived, and Tom had the music and played the timber flute and his son was Thady who had the timing in him and it was said could pick a tune out of the breeze. And though Garrett would die in the Ennistymon workhouse and be buried in an unmarked grave in Inagh, before he did he left the tunes after him so Thady Casey became a dancing master travelling around and teaching the Caledonian and other sets and making step dancers with a twelve-inch rule he struck none too lightly on the calves if the dancers weren't in the right time and getting off the ground.

Getting off the ground was an important thing.

Being in the right time, another.

The same Thady put buckets and saucepans under the flag-stones when he was laying the floor of his house in Annagh so the batter of the dancing would ring. That house is there still, I believe, on the road from the ocean.

Thady had a cousin Scully and Scully Casey on the fiddle became the mentor to many, one of whom was Junior Crehan.

Junior was Martin, but his father was Martin too and Martin Senior lived past ninety years so Junior stayed Junior. Once he heard a tune it never left him, they said. There were players everywhere in the townlands around him in Ballymackea in the parish of Mullagh. It was common to hear music played in the evenings, and he went out nights to play the fiddle at house dances far and wide, hiding his pyjamas in the barn so he could sneak in home at dawn, escape the look of Senior and snatch the small sleep of the raptured, the reels still spinning in his head.

And because the music was not written down, because it lived in the air in the moments of its playing, and then in that place between the fingers and the memory, the players were its custodians. In time Junior Crehan carried so much music in him he became a one-man repository, both modest and legendary, a walking encyclopaedia of tunes, dances, airs and stories, in whose playing was the playing of all those before him on into the mists of the long ago.

There were other strings. There was another dancing master Pat Barron whose father was a dancing master who had left the house one day to go playing and teaching and came back another day an old man. And Pat said to his father he'd like to go on the same job. But the father had pawned the fiddle before he came home and so he told the son where and the first thing Pat did was go and get that fiddle and that was the one he took on the road. He used to sing, dance and play fiddle all over. He played 'Top of Cork Road' and 'The Priest in his Boots' and 'Miss McLeod's' and many times he came into Clare, he came to fair and market days and horse races and football matches, he came to Fanny O Dea's in Lissycasey, played in Faha, played in what later became Mrs Crotty's on the square in Kilrush, he came to Miltown and played for a man Gilbert Clancy who was the father of Willie and who said the pipes recalled what couldn't be remembered, the old bard times, and in their melancholy and joy was this world and another.

And because Clare was the place for music, the travelling piper Johnny Doran got up on his caravan and travelled out of Dublin and came the way and parked near Miltown, and he was the one Willie Clancy heard when Johnny set up playing, standing up, at the races on Spanish Point beach, the box under one foot. And all that afternoon, evening and night Johnny played and gave a wonderful exhibition of music that passed into legend so that the whole populations of Miltown and Mullagh and Cree and as far south as Faha said they were there. And, years later, on Johnny's last day in this world, Willie came to visit him in his hospital bed in Dublin and they recalled that day and Willie took out the pipes and squeezed the bag for Johnny's fingers to play.

That Willie Clancy lived not five miles from Junior Crehan was neither coincidence nor design. It was in the air is my point. The music was a feature of the landscape and as such not pass-remarkable. There were many fine players, most of whose names were unknown. It would be years before I would realise that I had heard Elizabeth Markham who became Mrs Crotty play. I heard Micho Russell, and Tom McCarthy, Micko Dick Murphy, John Joe Russell, Peggy Healy, Solus Lillis from Kilmacduane, Nellie Fox, the Neylons, Timmy Tom and Tony, The Captain, Manus, Cissie, Josie, a world of them, and I saw the set dancing Penders in Galvins of Moyasta when the air was thick with smoke and loud with battering and the entire place rose, holus-bolus, six inches off the ground.

Although we didn't know it then, that summer, a young man, Ciaran MacMathuna, would roll down from Dublin to Clare, to call to houses, to step inside back doorways into flagged kitchens with open hearths and no electricity, and with the help of the country's first mobile recording unit start to record the players. He'd be received with the venerable courtesies of country people, cups of tea that hills of sugar couldn't sweeten, cuts of ham and griddle bread. He would put on a stone that summer, he'd say, because each time he would be feasted before he could get around to requesting a tune. And then, with the natural bashfulness of those who in the purest sense were amateur and believed there were better players elsewhere that he should be recording, aware that they were carriers of a tradition that was passing through them, but reserved and absent in vanity, they would be coaxed an hour, two sometimes, but at last, in the dim light of their kitchens and parlours, play. And in that playing another time would be summoned, the time of dancing masters and travelling pipers, because in it was a threshold, across which it was still possible to pass and be at the races on the sands at Spanish Point or the fair days and football matches along roads and across fields and time and still be where, in the playing now of Junior Crehan and the like, was recalled the soul of a people, the pulse of a place, and a hundred years of music.

To hear Junior play, Christy and I took the bicycles in the fall of dark. A small thing will feed a lover, and the thought that Annie Mooney had recognised him in the church that morning was enough to keep Christy's heart high and his eyes glossed. He was a chronic optimist and, as I would discover, a pathologic romantic. That he added to this an old man's affliction of sentiment, I can't blame him. We spend most of our lives guarding against washes of feeling, I'm guarding no more.

The thing about music in Clare was that its location was always unknown. There were not set venues or session times as such. Places garnered reputations because of music that had sprung up one evening, and become in memory legendary, but you could as easily arrive in the door of the same place to see three men sitting in a dim silence and, as if it was somehow vaguely your fault, be told by the barman *You should have heard the music that was here last week.*

Without specific destination, but the knowledge that the heartland of the music was north of Kilmihil and south of Miltown, we pushed the bicycles out of Faha along roads hard and curved like bones in the moonlight. We could see a silvered way and the gleaming of figures well ahead of their actuality. In the bounty of his good humour, Christy saluted all, inspiring by surprise a good number of salutes back and many a *Fine evening, thank God*. In the balmy dark there was a sense of holiday and, after the privations of Lent, something of a people unshackled.

By Commodore's Cross, where for once Greavy was not on guard for bicycles with no lamps, links of laughing girls in clacking shoes hurried behind a bobbing torch beam on the rumour of a house dance. A gate shouldered open, loose on the road ran little clusters of back-kicking cattle, going from dark into dark on adventures of escape. An occasional car announced itself in sound and light long before its appearance, the eyes of the headlamps opening the countryside, making brief orange discs of a fox's gaze, before leaving all back where it found it. Each car that passed was window-steamed and packed tight with passengers. A sleeved arc in the windscreen, it motored down the centre of the road on an Easter excursion of small revelment and loose steering. In its aftermath, the quiet was quieter, and sometimes in the silence that reassembled you could hear from across a valley a solo music played outside a front door for no audience but the night, a concertina, and one time a timber flute, travelling from the unseen player across the fields. It travels still, and of all the things I have forgotten that survives.

As before, Christy and I walked up hills and freewheeled down them, so on the rises there was opportunity for talk and on the slopes a chance to escape it.

'Tell me again how she smiled.'

'Why do you care?'

'I wronged her.'

'Fifty years ago?'

'Yes.'

'How?'

The history of it passed across his eyes but not out of his mouth.

'Tell me how.'

'I want her forgiveness,' he said.

'For what?'

He angled over the bicycle to mount it. 'I broke her heart.' He pushed off and sailed ahead of me down the hill.

As though an infinite store had been discovered, more and more stars kept appearing. The sky grew immense. Although you couldn't see it, you could smell the sea.

With the common excuse of slaking the dust of the cycle, we went into a place called Pyne's. There was a Sunday-evening gathering and a man being coaxed to play the tin whistle. We stayed the while and drank from bottles. The player was being coaxed still when we left. It was a given then that with musicians in Clare it was difficult to start them, to stop them impossible.

In McCarthy's further on there was a crowd and a sing-song and we had what Christy called a drop and after a time I thought he was on the point of bursting into song himself, but a fiddle was found and, because it is a true fact that women live for dancing, a set was called and the women formed into pairs. They spun and stepped, dancing with each other in loose embrace, their faces flush with faraway looks and their feet like a native clockwork, slipping them free for now of all hardship and chores, stepping them into that else-where from which all music takes its origins. Christy made no bones about admiring the women, or letting them know either, a behaviour that not only made me uncomfortable but confused. The women smiled or laughed or threw back comments and nothing came of it. I'm not sure if more was intended.

In Cooney's there was no music, but there might be later. It would be discourteous to come in and go out without having the one. Mrs Cooney behind the counter had a smile would defeat a bishop, Christy told her.

After, we mounted the bicycles, and got off them fifteen yards further, to try O Connor's, where the same courtesies applied, and where, on a stool by the counter Denis Doohan, a precursor of future times, made a living off his celebrity. Doohan had a share in a minor prize in the Sweep, and, because luck like leprosy passed by touch, for a small fee would let you have a rub of him. Christy paid him thruppence, got five seconds' worth, and at once felt lucky.

Junior Crehan was maybe in O Connor's, he was sometimes in O Neill's, he was known to have played in Moloney's. But that night he wasn't in any of them when we were.

The pubs that followed those have folded into the night and lost their names. In many there was music, all of it played by suited figures earnest and excellent and entirely absent in vanity or showmanship. It was a mystery to me how before they took up their instruments you could not tell the musicians from the audience. They looked like farmers, grounded ground-men, shy and unshowy, smoking cigarettes and hunkered silent or small-talking over pints, with no evidence at all of their gift. They had no apparent inclination to take the instrument cases out of where they were stacked in the windowsill, until they did. And when they did, the air was changed. There's no other way to say it. The smoky, dark corner of a dingy pub forgot that it was a nowhere. It became a locus, a centre, and we became a company, focused around tables where, behind abandoned butts smoking in ashtrays and pint glasses paused in mid-tide, two fiddles, a flute and a concertina made time stretch so it was now and back across the ages in the same moment.

Not all the music was excellent, but it was to Christy. He was moved by it, and sometimes, when a reel would end and a jig start up, I'd hear a *Good man* or a *Yes* or a big clap out of him.

When the music ended the players lowered their instruments and took up their glasses, resuming their habitual shyness but allowing a glint in their eyes now if they met another's, a silent acknowledgement, not so much, it seemed to me, that they had played the music, but that they had been there when it happened.

The instant the music ended, time was turned on again, with subsequent rush for the bar, and I'd be witness to Christy's shouldering in to the counter and his helpless munificence as he bought drinks, porter, shorts, port, minerals and cigarettes for those around him in what seemed to me a fairly decent attempt to rid himself of money.

Coming back through the throng, drinks at head-height, like things rising or rescued, he had a dozen new friends. 'People here are wonders.' Unsurprisingly, in all the pubs he grew an instant popularity and was to come back, and soon. Women twenty years younger than him told him he was a melted rogue but they were laughing when they said it. In Burke's we were told Junior Crehan had recently played. *O God he did.* But the rising curtain of the dawn and the drawn limits of human tolerance defeated us and that night we did not make it any further.

When at last we came outside to the bicycles we were in the blink-and-head-scratch of that well-known location

Who-Knows-Where, abroad in the back country of west Clare, the ocean near and pounding. By which time I might have believed my mother forgave me, that Annie Mooney had in fact smiled, and that in the days ahead lay the happiness found only in stories.

———

Ambushed perhaps by the Wild Colonial Boy, the Minstrel Boy, and Kelly the Boy from Killane, inspired by the near and distant company of smiling women, and with the rub of Doohan's luck still on him, Christy succumbed to a fevered dream, and by the flawless logic of those out of their minds we arrived back in Church Street, Faha, and outside the chemist shop.

The birds were awake but the street was asleep. The first rays of the sun were taking off a pale scarf of rivermist. As if conspiratorial, the scene was painted. I wasn't sure what Christy intended. I remember we left the bicycles by the church wall, and that he walked his square-chested walk ahead of me across the street. He was this solid block of human emotion with the short swallow and shone eyes of a man resolved on a tactic of all or nothing.

'Wait!'

I'll give myself that. I called out *wait*, not because I knew what was about to happen, not because I had insight or foreknowledge, not even because I knew I had to confess the lie before he acted upon it, but because catastrophe is in the air and in your blood a moment before it happens and your mouth falls open helpless with doom because *O God here it comes.*

Already he had assumed the position he had taken in Craven's, head back, chest out and fists pressed down, and at once he was singing. He was singing that same sad love-song with shut eyes and a full-throated volume to which Nolan's dog in Nolan's yard responded with a low whimpering, as if it knew that, although the human need for music was both mysterious and universal, this was a frequency unheard in the street in Faha and that there was ruckus and rira and danger in it. The singing was all the louder for the stillness of the morning after the Resurrection, the sliding slope of Church Street like a crooked yawn, the misaligned huddle of the shops and houses curved into a comma, paused beneath a sky now both opal and pink, the picture of actual earthly peace, or as near as.

Christy sang the song up to the front windows of Gaffney's chemist shop. I stood a little ways behind, like one holding the horses.

I can't say if he sang well, I can say he sang loud, certainly louder than any had sung a dawn love-song in the street of that or any parish in west Clare. He sang it shut-eyed, but aimed, his face tilted up like a priest. In his mind he was seeing her. I am certain of that. If you came into Faha at the moment, if you came into either end of the sleeping village, in the grace and the repose of the just now delivered dawn-light, the two parked cars, the tied bundles of news-papers outside the post office, you'd hear him singing and you'd be certain too. With screwed-up eyes and throat-cords bulging, with bubbling porter-sweat and cuckoo-spittle, he was singing her into being and, by the power of an antique passion, porter and the potency of an old song, seeing her too. Whether the Annie Mooney of years earlier or the one in St Cecelia's that morning, I couldn't have said. I was not even an amateur in love and understood nothing of emotion that could endure deep below the tides of time.

But I think I knew that while he sang he was in thrall to a fiction, and on the thin foundation of the lie that she had seen him in the church, recognised him, and smiled, like all male lovers he had quickly built a rose-coloured version that matched his own hope: how Annie Mooney had hurried into the chemist's after Easter Mass, turning over the cardboard *Closed* with a frantic heart, questioning the evidence of her eyes, *Had it really been him? How could he have found her?* How she hurried upstairs, along the landing with peremptory step and into the front bedroom to sit on the pearled ridges of the chenille spread and watch through the veiled privacy of the net curtain as he and the young man moved out the church gate; how she let out an involuntary gasp that her eyes had not been lying, that it *was* really him (and that the decades had not withered his bull-chested captain's handsomeness); how her cheeks flushed, pinched with memory, and her right hand moved to her breast; how the rest of her day was upturned; how later she sat stiff and polite in the dull, cushion-less small talk of her husband's distant relations, found her appetite absent, her taste metallic, and her mind edged by sickles of questions; how she came home early in the late afternoon, sought a palliative among the powders of the pharmacy, chastising herself for foolishness even as she opened her mouth in a young girl's vain attempt to release the butterflies in her stomach.

All of this, I imagine, Christy pictured as he sang. The plots of cheap romantic novels were known even by those who never read them, and a serenade was venerable enough to have become a cliché before it was thrown in the dustbin of the world.

Now Christy was going for it.

Giving it everything grew him by two inches. They were two inches he was unaware he had, but we all have them, folded up on themselves inside the purse of the heart. He was picturing Annie's distress and had come to relieve it. That was what I understood. To announce himself. And, because I was not immune to the force of his feeling, because of travelling through the starred night, because by drink and dream I was so far removed from myself, or because of what would become a lifelong weakness for fine words and minor chords, I think I believed not only would calamity pass but the tactic would prove ingenious. In a moment the curtain would move aside and Annie Mooney would appear at the upstairs window and bring her hands to her mouth, helpless in the face of so naked a declaration and a ballad behaviour out of a sunny clime in the seventeenth century.

To the serenade, Nolan's dog was not a convert.

Nor, it turned out, was Bourke's.

Nor Cleary's. Nor Ryan's.

This too was traditional, but in the case of Faha was augmented by Clancy's cock, Hayes's hens, and then, wait, Healy's ass in the half-acre behind the hardware shop. In truth nothing in creation could be declared a fan, and, though the singing was neither drunken nor loutish, soon enough a rough chorus was barking and braying and the village was started from sleep with the forked hair and quizzical eyes of the burgled.

Christy didn't care. Old songs had the uncertain virtue of many verses and he was pressing on right to the end.

Cleary opened his front door.

Ryan opened his back one and yelled at the dog. Faces came to windows, Mona Ryan's curtain moved. But not the one above the chemist's.

Sentry to this Church Street display, I had been certain that at any moment Annie would appear. If only to throw something. But not for the first nor last time, certainty proved a bad bet, and at her curtain there was not the slightest movement, and now the song had ended.

At his front door Cleary scowled and by way of review delivered his catchphrase, 'Thank God for small mercies,' large mercies being unknown in Faha.

Returning from the passionate elsewhere of the song, Christy opened his eyes and looked up at Annie Mooney's window. I haven't the skill to describe the expression in his face. He turned away from the chemist's and took his bicycle.

'Maybe she isn't there,' I said, and, to make less excruciating the failure of the moment, suddenly found myself speaking quickly, doing that thing people do when faced with the mystery of another, prescribing to them your own emotions and behaviours. 'Maybe she was embarrassed. Maybe she was about to come down but then she saw the doors opening.' Out of me ran a mouthful of maybes. We were walking the bicycles out the end of Church Street. Like Butt, the blubbering barrel of the County Barrister, I rested my case by concluding: 'There are many plausible reasons.'

'None of life is plausible, Noe,' Christy said. The eyes, in which I expected to see distress, were the blue of a Mediterranean June, and I realised that unlike those of us whose hope only came in one size, slim, Christy's was still broad enough to survive the failure of his first approach.

'She heard me,' he said. 'But she won't forgive me as easy as that.' He swung his leg over the saddle. 'Neither would I.'

He pushed hard on the pedal and I the same and we cycled past the forge and out of the village, leaving behind us the operatic scene, the singing of the love-song, and a story that I'm assured is still told, embroidered into fable, sixty years later.

19

Easter Monday may have existed, I've no proof or recollection. I stayed above in the bed. Christy, sleep defeated by the aches the Good Lord sets into old men's bones to make appealing Eternal Rest, rose after an hour and went I never learned where.

Doady and Ganga journeyed to the park for the holiday renewal of the challenge match between Boola and Faha. Under the auspices of Gaelic football, parish rivalries were unbounded and in the warm, milky bath of an April sunshine the bulk of the populace could go to Mulvey's field and enjoy the capriciousness of the high ball and the Homeric spectacle of men taking lumps out of each other. It was a game rough and ready which found many devotees, particularly among the clergy. Years earlier, the villainous Father Sully, perhaps knowing he was Hell-bound, had seized an earthly immortality by donating a trophy, the Father Sully Perpetual, and there were medals somewhere, if only they could be found. Enjoying the animation of the rivalry and the pulse in the blood that was not available to them in the Church, priests came after the jelly of their desserts, some doing the rounds of Mulvey's tin-roofed shed which passed then for a changing room, in the mustard air of embrocation smacking their hands together and administering the age-old exhortation of *Come on now, men.*

And these were *men.* Neither team had youth on its side. England and America stole the young on the cusp of bloom and emptied the parishes of all between the ages of seventeen and thirty, a truth made evident by the sight of the Senior men trotting on to the pitch in the short shorts and chest-compressing jerseys of youths. Still, this was Faha versus Boola, and once the ball was thrown in, the players forgot their antiquity. Showing the native love of the literal, they marked their marker, saying hello the Spartan way, with a dig in the ribs. Ahead of the funds for the purchase of a pitch proper, funds that, like everything else, were on their way from Dublin, Mulvey had given the use of his field and allowed the goalposts to be erected but saw no reason why between games his cattle shouldn't graze. The result was ground pocked with ankle-breakers, bounce-unpredicters and Friesian plops of local hazard.

In an effort to elevate the status of the game and replicate the wireless commentaries on Radio Éireann, Thomas Nally employed a bullhorn and ran up and down the sideline broadcasting a pro-Fahaean version of what was happening. Not to be outdone in the battle for reality, Boola had a Brophy with a bullhorn who did likewise, running up and down the same sideline, describing the same action with battalions of superlatives but with a partisanship so blatant that no one could believe the evidence of their eyes.

In the long black coat and wide-brimmed hat of the poet, hands clasped behind his back, Felix Pilkington paced the pitch, throwing the blackbirds of his eyebrows hither and thither. After a heavy tackle from a Boolean, he stopped, threw his hands in the air and cried out, 'Elvish-mark'd, rooting hog!' and 'Bull's pizzle!' for those who preferred their commentary in longwave.

This year the sun made hard the ground and high the bounce, Ganga reported. Boola, once they got ahead, took a low tactic of driving the ball into the river to preserve their lead, but two of the undrownable Kellys were positioned, and plunged, plashed and made short work of returning it, he said. The referee, a martyr called Tuohy, who came by bicycle and hoped to depart that way, had two watches, was sole adjudicator of time, and, no matter how long it took, always endeavoured to bring the game to the fair conclusion of a draw. 'The sides could not be separated,' was his hasty annual review before he pushed off, pedalling hell-for-leather out of the many erupting disputes.

By which I mean, ordinary life carried on. By mid-afternoon the July sun that shines in the memories of grandfathers was in April attendance at Mulvey's field. Three months ahead of his habit, Hickey of Miltown dusted off his ice-cream van and met the crowd coming out with the offer of a threepenny vanilla and a squirt of what it said on the bottle was strawberry. From the fever of the match and the feeding of a hungry sun on skin rain-soft and sun-virginal, the supporters of both parishes were pinked like salmon. The Booleans, whose options for entertainment were few in Boola, hung around in Faha, and in the same way that they landed holus-bolus whenever there was a gamble or a bingo or a card drive, employing a schooled practice of cheats and tokens to take the prizes back with them, they sought out whatever bounty the parish offered.

The episode of the dawn singing was not discussed until after the game, when it made its way sideways into the talk, first by way of Kitty Meade who with vividness, exactitude and dramatic pause described to Dympna Fennel in Bourke's what she had not witnessed, and then by Dympna who, in telling Cissie Casey, added the flourish of Christy's dropping on one knee and sweeping from his head a straw hat.

Once standing, any decent story has a life of its own and can run whichever way it wants. So the details that Doady came home with, Christy's calling out Annie's name, his beating the chemist's door with his fist and crying against the glass, like a child with a runny nose it may have picked up anywhere.

The point is, the story was alive and kicking, and although she was too crafty to say anything once she got home, it lived unspoken in the glassed look of Doady's eyes at teatime and in the Do Not Disturb imperative with which she flattened the paper and dipped the pen to draft an epistle to Kerry that evening.

20

By some mechanism of the heart that I could not have explained then, and cannot explain now, the second time my mother fell, I felt it was my fault. I was twelve. I was alongside her in town. We were on an expedition for long trousers. I had come into a cool and distant personality which was marked not by sullenness but by silence and remove. I had an affliction that is more common than generally understood, I was terrified of people, and of my own strangeness. So, I was alongside her, but not with her. We came out of a shop on Harcourt Street.

'Oh,' she said. Just that. The smallest round of sound, that she would have swallowed if she could, to save herself from making a show in the public street. I looked to her, and what I saw I would never forget. Her eyes seemed cellophaned, something had entered her and screened off the world, and she reached out a blind hand to reassure herself and maybe to reach for me. But she was already falling. *Your mother is falling.* And in all the times you replay that instant you can't quite believe the simplicity of it, the unannounced arrival of calamity on an ordinary day in the ordinary street, and in all those times you make the move you didn't make to save her, it's just a shudder, a spasm of rescue that's in the pulse of humanity but in the dream version you do make it, you push aside the idiot embarrassment you're feeling and you reach out a hand that can't save her from crashing on to the path, but you reach it and maybe sometimes you jump forward and you get your whole body in the way to break the fall so that your mother and you fall together on to the cold indifferent concrete of Harcourt Street and her head does not go *crack* like that, *crack*, so sharp, so violent and unexpected that in the same instant your stomach turns and you vomit in fierce convulsions as if a foulness is being pumped up out of where you knew it always was, and there's nothing you can do, because now here it is, here is how the world goes, your mother fallen and you throwing up but keeping your head forward to save your new secondary-school shoes.

In all those times, my mother doesn't just say *Oh* and then fall in the street. But that is what happened. I don't move to save her. I don't save her. She falls. I get sick. For a long time, that's all there is. Later I will think this was the time the angels were coming. Because although my mother does not move, although I look sideways from the fawn sput of the paroxysm and see that she is not moving, my mother is not dead. She is to be saved. And there is a man bent down to her, and he looks over at me not moving towards her and then looks back to her in that slow and serene dreamtime that surrounds catastrophe when a breach has opened in the everyday and a bridge is still some ways off.

My mother does not die. When she comes home from the hospital she has lost her walk, but she may recover it. To absolve me of the stained feeling that her fall was my fault, and to bring her back to full health, I open a round of night-time negotiations, which take the form of prayer.

When she starts to lose her speech, I realise that prayer is not going to be enough.

21

There was no reason to suppose the fine weather had only come for Easter, but if reason accounted for all that human beings did the history of the world would be a straightforward telling. Everyone in Faha supposed it. *Wasn't it lovely it stopped raining for Easter?* Blessedness was not only still in the vocabulary of the everyday, but in its actuality too. So, when the same sun rose over Tuesday, the same sheet of blue stretched over the river and gave the grass the green of May-time, people who lived then in the weather, and were of it, felt the silent lift in their hearts and the sense of grace that in my mind is linked with that old word, bestowed.

Something was being bestowed. Not that many dared say so outright. Perhaps because of a not-yet-eroded belief in the nearness of the unknown, and an unknown with a broad yellow malicious streak in it, people didn't tempt bad luck by claiming good. Things said out loud had a potency, a man on a high horse was easily knocked, and no one wanted to say *We are blessed.*

But it was felt. The five days of sun were already enough to be a good summer in Faha most years. And when Christy and I went about the townlands with the memorial there was no one we met who was not livened by the light and the warmth. To some, of course, blessedness is a curse coming. *It's not right at all, this weather.* And, as though playing a close-to-the-chest card game against an opponent deep and devious and invisible, people like Maureen Tohill and Timmy Hayes gave out a contrarian view, *It won't keep up*, and *We'll be paying for this yet*, bluffing the Almighty to show his hand and keep the sun shining just to spite them.

The sense of the new was doubled by the arrival of the electricity crews. Faha was not a parish visited by strangers, those who did come were mostly lost or looking for gravestones, and the sight of the Fordson vans, the small brigades of men ready and robust and confident, sharpened the air and made real the feeling that something was happening.

As with everything since the seven days of creation, work was behind schedule. The confirmation of the signatories to the memorial, a foregone conclusion, a dotting of i's and crossing of t's according to headquarters, was to have been completed before the poles went up. Christy was to have secured the agreements and delivered them to the District Office where they would be locked into a drawer ironclad as affidavits should any of what Harry Rushe called back-sliding happen. But by the time the crews arrived there were still gaps in the forms. Holding out was a quirk in human nature and those who lived in the Last Minute had found not only was there no penalty in lateness but often a bonus not granted the timely. Besides which, because nothing in Faha ever came on time, because like in all distant places where insignificance was countered by seizing small controls, in a time where clocks were individual and wound by hand, where Considines ran later than Clearys who ran later than God help us the O Malleys, where *What's your rush?* followed the offer of the second and the third mug of tea, reasons for haste were harder to find, and the need to meet a deadline was understood to be an invention of convenience.

Not for the first or last time, correct procedure was disregarded and the crews were already in fields and holes for the electricity poles being dug when the dawn birds were resting from their chorus. Vans, one, two, and now a third, came past open doorways, making a first noise of traffic and rising a cloud of dust off the backs of boreens whose bramble and thorn bushes were soon wearing the pale brown petticoats of an imperishable dirt. The poles, felled in Finland, carried a foreign scent and when ten of them were brought past on a labouring lorry the purity of their pine escaped the creosote and in the parish mind became for some time the smell of electricity.

People came out to watch the vans and lorries pass. Grandmothers were sat outside in armchairs to wait for the next ones, and when the news came that one of the vans had driven over Dilly Conway's hen, or sent Honan's cattle three miles down the road, these only made more real the air of change, and the truth that the parish had arrived on a threshold.

In the way that these things happen, without an order or contract, one man offering and another saying *All right so*, horses were called up for the same tireless and unpaid duty as had been since the Flood, and Sean Conaty led two draughts up to Whelan's place to drag the timbers, and Matty Keane had another horse over in Ryan's doing the same and neither Sean nor Matty were conscripted or salaried but doing what they considered their bit, because *Why wouldn't you?*, because, despite what an old man might fall prey to thinking in the grey afternoon of the world's saddest days, goodness is native.

Besides which, Sean and Matty and others too were alike infected by the same enthusiasm and belief, that they were part of the engine of nation, and that that engine had arrived in Faha after nearly a lifetime of coming. Playing your part was a valid notion then. The country wasn't forty years old yet and hadn't the exhaustion of midlife.

So, as Christy and I went about making good the gaps in the memorial, there was electric business going on about us. Christy showed no sign of the failure of his dawn singing at the door of the chemist's, and because of a pimpled petrification of the awkward I did not bring it up. I chose Ganga's method for dealing with catastrophe and pretended nothing had happened. It wasn't so easy. The scene not only stayed with me, it grew larger for not being spoken and proved perhaps the theorem of imaginary numbers by showing that the imagination is many times the size of reality. I kept looking sidelong at Christy as we walked the bicycles or came in and out of houses. What was he thinking now? Had he accepted the defeat of his tactic and was he now resigned to leaving Annie Mooney alone? Had the singing somehow absolved him of whatever wrong he thought he had done her? Warming in the sun, the questions multiplied, and by the time the sweat of noon was falling off our foreheads and we were laying the bicycles in against the wall by Master Quinn's field, I had to abandon Ganga's philosophy.

We were inside the baked top corner of the field with a view of the valley. Christy sat on his jacket, leaning back for support on one elbow. Though a big man, he had a natural ease in how he lay himself. It was a thing I noticed, mostly because it escaped me. To sit on the ground and look natural, and not, as I seemed, to be missing a chair. He lay propped and easy while I unbound the cloth about the egg sandwiches.

'Here.'

'Beautiful.'

He ate the way he always ate, heartily. I was looking for lovesickness. I was looking for heartache, for sorrow or self-reproach or the sour stomach of contrition. But I saw none and after a time decided to approach the matter the Fahean way, by coming at the thing the long way round.

'There was good music the other night.'

'There was.'

I let the birds have the interlude. In urgent conclave, they were doing a demented singing, half of them trying to convince the others this was breeding time.

'No sign of Junior Crehan, though,' I said.

'No.'

'No.'

'We'll hear him yet. Don't worry.'

'Yes. No.'

I can't say I was schooled in what it looked like to see a woman in a man's mind, what or even where she might be remarked, in the lips, the flesh of the cheeks, the small wrinkles at the corners of the eyes, the eyes themselves so blue and deep. I couldn't say how exactly, but after a time I knew she was there, and that like a salmon rising up through the rivers of him, if I waited she'd leap out of his mouth.

The sun bore down, Spanishing the air. Swallows, returning, must have questioned their coordinates. The birdsong was just hectic. Though the day was already warm and the sky cloudless, people still lit fires for cooking, pale turfsmoke sitting in small plumes above the chimneys wondering where the wind had gone. It made for a dreamlike scene, if your dreams ever take you to idylls. Down the valley you could see the townlands of Kilmac and Corry, the fine hill fields of the Murrihys, the bad bog ones of the Murphys. There were cattle standing in the puzzle of puddles gone, the ground hardening and the grass sweetening as it sucked the sun out of the sky. You could almost hear it happening.

And because old men no longer need adhere to the convention of time, and because memory dissolves it, I can be there still. I can be sat on the grass at our lesser picnic on the top of Master Quinn's field and feel the sun striking down and know something of the peace of that pause, the dawning that opens in a person, which is not yet at the point of understanding, not yet anything solid or sure as a thought, but happens in a way that you may not realise until years later and miles away when it comes to you that just then, just there, you were brushed with nothing less than eternity, catching a sense of a place that has been before you and will be after you, and both were contained in that moment. In the mid-distance birds landing and lifting that were the same birds since forever and would be forever, and you in that forever too, sitting on the dry grass of a hill field in Faha aware that your whole life is an instant, knowing it for what it is, and so too then knowing something of the deep sleep of the fields, the smile of spring and what mercy there is in a fall of sunlight.

Patience is the hardest virtue. I couldn't hold out any longer.

'You sang well. The other night,' I said at last. 'At the chemist's.'

Christy palmed his beard. The chamois of his face crinkled in a wince. 'I'm not sure I did.'

I was already committed, I might as well go further. 'Is that what you planned? To sing for her? Mrs Gaffney. Is that what you wanted to do? Is it done now? Are you done? I mean, is that it?'

'No. No. That won't do.'

'Why?'

'Well,' he looked a small ways in front of him at a bare truth, and then turned to me and said, 'because, I told you, I broke her heart.'

I couldn't meet his eyes. I took a bite of the bread.

The thing about Doady's brownbread is when you take a bite of it you've taken a bite out of the elements, earth, air, fire and water all, and while your mouth negotiates with the grainy dryness now made a ball by the moisture of the butter, while you realise that by an alchemy of bakery the lump of the bread in your mouth is bigger than it seemed in your hand, *keep chewing*, and that there's nothing you can do now because you're getting a first-hand practical demonstration of what Duns Scotus called Thisness, *keep chewing*, the dense solid mass of the undeniable, you can say nothing for a bit. You can wave at a couple of drowsy bees warmed awake and delirious on the early coconut of the furze blooms. You can make a low throat sound to signal you'll say something shortly, but while you're eating Doady's brownbread, *keep chewing*, you're gagged by the essential stuff of substance, that insists on its own primacy, that, like life itself, is partways laughing at you and partways saying *Take me seriously*, because otherwise it may just choke you. So, I said nothing for a bit.

Christy leaned to one side and took out a crushed pack of cigarettes. He tapped one out and rolled it between his hands, all the time looking down the Master's field. He put the cigarette to his lips and by instinct more than intention patted the pocket of his jacket on the grass beneath him. I had the matches and struck one and the smoke veiled his face and lent him that look that smokers have, when their thoughts seem visible and there's a door open to intimacy.

'How?'

He drew on the cigarette, watched the smoke move away from him. 'In St Michael's church, Sneem, County Kerry, I left her at the altar.'

22

There was nothing to say to that.

At least nothing I could come up with. The idea of it landed in my brain and blew everything else aside. It seems an obvious point now, but I hadn't lived long enough to know there's an infinity of ways to tell the same story, that human failure is a history without end, but so too human endeavour, and that between both lies the lot of the living. Nor did I know how an older person must accommodate the younger one inside them, and the first part of my reaction was an inner violence as I tried to reconcile the Christy I thought I had come to know with a man who could leave a woman at the altar. I was all absolutes and ideals, remember, I had been nowhere, knew maybe half a dozen people, none of them well. So, without knowing any further details, I made a proverbial rush to judgement and stood up with the sinking feeling that was Christy free-falling off the silver ladder of my estimation.

Doing the Christian thing, I was to realise, was maybe only achieved by Christ. What settled in me was the bilious soup of disappointment. I turned away, took up the bicycle and cycled ahead, head up, glinting in the sunlight, a skinny Fahean version of a latter-day knight, carrying like a badge of honour the fifty-year hurt of the spurned Annie Mooney.

Over the next few days, Christy made no further progress in his personal atonement. As when, over the draughtboard, Ganga put his two thumbs inside his braces and gave small outward pulls, he was considering his move. I was small help, which is charitable for none. We went about the business of securing the signatories and, as though sealed inside the inviolable privacy of males, for a time said nothing more about Mrs Gaffney or Annie Mooney or fifty-year-old broken hearts.

But in all parishes stories have their own legs. Though tele-communications were still in their infancy, their invention already seemed redundant, because often when we stepped on to a flagged threshold I had the sense the story had got there before us. It was in the tremulous pulse of a curtain as we leaned the bicycles, and in the curious look of the wife or eldest daughter drying their hands on a teacloth and coming from the shadows inside with a *So, this is the man* in their eyes.

Christy met all with the same geniality and warmth. He showed no awareness of my coolness and introduced me with 'You know this man.' To which the reply was often: 'I knew his father, and his grandfather.' By which method, simple and old as nature, I was stitched into the fabric of Faha. Though we sometimes met with a trio of the dogged, the bull-headed, and the out-and-out mulish, Christy took none of it person-ally. He adopted the native policy of avoiding confrontation, and most times when people spoke against the electricity he listened, nodded, noted, and said we'd call again.

Because the machine of State forgets that it was built by people, poles were being erected in fields where permission had not yet been granted, and there were disputes, work held up, and the memorial called for. The document had no legal

174

status, but because they were so rarely given – birth, marriage and death certificates accounting for the threefold circle of life – most people were persuaded by the authority of their own signatures. In Cregg's the hole had to be filled back in because Sam said he hadn't given permission. The crew shovelled it in like a grave, then stood by as Christy showed the form. Sam studied the unfamiliarity of his own autograph, the inked validation of himself in fiercely concentrated, upright primary-school penmanship that I imagine recalled in him the hardship of learning handwriting, his mother rapping his knuckles with a rule and forbidding him the freedom to play outside until his name was wrote right. Sam studied, swallowed the pride of that childhood victory. He said something but spoke with the mumble in-speak of a people who never believed they were heard, and Christy had to ask him again, and this time he nodded, and the boys unburied the hole again.

In my grandparents' house, perhaps because the rearing of twelve contrary children had taught them to live by swallowing the stomach acid of first reaction, the news of what was now a dawn opera had settled without disturbing the status quo. But in Doady there was a fresh proof of the universal truth that a man becomes more interesting to a woman once he is shown to have a heart. A reply to her letter about the singing episode had already come from Kerry, in it the triumphant results of a cross-mountain multi-parished *rútáil*, a rooting operation of detection, a *Do you remember a story about a wedding that wasn't?* and a *Was she a cousin to Peggy Taafe?* and a *Do you know who'd know that now?* as a Sneem-ish intelligentsia had unearthed the bones of the drama from under the stones of fifty years. And now that Doady had the whole tale up to that point, she relished the rarity of Clare trumping Kerry for once, having the hero under her own roof, and being uniquely positioned to tell them across the river what happened next. She said nothing to Christy, of course, but when we had tea at the table in the garden, the moons of her glasses kept him in scrutiny, as if for the next episode.

Since Christy had told me, I had failed several times to put aside the idea of him leaving Annie Mooney at the altar. A story grows in the gaps where the facts fall short. And maybe, in extravagant weather, grows faster. Maybe, the way people in Faha believe warm weather a breeding ground for germs, why the Digger Dunne put his pneumonic grandfather outside in his nightshirt in the frozen December of 1950, maybe the sun had something to do with how large the story grew in my mind.

I knew of only one instance to compare it to, and in the quiet of the hills and hollows as we walked or cycled or sat outside evenings playing cards in incredible weather, I tried to recall what I could of Miss Havisham.

At that time you read *Great Expectations* in school, and if it landed larger than your own life in the white rooms of your imagination, if it haunted your days, made you fear Magwitch, pity Pip and love and hate and love Estella until your heart was wrung and your own world less real than the one in the pages, your teachers didn't care, as long as you could summarise last night's chapter and pass the window-hawed time of Friday afternoon by reading out loud from wherever the boy before you had finished murdering Dickens. That in some schoolrooms Dickens survived was a miracle that endured a hundred years after his death, until the Minister, bound on a course of improving things for the worse, cut the throat of him in favour of more contemporary texts.

I was thinking of Miss Havisham. In my mind I could hear the creak of the gate of Satis House, see the weeds of the yard and Pip's candlelit ascent up the dark stairs behind Estella, I could see his rough boots, see the cards in his hand when he played with Estella and called the Knaves Jacks – the same as I did – but I could not quite picture Miss Havisham's face. It vanished behind a pale mantilla of cobwebs and shadows. It was the idea of her more than the image that had seized me, that she had been left at the altar, and that on that day her heart had broken, time had stopped, and she had survived in a grotesque between worlds, transitioning to a caustic powder.

Because this was my only reference, because when I read it the story imprinted itself in a way that would last a lifetime, and because we want to believe the world goes how we imagine, I supposed Annie Mooney's life must also have been devastated by being left at the altar. The person she recalled now was Mrs Blackall, and at once I thought I understood why Christy had been so affected by her and why we had done her whitewash.

Annie Mooney had fled from the eyes of Sneem after the failed wedding, how could she have stayed? No, she had abandoned her wedding dress on the bed – her sister Dympna wore it two years later in the renovated church of St Patrick's at Tahilla Bridge, Doady reported, where the twenty-seven windows caught the other-worldly splendour of the west Kerry light and let love seem burnished and by God bespoke – Annie left in the night and came like all of Kerry to Killarney and was working chambermaid in the wood-and-pipesmoke of the Lake Hotel when Gaffney the chemist found her. He was eighteen years older than her. She could not love him the way she had Christy. That human beings loved truly only once was an unwritten tenet when the world was young, an idea fostered by the Church, supported by the coming knowledge of heart trauma, and by the bookstall of Spellissey's where all the second-hand paperbacks told of First Loves. Second loves had small l's, they existed, but were in the lexicon of male weakness where woman's bottoms were buttresses against loneliness and the emptiness of men's stomachs made fine words come out their mouths. For women, second loves were accommodations of convenience, not great passions like the ones in the picture houses. So, first off, I had Annie Mooney reject Arnold Gaffney's proposal. She had said goodbye to all that. She thanked him for his attentions, but no thank you, and he blinked at the beauty of her and stood in his black suit, slack at the knees because he always hoped to be taller than he was, and because in Todd's in Limerick Mr Mason hid the inch-mark on the tape and tilted the mirror to show his customer a taller version of himself. Arnold had no experience in courtship. He had put it aside in the dry years of study in Dublin, and it had put him aside after that. But he was fascinated by reactions, by the working of one chemical on another, and knew that in many cases nothing happened until a catalyst was added. He left Killarney, not with dejection, but with the clear brow of a scientist who knows the experiment is ongoing, that somewhere out there, X always exists, and in the time of Y eventually the catalyst will be found.

Then, Doady said, he had a share in a chemist shop in County Limerick which was flooded five years out of six and where all around them were dropping like flies with a watery flu. They had a doctor there, a Cleavy quack from a duck pond in *Cork*, Doady said, using a Kerry pronunciation to let that speak for itself. So, Arnold Gaffney had a fair battle on his hands. But he was a diligent chemist and eventually the waters and the flu retreated, and in reprieve then, in a time-honoured tradition old as the Kerry invention of tourism in the tenth century, to recoup his spirit he came to the waters of Killarney.

He had a touch of the rose, Doady said, across the uppers of his cheeks. But more importantly, although he didn't know it, his expression carried a new understanding of the frailty of the human constitution and the brevity of life.

It also carried the first instalment of a philosophy of luck. Arnold still hadn't found the catalyst, but he found his feet walking across the creaking twelve-inch floorboards of the lobby of the Lake Hotel, which were only just drying out with the roaring fires necessitated by the reopening and living inside a waterfall. He came to the reception desk, was given the key to Room 7, and when Arthur the big-eared porter bore his case up the stairs, at the turning Arnold Gaffney passed Annie Mooney with her bucket on her way down, and he said, 'Hello, Miss Mooney,' and nothing more, touching the black rim of his too-big hat, flushing rose, blinking his too-weak eyes and looking at her with a look that told her she was as wonderful as he remembered.

And something in her surrendered then, I decided. Right there on the turning of the stairs, between Arthur putting down the case and picking it up again, pushing back his ears to resume his ten-thousandth ascent, something in her saw the recent life experience in the chemist and that it was an experience of grief or failure or both, and she knew that if he asked again she wouldn't say no.

The wedding was in a small church north of Killarney. Her mother and father came in a horse and cart with her two sisters, all of them wrapped in blankets saturate with rain, the length of the liquid journey giving them a drowned look and making loud the squeak of their shoes in the small congregation. By an impulse both characteristic and contrary, Annie Mooney had chosen to walk to the church in the rain. By the time she took her father's arm for the second time at the church door, the ivory of her dress was silvered and her hair pearled.

Like most people, Arnold had found Faha by accident. He was a Sunday motorist. Motoring for pleasure was still a novelty then, the roads were rough but empty and for a scientist carried the fascination of the undiscovered and a mechanised victory over the drawn limits of human distance. Besides which, Arnold was taller and younger in a car, and a drive in the country was discovered the perfect means to conquer the deflated time of Sunday afternoons. Being in motion, it turned out, up to forty miles an hour say, resolved the feeling of emptiness, and for the duration of the journey salved the spirit-wound that they seemed unable to have children.

One wet June day, he came west with his young wife in a black Ford, wipers spasming over and back in what Arnold, God love him, thought a temporary shower, roads unspooling through mad green growth, motoring along grand until the engine overheated and he turned off the main road, came down by Commodore's Cross and Cotter's, pulled over by the forge and dashed through the rain in to Tommy to ask for water.

And because he was given it, and because Tommy's wife was a saint called Mary who insisted on them coming in for the catalyst of a mug of tea and a cut of boiled cake while the car settled itself, Arnold fell in love again, this time with Faha. Without it ever clarifying itself in the front of his mind, without recourse to considerations of commerce or weighing the reasons for and against, but maybe following the deeper rationale of unreason that rain would always remind him of his wedding, in his case rain and love being inextricable, he finished his tea, looked out at the gleamy water rivering down the crooked smile of Church Street, and thought: *We can do good here.*

23

I didn't of course know, or even imagine, all of this yet. But I would eventually. From the distance of half a century it's impossible to remember which bits came from which sources, and in which order, and I'm not alone I suppose in sometimes thinking a thing I've imagined happened. I may be alone in thinking that doesn't matter.

Through a combination of conjecture, Dickens and details that leaked sideways out of my grandmother, I had my version. Now, with the flawless clarity with which we see stories of our own construction, I saw Mrs Gaffney again at Easter Sunday Mass, reinterpreted the dignity of her bearing, and found myself moved by an imagined life.

I say this to explain to myself what happened next.

In the way one person can fall inside the spell of another, I was attached to Christy. In the immediate aftermath of the street singing, I expected consequence, not to say calamity. That's how these things worked, this happened, and so then this. But not in Faha, where a deeper truth of human behaviour prevailed, and in the same way that nobody mentioned what all knew, that I had been earmarked for a priest, the singing story slipped behind the eyes of everyone and, once more, Faha resumed its natural torpor. Without jeopardy you could have erected an arch over the entrance to the village with the irrefutable declaration: *Nothing happens here.*

But a dangling thread is intolerable, who knows why exactly. Through the next few days Christy and I went about the townlands with the memorial as before. Evenings he swam in the river and after we played cards in the garden with the wireless playing a scratchy music out the door, or we took the bicycles and resumed our liquid quest to hear Junior Crehan. At no point did Christy announce the next stage of his plan, an intermission I found unbearable. Then, because you can't easily escape a religion of resurrection and redemption, I decided I had to go and see Annie Mooney for myself.

After the death of Arnold Gaffney, it was soon realised what a wonderful service he had provided, and the foibles of his person, his slow scrupulous attention to the details of prescription, taking down a volume from the backroom and reading up about the effects of a medicine, both frontal and side, while his customer stood waiting or was sat in the red leatherette chair, *Just let me have it, will you, Mr Gaffney?* his un-Fahaean exactitude, his *Limerick-ness*, his religious maintaining of the half-day Wednesday, the compensatory use of a French cologne he sold, every curse, criticism and complaint was washed away the flood day of his funeral.

Faha woke up the next day to a *Closed* sign hanging on the door and the awareness that the nearest pharmacy was miles away, a fact that soon proved Mrs Moran's theorem: the further you live from a doctor the sicker you feel. Not only did the chemist's operate in conjunction with Doctor Troy's practice, perhaps more tellingly it provided a veterinary service to farmers who knew what their animals needed, and, because of a crossed wire in their make-up, could be dying of four illnesses but still be in Gaffney's looking for something for a cow, calf or greyhound.

A week after the funeral the *Closed* sign hadn't turned and Faha began to fear for its welfare. As was customary, the parish sent word to the priest, through the emissary of Master Quinn, and the parish priest passed the ball to his curate. Father Coffey was in a vexed state at the time, by night writing long letters to the Bishop in which he vented all his outrage at what was wrong with the Church, then tearing the letters into minute pieces and posting them into the vegetable waste of the hens' feed. So, with the need to achieve an actual result, he approached Mrs Gaffney the evening of the Month's Mind, pinched the creases of his black trousers to sit in her small parlour, talk around the thing at hand and wait for the tea that was not forthcoming. Mrs Gaffney defied convention by being direct. 'What do you want, Father?'

'Oh, it's not what I want,' he said. 'It's the poor parish.'

He let that do the talking, I'm guessing. He let the sick of the whole parish rush in and sit some moments, the phlegmy, the fevered, the dry- and the wet-coughing, the asthmatic, the chronically bronchial, sufferers with chests caught in a mazy syrup of catarrh, all kinds, chilblains, all kinds, stalled circulation, all kinds, and the infinity of other ailments that came from living inside a cloud. Father Coffey let the damp grey mass of them take up all the air in the parlour until he supposed that point was made and he waved a vague hand to vanish them, leaned forward, shining his earnest eyes to ask, 'Were you thinking of advertising for a chemist, at all?' And before Mrs Gaffney could answer, he slid in with, 'Wouldn't it be a way to carry on your husband's spirit?'

When he left later that night Father Coffey's eyes were shining some more, because although he had caught a headcold he had secured the welfare of the parish in the handwritten wording of an advertisement for the *Champion*.

The ad appeared in the paper the following Thursday and gave Faha the swell of pride that used come from seeing your own place in print. There was a full two weeks to lord it over Boola, before the news spread that no chemist had applied and the Boolaeans made a crowing dance out of that, before they too started to feel the pinch and a sad truth was revealed: human beings care first about themselves. In any case, the news was not technically true. There was one applicant who had travelled all the way from the unlikelihood of Longford, a gingernut by the name of Spriggs with green eyes and corkscrew body. He had leanings towards the imaginative, and a philosophy of intuiting the patient's ailment, receiving the prescription from the greater universe by shutting the emerald eyes and holding out his hands to the shelves like a blind man to 'see' what the patient required, a philosophy that made its way to the church gates on Sunday where it translated into the Fahaean shorthand: *There's all kinds*.

Spriggs did have the soft white hands of a chemist, but in the upshot was found wanting in manner, knowledge and qualifications, and Mrs Gaffney said she'd be sure to let him know.

The parish had no chemist for the first time in thirty years, and, like Mikey Boucher when Doctor Troy told him his pistol wasn't working, the flag was lowered.

Eventually, as with all things in Faha, a homegrown solution was found. Following a further visit from Father Coffey, Mrs Gaffney agreed to reopen the shop herself. There was the clear understanding that it was only temporary, while awaiting a qualified pharmacist. But in all western parishes the temporary was unhinged from the temporal by the fact that it was the term used by Government to account for the short-term, slapdash, second- and third-rate solutions that were applied to bad roads, school buildings, hospitals, and the like. The people lived in the permanently temporary. They were facilitated in this by both the ferocity of the Atlantic and the teachings of the Church, both of which taught the same lesson: *You're only here for a time.* In any case, as I've said, time itself was an unstable entity in Faha, Prendergasts in the post office the only ones who set their clock by the pips on the wireless.

Temporarily, then, while waiting for the authorities to discover the anomaly and shut it down, the chemist reopened. Mrs Gaffney operated it along amateur lines, informed not by book-learning but life and decades of marriage to a diligent mixer of powders and dispenser of pills. To the locals, that it was illegal to dispense was neither here nor there once she had Greavy cured of the gout.

In the three years since Arnold Gaffney had died, no new chemist was found, and soon enough none was looked for. Having little appetite for remote places, the authorities looked the other way, and temporarily, for the time being, let the situation prevail, taking a parental tack: things would sort themselves out. As always, to the problem Faha found an organic solution, turning the deficit to advantage by saying that after so many years Mrs Gaffney knew their complaints better than themselves. She worked in conjunction with Doctor Troy, who visited the chemist's in the evenings and filled the prescriptions, lending some credence to Maura Dunne's theory that he was himself secretly in love with the widow. For common ailments Mrs Gaffney knew the common creams and cures, as did the patients, who often asked for them by name. Names retained their original magic. The first time that people encountered a product that worked its brand name became inseparable from it, *I'll take the Vicks. They have a good name.*

So, on the afternoon when I left Christy early to cycle to the chemist's, I knew that Annie Mooney would be behind the counter. I invented a headache that was behind my eyes, then in my temples, and went with the high seriousness of the vocational, not a little flustered by the comedy of being chosen by circumstances to play Cupid. If that was what I was.

The little bell above the door jingled and I stepped inside a space of honeyed light and trapped sunbeams. The shop was empty, smaller than I remembered, and stopped me at once with the smell of my mother in her last days.

The shelves were well-stacked, the multitude of things that could go wrong arranged chasteningly under broad rubrics, Head, Ears, Nose & Throat, Eyes, Teeth, Joints. Because they were a sex that concurred with Aristotle, having more to them than the sum of their parts, in their own category: Women. Furthest from the counter, as ordained by general backwardness in matters of the body, a small shelf: Men. Beside the Men, Animals.

Behind the counter was a curtained doorway into the main house. Annie Mooney was in there. My heart hammered. I waited some more. *What was she doing? Why had she not come out? Had she recognised me holding the bicycles outside the church?* In the prolonged pause I found I was suffering from Head, Ears, Nose & Throat, Eyes, Teeth, Joints, and maybe Animals.

I went to the door, opened and closed it on its jingle again. 'Yes?'

'I have a headache.' It was a blurt.

'I see.'

It's not an easy thing to capture the effect of one person on another. She had appeared silently behind the counter in a dark green dress, an apparition both grave and serene, her long silver hair tied down one side in front of her and her eyes steady and deep and sad, and instantly I was out of my depth.

'Is it bad?'

'Yes.'

'I see.'

She hadn't moved. She was a woman with an unearthly ability to be still, and serious, and in those first moments I think I already knew she was as unlike any woman I had met, and also that she would be impossible to persuade.

'Is it on one side?'

'It's everywhere.'

'I see. You've had it a while?'

'Yes.' And then, fearing that she might send me for further investigation, 'No. I mean not really.'

'I see.'

'A short time.'

'I see.'

Each time she said it I thought she was seeing more. Each time I thought: *She knows who you are and knows you're lying and now she's only waiting to see how deep you want to dig.* And because your mouth is often ahead of your thought, I said: 'It comes and goes.'

I looked up at her. 'It's gone now.'

In the afternoon light now amber, she looked at me, and because that look moved me in a way I couldn't have explained yet, because I knew then that long ago she had left Annie across the bridge of girlhood and was simply Ann now, because I myself was an innocent indebted to storybook valour and rescue, I said the thing I had already decided I wouldn't.

'Christy McMahon,' I said, and then couldn't believe that I had actually said it, because nothing had changed. Nothing at all that could be seen or heard had happened, and so, maybe only to reassure myself of the certainty of my own existence, too quickly I went further.

'Christy McMahon is staying at our house.'

Maybe because of my mother, maybe because one day your mother falls in the street beside you, I had a chill fear of the unpredictability of life. That at any moment a terrible thing can happen was a fundament of how I lived then, and some part of what had sent me to the seminary. The only way to cope with it was will and control. The way to survive was to think a thing through, you plan what will happen and what after that, and after that, and you follow the sequence as far as you can, that way erecting a series of shields through which life itself was unlikely to pass. So, I had imagined what would happen when I told Annie Mooney about Christy. I had rehearsed the scene silent and with sound. She would put her hands to her mouth to hold in what couldn't be said. She would look at a space above and to the left of me, for a moment unable to meet my eyes, looking into that place just above where the past was rising like a flood tide so fast and full that she would need to touch something so as not to be swept away. To reassure herself of the solidity of the now, she would lay a hand on a shelf of medicines, sunbeamed dust dancing as the sound of the name she hadn't heard spoken aloud in fifty years filled the shop. She would wonder how I knew and what I knew, questions would be bubbling up off the tide, but she wouldn't be able to ask them right away, because, soft wheel and hoof noises slow and unreal outside in the street, time would have folded back on itself, and it'd be as when you are returned to a moment buried in the first corner of your heart, returned to a feeling that pierced you once so profoundly that just to survive the loss required everything you had, just to breathe, just to go about in the broken world in the pretence of the ordinary, because she wouldn't have forgotten him, she wouldn't attempt to deny it, I knew she already had too much grace and honesty for that, but, I decided, she'd need me to say nothing more, to ask no questions, to allow her to see again the young man summoned by his name, and feel the rage and hurt and begin the rough negotiation we all have to make with failure, blame and loss, in her case more grievous because there had been no explanation, no argument, because he had just vanished, and because *I loved you once* is among the saddest lines in humanity.

I was prepared. From the readings of melodramatic novels, words of ballads, and the things your mind makes up when it has no knowledge of real human beings, I had imagined all outcomes, wore a nineteenth-century cloak of black velvet and had my full set of responses to try and help Christy's cause. But I lost them all now in the face of this actual woman and what she said next. Because, although she didn't take the worst option, she didn't snap the heart of Christy like a biscuit, she didn't say *Who?* She didn't laugh, she didn't frown, she didn't ask if I was joking or how I knew their connection, she didn't say *Only a child believes in an imperishable love*, instead, the fine wrinkles at the corners of her eyes pursed a little, she looked directly at me and, in a quiet voice, said the last thing I thought she would say: 'I know.'

I didn't move. My lips were dry, my throat tight. A crescent of sweat came beneath the forehead-fall of my hair.

With untimely gaiety then, the bell jingled, the door opened on a parallelogram of pale reality, and, like ones marooned from a rain-land, in heavy overcoats unsuited to the sun, Mrs Mungovan, Mrs Moore and Mrs Mulvey trundled in together in a hot bundle that broke all spells and I lowered my head and pushed out past them into the street.

24

'She knows you're here.'

It had taken me three unreconciled days to confront Christy. For three days I twisted over and back on the hook of whether to tell him I had gone to the chemist's, for three days I said nothing, opening and closing my mouth like a trout and twisting some more. Sidelong I studied him, watching to see some shift, some evidence that he was ready now to move on with his atonement. But there was nothing, or nothing obvious. Having gone to see Mrs Gaffney with the intention of pleading Christy's case, I found that when I came home I reversed myself and wanted to plead hers to him. By her air and manner I had been moved. It was not as obvious as disappointment or grief, I had no sense that her entire life had been unhappy, it hadn't, or that she would have thought Christy a great opportunity missed, it was not sentimental or trite – but something in the deep moment of her eyes caused me to resolve that Christy had to talk to her. Listen, I was young. Rashness and fixedness. In my breast pocket silver absolutes, pentangle on my shield. I was angry with Christy, galled by his delay. I laid the bicycle against the cow cabin at my grandparents', determined to tell him to go, go to Ann Mooney at once, but when I came in the door and saw him helping Doady with the ware, saw the gentle ease, the body wisdom of him, instantly I lost the pulse of action and adopted perhaps a philosophy of Saint Placid, hoping the thing would happen by itself.

The fine weather that sat over Faha sat there still, each morning the flying boats coming up the estuary gleaming like great gannets as a veil of mist lifted revealing cattle standing in silvered grass that was sweetening by the day.

Knowing that the opportunities of novelty are short-lived, salesmen had appeared in Faha with wares of exotica, straw hats, some soft-brimmed and floppy that looked like upturned basketry and lent the look of a Provençal Van Gogh, others, boaters, suggestive of unknown regattas in a more elegant elsewhere, and from further afield cone-capped sombreros that escaped a dressed-up look of Mexico by being customised with a ribbon of green-and-gold in the Faha colours, Tommy Fitz the first to wear one, the tops of his ears already gristle. Waxen navel oranges appeared, each one a jewel wrapped in dark blue tissue paper, also shorts, sandals, and elegant ladies' fans from Tennessee, which when extended depicted a scene from the Bible. There were sun sprays and oils, not to protect, but to help penetrate and make last the look of burnt freckle that was translated locally as tan. The sad truth is that, like fish, the looks of the Irish are not improved by sunshine, and if you ever see the photographs Mick Liverpool took when he was visiting his mother, in every one of them there's a scorched squinting look from what Ambre Solaire called *coups de soleil* and the sense of a people dazed and displaced.

So, after ten days of the blessing of fine weather, there were silent prayers that the Lord take his blessing elsewhere for a while, refill the watering holes for the cattle with a small downpour and come back again the following Tuesday, say.

After the same ten days the parish was already stippled with electricity poles. It was remarkable to look across fields where nothing had changed in a thousand years and see the stuck-up fingers, not yet wired or connected to anything, and not unlike the totems of a tribe landed from elsewhere and claiming territories by lines invisible and arbitrary.

On the bicycles Christy and I came up where Patsy Phelan in his three-piece suit sat on a small carpet on his front wall. Patsy enjoyed the privilege of stillness, most days did absolutely nothing but breathe and look and hear and smell the world turning. A self-appointed Judge of Existence, at noon he went in for his dinner, then came out again for the second sitting. He had a big florid face pumping out sweat, and when we passed he offered a greeting hitherto unknown in the history of Faha, 'Savage heat.'

And, as if suddenly aware of the uniqueness of the time, and foreign behaviour condoned by sunshine, walking the hill at Reidy's after, I turned to Christy and said: 'She knows you're here. Mrs Gaffney, she knows.'

'I know.'

'You know?'

'Yes.'

'And?'

'I'm not sure.'

'What do you mean?'

'I'm thinking, Noe.'

'Well, what did you think, beforehand, what was your plan?'

'To see her and say I'm sorry.'

'So?'

He looked up at the sky, his eyes small and his face crinkling, as if momentarily he was in collogue with the sun.

'You have to go see her.'

'I'm not sure I do.'

'You do.'

I let that statement stand there, bald and barrel-chested, its feet planted and thumbs tucked in the lining of its waistcoat like Butt, and when that brought no response I pushed further: 'You do. That's all there is to it. Or what? You came all this way just to sing in the street outside her window?' I regret the scorn. It's an acid vice of the high-minded. It belonged to Butt. 'Are you afraid of her?'

We were near the top of the hill, one of the Kilkenny girls sailing a white sheet up and over the line, a grace note not lost to me in its simplicity and beauty, in my mind it's sailing still.

Christy watched it too. 'Contrition is more easily said than done,' he said.

We went a little further to the crest.

'You have to see her.'

I looked across at him and, as always, while waiting for something to happen, I realised that something had already happened. He had lost his faith.

'I don't want to hurt her any more than I already did.'

'But she knows you're here.' And, because in the end revelation is irresistible, I added, 'She told me.'

Taking a final page from Butt's practice which was predicated on always having the last word, quickly I mounted the bicycle, pushed off and the downhill took me past the *consequiturs*, as Felix Pilkington says.

When we came into Quirke's there was a quorum in shirtsleeves gathered around a fresh hole in the front field there. Quirke's was mostly stones and the pole was on the ground while the men assessed whether enough stones had come out to make a third attempt to stand it. When Christy and I came into the avenue our arrival seemed propitious and we did the thing all men do, we came over for a look into the hole, nodding the tight-lipped nods that masqueraded as expertise. Two long lines of rope ran across the grass to a jittery grey horse waiting with Quirke. The third attempt was decided by a smack of the ganger's hands. Christy threw off his jacket and, because there are coded imperatives in the company of men, I did the same, and we stood in to raise the pole.

With a sharp *hup hup* from Quirke and a worry from his rod of osier, the horse took the tension. Head down and hands out on the sticky sweat-melt of the creosote, I saw nothing and heard only the grunts of effort and the *come on come on* of the ganger, the *now now, men* as the shaft of timber sank into the hole and then began to rise like a giant's needle into the sun. It was wonderful. I felt a surge of joy, the simple, original and absolute thrill of a physical victory over the ardours of the terrain, a pulse so quick as to pass instantly in through the arms of each man, into the blood and brain at the same moment with the pole triangled now at nine o'clock, now ten, *Come on come on*, effort increasing beyond the point where no increase seemed possible and yet was found. And because of that surge, because I was given over completely to the thrust of a communal triumph I had never experienced before, I didn't hear the rope snap. I didn't look up or across at where Quirke's horse had reared, where a welting lash of the rod had assailed its dignity and refusal flashed into its dark eyes, rearing and rounding, dissolving the tension on the rope in the same moment it realised it was no longer mastered. I didn't see Quirke raise his arms in a misplaced, hopeless hallelujah gesture to make himself bigger than a horse on its hind legs. I was only aware of cries of alarm, and the clenched jaw that is the last denial of victory slipping out of your grasp.

There must have been a shout of *Away*, or *Run* or *Christ*, I must have been aware of the men letting go, getting out of the line by which in this moment the triangle of pole to earth was tightening, and even to say *in this moment* takes too long for what was actually happening. I must have been aware of Christy jumping to the side. But if I was, that awareness didn't translate into one of the fundamental reactions by which mankind continues on the planet: I didn't get out of the way.

Instead, suffering a heroic disorder, that was part not wanting to leave the only moment in my life so far when I was at one with other men, when the profound loneliness I lived in had been assuaged by the communal, and part unwilling to be the one letting down the side, I leaned in to the pole, believing for one blissed-out breath that I could defeat gravity and hold it upright myself. I was looking at my hands. I remember that. I was looking at the splayed whiteness of my hands on the creosote that was the most real thing I had encountered, and my hands were coming back against me on the hinges of the wrists, my shoulders withdrawing like ones in audience to an immense power, the whole of me about to be crushed, now thinking *Ground does not give in*, planted thighs and locked knees taking a weight that gave reality to the word colossal, Christy calling my name and both my wrists breaking, the pain so extravagant it produced in me a laugh, I don't know how or why, just a *ha* half-gasp half holy with amazement that a human being could feel such a thing, tendons twang-snapping, releasing an arrow of realisation that God made man out of elastics and sticks, the pole still falling, filling your mind with ideas both clear and abstruse which could not then be catalogued, because so many things were happening in the same time, because maybe your back was breaking now, a pole from Finland falling being non-negotiable, because your hands gave way and your head took the blow and because now, almost exactly in the same time as victory, came complete and final defeat.

And then dark.

25

Before Avalon House was Avalon House it was Penniworth's Hotel. This was back in the time when carriages coming west looked for halfway houses off the main thoroughfare. After a few hours bone-rattling along the skeleton roads, passengers needed facilities, drivers drink, and horses watering. Hotel was aspirational. Penniworth's didn't look like a hotel or act like a hotel except in the provision of rooms, neither too spacious nor salubrious according to legend. Mr and Mrs William and Wallis Penniworth had arrived from England and bought the building from a fleeing family of Henshawes, the father a Horace whose Christian act was to point out a sash window on the upstairs landing that might, might mind, need replacing, and whose pale water-coloured children had been warned not to mention the rain. The Henshawes escaped out the avenue under the twisted blackbirds of broken umbrellas, *Keep going, children, keep going*, and Penniworth put up his painted sign of the only ever, previous and since, hotel in Faha. It was the same sign he had put up in Southwold, and, when that went bankrupt, in Robin Hood's Bay in Yorkshire, and, when that burned down, in Porthmadog in Wales, as he succumbed to the immemorial dream of migrating westward, towards ever cheaper properties, looking for the magic formula by which hospitality is turned into money.

In Fahaean history, written for the most part by the forgiving, Penniworth is remembered as a very intelligent man, he had a forehead, and spectacles. His wife is not remembered, but for a sniffle. At first, Penniworth had the classic infatuation of the Englishman in Ireland, finding in the ease of the people and an absence of regulation the heart-opening freedom which is one of the hallmarks of paradise. He was not alone in this, in Dutton's survey of Clare in 1808: *The low grounds of the Shannon are equal to the fattening of the largest-sized oxen.* In Samuel Lewis's *Topographical Dictionary* of 1838: *The best soil in the county is that of the rich low grounds ... which extend from a place called Paradise to Limerick.* In fact, the estate and twin-turreted towers of Paradise House itself, last seat of Thomas Arthur Esq., were not far down the road from Faha. Sometime look up the photographs of Brigadier Henn there and don't think too deeply about the descriptions that mention the aqueous expanse. Despite the aqueous expanse, and his wife's sniffling *Quite a few puddles in the front fields, dear*, Penniworth was fairly sure he had arrived at last in paradise. At the moment it was raining, but that was a small matter. The Irish exaggerated everything, William told Wallis on their first evening in the umber gloom of the drawing room whose chimney was just now struggling to draw. Wallis had a handkerchief to her nose, and between nasal drip and rattling wind-rain couldn't quite hear him.

'The Irish, I'm saying, they exaggerate everything,' he called across to her. 'It is really quite charming.'

Charm, however, was soon enough discovered soluble, and slowly William's expression turned to that of a man sucking sloes. Whatever the actual formula for success in hostelry, by necessity Penniworth's version required that no funds be spent on the building or facilities. The hotel responded with a diva's tactic of theatrically falling apart. Guests did arrive, a dreary selection of the damp and the near-drowned, dripping inspectors, itinerant salesmen, and the lost, who shook off the weather but not the sense of having arrived in a place of last resort. From the traffic of wet boots in the front hall the floorboards rotted, a remedial Persian rug of Limerick origin was Penniworth's solution, but the rain ran the dye then ate the fibres, two of the boards surrendering foot-sized portions, *plop*, to the pool in the basement, offering up a child's smile of gapped teeth. Two chopping boards did emergency dentistry while Penniworth waited for Mr Doyle the carpenter who had sent the perennial message that he would be coming any day now, a day not listed in the calendar. Capriciously the roof leaked, but the drip missed the bucket, and then the buckets, and then the bathtub, moving around the room in a rain-game familiar to those who've experienced the sense of humour of the Almighty when He comes to Faha. The bannister of the stairs came adrift from the rails, if you held on to it for support you had the sensation of a ship in rough seas.

Despite, or because of, the conditions, a sixpence of Penniworths were minted. Three long-nosed daughters, and three myopic sons, they had doting nannies and visiting tutors and went off to boarding schools and had no more truck with the parish until their parents departed this life and went in quick succession to be buried beside Purtills in the Church of Ireland cemetery Kilrush, after which the eldest, Philip, put the hotel up for sale and the parish came through the front doors to take a look and had the humbling experience of having to surrender its prejudice that every Englishman in Ireland was a millionaire.

Doctor Troy, Senior, it was who bought it.

(Pru, the eldest of the Penniworth daughters, had taken down the sign the day after the sale. She took it with her to two maiden aunts in Bath, preserved it as a token of what she remembered more and more fondly as her time in paradise, and like a sea-salvaged treasure or slow-dying dream it was in the back of the closet in her nursing home in Tetbury when she passed. Fact.)

Doctor Troy was from one of the better families in Dublin. Brusque, moustached, and with the natural aloofness of the Royal College of Surgeons, he suffered a smaller case of idyll-icitis, took on the property like an enfeebled patient, addressed the umpteen crises of dilapidation in all rooms and, perhaps ironically, renamed the house Avalon.

By a medical osmosis at that time, whereby the sons of doctors became doctors, young Jack Troy became Doctor Troy and, by the time his father was gently losing his mind to addictive trances of fly-fishing and gin-soaked games of bridge that were played not according to Hoyle's, Faha enjoyed a continuity of care, and grown children could copy their grandparents by saying they were going to see Troy.

All of which to cover the black time in which I lay unconscious.

I awoke in the nineteenth century, on a leather divan in a room of significant disorder, stacks of books, newspapers and journals had fallen over, a tower of suitcases had not, two bureaus appeared to have been carried just in the doorway and carried no more, possibly because of the obstacle of one of Hartigan's pianos, purchased because *Doctor, a fine house like this is crying out for one, just crying. And did I see – was it three? – beautiful young women going up the stairs just now?*

Well now. The house's crying out was not assuaged by the stiff un-music of the sisters' practice and scales, and soon enough was crying louder as Mrs Troy took ill and all practice stopped. The day of her funeral the out-of-tune piano was shunted down the hall to make room for the blackbird of grief and the trays of sandwiches that kept appearing. That piano was still there in that halfway station when years later Doctor Troy himself passed, and the vast population of patients, and their relations, and their neighbours, and their acquaintances, came out of the not-quite-woodwork and arrived like the testimonial cured in Avalon. Hartigan himself appeared, thin and yellow as sheet music two years after his rumoured death, enduring it seemed by virtue of long association with imperishable art. There, in the hallway of the surgery, the demisemiquavers of his eyebrows rising, out of the black-and-cream keys he knocked a Count John McCormack tune that all of Faha recalled as just beautiful.

I lay on the divan and looked about me, trying to recall what had happened. There were various armchairs, each occupied with dusty collections of what to Doctor Troy must have once been curiosities, the room a hodgepodge of interesting chaos and a fair replica I'd say of the contents of the doctor's mind, but all beneath a high ceiling with plaster egg and dart cornices, brocaded curtains and a blazing fire of sycamore logs. The long window looked without interruption down a lush meadow to the river. Evening had fallen, the river silvered. I lay and stared at that river a good while and understood something of Doctor Troy Senior's condition, because it just kept moving and I kept looking without any notion where I was or how I had got there.

The chimney was a poor drawer unless blazing, and from its lighting, and all times before, invisible ribbons of woodsmoke had settled about the nooks of that room. Coming to myself, the smell lay across my nostrils, sweet and deep and *foreign*. In Faha, turf was burned, and perhaps because turf recalled its more glorious past as forest, and resented its fall to a fuel somewhere just above cow dung, or because in Faha dry turf was never actually dry, it burned poorly and every house smelled of turf until no one could smell it any more. Woodsmoke was the smell of money, of big houses and the gentry. Now, lying in that room, that was the first thing that struck me. From that moment, I think, woodsmoke became one of the signal scents of my life, and I never again smelled logs burning without being helplessly hopelessly returned to Avalon House, and all that came with that.

Lying flat, I lifted my right hand to a shooting pain in my temple. But that hand was unavailable, and because I was under the lunatic jurisdiction of a cocktail of medications, my first thought was not to question that, but to say *OK* and try to lift the other one, which was also unavailable. I raised my head to look down and saw both wrists bound in a plaster if not of Paris then of Limerick say, that is, a bit greyer, and made immobile by two grocers' lead weights. I looked at my hands pinned there and then the electricity pole was falling on me again and again I was trying to hold it up and I was thinking *You'll get out of the way* at the same moment I was realising that I hadn't.

The imaginative suffer more than the grounded. That's my excuse for moaning then, feeling the stabbing in my head and the gourd of shame. But it had the result of turning the cream porcelain of the door handle and bringing a girl in a blue dress into the room. She was about my age, or a year younger, her hair long and fair. She was holding a book, *The Modern Home Physician*, a finger inside the page where my cry had stopped her reading in her amateur nurse's chair outside the door. Nothing about her entrance, nothing about the soft sound of her dress and the hard one of her shoes on the floorboards, disabused me of the notion that I was in the nineteenth century. She had a grace and ease of movement that made her seem to glide, made it seem in her case the laws of physics did not apply or had been surpassed without question, because now she was at my side and, though air-swimming through a fog of medication, I was aware of being in the presence of extraordinary beauty.

'I'm Sophie.'

Though I opened my mouth, I had lost the power of speech.

'Doctor Troy's daughter,' she said. 'You were knocked unconscious and brought here.'

I heard her, I understood the words, but couldn't respond. I was in soul-disarray, experiencing something for the first time, that is, a kind of dazzlement. I couldn't look at her. I just couldn't. If I hadn't been bound on the bed I couldn't have been in the same room as her. None of which would find its way into words then, none of which I could have explained to another soul.

You might think that in sixty-odd years I'd forget, lose the memory in my blood and in my bones of what that felt like, that the feeling would be lost, and my only recourse to invent a second-hand version or erase it altogether from the story. But you'd be wrong. Sometimes a moment pierces so perfectly the shields of our everyday it becomes part of you and enjoys the privilege of being immemorial. I remember it as though it were today. Honestly. I remember the canal of my throat closing, I remember riots breaking out, sea in my ears, sweat on my lip, fish-hooks floating in my eyes, and the reflex that was general and immediate, crawling beneath my skin and birthing in me the archetypal response to great beauty: the overwhelming sense of my own ugliness. I remember.

Sophie Troy was beside the divan, her hand holding the book, a forefinger still on the interrupted line. She was gentle, everything about her simplicity and kindness, but I couldn't look at her. 'You mustn't move your hands,' she said, 'not for a little anyway.'

Her voice I have lost now. I can't hear it, a desolation. I've tried, I try here now. I can shut my eyes and see her, can remember things she said, but I can't hear that voice or recreate it for you.

She took a taper from a side table and placed it inside the page, put down the book and from a pewter jug poured a glass of water.

'My father is out on a call.' She came back to my side. 'When you woke he said to give you these.' In her palm, two white pills. 'You'll have a headache, he said.' She studied me with a nurse's curiosity and dispassion. 'Is it awful?'

Let's say I shook my head.

'Put these on your tongue.'

Her hand was two inches from my mouth. It smelled of almond soap. It sent me somewhere. The pills, I tried to look only at the two white pills, not at the pink creases on the inside of her fingers or the five lines of her palm.

'Open your mouth a bit more.'

Gullivered, hands weighted down by my sides, eyes closed, I put out my tongue. Time stops on this moment. Somewhere clocks are ticking, sand is falling through the ampoules of an hourglass, and the river is flowing, but not in that room right then. And though it is absurd, though it is ridiculous, it is the absurdity and ridiculousness of real life, and I am surrendered, offered up to it, then feel the small pressure of Sophie Troy placing one of the pills on my tongue.

'Good,' she says. She is small and light and all business. I am her patient and nothing more. She is a girl lost in fascination to the workings of bone, blood and muscle, the convoluted and intricate mechanics by which a body functions. She sees nothing else. The injured body in front of her is in her duty of care now, there are procedures to follow and she adheres to them closely, concentrating on physical realities and lending truth to the threadbare axiom that women are the practical sex.

Her hand comes behind the back of my head and she leans in to lift me towards her to drink.

The firmness of her hand at my neck, the bareness of her arm, in the fall of her hair a smell I cannot name and some part of me goes scrambling after it, goes through meadow-scents, honey, something paler, falls into an exotic of coconut, and is still scrambling when the rest of me is trapped by the small crinkle sound like a starting fire in the stiff fabric of her blue dress and I realise with a shock the sheer *nearness* of her as she lifts me forward and towards her breast. For the first time in my life I am stopped in the thousand sensations, in the intoxicating *strangeness* of another person. Her breath is warm, and other. Her eyebrows are dark, and, combined with her fair hair, have a force of attraction that can't be measured, but against which I became then, and remain now, defenceless. Right then, more than anything, I want to be a better version of myself. I don't want to be this stupid injured, I don't want to be the failed priest with hands bound and weighted who tried with an idiot's certainty to hold up a falling pole from Finland. I want to be a knight. I want to carry the book of virtues and be honourable and wise and kind and heroic and whatever handsome is, and because I am not, and know I cannot be, the pain is sharp and true and all-consuming, because it is the pain of yourself.

Of course, Sophie Troy knows nothing of any of this. She furrows her brow slightly holding my head, her lips purse to get the patient to drink. Only the cool of the glass against my mouth keeps me in the world.

She watches as I swallow the pill and then repeats everything for the second one. 'Good,' she says. 'They will help.'

She puts a palm against my forehead and looks into the upper air, as if reading there an air-extension of my well-being, and for a second I think she can and will see there what I am still too confused to realise is happening, because maybe, maybe it is the medications, maybe I am in thrall to a pharmaceutical fantasy and my feelings are not mine but borrowed from chemicals and in brief time – I blink, and blink again – they will take them away and this breathtaking sense of an infinitesimal beauty will pass, and I will be back in an ordinary whose doorway right now I cannot imagine ever finding again.

Sophie Troy takes her palm from my forehead and, with the satisfied *quod erat demonstrandum* of a sophomore doctor, concludes, 'You have a fever.' She is confirmed, not alarmed. I am a textbook case. 'It will pass.' Briefly she looks at me to see if there is anything she has missed. Her seriousness pins me to the bed. I can't look at her or I fear I will betray myself. I look past her to the window and the dark meadow with the night in it and the river running with silver mockeries of moon.

'You're to be kept overnight for observation,' she says, by way of conclusion, then adds: 'Your grandfather is here.'

'Ganga?'

'I'm sorry?'

'Sorry. Grandfather.'

'Yes. He's been waiting for you to wake. I'll send him in.' Sophie Troy turns back to the side table then, removes the taper bookmark, reinserts her finger in the pages of *The Modern Home Physician*, walks to the door with it, stops, turns, and, without the slightest trace of what was once called intrigue, says, 'I'll be outside if you need me.'

She steps out the door. Not once has she smiled.

I hear her say, 'Now, Mr Crowe,' and, because my ears have followed her, hear when in a lower voice she says, 'I think he'll be fine.'

In his best suit – he has three, the worst one, the better one, and the best one, which will become the worst one in time – the white shirt and black tie he thinks mandatory for the formal occasion of a surgery visit, Ganga steps in. From big-heartedness and gratitude, his eyes are shining. His hands are holding each other in a knotting twist in front of him. He stands a moment to take in the fine dimensions of the room, helplessly flash-remembering the days of Penniworth when he himself was a boy, the rumoured grandeur of the hotel that no one in Faha ever set foot in, finding something of that in the foot-wide oak flooring-boards. Standing, he takes in the pleasing prospect down the meadow towards the moon river, and though there is presently no aqueous expanse coming towards the house, he can see how it could have, how the infamous floods of 1827, '29, '33, '37 – years spin-rolling now like a wheel of misfortune up to the floods of 1953, '54, '55 and '56 – could be a challenge right enough. All of which only takes an instant, then he comes to the bedside, looks at my bindings, slowly shakes his big round head, and beams.

'O now, Noe!' he says. 'O now.'

26

Once he got going, my grandfather's way of telling a story was to go pell-mell, throwing Aristotle's unities of action, place and time into the air and in a tumult let the details tumble down the stairs of his brain and out his mouth. He had grown up in an age when storytelling was founded on the forthright principles of passing the time and dissolving the hours of dark. In Faha's case, this was a dark permanently tattooed with a rain that insisted on its own reality, trying to get into the house any way it could, and doing a pretty good job too, pooling inside the front door where a soppen grey-black towel did nightly duty, weeping along the sashes of the windows, spitting down the chimney, bouncing black hailstones down through the fire and across the hearth, and invading on a rising water table below the grate so the embers hissed when they fell and all boots lifted an involuntary inch, thankful for the foresight of ancestors who put the slope in the floor. My point, the story had to compete with an emphatic actuality, and defeat it by an air-construct of the imagination, adhering to the Virgilian principle that if you can take the mind, the body will follow. To conquer both time and reality then, one of the unwritten tenets of the local poetics was that a story must never arrive at the point, or risk conclusion. And because in Faha, like in all country places, time was the only thing people could afford, all stories were long, all storytellers took their, and your, and anyone else's, time, and all gave it up willingly, understanding that tales of anything as aberrant and contrary as human beings had to be long, not to say convoluted, had to be so long that they wouldn't, and in fact couldn't, be finished this side of the grave, and only for the fire gone out and the birds of dawn singing might be continuing still.

As, from this, you can probably already tell, for storytelling, there were two principal styles available in Faha, the plain and the baroque. Plainness wore the guise of truth but was soon corrupted by politicians, *Let me speak plainly now*, and avoided by true storytellers. So, Ganga, like me I suppose, chose the baroque, first because of the native precept to enjoy the music of telling, second, because English was a stolen language, and third, because the baroque offered a truer reflection of life as lived in Faha.

'Wait till I tell you now,' he began, drawing a chair to the bedside and grasping on to the balls of his knees.

What followed followed in tumultuous fashion, a single sentence, quick-spoke and eye-popping and miraculous, bypassing both the principles of pauses and the mechanics of breath, my grandfather going for it, and in telling his side of what happened building a tower of description that was in constant danger of toppling over as more and more clauses were thrown on to it, adjectives and adverbs, *bounteous, haltingly*, found in pockets and pitched on, similes not spared, prepositions dangling and otherwise, metaphors throw them on there, in a telling urgent and excited and edged with the real danger that I could have died – and nearly did now in mid-sentence (and, in exuberance, and the irresistibility of funerals for Faha, might have, *killed you were*) – only to be rescued by *Or so I thought, Noe*, a running narration that attempted the same leap as all storytelling, to get the listener across the gap into the skin of the other, *Do you see?* not only capturing what it felt like to be him and be told his grandson might have died, but doing so in a style that was headlong and heart-racing, going both right ahead and roundabout and being in the end perhaps the perfect vocal diagram of the inner workings of my grandfather's mind.

The sentence ended not by design but by natural exhaustion. Ganga sat back from the edge of the chair to which the telling had brought him. His face was plum in the amber lamp-dark, eyes soft as a child's from the shock I had caused. He didn't need me to say anything. Once he had finished he was relieved not only of the story, but of the peril too, and his round smile came back and he rocked his pinching funeral shoes on the wax of the boards as though all was shipshape and sailing on once more. 'O now!'

It was only when he had left soon after, when I lay alone in the dark wondering if Sophie Troy would check on me again, that his story separated itself out into a chronology.

One of the young Kellys, Simon – I had seen him standing watching at the edge of Quirke's field, he was one of those boys that are always standing like lesser angels or demons in the vicinity of calamity – well, Simon, who was barefoot, whose shirt was a frayed short-sleeve Glynn & Sons meal bag put to emergency use, the blue ink faded but not altogether, he was the one who had come running to my grandparents with the news. *The pole, the pole came clean down on him.*

As always in moments of catastrophe, meaning was separated from the sounds of the words, and in the sunstruck slope of the kitchen there was a blinking gap of nothing, Joe being the first to respond, getting to his feet and lifting his head to look at Ganga with the depthless compassion of a dog's eyes. I had been carried to the van and Christy was gone with me. *They're taking him to Troy*, but Simon (who had the outlaw imagination and saucer-eyes of all the Kellys, who had watched cats kill birds, foxes pheasants, and, once, so far, the dawn raid of a pine marten in the henhouse) was full sure he had seen his first human fatality, declared *he looked kilt.*

Ganga took the news like an overwound clock, he had to get going at once. Doady, heart-scalded, but retaining the air of propriety, insisted he couldn't go to the surgery looking like that. *Like what?* A collarless shirt with three exclamations of egg-yolk and a fawn trouser, one left-leg piss-burnt stain from the dribblings of his waterworks. *That!* she delivered with a wife's lemon juice, and Ganga went down into the room, put on the funeral suit whose fly buttons defeated the excitement of his fingers, Doady catching him at the door in that state and without further comment doing them up.

The bicycle still lying in Quirke's front field, he took old Thomas and rode bareback with a fist of mane, urging Thomas just this once to outdo his arthritic amble, and leaving Doady to begin on the rosary which she cracked open right away and was at the *Salve Regina* by the time my grandfather rode up the avenue at Avalon.

They each had their reasons for believing me alive, Ganga, because through shallowness or depth, he believed the world will always try and fall right side up, and Doady, because Intercession of the Saints was available to Kerry people.

My grandfather left Thomas to the sweet grass of Avalon's lawn and burst in the front door, the clock still thrumming in him until he saw Christy sitting pitched forward, hands down between his knees outside the surgery door, and Christy looked up and said, 'He's knocked out, but he's alive,' and in the same half-breath added, 'I'm sorry.' And because he hadn't considered attaching blame, because he lived outside of the jurisdiction of all judgement and thought everyone was always doing their best, Ganga put a hand on Christy's shoulder and squeezed.

They attended outside in the once-spacious now furniture-crowded dimness of the foyer while inside the doctor had for once decided against the nitroglycerine for which he was famous and employed instead a remedy of his own devising to bring me back to consciousness: he pinched my nose and stopped my mouth, watching the patient go to the perimeter of suffocation until the life-force fought back with an outraged refusal that started my torso and shot open my eyes.

Ronnie, the eldest of the Troy sisters, brought Christy and Ganga tea in fine china cups that were mismatched with their saucers, but what of it, and if the tea was Early Grey and not in their acquaintance, what of that too, said Ganga, wasn't it kindness itself? By an un-ironable kink in the duties of daughters, Ronnie had become the mother when Mrs Troy had died. At twenty-three she took over the household in its absolute and fabulous disorder, the kingdom the doctor had let go to pot after the passing of Mrs Troy. Regina, her name was. Regina was the last one to call Ronnie 'Veronica'. The doctor preferred Ronnie, a diminution that began in affection, and was not knowingly to cover the small fall of his hope for a son when she was born and his having to go to tell Doc Senior, *A girl!*

Ronnie had the acuity, intelligence and even temperament of the best physicians but by era and circumstance lost the opportunity to go into medicine. She was diligent and caring and carried a burden of sadness she hoped you didn't see.

Ronnie was the one who came and told Ganga and Christy the doctor had wakened me but that my injuries were several and some severe.

It was also she who came out an hour later with the doctor's instructions that someone go to Mrs Gaffney the chemist's for the materials for the making of casts. Christy volunteered smartly, Ganga said, having no idea what a visit to the chemist had entailed for their lodger.

Christy would have gone, I knew, with a prime motive, any hesitations because of his own circumstances trumped by a duty of care he felt he had failed. He would have still been in the stalled time of the aftershock, still with the sight of the pole falling on me, but also the surge of spirit that comes on the suite of a kiss from death. As I imagined him, he went with both urgency and relief and was in the evening emptiness of Church Street before he had time to think fully that the fifty years' wait to see Annie Mooney was at an end.

In Ganga's version – *He came back soon enough with the bits* – the bit I wanted to hear was missing and, drifting down a medical river on which the injured parts of me floated at an analgesic distance, I filled it with a concoction of my own.

At the chemist's, Christy knocked on the locked door, first softly then peremptorily. He stood square-chested in the street. A grey eyelid, the edge of Mona Ryan's curtain stirred. A squat woman who grew a fearful squint, Mona was all the time receiving signs, if only she could read them. Her State glasses came the day of her funeral, and she was buried wearing them.

Annie Mooney came with the lamp. As the chemist's wife she'd known a lifetime of night calls, slept the thin sleep of those familiar with the clockless continuum of human woe, the multi-volume encyclopaedia of illnesses, infections, fevers that attack the hearts of the aged, the ears of infants, and, in general, the abiding and mysterious tendency of all living things to sometimes become inflamed. She was not alarmed. She had the tranquillity of the experienced and she called out, 'Coming,' which was the first word Christy heard her say in five decades.

And for a moment, I couldn't get him to move.

For a moment, by the magic of empathy and imagination, I am him, and I am the one come back and seeking forgiveness for a folly of youth, and the heartbreak is opened red and raw and forgiveness seems a thing too large for this life.

In the surgery in Avalon, I press my head back on the divan and open my mouth, as if, like a muted balladeer, to let out the ache.

Do I exaggerate? Of course I do. The truth doesn't care. Here's the thing life teaches you: sometimes the truth can only be reached by exaggeration.

At last, Christy turns to face the chemist's door, and through the opaque glass that Arnold Gaffney installed to protect the privacy of patients he sees the blurred illumination of her.

Inside, Annie puts down the lamp where she always puts it, on the edge of the sill by the cardboard promotion for Panacur drench, and her hand goes to twist the stubborn Yale lock that her husband had meant to oil in all the weeks before he died, and after which she didn't oil for reasons too deep to be fished. She draws open the door. The bell overhead jingles.

He sees her.

'I'm not here for myself,' he says.

She looks at him.

Both stories rush forward at the same time, the near one and the far one, the one that he is here because of an accident that is, by virtue of a breathtaking strangeness when it occurs, called pure chance, and has nothing at all to do with their history, that is simply of now, this pure moment, and the other one, the one where Annie Mooney is looking at him and seeing the work of the fifty years, and what life has done to a youth who had all this time remained handsome, animate, spry, quick-witted, big-dreaming, and infuriating, in the backroom of her mind.

'Step inside,' she says.

And there, imagination failed me. I couldn't quite believe any version I pictured, and the tissue pages of *what happened next?* came apart in my hands. I lay back, exhausted by being for a small time in the shoes of another. But, perhaps because Sophie Troy had already removed me from myself, or because of a white optimism attributable to the chemicals, I wasn't fearful of the outcome. I took comfort in thinking my trying to catch the falling timber had been instrumental after all, and for a time converted to Phil Moone's philosophy that idiocy has its place, that there are cogs and levers in the smallest happenstance, that our wrong turns are compensated for by our Creator who not only forgives them, but who put them there in the first place, and by which not-to-call-it-logic, all plots turn out right in the end.

Sometime after midnight, the surgery door opened and all of me leaped.

But it was Doctor, not Sophie, Troy. He came briskly to the bedside, carrying a smoking lamp whose wick needed trimming. A taciturn man of fifty, he was compact, with studied, careful movements, and wounded blue eyes. Human sickness was vast, and not as easily explained or remedied as in medical school. Doctor Troy was never seen out of a white shirt and waistcoat. He didn't look like his father until he sat with the old man's portrait on the wall behind him. Senior had the same handsome face. Like many a bald man who missed the small ceremony of barbering, the old man had grown a beard. He looked out from his portrait in the beard of Bernard Shaw, a look his son hated for its extravagance and suggestion of untamed. His own hair blown backward into an iron grid by Atlantic storms that never failed to attend his call-outs, Doctor Troy grew no beard, but made do with a shoe-brush moustache that was both assuring and combative. In his practice, the doctor's dictum was famously threefold. He sat in a winged armchair of life-distressed leather, listened to the patient's complaint, took a pulse, placed the cold diaphragm of the stethoscope on the chest with the instant life-affirming result of making the patient gasp, sat back, fore-finger-brushed the bristles, and said: 'It will either get better, stay the same, or get worse.'

Doctor Troy put the lamp on the side table, releasing a tongue of black smoke he didn't appear to notice. He didn't say hello, he didn't say *Has my daughter taken good care of you?* He just came to the bedside in his worn shoes of tan leather, put a hand on my brow and looked away into the upper air just like his daughter.

'You were an idiot,' he said to that air up there. 'They should have been broken. They're not.'

His hand smelled *grown up*. It smelled of whiskey and white cotton and woodsmoke and sandalwood musk, and instantly I thought *This is what men should smell like*, but how you came by it, by what gravity, engagement and life experience it entered your skin, seemed in the same instant beyond the likes of me.

'I have a pain when I breathe.'

The doctor made a short air-laugh somewhere in his nostrils, it made it as far as his moustache but not to his mouth, which may have been the reason for the moustache, which trapped the snorts of caustic that were a contingent peril of General Practice. He turned the wounded eyes on me and delivered his dictum. To which I gave the traditional Fahaean rejoinder and said nothing.

'Sleep. Don't move,' he said, and left, taking the lamp with him.

27

Now, I should say something here about the state of my mind when I woke the following morning.

First, let me say that I knew nothing of love, except that it belonged in a higher realm. On Marlborough Road in Dublin I had loved the girl next door. Her name was Helen. I loved her as wholly and purely as I think humanly possible when you're twelve years old. Of course, I never spoke to her, and don't suppose she ever knew. So, yes, a higher realm. I had no understanding yet that in this life the greatest predicament of man and womankind was just how to love another person. You knew in your blood it was the right thing, you knew somehow without ever having had a single lesson, without it ever being mentioned once in thirteen years of school, without your mother or father saying the word out loud once you passed the age of four and went in short trousers to the nuns whose only use, not to say knowledge of it, was in reference to God, so it seemed both supreme and unreal at the same time, and lived in an aura of aspiration, a place inside you that aspired up in a spire nearer to heaven maybe, and not the actual ground of dirt and puddles and broken pavement you and your heel-broke shoes lived on. You knew, you knew the Commandments, had learned them out of the missal-thin pages of the green Catechism, where, in a genius move of utter simplicity God had set the high bar for Christianity by saying *Love your neighbour like yourself,* and you read that and looked over at your neighbour, Patrick Plunkett picking his nose and pressing the pickings on the underside of your desk, and by virtue of nothing more than carnal reality that bar got that much higher. Still, *you knew*, you knew that the purpose of human beings was to love, just that, and though you knew it, though it was maybe the only given in the ceaseless search for purpose, the evidence of the perplex of love was all around you, so that though there were weddings and white dresses and roses, though every song was a love-song, there were black eyes and bitter words and crying babies too, and every heart got broken sometime, yet, and yet, and yet still again, because you couldn't deny it, because, if anything was, it was a fundament, it was in the first intention, part of the first motion when the first key was wound and the whole clockwork of man and woman was first set going, love was where everyone was trying to get to.

Forgive an old man. I say this here because pretty soon you get to a place where you're not sure there'll be a tomorrow, where you think *I better say this now*, here, because not only is time no longer on your side, you realise that it never was, that things were passing by faster than you could appreciate, and whole marvels, the quickening green of springtime, the shapeless shaped songs of unseen birds, the rising and falling of white waves, were passing without you noticing.

So, first, yes, flowing inside the rivers of my bloodstream I had the vague universal longing for love, without any idea exactly of what that entailed, or in my case looked like. And because I was still that young to be in rebellion against my own body, to be repelled by mirrors, to be nothing but a raw and urgent yearning to be other, because what arms and hands and shoulders, what mouth and eyes these were that bore not the slightest resemblance to what I was feeling inside, I had the certainty that I myself, that Noe Crowe could not be loved. I wasn't alone in this. As I think I've said, unworthiness was a birthright then. It was born of religion and history and geography too, the thorns of which have thankfully mostly been plucked now, but then were real.

All of which is to say that, that morning, waking in Avalon to the birds singing, turning my head to first light on the river meadow, the first thing I thought of was Sophie Troy. (To say *thought* is a lie, it supposes a vacancy and then a conscious act, but she was there before I was aware of the words to think or say she was. To say thought suggests a singular act, *I thought of her*, but the truth was she was universal not singular, that is, she was all my thoughts and at the same time, so that they were not separate, not measured or measurable, not individual like memories, not how her hand felt at the back of my neck, not the smell of soap on her fingers or the scent of her hair, not the crinkle sound of the fabric of her blue dress, not the firm resound of her shoes on the oak floor, not the dark line of her lowered and grave eyebrows, the kindness of her voice, but all of these, and more, and all somehow already inside me, flutter-ing and spinning and hopelessly rendered by the poor phrase, *I thought of her.*) And so, before the light had travelled up the meadow and the sun made glisten the grass, before the first pilot boats passed on the permanent slow-motion of the estuary tide, I knew I was in a state, if not to actually love, then certainly to give myself to that for which my temperament and education had prepared me, which is, to adore.

Sophie Troy did not appear in person that morning. By noon my period of being under observation was over. Doctor Troy brought me home in the green Hillman Hunter. He drove it down the middle of roads with an ambassadorial confidence, carrying the patient past the houses where the patient's story was already sitting, and where this next bit was added now, *Troy cured him*, or, because some craved catastrophe, *Crowe's fixed, but he's not right. Sure, he'll never be right again.*

The doctor drove me home without a word. He was not from the parish and hadn't the local idiom of speaking without saying anything. The holes in the road he may have considered emblematic of life's melancholies – he went in and out of each one – shooting jolts of pain into my wrists and up to my shoulders and reminding me I was not only an ardent essence. The day was again dazzling, the sky the same blue that could not be believed, but which, like any wonder that lasts, was already moving from the centre to the edge of conversations in Faha. But to me, turned to the side-window and watching through the reflection of my own face, the country had new lustre. Though I would like to prove the authenticity of my person and the originality of my heart by saying here that no, for me it was different, the truth is we all sometime confirm the durability of clichés. So yes, the grass did seem to have greened overnight, the birds to flicker, the gorse to be flecked with gleam. Even the poached rush-lands of Slattery's looked pastoral, if you can credit that.

We passed Tommy Leary leading two horses, we pressed ahead of us in quick-trotting alarm the loose cattle of Cussen's whose grazing was ditches but whose numbers came up when they turned in the left-open gate of Twomey's meadow. We passed Hayes's and Hanway's, saw an electric crew gathered in the Fairy Field of Naughton's discussing the rights of way of the invisible. (Later, when I mentioned it, Ganga told me Naughton's grandfather had operated a poteen still out of the Fairy Fort there. By way of both respect and payment of rent he always let the fairies have the first glass. His first practice had been to toss the poteen into the centre of the ringfort, but his luck went awry and then awry-er, until my grandfather, my grandfather said, told him he was tossing it into the faces of the fairies. He poured the glass and left it on the ground after that. There was no day it wasn't drunk, Ganga said, and his luck came right after. That's a true story now for you, he said.) The doctor took and returned nods but was in a silent elsewhere and said nothing until we pulled up in my grandparents' yard when he turned to me, sniffed some authority off the bristles of his moustache and said: 'Don't alarm the old people. You're fine.'

Ganga was out to meet us, 'O now!', Doady with arms crossed watching from the front door.

'I'm fine.'

'Thank you, Doctor. Doctor, you'll come in for something?' said Ganga.

Doctor Troy raised a hand, smiled his sad smile, got back in the car and drove off, rising for the first time on that road a chariot's plume of dust.

'Come in. Come in now,' Doady urged, as if I might be struck again in the sunlight. She looked at me with large eyes and some shyness, a behaviour borrowed perhaps from the sister of Lazarus. She stood aside to let me in the door, shooting two fingers of holy water and then following in ahead of Ganga, keeping close to me and already composing the next instalment for that night's epistle to Kerry.

'Are you all right?' was her approximation of nurse ways.

'I'm fine.'

'Course he is,' said Ganga, and patted the wood of the table. 'Course he is.'

'Go up and lie down,' ordered my grandmother.

Lying on the bed, both wrists bound, head thrumming in three-part rapture, pain and pain-relief, I was in that unreal time that passes and doesn't pass, when you're off the ground, ungrounded, in a pale smoke-like drift of wakeful dreaming where images, smells and sounds become part of each other and are too swift and numerous to be singled but all which combine in a sweet ache of yearning, which in my case was composed of Sophie Troy, and of Annie Mooney too.

'You go up and check on him,' I eventually heard Doady say through the holes in the floorboards, turning reality on again.

I came down, holding my hands in front of me like the handcuffed.

'You'll have tea.'

'He'll have something stronger,' Ganga said.

'Go away and make tea till I look at him. Sit here now.' My grandmother pointed to Ganga's armchair with the incompetent cushion of ten *Old Moore's* and sat herself beside me. She folded her arms on the tiny blue flowers of her housecoat and looked so directly that I soon realised she was scrutinising me for signs of idiocy.

'Drink that now.' Ganga put the tea on a footstool and stood there to watch me drink it. It was the worst tea I ever tasted, being some part, maybe most part, whiskey. His whole face inflated with a pink mirth and my complicity in hiding it from Doady.

'What kind of tea did you make him?' she asked.

'Tea,' he said. 'What kind only tea.'

She got up from studying me and went to the far side of the room where she made a clatter music of pots that in wife-language signalled the deficiencies of her husband and that she alone knew what was required, in this case carrageen moss. Cooking it filled the room with the smells of warm honey and a tide gone out. I sat and watched the fire and found the tea not as terrible and realised custom is half of taste.

I was negotiating the cure-all of a carrageen both sandy and salty when Christy came home from work.

'Noe!' he said, large and open-hearted like that, letting his eyes say the rest, then standing back to show the squat figure in the doorway behind him. 'This is Mr Rushe, the boss man. He wants a word.'

Rushe had a face on him like a wasp in October. It may have been customary with him, I can't say. It combined poorly with the corrugated ginger hair. He had a dull suit of grey tweed and a felt hat. His eyes were grim. He shook hands with Ganga, and, with lesser interest, with Doady, who first cleaned her clean hands on the teacloth. By reflex, my grandmother offered tea, and had to readjust her role when it was firmly refused.

A figure of officialdom, Rushe's appearance in my grandparents' kitchen had the same effect it would on all the old people, it made them shy and somehow smaller in themselves, as though they were in the company of critical judgement. Doady blinked, as if before a blow, and missed the one opportunity to usher all into the parlour. Ganga rocked on the balls of his boots.

Courtesies over, Rushe turned from them at once, making clear that he was there to see me. He planted his feet with the square stance of a man who had made it to the top of a turning world and wasn't going to slide off. 'Mr Crowe.'

'Noe, he's called,' Christy said.

'Mr Crowe.' Beneath his hat Rushe's face was crunched together, as though hastily assembled. He had the small mouth of a smaller man or one who distrusted words. 'I am here to clarify one thing. You were *not* employed by the Electricity Supply Board when the accident happened. You were *not* under any contract, directive or understanding, formal or informal, written or verbal, stated or unstated, and therefore not authorised to interfere in any manner with the works as being carried out in Quirke's. Is that correct?'

Somebody had to take a breath. I took one. I looked across at Christy.

Rushe lived up to his name, didn't need a breath to continue: 'Further, if you were under any misapprehension, instigated on the part of Mr McMahon, for whatever reasons, none of which are pertinent here but will be dealt with in due course, *internally*, that you were in fact in the employ of the Board, then I must tell you that any liability for what transpired, any liability at all, must lie at the feet of Mr McMahon personally and not at the feet of the Board.'

Rushe looked at the witness. The witness considered the feet of the Board.

Ganga had narrowed his eyes, as if trying to see what had been said. Doady stood with her arms crossed, waiting to be knocked by a feather. Christy coughed into his fist and sent me a message with his eyes. I wasn't sure I got it.

'If Mr McMahon let you believe that you were in fact in the employ of the Board, if he misled you, then you should say so here and now.' Rushe's chest had grown larger as he advanced up the corporation, with the effect of making retreat his arms, which, from whiskey-tea, medication, or the unquantifiable hallucinogen of a yellow seaweed, now seemed half-sized and stuck on somewhere behind him. He pushed the block of his head forward on his no-neck to conclude: 'So, son, think clearly now.'

That *son* started spinning like a coin inside me.

'In short, did you think you were an officer of the Electricity Supply Board when you stood in to assist with the erection of the electricity pole in Matthew Quirke's field, or were you a bystander who chose of your own free will to interfere and thereby injure yourself?'

It's hard not to despise officialdom in all forms. The retreat of human beings behind it diminishes the nature of what we are. I've never known a man or woman to be better for the wearing of the uniform. I've known them to be different, but not more human. I dwell a moment on this scene for two reasons. It's one I've returned to several times in my life, not because it struck me at the time as an axle. Like most, I was not aware enough, or distant enough from the immediacy of things, to assess or see meaning. But it did eventually occur to me that that afternoon when Rushe appeared in my grandparents' house he brought with him more than his person. In his manner and im-person, he brought the State, and in doing so, in his standing there, squat, rigid and bull-headed, in his use of a tone and language hitherto unknown inside the stone walls of that crooked house, an easier and more natural way of living was nearing its end. Because, it occurred to me, in Faha, and places like it, people had been making it up as they went along and making it up out of no rule book but the one they had been born with, that is an innate sense of right and decency, the rough edges of how to live alongside others having been knocked off not by ordinance or decree but by life.

I may have the rose-tinted glasses on. There's no great harm in it sometimes. The thing I'm trying to capture is the foreignness of Rushe in that kitchen and talking that way, the open front door letting in a parallelogram of sunlight and catching the turfsmoke halfway up the blackened wall of that hearth of the eighteenth century, and that he signalled an ending.

The second thing that occurred was more personal. It was that when he called me *son*, everything in me baulked. Not for the obvious reason, I think, but something deeper, which began there but I would only flesh out much later, that is, to the role he was consigning me, I would not serve. There in the kitchen, I flushed into the roots of my hair and felt the stirring of a family trait I hadn't realised I possessed until right then, but which would inform the kind of life I would end up living, that is, what authority provoked in me was a desire to be an outlaw.

'Well, son?'

'It was my fault, Mr Rushe,' said Christy.

'No, it was my own fault.'

Rushe's head didn't turn, his eyes didn't leave me. 'Well, which is it?'

'Mr McMahon did not mislead me.'

'You did not think you were in the employ of the company?'

'I did not.'

It wasn't the answer Rushe expected. He pressed just the tip of his tongue through the small lips. 'Were you paid for the work?'

'I was.'

'Who did you think was paying you?'

'Mr McMahon.'

'Out of his own pocket?'

'Yes.'

'Why would he do such a thing?' Rushe shot the square head forward to headbutt the stupidity of my position. He had me, until I answered.

'Out of a sense of goodness.'

A parcel of silence landed between us then. It was as though I had opened a box from which a white dove had risen and flew now about the kitchen, the sense of goodness being just as outlandish.

O now! Ganga mouthed but didn't say and rocked back and over on the up-curve of his boot soles. He nodded a nod to Doady who blinked, transfixed by a scene she couldn't unravel but which she knew would necessitate several pages of the Basildon Bond.

Rushe found an itch in his temple just below the hat-brim that caused him to smile, or his version. He scratched it once waiting for the dove to pass then continued with an amateur legalese borrowed from Perry Mason novels. 'So, just to be clear, you were acting of your own free will?'

'I was.'

'Good. That's good.' He let that sit. He lent it an air of conclusion, not to say defeat, by nodding slowly. We were done. He was about to turn away but turned back and brought his head closer. 'Well then, the Board could find *you* liable for interfering with works, causing loss of a day, and endangering crew.'

'Mr Rushe,' said Christy.

Mr Rushe didn't turn to him but raised a finger in the air to hold the speech there. He peeped the tip of his tongue out through the pale lips. 'Unless, that is, you were ignorant of the law.'

There was a cold sweat lying along my hairline.

'So, were you? Ignorant?'

'No, I...'

Christy coughed into his fist.

I looked at Rushe with as little respect as I've looked at any living thing. My grandmother and grandfather were like figures in a painted scene.

'I was,' I said.

'Ignorant?'

'Ignorant.'

'Well,' Rushe let out a breath and diminished by two inches, 'that's all cleared up then. We won't be hearing any more of this, from any side, and you won't be interfering in any sites where trained crews are working. Thank you now,' he said and touched the rim of his hat in salute or riddance hard to say, then he was out the door, leaving the household in the shook air of aftershock and with an unsettling impression that in a manner peremptory and cool, and without so much as a by-your-leave, the State had invaded.

28

That evening, after a muted tea outside in the garden, Ganga found he needed to go talk with Bat Considine. Bat would have newspapers for him, he said. I can't say I saw the upset in him. It's a true thing that when you're young your grandparents can seem fixtures, in their advanced age already beyond ageing, and to stand over the world like two colossi, immune from the daily turbulence below. So, no, I didn't notice the effect of Rushe's visit on my grandfather. I only knew it later.

Ganga went off down the road in the failing light, and, after a last good look at me, as though she were a portrait-painter and wanted to secure me in her eye, Doady withdrew to lose herself in Bond paper, Quink ink, and a single sheet of blotting paper that in blue hieroglyphics left hints to the future of what happened in the past.

Christy and I sat on at the table. He patted for his cigarettes. I leaned to fish the matches from my trouser pocket, until I remembered my hands were lost to fishing now, and said, 'I...' and no more, because no more was needed. I held my hands up, and, wordless, and with not a little delicacy, Christy reached over and fished the box of matches from my pocket.

It was the early part of the evening, the birds singing their accounts of the day and the whereabouts of night dwelling.

'I'm sorry about all that,' Christy said after a time.

'I'm sorry.'

And that was where we left it. He smoked, studying the river vanishing into the coming dark. A calf was making a ruckus beyond in Furey's, and soon enough from a field over its mother started. It seems I remember that. It seems unlikely too.

I wanted to tell Christy what had happened to me. But the dimensions of it seemed large and amorphous. I was in the grip of a compulsion to do something I had not yet done in this life, that is, to say the name *Sophie* out loud. Overwhelmingly, I wanted to sound it, I wanted it to be in my mouth and then in the air. I wanted to hear what it was like to hear her in my voice, to have that connection, not just because it was a name outside of the realm of girls' names I had grown up with, in Sophie was sophistication, and an air foreign, intelligent and compassionate, the music of it was beautiful, but also because to say *Sophie Troy* out loud was to summon her into my space.

I opened my mouth to say it, but, silent as a fish, closed it again.

To escape feeling that I might float belly-up, I said at last, 'Thank you for going to the chemist.'

'No need for thanks.'

I looked at the sky, he looked at the estuary tide going west. 'You saw her?'

'I did.'

'And?'

'And...' He drew on the cigarette. He pulled the smoke inside him, making the puckered sound and squinting one eye, shooting or shot, before leaking it slowly then pushing away from him in a backhand gesture cigarette, smoke, and the scene. 'She filled the prescription.'

'She knew it was you?'

'She did.'

'And what did she say?'

He studied the tidal river that was all but invisible now. 'She said, "Wait here."'

'That's all?'

He nodded towards where the river we knew was there was not there now. 'That's all.'

It was like something had fallen from the sky. It plummeted down and landed *thump* on the ground in front of us, feathers, bones in a twist, neck awry and blood from the beak. I tried to swallow.

'She saw you. She knew it was you. And all she said was "Wait here"?'

He nodded once and, after a time, I realised he was reliving the scene when he added: '"Here," she said, when she came back with the things.'

'And didn't you say anything to her?'

'She opened the door. "Goodbye now," she said.'

I can't say he looked sad or hurt but I felt he was. I had ruined the reunion. This was not how it was meant to go, this was not what you waited fifty years for. I had that sickening feeling in what they say is your stomach but is in fact your soul. Annie Mooney had been neither pleased nor angry to see him, worse, she hadn't cared. It had meant nothing to her.

Night fell on us. The river was gone. In the dark, only the red tip of Christy's cigarette.

'We'll hold off our quest to hear Junior play until you're able,' he said at last, by way of closing the evening.

———

Those who sleep in snatches say they get none, so I may or may not have slept that night. It's a fact that the heat of the day was trapped under the thatch and the midges whose day had been destroyed by a foreign sunlight found their way up the Captain's Ladder. Christy's snores serenaded them. Lying awake in a sleeping house is sometimes peaceful, sometimes not. I couldn't list all the things that were agitating inside me. I lay there, both bound hands flat out on the blanket and sort of singing with under-pain, reminding me I had a body not just a mind. Reminding me too that I was an idiot.

After a time, I held up my left wrist, and, with the fingers of my right, from inside the bindings drew out the taper that had been Sophie Troy's bookmark. I can't do justice to what it felt like to hold it. I can't do justice to the notion that that thin wand that had been in her hand was the thing that held me on to the world.

Now, I had abandoned the practice of praying at that time. But I don't mind admitting here that, under the influence of an encounter with extraordinary beauty, and dejected by the failure of Christy with Annie Mooney, I held that taper a little aloft and to the dark offered a silent prayer: *Good things coming for Noe and Christy.*

In the days that followed, Christy went to work, and I stayed in and around the house, lost to the dream-blank of the bereft and the mute mope of a heart given away. Because I was incapable of inventing a unique behaviour, or the world had used up all its originality, with a sugared irresistibility, all the clichés of lovelorn behaviour stuck to me. I didn't mind. There's honour in the ghost-company of the unrequited.

The rain was still postponed, and, by a grace in time and memory, was already passing into a fonder reality where the rain had never been that bad, *There'd been a drop now and then, yes, but what harm?* and people forgot the floods, leaks, puddles, drips and drop-downs. From the front of their minds they let slip the constant drumming of a falling sky, living damp to the underpants, the watery squelch in their boots, and the green fungus that grew to the height of a small child inside the walls of some houses strongly denying they were stone submarines. Because of a kink in human nature, where the new becomes old, people were already asking when this terrible hot weather would pass. For the first time in Fahaean history the ridges of potatoes would need watering, and all times now you'd see women and children bearing buckets and cans along the roads back and forth from wells, with sun-blistered foreheads and freckled arms.

In Faha *pure* was an adjective of negativity. In circulation now, from the weather: *I'm pure burned.*

At my grandparents', a number of the burnished came to make calls on the telephone, and enquired after me, and repeated versions of what they heard had happened, adding details and leaving out others in a living demonstration of how reality was made up. It was a true thing that all incidents in the parish then had an afterlife and were tirelessly reanimated with an interpretative emphasis or edit. It was one of the threads that tied community and whether or not you had heard the story already didn't matter, you listened to this version and nodded and said, 'I know,' and let that knowledge be a comfort between you for a time.

One afternoon the stools and chairs were brought in from the garden and set around the kitchen because a summit of the neighbours had been called. Moylan, a salesman from the electricity company, was doing the rounds. A victim to the cult of his own personality, to maximise the effectiveness of his pitch and to showcase the skill of his performance, Moylan wanted

236

the largest audience. Because it had the telephone and the air of unofficial post office, because it was already deemed connected, and as I've noted was a kind of locus in the townland, my grandparents' house was chosen for the demonstration of what the future was bringing.

Ahead of the event, my grandmother's nominal house-keeper, Mrs Moore, arrived in green gaberdine and orange headscarf. Like her, her costume was immune to season. From her large bag she took out Flo the duster, placed her on standby on the dresser, an act she made seem part of her working, as though the dust was now on retreat and the house already that bit cleaner. Then, signalling the notability of the upcoming occasion, she took off her boots, a labour of angles, her body inflexible as an old oak, and, since yesterday, her laces much further than her fingers. Then she pressed her feet inside what appeared to be balls of rags, a genus of slippers of her own construction, whose purpose was twofold, first she would be dusting as she went, and second, she'd leave no boot prints on the wet flags. 'So,' she told my grandmother, 'it will be like I was never here.'

Before she went wax-papering the stove, to catch her breath, she would have just the one Wild Woodbine. Doady would have just the one too, the two of them soon puffing away in a wood-bound wilderness found savoury and companion-able. While Mrs Moore smoked, she looked out at me in the garden. I had been to where all of her family and most of her acquaintance had gone, but I alone had come back, and resurrection, as I was soon to find out, has its own allure.

Because of an unwritten rule in country living, ahead of the summit, there were hills of rough sandwiches to be built from home-made bread, and a cake to be boiled. In these Mrs Moore was no help, but she offered an imaginary version, standing alongside Doady, the fifth of her just-the-one Woodbines held out and doing its tower-tilt above the makings while she relayed who else was now ashes. (She herself had been unwell all her life, she'd say out loud, she could die at any moment; it was a gambit that worked until she was a hundred and four and God caught on.)

The meeting had been called for three in the afternoon. Moylan was a nine-to-five man, three was when he was at his peak, and country people had no work that couldn't be left aside for something as essential as electricity, was his position. A Limerick baritone with a magnificent sweep of black hair, he arrived in the yard in a van. 'Sonny, help me carry these in,' was his greeting. I could carry nothing and his entrance was stymied by having to be his own prop man. When he saw the smallness of the kitchen – the slope of the floor doubling the cramped illusion – he had to overcome the familiar fall of his heart that this was a lesser stage for his talents, and not let it impact upon his performance.

'Where is everybody?' he asked Doady.

'Everybody is coming,' she said.

Into the kitchen on a handcart Moylan hefted a selection of machines whose existence to that point had been notional. Many were white and of such a gleaming newness it seemed nothing in the parish was as white as had previously been thought. All had a black wire coming out the back with a three-pin plug that looked both imperative and nakedly masculine, as though in urgent need of finding a three-holed female. Moylan laboured to get the washing machine in and around the turning of the front door whose jamb was predicated on human dimensions. Doady said it was a shame Ganga wasn't there to help. The turf needed turning, he'd announced abruptly that morning, and headed with Joe to the bog.

In clusters of shyness, the neighbours began arriving.

Moylan had already given a performance in the village, and the reviews were good. 'Nice little house you have,' he said to Doady, the sweat shining off him standing in front of the twelve-foot hearth where small sods were sighing a complacent smoke unaware that their time was running out. He was a desperate *plámáser*, a pure flatterer, Doady'd tell Mrs Moore later, and rebuff his recalled compliments with one back-toss of her head, but right then it looked like she ate and drank them. 'It's very, I don't know, home-like,' he said.

The centre of the room was taken with the machines and the neighbours came in around them muted and respectful the way they did when there was a body laid out. They settled into the chairs, on to the stools and benches, and let their eyes do the talking for a while. Mostly it was women. Those who were not eyeing the electrical equipment were taken by Moylan's shoes, which were two-toned, extra-terrestrial, and with an air of Hucklebuck. Maybe the Shimmy Shake too.

While the practical business of bringing the electricity to the parish was almost exclusively the domain of men, inside the houses the jurisdiction over electrical equipment, kettles, cookers, hairdryers and washing machines, was conceded to women. Only two men came to the summit. First, because it was taking place in a kitchen in daytime, and second, because men refused to be summoned, it outraged their dignity, and nothing in the known world had yet required that absolute submission except Christ, and even with Him there was leeway. The two men were Bat from back the road who came in, God bless all, with cap low and eyes down, and Mossie O Keefe who was the Job of Faha, a man so hexed, not only dogged but whaled by bad fortune, that eventually, by a Fahaean genius for latitude in language, his initials became the thing people thought when things were not OK. You hit your thumb with the hammer, you went over on your ankle, you thought of O Keefe and said, 'OK!' (I remembered this years later in a coffee shop on 14th Street when a senior waitress spilled coffee and her curse was 'Oh Finkelstein!' and I said 'OK!' I couldn't translate and her look said she didn't much appreciate it.) O Keefe's mother died when the cart turned over on her, his father went into the bottle, he himself married the woman in love with his brother, one of his sons went in a threshing machine, the other drowned in a ditch. A Stan Laurel, with abbreviated eyebrows like a pair of French accents, both pointing haplessly in and upward, Mossie took it all without complaint. His good luck was going to someone else, he'd say, and the eyebrows would go up a little and you'd feel that whoosh inside you that comes in the company of something larger than yourself. From his job keeping the grass down on the graves, Mossie's head had been savaged by the sun. As shield against the sores he now wore a four-knotted handkerchief that had a look of poultice.

Bat sat alongside him and grasped firmly the balls of his knees. His suit was a brown that had turned a glazed plum. It bagged at the knees and flagpoled his shins, lending him a look ceremonial and derelict. Bat was a man who tried in vain to make himself believable. He often looked like he was in mid-sum and realising he had forgotten to carry the one. Keeping his eyes on the floor, he shook his head slowly and said, 'If only Napoleon had invaded.' It was a starter for which there was no finisher, but for the occasional muffled artillery of his gas. Next to Bat, Mary Mulvey performed a little pulling in of herself. She'd had two bits of bad news and was waiting for the third. Mary Bruff, who never went anywhere without her cough, let it off now, and all of Moylan withdrew an inch, as though he were behind a curtain peeping out at the horror of the public. The impossibly pale and thin figure of Jo Ryan slipped in and stood just inside the door. She had a beaten air, a small sensitive mouth and the timidity and shame of those who feel the scars on their soul visible. At the age of thirty, Jo had succumbed to the false coinage that a bad man is better than no man, and married Pat, a cur, who is roasting somewhere now.

There were others, the room filled and the sunlight blocked at the window, but Moylan couldn't wait forever. Emboldened by the air of event, and with the fattened authority of farm-yard matrons, three hens came inside the open front door, nestling down in a bath of sunshine to watch. Neither in nor out, I was perched on the back step.

To give Moylan his due, he had his routine down pat, *Now I want you first to look at this*, a combination of science and circus in an actor's boom, *This, this machine, will do all the work. It will wash your clothes for you.* He lifted the lid and drew out a white towel, as though the washing and drying had happened in the time it took him to say the sentence and here was the proof. He had devised this touch himself and was proud of it. It was the only proof possible without electricity and had the added boon of making it seem as if he himself was the current or at least its conductor. Further to this, ten seconds into his pitch a film of sweat was glistening on him, lending him a shine which he didn't dab away, believing it translated as electric excitement and disguised the actual truth, that he was being cooked by the fire.

Moylan had all the tools of rhetoric. If you stayed in school past the age of twelve you learned them then. Things like Johnson's *Letter to Chesterfield* or various bits of Swift were taught, you knew your clauses and subclauses and had

homework parsing sentences. You knew everything from allit-
eration, allusion, amplification, analogy and anaphora ('If you
prick us do we not bleed? If you tickle us, do we not laugh?'
I could recite every speech of Shylock's once. God bless the
day) to metonyms and metaphors, oxymorons and similes.
After *Gallia est omnis divisa in partes tres*, the next thing you
learned in Latin was *non solo sed etiam*. What I'm saying is, it
was foundational, and admired, the bit of flourish.

On Moylan went, letting fly with antanagoge ('This heater
is not as beautiful as your fire, but it puts out more kilo-
watts'), enumeratio ('The motor, the pump and the drum, all
the very latest') and epizeuxis ('Power, power, power').

His audience was rapt by the important and foreign sounds
of spec and kilowatt in that 200-year-old house, and by touch
and look Moylan kept relaying the words to the magic of the
machines that sat mute but powerful like idols.

From time to time, because I was from Dublin where they
had been using such things for twenty years, the neighbours
kept looking at me to confirm wonders, and Moylan, sensitive to his audience's every breath, caught on at once and with
a looping gesture roped me in. *Tell them, sonny.*

Knowing the mystic power of jargon, he wasn't shy about
employing the Germanic language of electrical engineering, letting it do the business of marshalling his audience,
making them a little afraid and abashed, as though everything they had known, they were just now realising, was not
so known.

Moylan said the first law of engineering was to make the
world a better place. (He didn't state the second law, that without exception everything that was engineered would one day
break down, that sometime, and usually one day after each
machine had become indispensable to living, that machine

would abnegate all responsibility and not turn on, you'd press its red button and it would just sit there looking at you, and you'd press the button a second time as though excusing it that one time it had forgotten its job and forgotten that its whole purpose was to serve this one simple function, and you'd press the red button or throw the switch and an absolute nothing would happen, a less-than-nothing, a minus action because it would seem you were in a worse-off place than nothing happening because now not only had you forgotten how you lived before but you had to find a service man, and while some part of you always realised that you were living in the forgotten edge of nowhere you didn't have the hard proof until you tried to find a service man to come to Faha. *Where?* Oh there might be one coming next week, definitely the week after that, or the one following, and, as it slowly dawned on you that to make his journey worthwhile the same individual was waiting for more machines to break down, you kept pressing the red button because maybe today after the bit of a rest you never know it might turn on, and when it didn't, when you'd tried the pressing combined with a small shove, with a more serious shove, with a shake, descending through the whole sorry declension until you'd arrived at a kick, when the stubbornness of the stupid machine seemed so defiant as to not only lower the flag on the flagpole of manhood but take the flagpole too, sundering marriages by the blank white stare of an unwashing washing machine, any number of men, and some women, would choose to have a go at it, going with the crude iron tools of an earlier time and a zero knowledge, the guts of the machine spilled on the floor and the red button somewhere over there by the time the service man came in the door with his sponsored smile. *Is she giving you a bit of trouble?* taking a good gander at the home-made devastation before nodding slowly and telling you the third law: *Afraid this is going to cost you a fair bit.* The fourth soon after: *I haven't the part with me.*)

These laws Moylan forgot to mention. When he had finished extolling, when he was certain his audience was in his hand and like a sugared air could sense the desire of everyone there, he paused. He swept back the magnificent hair, eyes dark and glazed as Pilkington's glasshouse grapes. He turned the toe of one of the two-tones over and back and looked down at it as though recalling or anticipating a dance and then he clapped his big hands together.

'Well. I don't need to tell intelligent people like you, do I?'

Now this was a risky play. Matthew Poole, you may recall, was the lad who was often to be discovered having a bit of a laugh to himself. Well, in Faha the thing most often said about Matthew was that he was fierce intelligent, the word *fierce* used dexterously so that it worked two ways at once, was understood to be wonderful and terrible, intelligence in its ferocity a gift and a burden, something difficult to handle and extraordinarily sharp, like a sword in the soft tissue of the mind. In general, better not to be too intelligent, was Faha's philosophy, and though then I considered this backward, soon enough I came to understand the wisdom and recognise we are not all mind.

Bat was on the point of answering the rhetorical, but Moylan cut him off with his follow-through: 'The hardship of your lives is over.'

It was a breathtaking sentence and the summit took a moment to take it in. From my place on the back step I glanced at them. The idea was too enormous, or the reality of experience too sharp to be digested. It was as if the hardship of their lives had been summoned, had come in the open front door, a history of cold and rain, of muck and puddle, dark, disappointment and struggle and disappointment again, and was face-to-face now with an army of gleaming white metal. As always when confronted with compelling fantasy, nobody knew what to say.

'If only Napoleon had invaded,' Bat said under his breath and shook his head.

Moylan drove on to the final curtain by delivering the news that any of the machines there could be purchased. 'You could own one of anything right now,' he said. 'One of everything, why not?' He smiled his winning smile at Doady. 'Beautiful cooker like that look well in a lovely homely home like yours, Missus. I can see it over there. A nice toaster on the table there for your morning toast. No more lighting the fire, waiting for the flames, and sticking your bread into the smoke. No more smoky toast,' he said, unaware that no one in Faha ate toast and that smoky was not a term of denigration.

Doady blinked at him but didn't smile. She may have been engaged in an act of the imagination, trying to picture the totems of the modern in a room with crooked floor and walls, a twelve-foot hearth with fire on the floor and sunlight coming down a stone chimney wide enough for Ganga to climb up and out the top one year winning a Stygian dare with Bat about flue masonry or passing through purgatory. Like others there, I think my grandmother may have been chastened by a feeling the machines were looking at her, and her life, with cold judgement. I couldn't help thinking of that moment when Pip looks at his boots and realises how crude they are. My wrists stung. In defence of my grandparents I felt a flare of outrage and wanted Moylan and his machines gone.

Then, as the audience deflated, as the gas of the performance bled away, and people were being stitched back into the straitening of their circumstances, where the cost of purchasing anything was prohibitive, Moylan opened his arms like Christ in the picture above the window and delivered the *coup de grâce*. 'Any machine you see here, you can buy, *on tick.*'

Tick. It was the jump of a clock, and a ransom note from the future. Instantly, I had a grey uneasy feeling, knowing that hardship could not be overpowered by a three-pin plug and the future was not free. I think I understood too that I was living in the vestige of a world whose threads were all the time blowing away, and some blew away right then on that *tick*.

The summit ended, the women went for the hills of rough sandwiches and the boiled cake, which was adjudged *Just beautiful*, and Moylan circulated with a form on a clipboard. O Keefe stood up and hit his handkerchiefed head off the underside of the Captain's Ladder, grinned at the familiarity of misfortune, as if it was God who was all the time knocking his head, as if it was twisted affection, and then he and Bat went out to the gable to make their water.

29

Sophie Troy.

A name is a thing of immense power, the saying of it both a summoning and summing up, so that standing on an empty road and sounding it is a kind of conjuring, or was in my case. It seems there were some days then when I did little else. I went out of the house and walked, my bound wrists smarting, the sun glancing off my forehead while I thought of Sophie Troy and spoke her name and took from it a kind of consolation which lessened loneliness. In a twist of fate preserved for lovers, loneliness was more profound now, as well as darkly delicious.

Now, I am aware it may seem far-fetched that any emotion, never mind love, could be built on so slight an acquaintance. To which the answer is yes, yes it *was*, and absurd too, in the way life often is. I am aware too of the dangers of using the word love here, but I am trying to be true to who I was and what I felt, to see that grave and angular youth who had come from the seminary with no map for living, allow him his own blunders, and forgive him for them, which may be the point of old age.

As will be clear, I was an amateur in this, and to me fell the amateur's lot of making every available mistake. I suppose I knew that the word most associated with romantics is hopeless, and that the end for the ardent is disillusion, but what I was feeling I couldn't deny or banish. I said her name, and, like the first man to eat the egg of a bird, felt a little ascension, and like him wouldn't have been surprised to find feathers at my back.

Only one thing was certain: I had to see her again.

To be clear, in the risen and white-linen state I was in, that was all I wanted, just to see her walk past. Conversation, company, the touch of her hand, these were not even on the edge of hope. The truth, as I knew it, was that I did not harbour the slightest aspiration to be her lover. That was an obvious impossibility. In the context of Sophie Troy, the word boyfriend was somehow abhorrent. What I wanted was to be her Lover. I don't know if I can convey this state of mind exactly. I don't know if notions of worthiness and unworthiness remain in the world or are gone the way of knights, and the Church, but honestly, it was enough to be in the world that she was in. Just to see her again would be enough.

Sophie Troy.

On Sunday I decided to follow the Fahaean way by which men were licensed to be in the company of women, and go to Mass. I washed in the basin and fought with my hair. I had dull, forgettable hair that for some reason I couldn't forget. I thought my quiff should fall just so in a combed curve across my forehead. Generally, I considered myself if not exactly ugly certainly somewhere below plain (and plainer now since I had seen Beauty) but if I got the curve of my hair right it would render me tolerable. Of course, I could never get it right. (Here's a grandfather's laugh: I would live another thirty years before baldness took away the hair to show me what had been staring me in the face: the hair *was* forgettable, the forehead spectacular.)

I was upstairs in the bedroom finger-combing the C into place for the fourteenth time when Christy noted it and smiled. 'Well?' he asked.

'What?'

He invited me to tell him what was happening by a look.

'What?'

Now, I didn't draw the corollary then that the failure of his fifty-year love had provoked the birth of mine. I didn't realise any connection, didn't admit the vanity of all lovers, that I was imagining myself a flagbearer, that mine would be different to any that went before, and where he had failed I would not.

'What?'

'Nothing. Nothing at all,' he said, offering a comb from his jacket. 'Never aim for perfection,' he advised. 'We are human.'

I went to Mass with Doady and Ganga on the horse and car, my grandmother tight and erect and behind her glasses individually thanking her saints that my crisis of faith had passed and I had refound religion. Christy took the bicycle and travelled at one-horse speed just behind us like a wavering escort.

St Cecelia's was hotter than a church in Tennessee. Day after day the air inside it baked. There were hooks for opening the high stained-glass windows, but no pole long enough to reach them. Life in Faha fostered the skill of getting round most things, and in the pews mimeographed copies of the Bishop's latest *Pastoral Letter* were employed as ecclesiastical fans, and on the altar, when not ringing the bells or attending at the Consecration, two of the Kellys tried to cool the empurpled face of Father Coffey with slow-motion palms, as though he were the King of Siam. The church was packed, numbers swollen by the addition of some of the electricity men lodging in the parish, who, by the twin merits of being foreign – from outside of west Clare – and working with conductive cables, added a live charge among the females, some of whom I believe later found earthing there.

The scent of the Easter lilies had outlived them and, as was apt, risen to the rafters, from which every so often a dove-like remnant floated down with a white memory of Resurrection. For once, overcoming the native fear of a chill, the three sets of doors were left open and, by virtue of self-diagnosed blood pressure, vertigo and fainting spells, some of the congregation took medical dispensation to stand outside in the shade where, in the absence of electric amplification, Tom Joyce did loud-whisper duty relaying the Confiteor, Kyrie, Sanctus and the rest, so the sacrament was both inside and outside.

It was the Feast of the Divine Mercy.

Though I scrutinised the pews from the poor vantage of where Doady parked us next to the Cotters, though eventually I made out the silver spines of the doctor's hair and the green pill of Ronnie's jacket next to him, it wasn't until Communion that I saw Sophie. The skill of looking while not wanting to be seen looking is in Ovid's manual of lovers, I suppose. I didn't have it. She stepped out along the pew and I fairly jumped forward. At least everything inside me did. Boom, just like that. It's a thing that can't be told rightly, because in the turbulence of life we have to cling to the notion that human behaviour is governed by reason, but when you feel a force like this, a thing that just picks you up and throws you over here, takes the whole of your intelligence, judgement and logic, balls it up and says none of that matters right now because, despite the voice, loud enough too, saying *this is impossible* and *don't be an idiot*, despite all wise and winning arguments to the contrary, you've already jumped the barricades of propriety and embarrassment and ceded to something compelling which can be nothing more than mystery, and the mystery of another, and the next moment you're pushing out past all the doe-eyed Cotters who are on their knees in the devout last stages of the Prayer Before Communion, and you're brushing aside like a thin filament the iron commandment laid down in you since you were seven that you never, never take Communion if you haven't first gone to Confession, and now you're thinking *It's true, mercy is divine* because you're in the line of communicants shuffling slowly forward in a red-stained sun-lanced aisle eight back from Sophie Troy.

Martin Hanway, Mary Hanway, Mickey Riordan, Jack Mannion, Mrs Mannion, Pat Greaney, Mrs Jo Greaney, and the blue-and-orange-feathered Caribbean that was the hat of Mrs Sexton, all obscured me from seeing her. We inched forward.

At that time, people in line for Communion bowed their heads and prayer-palmed their hands. Aware of approaching the consecrated, they didn't look about them, and landed at the rails with a bare and absolute vulnerability, the crucifix hanging overhead. I did neither. Light with an outlaw emotion, I kept my head up, my wrists stung if I pressed my palms.

Father Coffey had yet to make his first attempt to implement traffic regulation on approach to the rails in St Cecelia's, Father Tom's free-for-all still held the day, so people came up and down both sides at the same time, with jostle and press, as though the idea of a queue had not yet been invented or was dissolved under the imperative to receive. Just so then, stepping into the crowded two-way, three-way middle of the aisle to make room for a troop of Twomeys, I looked ahead and saw the gold of her hair.

I might have pushed then. I might have cheated the line and, sanctioned by my injured hands, the holiness of the heart's affections, and a primal urgency, slipped ahead of the Greaneys and the Mannions and the feathered Caribbean, because now I was at the rails where, a little further along to the right, the three Troy sisters were kneeling and waiting, God forgive me, to put out their tongues.

The candles took on a shimmering intensity and made the air before the altar dance. I could feel the heat of them on my face, breathe the honeyed scent of the sanctified beeswax, and the cloying afterlife of the frankincense, all of which combined by canon strategy to confirm that when you approached the rails of the sanctuary you had left the world proper, you were no longer in the place of daily life.

The Troy sisters received and rose and turned back into the fold of communicants. I might have got off my knees and followed them. Fixity and rashness, you see. But now Father Coffey was paused before me with the ciborium.

A braver man than me might have said *Sorry, Father, I no longer believe*, might have said *I'd like to, I want to, but it's gone, I have lost it*, might have confessed out loud right there at the frontier of the divine that *My soul has been taken by a new religion* and accepted the consternation not to say apoplexy that would ensue. But all that I managed was not to close my eyes or put out my tongue. By reflex Father Coffey dipped to choose a host and had it between thumb and forefinger before he noticed. He looked at me but still I didn't shut my eyes or stick out my tongue.

There was a held moment. In it was a kind of suffering.

Next to me, like a Communion clockwork, Geraldine O had already closed her eyes, tilted back her head to receive. I think I probably wished I could do the same, and by all reason should have. It was a small thing, and an enormous one. In the instants in which I was paused there, and they were only instants, my mouth dry, my forehead blistering a cold sweat, there was nothing apparent of a private agony or crisis of spirit, nothing but for what trafficked between my eyes and the priest's. And then Father Coffey, glazed and ruddy from the heat and his Wilkinson blade, gave the lie to his youth and inexperience and transcended the rigidity of the Church by doing the most remarkable thing. Understanding that I would not open my mouth, the host he had chosen for me he brought towards my closed lips and, when it was near enough to touch, in a fluid arc, as if nearness was enough, he brought it back and laid it in the ciborium and moved on to Geraldine O. So simple, graced and generous a gesture was it that not a single person in St Cecelia's noticed. It was as though by mime I had received.

Returning, I didn't slide into my place the far side of the Cotters but sat instead on the outer edge of the pew and let them in past me. There were precedents, after Communion frequently a muted Musical Chairs where people landed back in the pews in reshuffled order. No one objected, smallness of mind the first casualty of Communion. I wanted to stay where I could be seen. I thought that perhaps when the doctor and his daughters passed on the way out he might stop and ask after me or tell me to come for a check-up to the surgery, and Sophie would be by his side. I pushed into place the fall of my hair. Soon enough Father Coffey brought the Mass to an end and under the solemn intonation of the Latin the congregation did a synchronised blessing, or the Faha version. Then the church rose as one, or Faha's version. I watched for the Troys, but the doctor had the besieged air of the General Practitioner who, because of the ubiquity of human ailment, knew every person there had something they'd like to have just a quick word with him about, and he led his daughters quickly out the door and was away in the car before Father Coffey was free of the embroidered weight of his vestments.

In passing, Ronnie, I think, did look briefly in my direction, but it was a look I couldn't translate.

We came out into the day that was always different after Mass. From the intercession of her saints, I think, Doady was light in herself and looked at me with the prodigal beaming reserved for one come back into the fold. She had to go to Clohessy's for the few messages. A sliced pan was something not yet in demand in Faha. Throughout the parish, women, and in fairness some men, baked their own bread, but an unforeseen consequence of Moylan's performance had been to make my grandmother realise she lived in a fossilised cave. When the machines were taken away on the hand-cart and her kitchen returned to its former self the room seemed lesser and could not easily recover what seemed to have been silently robbed. Moylan's pitch, his evangelist's conviction and rhetoric had their own afterlife, made Doady look askance at her life and circumstance and release a host of hooped taupe mealworms into her belief in the pre-eminence of the home-made. She was not alone in this, a flaw in our nature makes the glamour of the new irresistible. At the summit, several of the neighbours had signed up to buy machines they couldn't use, or pay for, but whose value was already felt as the ouster of the antiquated, the inviolable authority of clean-line engineering and the airy promise that the days of hardship were numbered.

'When we have the electric we can have toast when we get home,' Doady said, a non-sequitur that had a sequitur in her look at Ganga. He smiled haplessly and let her off and stood a little after on the open slope of where the church gates were supposed to hang if only the committee could agree on a smith and the ground made to stop sinking. The *Closed* was hanging in the door of the chemist's across the way. Christy was nowhere.

'Ganga, I'm going to walk home.'

He didn't say *O now*, he didn't ask me if I was sure. He just nodded absently, trying to undo the knot of his brow.

I walked out the road in the small traffic of departing cars, carts and bicycles, and in the stillness that fell after, at the unmarked shrine of a country boreen, found the only relief by the original method, the saying aloud of another's name.

'Sophie Troy.'

30

But what of Annie Mooney?

I know, I hear you. Bear with me. It's a fact that that Sunday I didn't look for her or think of Christy. I was lost to the breathtaking selfishness of the enamoured. Solitariness is a seedbed for absolutes and by the time I had got back to my grandparents' I had resolved that the rest of my life would be lived in proximity to the youngest of the Troy sisters.

Sounds mad when you say it. Seems sane when you feel it.

That boy is out of reach now to shake him by the shoulders. He would give you the pips, was my mother's expression. But he and I have come to an accommodation, as Thomas Brennan used say. God bless him.

With that graven predictability some find comforting, in Faha the sun had already performed the first and oldest transformation it had enacted since the species discovered dry land, that is, it provoked a profound laziness and made man want to curl up in an afternoon sunbeam. Women, being moon-borne, or more endurable, suffered this less. By the second week of Spanish sunshine a practice of unofficial siestas had become established in the parish. Some employed medical arguments, the Fahaean flesh pale, the fireball of the sun fatal, but most simply slipped away into a meadow when they felt their energy stolen and a warm blanket of lethargy come over them. In fields of now parched ground from which the frogs had at last departed, and to the hitherto unknown whisper-music of crisp grass, men slept the impossibly deep sleeps they would remember in old age when summers were no longer sunny and sleep only came in snatches. (There were some of course not sleeping, the primary aphrodisiac of the sun proving irresistible, and sometimes you'd see a man or woman coming up out of the grass adjusting their clothes with a dazed look of shy joy that was outside the prescriptions of the time. That the children that came nine months later started life with a sunnier disposition is a gloss for which there is no statistic, but stands to reason, if reason is your measure of what's true.)

I had already found out that to the lure of the siesta Christy was defenceless, and that Sunday afternoon when he had not appeared at the house I went looking for him. I wanted walking anyway. All confines were impossible now. I went back along the road. The natural lassitude of Sundays was multiplied by the weather and the townland felt stunned and sleepy. There was nothing moving, cattle and horses saving energy in distant still-lifes and dogs in flat collapse in the sunburnt centre of the road chasing only in jerking dreams. You could hear the Kellys, by unrefereed dispute playing football in the distance, or, passing a house with a door open, the escaping commentary of a football match on the wireless, but nothing else. In a white shirt with the sleeves rolled and a felt hat rescued from a scarecrow, Martin Moran was standing at a gate looking into his meadow, like a figure in a painting. That he might have been there forever was the feeling you got. I didn't speak to him. I put him in here so he's there still, looking into that field which was his measure of contentment, and by virtue of that becomes part of mine here. If you follow.

By Cleary's big bog meadow, Ganga's bicycle was shouldering the ditch. On the upper slope not far in, Christy's crossed leg rose above the grassline, one bootless foot in the air.

'Was she there?' I asked him.

Lying back in the grass he had a rumpled blue defeat about him, like he was thrown there. His suit jacket was under him, his shirt open. But more, his eyes were changed. He hadn't the same shining. Before, I had thought him filled with impulsive energy, the switched-on optimism of fools or saints, the one that goes straight ahead without hesitancy into the chaos of everyday believing that because it is life it is to be embraced in all its contingency, and because God is watching and not off, say, spinning the rings round Saturn, the worst that can happen will not be so bad. For the most part we don't realise how fixed are our judgements of others, how founded they are in first impressions and the smallest evidences we seize on to prove to ourselves that, see, we were right. Standing alongside him in Cleary's, lambent sun-lances in both our chests, I understood that I had been wrong about Christy. I had come to believe his character irrepressible. I had thought of him as a force, with sureness of purpose, but, in doing so, I had robbed him of human dimension. The eyes that met mine were sad, his voice soft, and once it spoke I could hear the hurt disguised in it. He shielded the sun with a held salute.

'Was she at Mass, I didn't see.'

He lowered the salute. 'She wasn't.'

'What are you going to do?' I was more direct than myself, the condition of my condition unearthing caution and letting loose a livewire. Besides which, in Faha, the stuck plot is intolerable.

'There's nothing to be done for now but wait.'

When you're young, the old can disappoint. I remember that.

I sat down on the grass next to him. 'You came here for her. You said so.'

'It's true.'

'To ask her forgiveness.'

'Yes.'

'Well, then it's not over until she forgives you.'

He didn't have a response.

'You can't do nothing.'

'I have already done what can be done.'

'No, you haven't.'

Christy considered this, or I told myself he did, and while he did I followed up with a speech that embarrassment has dissolved, the gist telling him he shouldn't, couldn't, etcetera, because of this, that and the other, talking myself into a state, hot, absolute, adamant, and arriving by force at the thing I hadn't dared ask: 'So, why?'

He was propped on one elbow, the long meadow out before us, birds in a sun-stunned drowse not singing.

'Why did you leave her?'

He didn't move, but his eyes, his eyes were impossible to look at. I turned away at once. Another would have left it at that.

'Why didn't you marry her?'

I heard the movement of his large body on the grass as he sat up. He was facing down to the river. 'Some of the things you do when you're young are unforgivable to you when you're old,' he said at last.

Again, I might have left it there. But I think I already knew there are few moments in life when people can afford to be absolutely truthful, and this was one. 'She loved you?'

'I think so. Yes, she did.'

'And you loved her?'

'Yes.'

'I don't understand.'

'Sometimes neither do I.'

There are signals we send to say *Stop pursuing me*, signals to say *Leave off there*, but if I saw them I ignored them.

'What happened?' I looked at those deep and blue eyes that I can see now, here, more than half a century away. You'll find that hard to credit, I know. It's the truth all the same. And it was not just because of the beaten stillness, the birdless sun-haze, the burnt-off excesses of a Sunday afternoon that reduced the moment to essence, not just because we sat on the side of the gold chalice of that sloping meadow, in an elliptical time, other and alchemical, or because of the over-whelming need I now felt to, for want of a word, *fix* what was broken, to connect and make live, alive, what was dead, though all of these would in time come to seem part of it, it was mostly that I knew then that I was as close at that moment to another human being as I had been in this life, and that that closeness was in some way part of love.

The air was turned off. The bee-drone muted. I don't believe I could breathe.

Christy looked away from me, broke open the cup of his hands, lowered them. He rocked slightly, rocking on the spike of the question so it went deeper all the time. There was suffering in it, I knew that, and was realising that when you're seventeen the suffering of a man in his sixties can seem monu-mental, and till that moment you thought soul-torment the territory of the young.

'I was afraid,' he said at last. His whole face was a wince, wrinkles running off like wires to nowhere, the eyes I couldn't look at. 'I was afraid of what I felt. I thought it would swallow me up. It already had. I only wanted to live for her.'

He offered nothing more, and this time I didn't press him. There had been no row between him and Annie Mooney, no breakdown, none of the surprises or reveals by which a thing can be explained and wrong behaviour understood. I had wanted to be able to blame someone. I had wanted an incalcitrant father, a possessive mother, a wild and violent argument. I wanted him to have been forced into an impossible situation, to be the victim of circumstance, and realised that on a stage somewhere in my mind, against a backdrop of Kerry mountains and wild rain, I had set an operetta, employed all the time-worn devices of melodrama to obstruct the love that should have been. But that was not what had happened. In this story there was no story. Instead, I had only a sense of ordinary human failure. He had run away. He had left her. He had loved other women, she had fallen in love with another man, and they had lived their lives as though that love had never happened.

'Well, that's not the end of it,' I said. 'That can't be the end of it.'

Christy made no reply, and we left it there, the sun laying a glisten ointment over the topic, letting us off to heal over what had been said and remake a version we could live by.

Later, both of us thrown there in the warm grass in that unlicensed place between sleep and dream, he asked: 'What's her name?'

'Sophie,' I said too quiet for him to hear, and then, with the feeling of falling, helpless and wonderful, and with no desire ever to break the fall, 'Sophie Troy, the doctor's youngest daughter.'

In the blue of the sky he studied all I didn't add. He palmed his beard back against his chin. 'It's likely your love is doomed, Noe,' he said, and then, with the blue glint of a Cyrano smile, added, 'We must make sure you give it everything you've got.'

Just so, in silence then, another key was turned.

'You will go see her tomorrow,' he said.

I invented a braver self and said, 'I will.'

We both lay there then, flattened by forlorn desire and the airless press of the afternoon sunshine. And because in our minds we could imagine ourselves knights of first and last loves, and because of the overpowering need for something to be done, I announced, 'Tonight we are going to hear Junior Crehan.'

In the upshot, we did go. We followed the recipe for comedy that is two men on one bicycle, starting off with me on the bar, switching to Christy on the bar and sparing my wrists by his operating the handlebars, attempting a third variant with me up front like a giraffe transport sitting on the handlebars, before we accepted defeat and walked the bicycle like an indulged idiot companion, going in and out of numberless public houses with thirsts corporeal and spiritual neither of which could be vanquished, hearing music of matchless skill unpunctuated by pause or applause or the naming of the players but ending up in the dumping ground of all good intentions, not discovering Junior once again, and polluting the adjective unforgettable by living an evening I have otherwise forgotten.

31

The time they were doing *The Playboy*, Mick Madigan of the Faha Players had to be told he was in a comedy. Because of the circumstance and stricture of his own life, Mick always supposed he was in a tragedy, always learning the lines in the evenings after coming in from the farm and taking up the book as he called the script with a high seriousness that was part passed-down reverence for the art of the Greeks, part triumph over the end of his schooling at age twelve, and part pride that he had been given a role. Every play he treated the same. Every year when he came home from the meeting of the Players in October he'd hang up his coat, sit in by the fire, cup his two knees, and, as though it were a birthday surprise, announce: 'The Master's given me a part.' He'd wait until Sheila asked, 'Has he really?' and he'd reply, 'He has,' and after a time add, 'An important part too.' And after another pause, dressed with small sighs: 'The Master thinks I can do it.' And Sheila would play her no-less-scripted part by assuring him he could, he could, and he'd counter with 'There's a lot of lines in the book this time, Sheila.' And then Sheila would say couldn't she help him learn them, and couldn't they do a bit each night (not noting it was what they did each year, not noting that the climbing of that annual mountain was embedded in their marriage, and that the nights she'd come to see him walk out on the stage, not missing a single performance he ever gave, were garlanded luminous vindication of her decision to say *Yes, yes I will*, feeling but not noting aloud the perplexed truth that by playing another he became the best version of himself), and then Mick would conclude the contract by saying, 'I suppose I'll have to rise to it.'

'You will. You will, Mick.'

Each year they learned the lines together, Sheila playing all the parts, a paraffin lamp standing in for the footlights, and Dunne their dog doing a passing job in the part of the audience in the hall. Each year, whatever the play or part, Mick Madigan brought to it the gravity of a tragedian. He spoke his lines with the deliberation of a town proclaimer, giving each playwright's words the weight of scripture and getting full value out of the long hard learning. And each year, Master Quinn, wearing the seven hats of leading man, director, producer, set designer, prop man, painter and prompter, would pull Mick aside and try in vain to get him to lighten. 'It's a comedy,' he'd say, and Mick would answer, 'O yes,' and not only look like he'd got it but that it had never been in doubt, and then he'd do the lines again in exactly the same way, fairly certain that he was on the money this time. Each play was rehearsed for six months for the eventual three performances which were sold-out events that made a mockery of the physics of space and Father Tom's ticket-only policy by the queue that swelled down Church Street and eventually, by an accordion magic, into the hall. The bedlam of the overcrowd was made worse by the fact that Mrs Reidy on the ticket desk, seeing the children sneak in for free, decided, because of the etiquette of theatre, because of a fox stole handed down from a dead aunt in Cork, not to resort to the bum's rush employed in the Mars cinema in town.

Each year, playing opposite Mick, on stage and in mid-scene, the Master could be heard directing him with an underbreath '*Light! Light!*' and each year it would be the same and have the same effect, which is to say none, in time the parish coming not only to expect but want the tragic tone of Mick Madigan, taking a dark joy from the truth of it and the fact that for some the world is without light.

I saw Mick play maybe three times but have thought of him more than that. I note this here by way of excusing my own character at that age. It took me many years to conceive of life as comedy, or tragicomedy anyway. The part I was playing always seemed grave and earnest. I always felt there was something I must do.

Which, in roundabout fashion, may explain why, three days later, in some part under the influence of Christy's directive to give it everything I had, I walked into the village seeking Sophie Troy with the tight lips and high head of Mick Madigan's torch-bearer.

I had never seen any of the Troy sisters in the shops. How they got their supplies was enfolded in the mystery of the beautiful. But everyone with a stolen heart sometime finds themselves leaning on a thin rail of chance and maybes. Maybe I would be lucky, maybe the very moment I would walk past a shop Sophie would step out the door. Why not? The world keeps spinning its raffle-bin. Why not me?

Sun-smote, the village was deserted. I had forgotten about the half-day. I went past the shut shops and the church and the net curtain of Mona Ryan wearing a disguised look of purpose. Past Pender's and Moran's and Dohan's and the creamery with its dried puddles of dung yoghurt. The important thing was not to look like what I looked like. But sometimes, by a treaty between body and mind, your feet have a way of bringing you where you need to go, and soon enough I was at the rusted gates of Avalon.

There was a gravelled avenue, worn in twin ruts, a ribbon of grass in the centre. It went like a tossed hat gaily up and off to the right towards where the house itself could not be seen. Just inside the gates the looming arms of the parish's most ancient and only surviving sycamore trees, not yet uprooted and sent sideways by the storms that would be unmatched until the millennium, not yet sawn down and cut up and sold off after the last Troy was gone and Bourke's son bought the house for the ground with the dream of building a second Faha there. So, overhead me that afternoon the tender and unreal too-green green of first leaves wondering where the rain had gone and for how long the old tree could keep bringing water up from roots that went further back than Parnell. I stood in the sweat-skin of my white shirt by the gates, pushed the damp quiff of my hair around, then decided that I should stand across the road a bit, as though torch-bearing over there would be perfectly normal and not at all like I was stalking that entranceway for an unlicensed glance at Beauty.

There was not the slightest breeze. Even across from the gates the trees threw thin unmoving lattices of light and shade and there was shadow-dapple cool and birdsong and the steady thrumming that is the air-engine of May. I tramped up and down with big Mick Madigan steps, as it seemed the part demanded. What I thought would happen if Sophie appeared, I am not sure. I am not sure if I thought it not only unlikely but impossible that she would, because imagination had only got me this far.

The vigil was an act of love. That was the thing. I had told Christy he could not do nothing and by the same sweet contagion nor could I. Well, this was not nothing. The something it was though was ill-defined. I would wait there, a sentry to Beauty, and wait until Sophie came or went, and I would see her pass. That was the full of it. That would be enough, and enough for her too to know that I was her servant. That was in the thinking of it. I would stay there all the rest of that day and afternoon and be there until dark if that's what it took. I was resolved on that, my vigil a thing naked and true that did not end when Doctor Troy's Hillman Hunter came flying along the western road, driven with the loose steering of a man whose mind was elsewhere, shooting in the gateway of Avalon but not before he had turned his hatted head sideways and clocked me with a look in which was translated his experience of every kind of human folly, a look which read instantly the nature of my vigil and in which there was not a little salt of derision.

I didn't walk away then. I took up a new position further along, bringing with me a fine host of flies that were already drunk on the heady stuff of vocation. In the distance O Leary's ass roared and didn't stop, the roaring of an ass savagely eloquent and immensely pitiful.

An hour or so later, the doctor drove out again, and again looked at me, and again didn't stop. For a time after I thought: She might walk down now. He might have told her, *Young Crowe's at the end of the avenue*, and she might have said nothing but gone upstairs to her room and looked out the top half of the sash window that couldn't see the gates proper but the turning to them and she might have imagined me standing there. She might have enacted in her mind the same encounter I did and soon enough be unable to leave it in imagination. Soon enough she might be coming in her low boot-shoes down the avenue, the hot gravel crackling and the birds announcing.

You see, I had a nineteenth-century imagination. I pushed the quiff. I took up a better position only to find it worse, picking another on the lumpish grass to the west and engaging there in a vain battle to stop sweating.

When the doctor drove back later that's where I was. He looked at me again as he turned in the avenue, this time stopping the car just inside the gates. For a moment it just waited there, exhausting itself in a vexed plume, the doctor's eyes boxed in the rear-view mirror. Then, with some resistance, the window was cranked down a portion and through the narrow opening came a hand. When it was just outside in the air, its forefinger beckoned a single beckon.

It was less invitation than command. I walked across to the car and Doctor Troy tilted back his hat to look up at me.

'Are you sick?'

'No, Doctor.'

He moved his moustache some. Since the passing of his wife his eyes had the tide gone out in them, what was left were suds of feeling, but one of them was caught in his vision then because he turned away and looked straight ahead up the avenue and looked at the next part of raising his three swans of daughters and all that would entail, and then he turned back and considering what to say moved the moustache a small bit before looking up at me and delivering his verdict. 'Go home, son.' He touched the rim of his hat a touch, cranked the window and coughed the car into gear.

It was both defeat and victory. I felt I had taken a step. I had announced myself and went back into the village not a little charged up. I had not planned to call on Annie Mooney. I think that's fair. But stand a few hours outside the gates of love, just stand waiting a long time anywhere on the planet and your mind will not be standing, it'll be travelling at a speed ten thousand times faster than it can when your body's moving. It'll arrive at places hitherto unvisited, which in my case meant north of renunciation, a refusal to let things unfold in what in those days in Faha was considered God's plan. If I couldn't do anything yet about Sophie Troy I could about Annie Mooney.

Now, as far as I was concerned there are two ways of living, and because we're on a ball in space these were more or less exactly poles apart. The first, accept the world as it is. The world is concrete and considerable, with beauties and flaws both, and both immense, profound and perplexing, and if you can take it as it is and for what it is you'll all but guarantee an easier path, because it's a given that acceptance is one of the keys to any kind of contentment. The second, that acceptance is surrender, that there's a place for it but that place is somewhere just before your last breath where you say *All right then, I have tried* and accept that you have lived and loved as best you could, have pushed against every wall, stood up after every disappointment, and, until that last moment, you shouldn't accept anything, you should make things better. This was more or less the philosophy of Tess Grogan, who, well into her nineties, kept the finest garden in Faha. We lost a garden, she'd say, speaking of the time of Adam like it wasn't so long ago, pressing gently the swollen joints of her arthritic fingers and smiling the sagacious smile of the nonagenarian, 'We lost a garden, our whole lives we have to remake it.'

The other thing is this. I was implicated in what happened between Christy and Annie Mooney. I hadn't intended to be but I was, the way you can be first through company, just sharing a living space with another human being and being drawn inside the ambit of their person.

Some of all this was likely criss-crossing in my mind the time I was standing outside the gates of Avalon. In any case, alive now with the jittered pulse that comes from acting on emotion, I was momentarily freed from fear of embarrassment, and so, as unlike myself as Launy-the-lover Logue, I walked up the winding slope of Church Street to knock on the closed door of the chemist's.

I forgot with my bound wrists I shouldn't knock, and the pain smarted nicely. When no response came at once I tapped two taps with my elbow.

You understand nothing in the time when it's happening. I've decided that's a fair creed to live by. Most of the time you don't estimate the good or the bad you do and you have to operate on a small and labouring engine of hope with a blind windscreen and pray you're going in a direction that not's too far off good intention.

When Annie Mooney unlocked the door she supposed I was in need of medication. She didn't question or hesitate and when I stepped inside she locked the door after me. She was wearing a long green cardigan and her silver hair was tied in a single bind midways down. Her face had the same graven look of ancient beauty and her eyes the same sorrowfulness that some call wisdom, but what struck me most was her air of stillness. Perhaps because it was the very opposite of what I was feeling.

'Do you have a prescription?'

'I want to talk to you.'

There was a pressed-down pause. It was as though into that single instant a long history had been compressed and between the tick and tock of the second hand all of it was there and she put both hands into the pockets of the cardigan and, in the trapped heat of the half-day in that armoury wherein was redress for all that could and did go wrong in man woman child and beast, read what was to be read in my demeanour and said, 'Come through.'

We went through the dry click of a ribboned plastic curtain, into and out of a stacked stockroom in which there were more medicaments than the population of Faha, across the once flood-swollen and now lifted-in-places linoleum of a back passageway, up three concrete steps foot-worn smooth in the centre and through a cream door into an amber sitting room of oak flooring and Persian rug where Father Coffey was just finishing his tea and cake.

'This is...'

'O I know,' he said, the sun-fired face of him flaming a little more.

'Father.'

'Mr Crowe wants a word.'

'Yes. Yes. I see.' He put his cup carefully in its saucer, backhanded a crumb off the crease of his trouser, and stood gravely.

'We can go to the Parochial House,' he said. 'Thank you for the tea, Mrs Gaffney.' He passed her a look whose meaning I couldn't make out except to know it was not about tea. 'Come on so.' He held out a shepherd's hand to guide me to the door.

'It's me, Father,' Annie said. 'It's me he wants to speak to.'

At that time Father Coffey was a poor reader of human nature. He was a better reader of divine nature was the corollary. But he didn't like to be caught out. He had supposed I had sought him out and that it was to do with the torment he saw in me at the altar-rail. He lowered the shepherd's arm,

271

gave me a hawkish, Thomas Aquinas look. 'I see,' he said, but he didn't and for an elastic second just looked at me with cheeks blazing, once more learning the hard lesson that the unexpected was a meaningless term in Faha.

Annie went out with him. They had a muffled exchange. I didn't think anything of it. I was standing in the sitting room gathering the bits of my speech.

'Sit, please.'

Some people have a gift of naturalness. There was something about Annie Mooney that made it seem no calamity could overwhelm her. She had what I thought then an improbable evenness of temperament, and when her eyes met yours what you felt was her clarity and calm, as though by life she had been distilled. This was not the girl I had imagined when I had first heard of her, this was not the impetuous girl in Kerry who could fall in love with a man like Christy, and, seated in the feather hollow Father Coffey had left, I found myself in the footless place between story and truth. For no reason I can come up with here I hunched forward and tapped the underside of his saucer.

'Would you like tea?'

'No. No thank you.'

'I feel I should sit down for this.' She smiled saying it and sat across from me and folded her arms and waited, as though there were a draughtboard between us and this time I was white.

'It's about Christy.'

She was thin, I was realising. The way she held her arms across herself showed her wrists and that she was even thinner than you thought. She had a pared-away sense, as though the features of her face had come forward and were of this startling lucidity. Her eyes were grey. Her voice was kind and indulging of me, but there was weariness not far. I'll say here that I sensed that. I may not have at the time.

'He didn't send me. He doesn't know I'm here. He wouldn't want me to be here. Not for him, not on his behalf. He'd probably, I don't know what, if he knew. But anyway, he doesn't, that's important. It's not that he… I'm here on my own.'

She was sitting upright on the edge of the armchair, her back straight, watching me the way you might watch a patient presenting, not wanting to jump to conclusions, or to show yourself jumping anyway. 'You're sure you wouldn't like tea?'

'No.'

She moved her upper body slightly, angling it forward, and the smallest crease of a wince parenthesised the corners of her lips. 'A glass of water?'

'Thank you no. I'm here to say something and if I don't say it quickly I… I'm here on my and he doesn't know, didn't suggest it, it didn't wouldn't occur to him to because he well he, what he, I shouldn't put words in his mouth and I'm not, that's not what, he put some in mine and that was fair enough I'm, but no nothing I'm here to say he told me.'

'I think I've got that.'

'I don't want you to hold it against him.'

'I won't.'

The room was grander than I'd thought, but more faded too. Its dimensions those of the few fine square buildings that had formed the first street of Faha and lent it for a time the air of a town, expecting for a time it might become a town too, and for all time after wearing the look of disappointed elder. The windows were long and the ceilings high. The furniture was heavy and dark and saw no sunlight, and since the chemist's death had not been moved or changed, so the room retained not only his ghost and the ghost of the village's

273

origins but that of something that was not yet dead too. In my memory it was late afternoon but may not have been that late in fact and may only have acquired that sense of lateness from the dimness of the deep room and the embers of love. Because of the room's dimensions Annie was sitting further across from me than usual, the gentry having longer legs or not wishing to sit too close to each other. The more I spoke the further I leaned out towards her and the louder my voice.

'The thing you're here to say?' she prompted gently.

'Yes.'

It's not that I had forgotten it. It's that I felt like Francie Dunne when he tried to eat the football.

'You're not unlike him,' she said. And some figment of that passed through her expression and she released the arms crossed on herself and drove a crease on her skirt down and away. 'When he was your age.'

I was too het up to decide if this was good or bad. I pushed the quiff across and blew out the football. 'He came here for you. That's why. There was no other reason. He came with the electricity but he worked it so he came to Faha once he knew you were here. You're it. You're his purpose. He has thought of nothing and no one else in coming here. He went to Kerry first looking, did you know that? He did, he wasn't even in this country but he came back and he went there and asked and heard that you were married here and he came anyway not because he wanted anything, he didn't, from you I mean, except to see you and speak to you.'

It was important to take a breath. I think that's in Cicero. 'You're the whole reason he's here.'

'I think that's probably true.'

'It is.'

'But it was foolish.'

Her eyes were still the same even calm wise eyes and her voice was still the same even calm wise voice but there was something extra in both, I want to say sadness but it was more than that, it was experience and knowledge, it was the world as it is and not how we wish it to be.

'It doesn't have to be foolish. Why can't it be that…?'

'Because he doesn't know me. Because I don't know him. Because we are strangers who know nothing about each other.' It was a three-part death knell and finished off with the cold truth of: 'It was several lifetimes ago.'

The lower half of the sash windows were raised but no air was coming in and nothing stirring in that wine-carpeted mausoleum except what I had been trying to resurrect by forced speech and forehead sweat. Outside, a horse and car came and went in rattle and clop and a clipping of conversation between Mona Ryan and Marie Sweeney rose as far as the curtain before transitioning into mumble.

'He didn't come for love,' I said, both surprised and not by a high tone and troubadour's diction spouting out of my mouth. 'He came to ask you to forgive him, that's all. He woke up six months ago with one thought. He wanted to ask for forgiveness of anyone he had wronged.'

Once I said it I knew I had reached her. She didn't react right away, didn't betray surprise or derision or disbelief at the idea both simple and grandiose, she had lived too long and known too much for hasty response, but I knew by the pause she gave it. I knew as Nolan's car purred down Church Street and idled outside the post office, the car door opening and clunking, and opening and clunking again once he'd dropped the letters in the box.

'And has he?'

'I think so.'

This time she couldn't help herself. There came a comment through her nose, a short puff of air. Later I would interpret this widely, as wordless expression of the vexing truth that all men are impossible sentimentalists, who invented a religion of forgiveness and grace in the full knowledge of their own waywardness, all sorts, who sought forever the consolation of clemency and the embrace of their mothers. Later I would think her comment stinging, but then she said nothing. She crossed her arms on herself and drew back her head a little, not unlike Ganga considering a position on the draught-board. Her eyes, whether from deep feeling or falling light, were striking. I hadn't lived enough yet to think of them as beautiful. Then the parentheses occurred at the corners of her lips again and she shifted her position and stood. 'Thank you for coming to tell me.'

She walked to the door and held it open, and soon we were back inside the shut chemist shop and she was turn-ing the Yale lock and opening the door on the un-humming humdrum of Faha where the scene just ending took on the swift dissolve of dream.

'Can I tell him to come see you?'

'I think it's best not to.'

'But just to talk to you? He just wants to talk to you.'

She smiled her no, then said, 'But you can come again.' And she touched my arm fondly, as though there I wore the armband of the ardent. Whether to be pitied or prized for it I couldn't rightly say.

32

The next time my mother fell I was not with her. I came home from school and found her on the floor in the kitchen. *I lost my balance*, she said, quiet and contrite and ashamed as though it were a thing she had misplaced and maybe I could find where she'd left it, and she reached out a hand that shook in the air, a hand that shakes in the air still as I tell this.

I couldn't lift her. She was not large but the parts of her seemed to pull in different directions and some element of the shock must have weakened me. I had never tried to lift another adult and never put my arms around my mother except to receive her embrace, already a long time since, and I was awkward and embarrassed I suppose and some ways wanting to pretend this wasn't happening. When I took hold of her it was around her back on the coarse stuff of a worsted wine dress. It was twisted up and showed below it the cream of a slip and the fawn of her stockings with fawn worms where the material had gathered, and there was shock in that too, in the rout of the private, in the disarray and helplessness. I was thinking to support her as she stood not realising all the power of her legs had left her and she would never walk on them again. I heaved up and she groaned out of the deep centre of her, and I couldn't lift her and had to let her back down on to the floor. *O Noel*, she said, *I'm sorry*. And she started crying then, small spouts of cries like a not-yet-running tap. She tried to choke them back, but that tap wasn't for turning, because she knew what this fall meant, knew it wasn't a misstep, uneven flooring, or any fault in the surrounds, but was in herself, and the knowledge of that was running and flowing fast now and couldn't be turned off. *Mam, I can lift you*. And I grappled on to her harder than I should have because of the crying and because of the wild terror that was in that box kitchen then. It was like a force had escaped its casing and been released.

When you try and lift your mother it's not the same as lifting another human being. The moment you do it you know you'll never forget it for the rest of your life. You know there's no frailty, nakedness, nor tenderness either, quite like this, and know that the moment you have her in your arms the feeling of it is entering you so profoundly that from here on it will form part of the knowledge of your blood and brain and soul too, whether you believe in souls or not. I didn't quite lift but half-dragged my mother off the floor and across the shining wet linoleum to what we called the soft chair where I got her torso half on but she slid back crying all the time now and I had to heave her twice more to get her up. *Mam? Mam?*

I got her a glass of water. Her hand came around mine drinking it and I could feel the jumping live quality in her fingers, all of her throbbing like that, her eyes wildly seeking mine, looking away the minute they found them. She didn't want me to call the neighbours. She was ashamed. So, we sat through the rest of that afternoon, waiting for my father to come home. When he did, he called the doctor, and together they took my mother up the stairs, her legs the legs of a rag doll dangling. *That's it, May. Good girl. That's it.*

When the doctor left, my father found me doing my homework. *Your mother*, he said, and immediately lost the rest of his sentence. He was younger than himself at that moment, smaller too, and briefly I could see him the son of Doady and Ganga and wanting to be in one of the lumpy brown armchairs in that immutable home on the far side of the country.

It's like she's been struck, he said, *by electricity*.

33

In the days after seeing Annie Mooney, the cabling started going up in Faha. All over the parish you'd see trucks tearing past in grave urgencies, huge spools of black wire on the back with any number of shirtsleeved or bare-chested men duskily blazoned by the sun looking like they were hastening to and from a game of giants. And walking down any road you'd wonder *What's that line?* running taller than three men, between the fort field and Meade's bog meadow say. The line of wire caught your eye, not only because your eye hadn't attuned to seeing lines but because these were the first drawn by man on the air over that landscape, and spoke, in some part unsettlingly, of the dominion of science over nature and the reality of future times. From baking in the sun, the cables when they went up smelled of India, Tom Sullivan said, as though he had been there. The rubber, it's true, had a burnt treacle about it, or was its near cousin, and the cable workers had it about their person, the smell slow to perish and in time the men stopped trying, taking it as a badge of honour, and adding I suppose to their allure. All of them were foreigners, that is, from outside the immediate locality, and foreignness of any kind being better-looking than Fahaean.

Once the cables went up the crows came down on them, proving true the safety testaments of the Supply Board by not getting electrocuted. (This was refuted by Martin Martin who was a bit of a *gligeen* and said the current couldn't travel through claws. If you sat a child on the wire you'd cook it nicely, he maintained, but was not pressed for a test case. He threw a pair of old boots laced together up over the line down near the graveyard, they were there still and they burying him.) Cattle, too dumb or discerning, took small notice of the lines and would graze in their vicinity and under them too, but horses, with their fabled sensitivity, blew their nostrils and high-stepped to the furthermost corners, trotting over and back and making a general ruckus as though they'd supposed they were living in the time of Homer, and the strung wires impugned their nobility. They'd come around, but it took time.

The lines went up quickly, the whole parish like a Christmas bundle getting strung. People thought little enough of trees then, if there was a tree in the way down she came. If there were branches extending they weren't extending long. Some of the lads were so saw-handy you'd hardly see the saw in their hands only the great wing of the branch whooshing down and some lad up the tree shown then by the white wound calling *Will I take this next one too?*

The fine weather continued to outlast all predictions and prove that even in these times there was such a thing as incredible. Flowers that had been forgotten because they were each year vanquished by the floods falling from upturned clouds now bloomed. They were small roadside blossoms, like the local character, neither showy nor brash, it took an eye to notice them. Maybe the heart-swollen see more. Maybe the world is not the same world when you're plodding through a pining May-time. Either way, there was a definite flourishing, and that's a fact. I'm not making more of it than that.

The annual plague of slugs that had become such a condition of living that in Faha it had passed beyond comment, *Bad year for the slugs* a phrase redundant in all parts where the river was licking the land and especially in that parish where for years the slugs slimed down the grey skies, this year was visited on a benighted elsewhere. Another boon of what, with Catholic caution and native understatement, was called *the fine spell*, was that in the press of heat the weeds didn't come up. Like all who have to swallow occasional curses of their climate, neither Doady nor Ganga ever spoke of the fact that what most thrived in Faha was weeds and rushes. In the normal sop of wet springtime, it could seem that, following some subterranean advertisement of places with saturated mud-soil, the weeds and rushes of several counties had come for their holidays. You could pass an afternoon crooked over in the garden with your grandmother pulling fistfuls and stand after with the small victory of the cleaned bed only to find the dandelions back laughing at you two days later. But this year the weeds were suffocated by an implacable sun and there spread instead a Spanish gardening, which meant a world of watering. It was always known who in the parish had the best wells, a good well being both pagan and Christian, luck and blessing. These were mostly just a wet eye in the ground, but they were respected, understood part of a beneficent covenant and no amount of bucket-dipping could dry them. Now you'd notice people heading here there and everywhere with brimming buckets. And soon enough too you'd hear someone ask the question that in Faha had not been uttered in the living (and also dead) memory of Mrs Moore: *Will we run out of water?*

Weather and wiring combined to verb the air and fabricate a sense of the novel. That's my point.

In those next few days I didn't tell Christy I had seen Annie Mooney again, and I didn't see Sophie Troy, but lived with the blocked arteries of both stories. To keep the pressure and the pain up, in secret I'd tour the memory of Sophie. I'd find some detail I hadn't realised I'd noticed, the golden almost-down on her face say, and the wonder of that would make a nice agony to be going on with.

Those nights Christy and I resumed our quest for Junior, knowing that he was likely five miles further than the reach of a cycling handicapped by having to stop every so often to slake an onerous thirst. On those night-journeys, he would enquire of my lover's progress, and I'd tell him the none I was making and he'd say *That's not good* and add breathy bicycle-counsels, most of which were versions of the earlier precis of: *Your love is doomed, you must give it everything you've got.* That he wasn't adhering to his own advice I let slip for now, the state of in-love granting all its citizens visas of self-centredness.

When I did think of it, I was surprised that Christy was not more downtrodden by the impasse with Annie, and one evening approaching the village of Kilmihil, where Michael the Archangel himself had stopped, and where every man we met was called some version of Michael, I asked him why. He explained himself in a single sentence. 'Noe,' he said, and took a theatrical breath, 'this, is happiness.'

I gave him back the look you give those a few shillings short of a pound.

'I know,' he said. 'Whenever I said that it used to drive my wife mad.'

'You were married?'

'I was. She left me for a better man. God bless her,' he said, and nodded down the valley after the memory of her. He smiled, quoting himself: 'This is happiness.'

It was a condensed explanation, but I came to understand him to mean you could stop at, not all, but most of the moments of your life, stop for one heartbeat and, no matter what the state of your head or heart, say *This is happiness*, because of the simple truth that you were alive to say it.

I think of that often. We can all pause right here, raise our heads, take a breath and accept that *This is happiness*, and the bulky blue figure of Christy cycling across the next life would be waving a big slow hand in the air at all of us coming along behind him.

'This is happiness,' he affirmed once more, pushing off and gasp-pedalling the uphill away from further enquiry.

Beneath the pinholed heaven, the night was God-dimensioned and monumental before electric light. In Breen's pub there was no sign of the Archangel that evening, but there was a piper in the corner, pipers then rare as hens' teeth, and he played a plaintive music that was like the salt wind singing, utterly strange and familiar, unlike any other music really, an absolute music, uncompromising as a blackthorn, ancient and elemental, and in the air he played was a whole history of the troubled heart, and when I looked at Christy I saw the sorrow in his happiness had made shine his eyes.

Now, here's a thing. Soon enough I had been three times standing outside the gates of Avalon, three times tramping up and down the tramped grass, six times seen by Doctor Troy coming and going on missions of mercy and not once stopping to enquire after mine, and none of these times had I seen Sophie. The truth, which was unknown to me at the time, was that if she had come down the avenue I would have died.

The apprentice lover has to make it up as he or she goes along, they think no one has ever felt like this before. *Others have loved, yes, but not like this* is textbook. We all feel we are originals, maybe at the moment when we are most universal. So, Noe Crowe's method was to stand sentry at the gates. Make of it what you want. He would stand and walk up and down and feel he was making a declaration. By farmers, and farmers' wives, and children, he was seen, saluted, nodded to, but in the broad church of the Fahaean way, which allowed all manner of human oddity, never asked what he was doing there. There were stories, he was sure. But none told to him. In his original thinking, he had thought it would be enough just to see Sophie pass. It would be enough if she walked down the avenue with her sisters and turned out the gate to go into the village. It would be enough if she was the passenger in the doctor's car and in the pause of the turn right or left he would catch a glimpse of her, and whatever it was that he had, by the sight of her it would be healed. That was his religion, as he was each minute inventing it.

All he needed was to see her.

From this distance, when you get past the hopelessness of him, there's something hopeful in that. In the cure of another.

Well, she never came. He didn't get even the glimpse, and instead of his heartache getting better it got worse. That's in the textbook too.

———

Now, in Faha at that time, there was one German. He was called The German. That was what he went by, and called himself too, after a brief failed season trying to get Faha to pronounce his Christian name which was Uwe, '*You-Wee*', but to Faha's ears came out like a command to pee. The German had appeared on a bicycle after the war. One day he'd started cycling west and kept going past the devastation of humanity until he came to the drowning edge of the furthermost that was Faha, got off his bicycle, took a look around at all that was green and dripping, knelt down on the ground and wept. Faha being Faha nobody said boo and soon enough The German bought Brouder's father's place. The German was the peacefullest man in the parish. He was a keep-to-yourself kind of man, though, who grew a very tidy garden. Very. Some of the Germans, it turned out, had a broad streak of the romantic in them, and The German had a little of Penniworth's idyll-icitis, Tess Grogan's Eden-itis, and what have you, because he never once complained of the watery spears falling on his head, the puddling of his furrows, and the river saying hello to the kitchen when it invited itself in around the back. The German just carried on.

In the parish history, no one recalls whose was the first bicycle he fixed. It stood to reason of course. A man who'd cycled across Europe had a certified knowledge. Well, The German fixed the first bicycle past the point of fixing, returned it somewhere past brand new, and soon enough he was like Cúchulainn with the three hundred wolfhounds, only with bicycles. You'd come into Brouder's and the bicycles would be coming out against you. They'd be laid in a line in along the boreen waiting their turn. If you lived within ten miles, you knew The German was the man for bicycles.

But not for company. He lived in the neat little house and he worked on the bicycles into the dark, and after by lamplight. He fished the river in season. But he was friendless.

And one day, some years ago, I can't say how, this struck my grandfather in the chest. Bam, like that, and Ganga took a fit of wanting to befriend The German. Now, he had nothing in common with the man. That didn't stop him. He could find no means, no language, no bridge, between them to cross, except by bringing The German his bicycle to mend.

And so, Ganga went out to the shed an evening, apologised to his bicycle, and took a spanner to her. Soon after he'd be pushing the banjaxed bike, wheel-groaning, brakes askew or bearings unbearing, crossing the drizzling twilight with Joe following, up the right-of-way gone now to Brouder's place. 'You won't believe what's after happening to the bike. Would you take a look at this?' the two of them going out to the tidy little workshed at the back where The German would set to, tightening, righting, mending, whatever, it didn't matter. It didn't matter either that there was little talk between them – The German worked in a studied quiet – because by the time he was going home in the dark after, Ganga felt that more than the bicycle was repaired.

The trouble was, for the companionship to continue, my grandfather had to keep breaking the bicycle.

And that's what he did, mostly hiding it from Doady who would have scolded him, but every so often scratching his big round head to tell her, 'The bicycle isn't right. I think I'll take her up to The German,' letting Doady think she'd married a class of *bosthoon, rúchach, gliomach* – they have more words for idiots in Kerry than anywhere else – so he could carry on with his visits. The German cottoned on, of course, but categorised it among the innumerable strangenesses of Irish people, neither man saying anything until, umpteen I think the exact number of bicycle repairs later, the eventual breakthrough came when in the shed Ganga spotted a draughtboard.

———

Ganga's German tactic was the only way I could think of to see Sophie Troy again.

———

Now, there's a cruelty easily available in mocking your younger self. Howanever, I don't want to fall to that here. I want to have generosity of spirit. I want to let him be as he was, honour him in all his innocence and, I'm going to say, purity.

For a moment so, pause him here on the top of the Captain's Ladder, and look kindly on the poor fool. It's the middle of the afternoon. Doady is out at the washing line where the clothes dry in jig-time now and the pegs turn brittle from the sun. Her hens are hunkered under the hedges. The fire in the hearth is just two sods leaning on each other but still a heat is rising from them. It gets trapped here at the top of the stair where he stands. His wrists are still bound, the bindings greyed and frayed some at the edges, but mostly white, so they look the long sleeves of a musketeer. He's on the top step, maybe fifteen feet of a fall to the slope of the floor. *O now!* His pulse is in his throat, and in his wrists too, and because just ahead of him is the certainty of pain, and because of what it takes to overrule your own instinct, to choose the way of suffering, he doesn't move. In a fast-forward not invented yet are the scenes of outcome, what he thinks will happen when he steps off the Captain's Ladder and lets himself fall. He will put out his hands to save himself, and the wrists will snap. He'll tumble head-over-heels, bang his head and shoulders off maybe two maybe three of the worn timber steps his grandfather built when he realised the house would need an upstairs to accommodate what kept coming from his loins. He'll arrive in a clatter ball at the bottom of the stairs, and be crying out with pain, and his grandmother will find him and call his grandfather and he'll be brought to the doctor. The scenes can be pictured, but not felt. In order to keep us living, actual pain cannot be imagined. It can be understood; your brain can tell you *This is going to hurt*, but it can't pre-feel it, not the lacerating outraged dimension of it, so, while to throw yourself off the top of a steep timber stairs requires a fair bit of negotiation, and I suppose some courage, the courage is based on a fiction. He doesn't know how much it will hurt. Not really.

But there he is. I won't say anything here about the aptness of a fall, only that he was versed enough and young enough, not to say conceited enough, *be kind*, to want his actions to be symbolic. So, face bloodless and forehead awash in apostle's ardency, he moves to the lip of the step, pushes across the curve of his quiff, and steps into the air.

The single second it takes for him to fall to the floor is a lie. There's too much to fit inside that single beat, the realisation that he's going head-first, the tilt, topple, and the swiftness that he goes over, the sensation of diving, not yet into a deeper life, not yet translated into meaning, for now only the exhilaration and terror, the blind white descent too swift even to say the word descent, and in that blindness the image that only comes to him now of his mother's falls, some part of him changing his mind mid-fall and wanting to save himself because, despite being too late by three years, in a twist of illogic that was yet true, in saving himself he would be saving her, then the first *bang* and the second *bang* and somewhere before the third the shocked awareness that these were not his wrists snapping, because his body had cheated or outsmarted him and before he hit the plank of the step, shattering it in a sharp *clack* that Doady heard coming in the back door, his hands had pulled in close to his body for protection and he was going, wings withdrawn, arrowlike and shut-eyed, in the cause of hopeless love, and, in the single second that endorsed the idiom by splitting apart, coming to understand *bang bang bang* that the part of him taking most of the fall was his head.

34

In many versions, all of life is a fall from grace. In this one, I'm hoping to go the other way. I'm working on life as a rise to grace, after a fall. After several falls, in fact.

I have little memory of getting to Avalon after the fall. I went with Ganga by horse and car. I had been knocked out and revived by whiskey, seen the uncertain edges of the world collapsing, wan and vertiginous, floating with fish-hooks, lost consciousness again and been revived again by Doady pinching hard my two cheeks and calling down a swift intercession of saints. How I got on the car, how the journey happened, Thomas at the trot, me wrapped in the boil and itch of a tartan blanket, passing water-bearers and cattle boys and doubtless making concrete my reputation as the odd Crowe, I haven't a clearer picture.

My brain was shattered; or felt like it, the split parts pressing against the bone of the skull; my own diagnosis, no charge. The pain gave new definition to the word sharp, the holes of the avenue adding a jarring agony as the old wheels went in and out of each one announcing us with a knocking-music and bringing Ronnie to open the door before we'd landed in the front circle.

'Knocked out,' Ganga said, employing the plain style.

Between them, I was brought to the surgery. Ganga hoisted me on to the divan and backed out. Ronnie said the doctor was on a call. She put a hand on my forehead and went away and came back with a cool cloth. She had the studied responsible air of an elder sister, and the melancholic maturity of the daughter nearest the mother who had died.

'You fell,' she said. 'It'll take a little time for things to come right. Rest now.'

I did not say to her *Please send Sophie* but my eyes did.

The hand that shook me awake later was not Sophie's but the doctor's. He looked at me with an equable look. As he was the father of great beauty, I had not a small portion of awe for him, and equal measure of terror. But he was one of those persons who give nothing away, as though the whole feeling part of them they keep elsewhere and only visit occasionally. He had a grown-up face, is what I thought. Doctor Troy was the finished article, a mid-sized man in perfect proportion, his silver hair forever in place, and with an air that he had come into the world that way. He stood close to the divan and said nothing. The grey eyes narrowed and took in the sorry truth that despite decades of General Practice humanity continued to have an inexhaustible imagination for harming itself. There was always a new one on him. The hedgehog moved over and back on his lip. It seemed to me the hedgehog was doing the diagnosis, but that may have been the split brain thinking. The doctor, I think, was mentally thumbing back through my case notes, pausing on the three days of my standing at the gates, adding this to failed priest and trying to catch a falling pole and coming, by circumstantial evidence, to: 'Son, are you an idiot?'

He pulled up my eyelid, shone a torch in my eyes, went by tap around the apple-swellings on my head. 'This hurt? This? This?' He wasn't listening for replies, like most doctors he had already come to judgement and was just going through the motions so it didn't look like he had magic discernment. He lifted each of my hands, let them back. 'You decided to save the wrists and land on your head?' He smiled a hedgehog-smile, prickly. 'How many fingers? Look this way, this. Down. Up.'

When he had finished, he stood back, put two fingers of each hand in the slit pockets of his waistcoat, and delivered a classic Troy-ism. 'There's nothing wrong with you, but for what's wrong with you.'

I had an unwelcome sense of being transparent and made the two-year-old's escape by closing my eyes.

'Open,' he said and palmed a pill into my mouth. 'Drink.'

He went to the long windows and tugged the curtains together, taking out the afternoon light and letting off a fine dust of yesterdays. Without another word, he left. I heard him in the hallway tell Ganga something and soon enough heard Thomas and the car wheels in clop and rattle depart, and soon enough too, by the grace of prayer and pharmaceuticals, I had assembled the split parts of my brain into a single thought: the surgery door would open and Sophie Troy would appear.

But prayers go their own way.

I opened my eyes from a sleep I didn't know I was having. And in the disorient realised night had fallen, and that there was a girl's face hovering close over mine.

It was not Sophie's.

It was still as a moon, studying me. The room was in the dark of after-midnight, the house asleep. From the girl's lips leaked a held smoke. From the perfect portrait stillness of her it escaped in wisps. Her eyes didn't leave me, and in the moments it took for me and the dark to grow accustomed to each other, she became Charlotte Troy. She lifted back her head and brought up a lit cigarette that had been invisible. She tilted back her face as though it were an offering, brought the cigarette like an adorer to her lips and sucked a pucker smoke out of it at an angle of eleven o'clock. The sound of her lips was the only sound, it was not nothing.

'I don't smoke,' she said, shooting the smoke across my body there on the divan. 'You didn't hear me come in either.'

She had a stance learned from Lauren Bacall, it came with the cheekbones. Sneaking back into the house after an evening whose entertainments all fathers drew a curtain over, she had craved the succour of one last cigarette and come into what she supposed the empty surgery to have it. She had first thought me a corpse.

The cigarette and her had their own thing going and for a bit I was inconsequential. My head had a bat beating it. I brought my hand up as a shield and felt the egg I had grown out of my right temple. She took notice and paused the cigarette to ask, 'Are you a bit touched?' She didn't wait for reply. 'You're the lingerer. At the gates. You're not simple or anything?' Her voice was a smoky chocolate, you wanted more of it.

I was already in some other place by then, inside the strangeness of the night and her perfume and her smoke and what I would come to think of as her *stickiness*, can't say why, but that was it, and it was so sweet and strong if you were standing you'd look down at your feet because they wouldn't be going anywhere. I managed a 'No' I think.

There was still something left in the cigarette and she let it come to the eleven o'clock lips once more, and held her face at that angle after, as though letting an invisible sun or moon bathe it. There was a consummate mesmerism to her. You couldn't stop looking, and she knew it, had the custom and entitlement both.

'Take me to the Mars on Friday.'

She said it twisting the butt into the ashtray on her father's desk, leaving the lipsticked remnant for him to find and know it was hers and begin the business of blinding himself to that knowledge.

'Seven o'clock. I'll order the hackney.'

There was an escaped flake of tobacco inside her upper lip and her tongue went to find it, pressing and pausing the moment with complete and unabashed confidence the way the beautiful can, before she brought it out on the tip, plucked it off. To confirm her invitation, she came close to the divan and looked at me a last time. In the sea of the dark her perfume swam, and I and the room did too, all of us lost. What she saw in the shadowed figure of a prone egg-head she didn't say. She kept the lustrous eyes on me another second, then turned on her heel and walked away to the door.

'I'm Charlie by the way,' she said.

When Charlotte Troy was born (*It's a girl!*) Doctor Troy told Doc Senior she was a boy. He had a son, Charlie, he shouted into the ear of the old man who was bedbound and deaf and dying, lungs stuck together by a tacky emphysema and two hundred seasons of rain. It was a small betrayal, but his father would be dead before he'd find out it was a girl, the doctor reasoned. He despised in himself the weakness of it, the embedded thorn, and when the old man didn't die, and then didn't some more, and when the child had to be brought upstairs in the swaddling into the roar and splutter of deafness and cough and be for the duration *A fine son*, that thorn went further down the doctor's bloodstream. He stonewalled his wife, Regina, had a policy of no way no how when it came to addressing why he wouldn't tell his father it was another girl, and hoped the old man would be dead before the time of dresses.

As it happened, he was. And Charlie, who was Charlotte to everyone else and in all other rooms of the house, died with him. Charlotte Troy was one of those luminous children that have the sunlight in them. She was fair-haired and quicker to smile than Ronnie, quicker to know the golden key of that smile, to understand all it could unlock in the world, and, first-off, that chores and homework were not for the likes of her. She defeated the undefeatable nuns by a mimicry of angels. While, under the crab-clawed tutelage of Mrs Dott, Ronnie played a diligent piano, Charlotte wanted dancing tunes, and when she didn't take the time to master them had her sister learn them so Charlotte could do the dancing. When she was thirteen, she pierced her father's heart at the dinner table by calling herself Charlie. He passed no comment but felt his father's thumb on the thorn somewhere behind his rib. She was Charlie thereafter, and who Charlie was was an April sun-shower, a quick and impetuous dazzlement, an untrappable tempered loveliness combined with a liveliness of mind that in those times the gentry called *winning*.

I'm aware I'm speaking across the years here. But Charlie Troy was, well, a goddess.

Now, I know, *I know*.

Fact is, I didn't see Sophie that time. She never came into the surgery. The doctor swept in in the morning said 'Go home' without punctuation or moving his moustache and swept out again.

In the lead-up to the following Friday I didn't forget Sophie, I didn't lose any of the shining inside me for her. A platonic love exists on a different plane, we had been told in the seminary, it's a risen thing, somewhere above the place of dirt and sweat. It cannot be touched by the comings and goings of ordinary life. I walked home from Avalon under a tight blue sky, a throb leaping like a trapped frog inside my temples. By the time I was turning in my grandparents' gate I had found linear the corkscrew logic that by calling at the house and taking her sister to the pictures on Friday I would be proving my love for Sophie.

I didn't announce the date, not in words anyway, but Christy translated my stooped revisions in the bit of mirror hanging on the rafter and rubbed his hands. 'You're seeing her?' He didn't wait for confirmation and I didn't put him right, but he got off the bed and came around me the way you might a beast due to the mart. 'You're not going like that?'

'Why not?'

He crinkled all the skin of his face, condensed his criticism and served it in the cold water of a single phrase, 'You look like a priest.'

On the Friday evening I set out in my black cleric trousers and one of Christy's oversized buttonless shirts. The shirt was more like a tunic, was tucked in on all sides, but on my journey to the village kept rising and inflating like a cotton balloon so I was soon a walking parachute. Staying true to form and the Fahean way, my grandparents had made no comment, but I knew that, inside, Ganga was all bubbles of glee – he slipped me a ten-shilling note, *Whist now!* – and Doady pips of dismay, for they sat either side of the argument for my return to the seminary. Before I left the bedroom, Christy had commanded, 'Wait!', splashed a spiced lotion into his palms and smacked it on both sides of my neck. Gently I had drawn the quiff across to re-cover the egg on my forehead.

Walking up the avenue at Avalon might have been one of the longest walks of my life. There were old trees left to themselves on either side, a fringe of ferns new-leafed and neon where they caught the sunlight, dark and fairy-taled where they didn't. I was halfway up when Heaney the hackney came past. The big powder of white hair on him, he wore an imperishable black suit as a nod to the venerable office of coachman. He didn't stop for me, but gave me a look in passing, and from it I understood he had been there before at the bequest of Charlie Troy, and that I was only the latest recruit in this particular game of soldiers.

Heaney kept the car idling in the front circle. He knew promptness was not in Miss Troy's nature, but he knew too that the Ford hated nothing more than being at the beck and call of a key, so they had negotiated this treaty. I came in past him. He had the window down against the swelter and the arm out resting. He preserved the chauffeur's code of keeping his eyes on the windscreen. I went up the steps I'm not sure how, pressed the door-pull, turned to the august and paradisal prospect from that front porch and was a pantomime of the young gentleman but for the frog leaping and the egg pulsing and the parachute that needed tucking.

The Shannon turned blue was like the sea lying on its back with its tongue out. The door-pull brought no response. All of Faha, but me, knew it was ten years since it worked. The doctor didn't care to repair it. 'The sick will get in anyway' was a Troy-ism.

After a time, I raised and lowered the knocker, the loudness of it startling the birdsong into another key and sounding more peremptory than I was.

Ronnie it was who opened the door. 'Hello.' She was wearing a sensible dress of taupe colour and holding in one hand the apron she had just taken off. She smiled the wise, soft smile she had and let me into the front hall. 'You're feeling better?'

'I am.'

'Good. I'll tell Charlie you're here.' Before she turned and went up the stairs there was the slightest hesitation, a sliver-moment in which she was looking at me, and I didn't know if it was that she was a sister outshone, if it was become a habit for her heart to fall a little at moments such as this, if there was regret or resignation, but her eyes were deep and full of telling, and then she pressed her lips in a closed smile and turned.

The foyer seemed even more crowded than before. The largeness of my feelings had given birth to an incipient claustrophobia. I couldn't sit down, but there was no room to pace. In response to the rainless season, a tennis net had been resurrected, and was on its way to Faha's only court round the side of the house, but for now was a great balled tangle on the floor, with a sizeable catch of last year's sycamore leaves. I stood in place, the sweat catching up with me and the 'chute clinging. *You are here.* That's what I was thinking. Just that. Then I heard the light footsteps come down the stairs, and Sophie was there.

She was holding a book with her finger in the page. She stopped on the last step. 'My sister will be down in a few minutes.'

I'd like to say I said thank you. I'd like to say I said her name, I'd like to say I knelt down, or did anything at all, but because of the transfixing anaesthesia of beauty, and the unassailable truth that Sophie Troy was incomparable to any human being I had known, I was dumbfounded.

'Soph?' In descent, Charlie's heels were attacking the stairs. 'Put the cloth over Percy later,' she said. 'I might be late. Oh hello. We need to go.'

Charlie waited at the front door and I opened it for her, the oval mirror showing a version of me I didn't recognise, Sophie going back up the stairs, and I heading out to get the car door, already tied up in scarves of scent, already lost to the game of soldiers in Heaney's look in the mirror, but aware that I was in the realm of the fabulous, in thrall to a family of swans, who had a grass tennis court, and a caged songbird whose name was Percy French.

35

Plato never made it as far as the Mars. If he had, his philosophy might have foundered. From the outside, the building was unimpressive. It had a plain face that hid the pandemonium of its interior and stood with pretend unremarkableness just off the market at the top of one of the broadest streets in Europe. The vista down the street was stately, had, if not a top-hatted air, a banker's waistcoat-with-pocketwatch one left over from earlier times. It said *Town*. In perfect Victorian, it said *Civility resides here*, and was found true too, not least during the regales of the annual opera season when the Mars put away the cowboys and hoodlums, forgot it was in a frontier town on the furthermost edge and transformed itself into the place of *Rigoletto* and *Tosca*. Because they kept company with beauty the opera singers were accorded special reverence, and for years later someone would summon the glories of the town's past with the phrase, 'When the operas used be on.' There was gravity and serenity in a street that ran down to the blue sky and the invitations of the estuary.

It had been a fraught car journey. From it my abiding memory is Charlie Troy having a deep but short-lived relationship with a smoking cigarette, rummaging after in the depthless depth of a shiny black handbag for a forbidden lipstick, finding it, applying it in Heaney's mirror with a magician's dexterity that defied the inconsistencies of the road, pressing, unpressing, and repressing her lips until the look came to her satisfaction and the bow was drawn.

When Heaney let us off outside the picture house he asked what time we'd want the pick-up and Charlie added a bandit note by telling him to be waiting by the bank after the showing. There was a loose interpretation of a queue by shuffle and press slow-motioning inside. Employing privileges of class and beauty, Charlie ignored it and we were quickly before a ticket desk whose glass was tinted by decades of human anticipation. Behind it sat the large ham-faced figure of Liam Looby, a lecher, on his lap three rolls of tickets he hadn't bothered to fit into the machine.

'Two one-and-threes,' Charlie said.

One-and-three was the price for children, two-and-six the adults, three shillings for the balcony. Admission at his discretion, Looby tore off two of the cheapest ones and slid the pink tongue of them out under the gap in the glass. 'There you are, Miss Troy.' Charlie paid him with a smile and stood waiting while I gave him Ganga's money.

Inside the foyer of the Mars the world was left behind. You transitioned out of the blue of May into an illumined elsewhere, both gaudy and glorious. In the heated jostle of the next not-queue queue, this time to have the ticket you had just bought verified by a uniformed doorman, the buzz of expectation was like a human engine that gathered force on a fuel of the communal. The more ticket-holders there were pushing around you the more precious your ticket, and the more urgent your need to get inside. Caught up in the pulse of this, I didn't distinguish myself by shoving ahead, Charlie following closely with her princess smile and right-of-way cleared by her vassal. 'What is that scent?' she asked, when she came next to me. But the crush of those coming behind made impossible any answer.

Seating was not allocated, and so once past the gauntlet at the doors, there was a frenzied rush down the dim corridor whose floor, once carpeted in a Persian crimson, had over time been tongued black from the tramp of wet boots. In the aberration of that season, the heat outside had for once penetrated the damp bunker and now released a brown air of boiled sock. The walls wore a weeping gloss of condensation. It made no difference. The glamour of the Mars was immune to human realities.

Like townies everywhere, to keep a grip on their own place on the ladder, the locals considered the country people living testaments to the cloddish, and were quick to the best seats, securing islets around them for their friends by embankments of jackets and leaving free the rows up near the giant screen where the antics of the country people could be monitored and tilted-back heads made targets if the picture dull. Charlie, of course, had her favourite seat, and like all things in her life up to that point the restrictions of our one-and-three tickets were only nominal, and when I was turning in the doors to the stalls she took my hand and led to the balcony. Her fingers were on mine for only moments, just long enough to guide me into the stairwell, but long enough to fizz all of me into a state I had, and have, no words for. All my awarenesses were heightened in her company. Every cell alive.

Like amateur robbers, we ran up the stairs. There was another uniformed doorman, but the perfect bow slayed him and he overlooked the one-and-threes and we breezed inside the balcony and up to the back.

Charlie Troy led the Resistance against the wearing of glasses. A pure and breathtaking vanity combined I think with a low appreciation of the value of clarity, founded perhaps on the looks of men thereabouts, none of whom came close to the idols of the silver screen. She had a pale cropped curtain of hair. It didn't seem like hair, it seemed like a lustrous helmet that came to just below the exquisite shell of her ear. She had been made perfect, and knew it, a knowledge that informed her every moment. The beautiful are different. The rest of us know it, that's what magnetises us to them. When Charlie sat down she peered at those towards the front.

'I have a beau, you know,' she said. 'Eugene.'

For an instant I thought she had seen him and my heart went crossways. But Eugene, it turned out, was a banker's son from Limerick, would be going into the bank himself, where his acquisitions would include a beautiful wife, and where soon after he'd start developing the soft, round bottom of a man who sat on money for a living. For his twenty-first birthday Eugene had been given a new set of teeth top and bottom. It was the done thing then among a certain class, and that was the one he was in, so the teeth were out, and he was out of kissing commission until the gums healed and he could say 'Charlie' without spraying.

As with the church, the cinema was full well before starting time, and as with the church, those who refused to surrender to clocks proved their singularity by coming in their own time. This accounted for the first of the usher's duties, which was a loaves-and-fishes job of making enough seats to go around. I say ushers because in the Mars they were not short-skirted usherettes in red-trimmed blazers but a big-shouldered fraternity, retired I think from the rugby club, who were not averse to the occasional mano-a-mano that would arise from the second of their duties, keeping the urgencies of frothing blood in order and the buttons of decency done.

When the lights went out, a high-pitched gasp escaped, and the torches came on. Thereafter all that transpired had the character of the illicit, which was the true worth of the price of the tickets.

'Chocolates,' Charlie said, ten seconds after we had settled into our seats.

I went and came back with an Eastersworth. She had slipped off her big-buttoned jacket of jade and was in a cream blouse from which her swan's neck rose with what struck me as startling nakedness.

The velvet curtains were pulled back in a series of manhandled jerks to reveal the scalloped one beneath. A kind only ever seen in cinemas, it had the sheen of a woman's slip, and rose now with slow reveal to bring us the advertisements and coming attractions, during which no one stopped talking. The whole cinema was abuzz, as though all conversation had been postponed until just now, and everywhere matches were being struck.

In the godlike beam of the projection, there were already twists of smoke. The focus was off, but only slightly, and under a cinematic spell, and in fear they might lose their seat, no one got up to complain. The less-than-clear picture was compensated for by a surplus of amplification. The volume in the Mars lived up to its name by being out of this world. The film stars' voices boomed like gods and masked the sometime squeals, shrieks and pants of astonished pleasure that rose here and there among the rows of writhing humans below the screen. The balcony was nearer the gods than those in the fervid skirmish of the stalls below, so up here the performance of decorum lasted a little longer. Eventually, the cabbage and onions of men's armpits defeated the artificial citrus of their pomade and from the stalls made rise a male fug that had the effect of the starter's pistol on the balcony.

It was a double bill, the first part a Western with Audie Murphy, who had the twin assets of an Irish name and an American jaw. The whole of the country was trapped in an incurable beguilement to cowboy pictures then, those who weren't secretly cheering for the Apaches were cheering for Johnny Reb, unless John Wayne was in the picture, in which case all bets were off, because he had a farmer's shoulders and your grandfather's walk. Audie was up to his silver buttons in an ambush and I was trying to figure out how to get Sophie into the conversation when Charlie leaned over and hissed a disappointed: 'Aren't you going to kiss me?'

For some things there's no accounting. Or the accounting that's done is not tabulated in columns of reason, but outside the margins and up and down in the swift squiggles of a heart monitor in a heart attack, because under that leaping imperative there I was, bringing my lips to the scarlet bow. It would be the first kiss of my adult life, performed to a soundtrack of cracking gunfire in a Martian elsewhere. Charlie Troy had tilted her head back and closed her eyes, for which I was thankful. I could never have kissed her if those polished jewels were watching. As it was, I was already battling with the ruby mesmerism of her lips. I couldn't take my eyes off them. Neither could I imagine damaging their perfection with any part of the likes of me.

The time it takes for one face to meet another's is in fact no time, it's so charged as to be outside of ordinary measure, fast, fizzed, and in a held suspension at the same instant, and in that instant I am leaning across, I am keeping my arms down as if to mitigate what I am doing, *no hands*, I am an awkward and unnatural bird in neck-crane with lips pursed, as though succumbing to some elemental suction by which human beings are to be stuck together, laughably, by the lips, crossing the no-distance that is also enormous, inside the age-old force field of a Provençal perfume of jasmine and rose, and the cloying burnt-gold seduction of cigarette smoke, and in that crossing aware of sensory explosions, all kinds, and in the flickering silver thrown from the screen see that in the seat alongside Charlie another girl is being kissed and under the pinned onslaught has her eyes open and is watching me with a mixed female curiosity and incredulity that says *This is who Charlie Troy is with?*

My kiss is the lightest touch on a surface soft and sticky. It's a kiss of imagination and worship. And mostly, it's a kiss trying not to damage the bow. But the moment my lips leave hers Charlie's eyes pop open, not with wonder, not with astonishment at such tenderness, but with the vexed puzzle-ment of a *What-was-that?* look, and her hand comes around the back of my neck and draws me smash bang into the bow, which proves a weapon of versatility, and is now knocking down the walls of everything you thought a kiss was.

Charlie's kisses, were, I suppose, in *The Book of Kisses*. But they'd be in the chapter called Devouring. There was biting and gnawing and teeth-banging in them, an urgent air of mouth-to-mouth combat, wild and violent and driving to an end that was out of reach, and known to be, but only the more pressing for that. And pressing was a big part of it. She pulled me against her in a mime of movie stars, but the three-dimensionality of our bodies made a bumping mockery of blending, elbows and knees proving extra to the parts required and noses on standby with an abashed air of being in the way. Of course, I was lost from the first moment, in a whirl carousel of taste touch sight smell, and sounds (all s's – *squelch, suck, smack*), a *carne*-not-*vale* but *salve*, a loud hello and hallelujah both, a dizzying lostness in which was found another version of yourself, one that was tasting smoke and chocolate and make-up, none of which you liked but did now, even as your wrists were singing, the egg on your forehead breaking, and your eyes agape from the out-of-this-world experience of your face eaten by a swan.

Charlie's kisses were so encompassing that one of them took the time for a main course. She had mastered how to breathe inside the face of another, I hadn't, and was glad when her teeth left the swollen rubber of my lower lip for a point of attraction I didn't know I possessed, the fillet meat of my earlobes.

My head sidelong then, I could see the whole of the back row was engaged in amorous acrobatics. The stiff outstretched armrests of purple velvet, like small bishops, were no obstacle to love's professionals, who got their legs over, their heads buried in white necks, climbing the ramparts of their part-ners like fallen-to-siege castles, enjoying the cinema privilege of a borrowed glamour, knowing there was nowhere else for love's declarations, but also that love was up against the running hourglass of how long it took Audie to gun down the Apaches and the lights come on. The professionals, I soon realised, had chosen the back row not only because, like the gods, you could watch the amateur sports below, but because unlike all other rows this one didn't rock, and the back wall of the Mars provided the resistance to force that multiplied the friction.

Life on Mars was not in the realm of the known. Nothing could be accounted for. Here was the flawless magnificence of Charlie Troy with eyes closed, pulling at the front of my shirt because, by an unvoiced directive, what she wanted now was to feel the flesh of my chest, only to discover Christy's shirt had no buttons, pulling it up, and pulling it up, chok-ing me on the last-line-defence of my scapulas, and pulling it some more, half undressing a surrendered parachute-mus-keteer until the torch beam found us and a rugby roar of 'You!' was bellowed, causing sidelong mid-kiss glances from our compatriots who wanted to witness the tantara but not disengage their tongues. There were drowned-out moans, outraged yells, and here and there the smacks that followed some fellow chancing his arm for a fondie. From the disap-pointed there were matches struck and tossed over heads like falling-star loves that weren't (*Who threw that?*), girls getting up and going to readjust themselves, like rough-handled equipment, in the thronged workshop of the Ladies where the competition for the mirror was a sport of shoulders, lads sending out fight invitations by putting their feet up on the seat in front of them, and bottles of minerals crashing, spill-ing and drooling down the slope of the floor where the drool would dry but never completely, Martian homage to the dark stickiness from which humanity sprang.

The second picture coming to climax (the prophylactic of the torch beams flashing more frequently but with less certainty of containment), there was a general rush into the caresses of last resort. Where the time had gone, none knew. The professionals availed of one last go at everything, in a condensed version. Charlie let me know she was done by a lift of her hips and a faraway look. We had not spoken a word.

There was a general hasty redress of decency once the credits rolled and the lights were imminent, buttons and zips attacked with a fierce and cleric urgency, me tucking in the parachute just as the lights came on.

How we got outside was also unknown, the after-Mars experience as perplexing as the in-Mars one, eyes blurred, ears singing, and feet not on the solid world of before. Propelled by the firm calls of *Goodnight now, goodnight, now!* of the ushers-turned-janitors, we spilled like the chastened on to the broad street, a mild night sky thrown over the town and an unreal ordinariness in every sight. Behaviours were instantly redrawn and, *The Book of Kisses* shelved, there were no intimacies of any kind. Under the steady gaze of the fine buildings, a buttoned-up code of respectability prevailed, betrayed only by the urgency with which cigarettes were lit, flushed goodbyes bid, and men walking away with the saddle-sore gait of a cowboy walk, as if they had tenderised steaks in their pants.

Charlie neither took my hand nor looked at me. She spotted the hackney idling outside the bank, crossed ahead of me and took out a cigarette while waiting for me to open the car door.

The journey back to Avalon was notable mostly for the awkwardness a person can feel. Charlie smoked. I had no idea if she was contented or not, no idea what she was thinking, and no way to begin to know. From time to time Heaney eyed me in the mirror and in that boxed rectangle his gaze had the weary glare of a confessor. He'd seen it all before, his eyes said, the cloud of his powdery hair lending him a look of evaporating wisdom. When we arrived at the foot of the avenue, Charlie was interrogating a hand-mirror and was as far from me as I imagine anyone in the world could be, a truth made colder by being together in the backseat of a bumping Ford.

The nearer we got to the house the more urgent my sense that I needed to say something. But, with a bewildering contrariness, the intimacies of the Mars were between us and too vertiginous to cross. I was too removed from myself to know what I was feeling, but wonder was part of it and fizzing in me along a cable of pleasure fairly thickly embraided with guilt and betrayal.

By the time the car came into the front circle and Charlie had posted her cigarette out the window I had edited a long

309

speech to what was most pertinent, *Do you think your sister Sophie*—, but Heaney thumped the brakes to let the gravel announce our return, Charlie turned to look at me a last time and my speech was slain by the indescribable eyes, and the over-the-shoulder command as she pulled the lever and stepped out, 'Next Friday.'

In a dark of cats and bats, the gravel soundless beneath her practised steps, Charlie Troy went around the house to slip in at the rear. The doctor opened the front door and looked out. Heaney put back a hand to be paid and I realised I was walking home. I gave him the last of Ganga's money, and stepped out, and was then in the scrutiny of the doctor from the top step.

There is no manual for how to greet a father after a debauch with his daughter. I improvised a musketeer's flourish salute. Doctor Troy didn't move, but returned only the dark beads of an appalled glare and let the stiff moustache say the rest, some of which was *That girl*, and more of it was *This idiot?*

36

'Well?'

'Well.'

'Tell me.'

My coming up the ladder had woken him. He propped on an elbow to look at me, though the room was in a blessed dark.

'Good?'

'Yes.'

'Good.'

After a moment: 'The shirt?'

I must have somehow indicated it was helpful.

'I knew.' He sounded a small laugh that began through his nose but defeated confinement and was soon shaking in his chest, his happiness for me like small white feathers of down in the dark, going everywhere.

I went to get out of the shirt but Charlie was inside it in a cling of her perfume and I left it on and got into bed with her.

'Sophie Troy,' Christy said gleefully to the thatched dark. 'Sophie Troy. She has a beautiful name.'

What exactly Christy did once he left the house in the mornings I classified under the inexact term 'work'. He was going about the parish with the memorial, trying to rein in the last of the hold-outs and negotiating the smooth passage of the workers through lands the State had gridded. This much I knew, but when he came home he told no tales, and when we went on the bicycles in the evening talk of work was outlawed by the exertions of the hills and the hope of hearing a legendary music. Now that the poles were strung and the parish wore at least the look of electricity, I knew his time with us would be coming to an end. And in this was a sour taste of failure. I had the classic impatience of the young, who want more from life, not yet realising that by that more is made. The more that I wanted I've already told, but between he and Annie Mooney was a sundered story and after the evening with Charlie Troy I had lost some of my certainty that two lines could be joined or love understood.

What in fact Christy was doing in those days I would only find out when he was gone.

During the limbo that was the wait until the following Friday, I adhered to the regimen of the spiritually unrequited by eating little, taking long, sun-blazed walks by the sparkling river, turning over the arguments for the defence and entering the difficult negotiations between morality and desire. The crux was, Charlie Troy had not replaced Sophie in my affections, she had joined them.

I was, I decided, in love with both of them.

One afternoon, exhausted from a muted dialogue with my selves, I came upstairs to find my fiddle case on the bed. In healing, my wrists needed stretching, Christy had been telling me, and I knew it was he who had put it there. I took it outside into the garden and, after the requisite agonies of tuning, scratched up one of the reels of childhood. I was not good, mind. Not good at all. But my playing was improved by the fact that there was no one to hear. The tendons of the wrists ached, but sweetly. Though the tune was simple and plain and a child of six could master it, the making of it was an air-ticket elsewhere. At first you were nothing but a side-chinned servant submitting to an instrument that would give nothing back but your own discord and inadequacy. You looked at your fingers and willed them to move to the places they were too stiff or slow to get to, the neck of the fiddle too narrow and the bow a contraption of capricious invention. But slowly, so slowly as to make new definition of that word, music emerged. It came through you and there was what I suppose was release, and soon enough release was its own end, and in the repetition and rhythm its own addiction too. And soon enough you were going into the attic of childhood memory asking *How did that other tune go?* and shortly after you were that fellow sitting outside in your grandparents' garden playing on the fiddle a recovered music, living in and escaping from the torments of your heart.

The infancy of my playing was fostered by an absence of criticism. The wisdom of the old people was incalculable. Ganga, coming and going from business with cattle, would cross from the yard with a mimed deafness. He would scrupulously not hear a note, and only when Doady, palms down and air-paddling a flotilla of hens out the front door, directed him by a head-beckon to the fiddler in the garden, did he stand and listen a moment before carrying on. At the tea later, he'd deliver his five-star review with the single phrase that was Faha's highest praise for musicians: 'You have an ear, Noe! By God, you do. You have an ear!' I would play the musician's part of denying it, but some element of the compliment would enter me, and when Ganga added, 'My father had one too,' and, after a bite of buttered loaf, 'This house often heard him,' it would go deeper still. It warmed me. But I didn't give it more weight than that then, not yet realising you can turn a corner and find your life waiting there for you, and that if you walked past it, it would come after and keep tapping you on the shoulder.

A different tap came from Doady, picking up the ware from the table, giving me the flashing-glasses look, and saying, 'I had a letter from Mother Acquin.' She waited for a response I didn't give and then added, 'She says to tell you your mother is in her prayers.' She knew that was all she needed to say.

That evening, when we were heading out, Christy said, 'Bring the fiddle with you.'

I didn't. Not physically, anyway. But, near enough midnight, when we were standing in the crowded sawdust of Looney's listening to an old man playing a timeless 'Rakish Paddy', I found I had the sharpened ears of the tune-hunter, my mind fingering and bowing goodo.

Christy didn't press me for details of Sophie, but from its thousand creases he translated the adventures of his shirt and told me to keep it. He realised I was dying of a hunger that could not be cured by food or drink, but, by an Apollo grace, could be stayed by music.

And music was plentiful that season, which was in itself remarkable. In general, there was neither as much music, nor was it as celebrated as it would be in the decade ahead. This is maybe a hard thing to appreciate, the music was there but under a bushel. The coming of modern times had made it seem a remnant, tradition belonging to a past the country was hurrying away from. But in places like Faha and thereabouts the music was one of the things the people had, it belonged to them the way the rain did, the way the blackthorns on the ditches did, and whether it was a poor thing or not was of no consequence. It was theirs, and it was free. In normal times it was often hiding, had to be coaxed out from under a low-capped shyness in players who were both Mohicans and Catholics, end-of-the-line and deeply restrained, who circumvented the sin of pride through a studied unshowiness, *Those old tunes*, and played only to their local audience and intrepid musical expeditionaries like Christy and me.

The fine weather, as Ganga said, had made mincemeat of the farm chores this year. The annual battle to secure a living out of mud and water was relieved by honeyed sunlight and a golden hay against which all future years would be measured, and about which Senan Hehir passed the immemorial judgement, 'You'd eat it yourself.' And so, because of the sun-lightened load, for the first time, farmer-musicians found their pockets filled with gifts of time. In fine form, they went abroad in the night, the result a jig-time after a slow air, and an aura of holiday where there was none.

Cycling home from Looney's you'd have a hundred tunes and not a small bath of liquid in you, with consequent chaos of feeling and thought. The code we had evolved was to concentrate on the cycling part, avoid discourse, and that way stay between the margins of the ditches. We were sometime successful. A loose pairing, by virtue of the singularity of souls, one of us would get ahead of the other on the road, and after a while realise it and slow down or stop altogether. Christy would prolong the opportunity to take breath by making one of the wise statements of the sloshed.

'That playing tonight, it was as pure as a bishop's rectum.'

An image I couldn't reconcile but found I could nod to.

Somewhere along the ribbons of the road, we left: 'A gift for the make-believe, Noe. The first requirement of saints', 'That barman was a poem to listen to', 'That other, did you

notice, built like a battleship but looked like he had a want'
and 'God is devilishly clever. You'd have to give him that.'

In the daytimes, in the broader parish, there was an atmosphere
of imminence. The electrification of Faha was not yet complete,
but near enough. The vans of electricians appeared for the first
time. The generalities of the national policy for rural parts was
made personal by their pulling into yards and coming in the
door to take a look at what wiring would be needed, Missus.
None of the electricians of course were local, the first electrician
in Faha old Tom Lawlor, who had no education only intelligence, who learned it by the antique method of looking, and
operated as unofficial electrician in the years while the trainees
were training, operated after that too when they learned the
first rule of their occupation, which was to be unavailable. The
electricians that came were schooled in the mulish practice of
shaking their heads when they looked at the job that needed
doing. The houses of Faha had a natural resistance to the new.
The interior walls of stone could not be drilled in channels for
the chasing of the wires, and instead would have to wear them
like string dressing. The cables could be housed in plastic, but
it cost extra. The electricians had perfected a tut-tut look and
engineered an air of superiority, leaning on the knowledge that
the local diet was to swallow all complaints except for things
Boolaean. People took the news of their houses' inadequacy
the way they did their penance, stoically. The cold assess-
ments of the strangers in their homes – 'Where does this door
go?', 'Does that table have to go there?' – were met with shy
acknowledgement and all demands accommodated because
nobody wanted the shame of being told their home was too
backward to receive electricity.

The electrician who came to my grandparents' was a long narrow strip with a tight mouth and slits of eyes. Doady traced him. His people were Purtills out of Tarbert, every one of them got the croup, she said, whatever way they were living. For a thin man, Purtill had a brusque way with him. The way it was, once a parish was declared ready for the final phase, it was a shooting-fish-in-a-barrel time for the electricians, and the more houses they could get wired, the more money they could make and the quicker they could move on. The individual character of the houses was their enemy in this, the character of the individuals in them another.

There was no actual electricity yet, mind. There would be an announced switch-on once the whole parish was wired.

Purtill posted his tongue out the corner of his lips while he considered the crooked kitchen. He banged his right boot on the floor, as though testing it was still true that flagstone didn't give. He went to the parlour door followed by my grandmother. He made the simplest thing sound outrageous: 'You want light in here, I suppose?'

'Yes please.'

The tongue moved some and the head shook slowly, words were spared. Although mostly silent, Purtill had a manner that was like he was salting your ancestors. His range of response went from *Could be a problem* to *Would take a small miracle.* He came back into the kitchen and felt the wall. He looked up at the temporary ceiling Ganga had built forty years earlier and which doubled as the flooring in my bedroom.

'Light up there?'

'Yes please.'

He took the small-miracle look up the Captain's Ladder. His boot stamped the floor up there and snowed the dust of her childbearing years on Doady and me. When Purtill came back down the tongue was posted out the far corner and in a coroner's tone he delivered a bleak verdict: 'That place is about to fall down.'

To which Doady didn't blink, but responded with a Kerrywoman's peninsular intransigence, 'Put a light in it all the same.'

As if accompanied by an invisible assistant, Purtill walked around the rooms, itemising, 'One bulb here, one light switch here, one socket,' affixing them with his gaze and leading my grandmother to look carefully to be assured virtual reality hadn't yet been invented and that they weren't already in place. A single light bulb was the most any room could want. *You wouldn't want it too bright*, a common judgement.

'Where will you put the Sacred Heart?'

Purtill cast the slit eyes along the ceiling. 'I'll put Him there.'

'We usually have His picture here.'

'He can stay there. The lamp will be over here, near the door. He can look across at it.'

Doady's blinking eyes didn't see the humour. Purtill moved away from them, he tapped the wainscot boards overhead the kitchen door. 'Your meter will be here. Light switch here.' A pencil materialised from under the hair that covered the top of his ear. He drew an X on the wall. 'Socket here.' Another X.

There was something of the slapdash about the way Purtill operated. The positions of the light switches were decided by his own height and reach. He put out his arm to where the switch would suit him, and that's where the X went. That my grandmother was much shorter than him didn't come into it. Either way he left his mark on the parish, and for years to come you could step inside a kitchen, find the light bulb hanging off-centre, the switch high as your shoulder, or higher still because that's the amount of wire Purtill had to spare – 'You can step on a stool and switch her on there, just as handy' – and the small gods of three-eyed sockets could be located anywhere. It was not unusual for a shelf for the kettle to be built in the immediate wake of the kettle socket going in along a no-man's-land of wall, and not unusual for these shelves, which had to be improvised at short order, to be uncarpentered constructs variously and ingeniously propped, tied, glued and hanging off stone walls whose last dignity was to refuse to be screwed.

Supposing homeowners would want to show off they lived in modern times, the socket was put in plain sight, a policy that in those doughty houses of earlier centuries would soon give birth to the Faha caution *Mind the wire*, rooms taking on the look of an elderly patient, resigned to wearing tubing, but liking it not one bit. By the time Bourke's and Clohessy's started selling adapters, the one socket in the kitchen becoming a kind of extemporised power station, men confirming their stereotype by finding sticking things into holes irresistible, one adapter going into another, and that into another, and fuse-blowing commonplace, well, by then it would be too late to call back Purtill.

Having X-ed all the rooms of the house, he was standing in the kitchen doing a tot, 'And seven and three is ten and two is twelve, and…' when Ganga came in with Joe. He was in his suit trousers and wellingtons, tops cuffed on account of the heat, and shirtsleeves rolled. His round face was florid, eyes shining.

'This is Mr Purtill, he's—'

'I've lost my place,' Purtill said, and went back up the sum in his mind, one finger pointing vaguely at invisible bulbs and sockets and ticking them off the mental audit.

Ganga was just smiling at him. He let the man do his business, one hand dropping down and making a small rubbing on the top of Joe's head. Joe's head had a way of always being under his hand. Ganga never needed to look down, he dropped the hand and scratched and the head was there. It was an arrangement they had, and when it happened here there was complicity in it, as though they'd both discussed the scene beforehand, worked out how it would go, and the hand was just saying *Hold on, hold on a bit, Joe* and all the time my grandfather's face just beaming away like he couldn't be happier, like Purtill was the Pope come to call.

'Not a straightforward job,' Purtill said. He let his slit eyes tell a vexed story. He was too skinny to amplify it, but from the back lean of his posture it was clear he mightn't be going forward, and in the balance was the possibility that my grandparents' house was too contrary for modernity. 'Not straightforward at all,' he agreed with himself.

The kitchen window was ablaze with afternoon light, the pendulum of the grandfather clock pending and pulsing in the timber throat of it.

'May be unforeseen expenses too,' Purtill said, and then defiled the adjective by adding, 'but there always is.'

Through the reflective moons of her round-rims, Doady blinked at him.

'I might as well make a start anyway,' Purtill said, and made the move to go out past my grandfather who stopped him with a short delivery in the plain style.

'There's no need.'

Purtill took a tone he employed on the dim. 'I don't start today you could go down the list.' And when that brought no immediate response, he underlined himself, 'I'd be gone. Don't know when I'd be back.'

'That's grand,' Ganga said, still beaming away, like this was the good news, like he'd been filled with it for a while now and had shared it with Joe and all the time been waiting for this moment when at last, with no trace of rancour or choler but with a kind of free-falling bliss, he could close the door on the future and announce: 'We're not taking it.'

37

Without further debate, the forum on the future ended there, and soon enough Purtill took himself off, leaving his Xs on the walls, where they'd be slow enough in fading. But I recall no argument between Doady and Ganga in the immediate after. That may be a weak spot in this poor act of resurrection, or my deaf blindness at the time to everything but my date with the Mars on the coming Friday.

In the lead-up, you can imagine the state of me. Add to it something of Haulie Ryan, who at fifty-two believed his parts had become fused by rust, the oil to free them not invented, until he met Marie Costello. And add to that a small bit of Jack Dunne who discovered a convex irony in creation, because up close all the things he most disliked about his wife Sheila when she was living were the things he missed most when she was dead.

On top of these, the out-and-out saintly beauty of Sophie Troy.

That Friday evening, as I was once more walking up the avenue, I think the final argument of my case for the defence was that I would take Charlie to the pictures but see Sophie when she came down to determine who the visitor was, and, like those in the films whose lines have been cut, my eyes would declare me.

The hackney drove up the avenue, Heaney adhering to the letter of his hire contract by not picking up the unpaying and once more honouring the coachman's code by acknowledging in no way last week's history of ravishment. He let the cloud of his dust speak on his personal behalf. He had pulled up at the foot of the steps and was idling as before, window rolled down and that same one elbow out that was so characteristic that McCarthy would consider accommodating it when they put him in the coffin. Heaney didn't turn the hair-cloud to look at me and I responded with a proprietary air, taking the steps quick and firm with an invented entitlement I instantly betrayed by pressing the door-pull like a stranger, following up with a too-loud hammering of the knocker.

I had a moment when I thought the doctor would open the door, another when he'd open it with his shotgun. The surgery was a citadel, but also came with a reputation for doom. *You probably caught it at the surgery* one of Faha's accepted wisdoms, following a cross-eyed unorthodoxy that people left their illnesses there like old rags to be picked up by whoever came next. Also, there were many whose last known appearance in Faha was at the surgery. *She went to the surgery* a calamitous pronouncement which meant that soon enough the choir would be put on standby for the funeral.

Sophie opened the door.

All of me knelt down. All of me bowed. Inside the chapel of myself, all my candles lit.

When Sophie Troy opened the door I lost language, I lost all bearings, and instead of kneeling and bowing, instead of the operatic gestures that belonged to the fervent, instead of a gloss-eyed poetry, I stood on the top step in the trouba-dour's shirt and said the thing I least wanted to: 'I'm here for Charlie.'

A quick furrow came on her serious brow, she kept the door half-closed against herself.

'She asked me. Last week.'

This didn't open the door. There was a further moment in which Sophie accommodated this news within the knowledge she already had of her sister, this next proof of the breathless and inconceivable recklessness of Charlie, and of which, vexingly, in equal measure, she disapproved and admired. 'You better come in.'

I stepped inside the furniture chaos of the front hall where the tennis net remained part floormat, part bench-occupant, its entanglement made worse by time and the discovery that it had been stored in a press with the netting for the fruit bushes, and by proximity and like-mindedness, they had married. Not to betray myself, I treated everything in Avalon as though it were the norm and stood on the net, its mouths taking my heels.

'In here.'

Sophie pointed into the drawing room. She had already picked up the book she had left down to open the door, and that was where her interest lay.

I like to think I was about to say *Can I speak with you?*

But I didn't, because as I came to the drawing room, she said, 'This is Eugene,' and stood a little to the side, a look in her eyes that wasn't exactly mischief, but play, and perhaps the entire history of her dynamic with an unlicensed sister.

There was no time to consider it, I was face-to-face with an America of teeth, coast-to-coast and sea-to-shining-sea, whose immediate effect was to make you keep your mouth closed on your own peninsular coastline.

'Sorry. Who are you?'

He was broad and fleshy and friendly with an open look. Not overly burdened by intelligence is a Fahaean phrase. He had a head of black curls and pursed pink lips. His eyes were the polished buttons of someone for whom the world has gone to plan. His suit was navy, his tie claret, his shoes tan, and the whole combined in an ensemble of adulthood that not only seemed much older, but in fact beyond me.

'Noe.'

'I'm being stupid. No, you don't have a name?'

'I'm called Noe, for Noel.'

'How do you do.' He shook my hand as though we were business partners.

Sophie was still standing inside the door, affixed to coming-on calamity. She had a scientist's cool regard for the free-for-all of her sister's love life and kept her finger paused in the book a moment longer.

'Who are you here for?'

There may have been quick or clever and witty answers. I knew none of them.

'He's here for me,' Ronnie said.

She had the knack of rescue and had been called on often I realised at that moment. She had materialised in the room the way good fortune might. I couldn't manage any words. The lie of course was unquestioned, because of the gravity of her person and her grown-up air of responsibility. She kept not only this household together, but the world, was what I was thinking. She managed everything, her father, the patients, the house, one wild sister, and one saintly one. She was not in any obvious way as beautiful as either, but there was a kind of steady and certain grace in her and the melancholy that people call wisdom.

'Hello.'

'Excellent,' Eugene said. Things always went swimmingly. He shone some America.

'You're all healed?' Ronnie asked.

'Nearly,' I replied, but the question was for him.

'Couldn't wait any longer,' Eugene said and raised his eyebrows in a pantomime *oh-oh*, as though he'd said a rude thing, and maybe he had, but it was all right among us chaps.

'Huge?' Charlie's heels clacked down the stairs.

Eugene chuckled at the calling of his nickname.

Sophie's eyes flashed a look at me not to betray either of her sisters. Then Charlie marched in and I was in a room with the three Troy sisters and as far out of my life as I had known.

'Oh, hello,' Charlie said. For one second, we exchanged looks, the rate not in my favour, I was left mostly with ashes. 'We can't dawdle, we'll be late, don't wait up, come on, Huge.'

He clicked the fingers of both hands, and came to her. 'Nice to meet you, Niall,' he said in passing, and none of us corrected him, and they sailed out the door like fabulous creatures from another world.

(In three years they would be married, a June day that would disappoint Faha, because the anticipation Faha felt on first reading of the engagement, *Doctor Jack Troy, Esq. of Avalon House is pleased to announce*, was swiftly knocked down by the news the wedding would not be in the parish. Already, there had been a flurry of planning. The paper with the announcement not yet a day old and, all of a shot, Mrs Queally had taken her big button to the florist's in town. She managed four ways to slip the phrase *society wedding* into the conversation on the bus. At the florist's she let *distinguished Limerick family* out, and sent a single nod after it, letting that speak to how beautiful the arrangements would need to be. There was talk of concelebration, there was talk of the Bishop, and of Handel, the choir was mustered and put on a regimen of double nights, all before Dilly Walsh who was all the time trying to escape the blessing of her fecundity came from the surgery two weeks later and delivered a three-word *coup de grâce*, "Tisn't on here.' In the event, not to lose face, Mrs Queally didn't cancel the flowers. A Fahaean solution was found whereby a floral archway, in name anyway, was built at the foot of the avenue to Avalon and the choir assembled and sang Handel in the rain when, in a hired dark green Riley car with biscuit leather, Heaney, in full wedding regalia, boutonnière and what-have-you, comedy of chauffeur's cap atop the cloud, drove the doctor and the bride out the gates on their way to Limerick, and Charlie delivered a slow Queen's wave that was part acknowledgement of retinue and part farewell and inspired John P's immemorial assessment, 'She's pure thoroughbred,' and the doctor was said to have just the trace of a smile lurking in the moustache, maybe because after a long-fought battle with a lawless daughter he could see the end in sight, and two hours later at the Redemptorist Church of Mount Saint Alphonsus he would hear it too, when Mr Eugene Hart would step forward, take his bride's hand and say *I take thee, Charlotte*, and Charlie Troy would be no more.)

'She's just terrible,' Sophie said. 'Terrible, terrible, terrible.' Verdict delivered, she turned and walked out of the drawing room with her book.

'I'm sorry,' Ronnie said.

'No. It's fine. It was my mistake. I misunderstood.'

She smiled at that, how Charlie was always forgiven. Her smile did to her face what May does to a garden. 'Can you help me hang up the tennis net?'

An hour later, after much tugging, winching, more tugging, one winder snapping at the moment of tension, a falling down, laughter, an agreement between Ronnie and me to declare regulation standard a net with an irredeemable bow in the centre, I walked down the avenue in a suffused evening sunlight, knowing that two things were now certain. I would never again set foot inside the Mars. And my doom was complete, I was in love with the three Troy sisters.

38

Maybe I didn't know it then, I'm pretty sure I didn't. Didn't know that there are times in a life that pass but retain a gleaming, which means they never die, and the light of them is in you still. There are many consolations in having a convulsed heart. Among them is being attuned to the music of everyday and awake to all that is shining, stirring, pulsing. I was not sad walking down the avenue from Avalon past the great trees in full leaf, their green heads full of birdsong. I felt not captured but freed. A door had opened, and the world was larger, fuller, more varied, complex and rich than it was when I walked up there. I also had a first understanding that, contrary to science, the heart expands more than it contracts.

Some of it too was that a shift had taken place inside me. I understood that I would not be marrying Sophie, Charlie or Ronnie Troy, but could love them all the same, and be happy in the misery of that.

All of which to say I came past the ditches noticing the knuckles of the blackthorns ruptured with blossom, and up into the village with the light step of the open-hearted.

The evenings that fell then were like embroidered cloths, warm and blue before the stars came out, a living embodiment of the soft permissive comfort in the sound *May*. Say it and you sound the evening coming down over Faha and the fields about, the cattle standing in them and the river behind the street wearing the navy sky like a favoured scarf. *May*. A sound that comes around you. A sound that has your mother in it.

Church Street was still as a picture. Ryan's dog lying outside Ryan's, Bourke's car outside Bourke's, and Clohessy's outside Clohessy's, two tractors outside Dolan's, too early yet for the main clientele who would squeeze the last from the extension of the daylight, not travelling out until the gloaming. Down the cracked slope of the churchyard, St Cecelia's had its doors closed but a lamp burning. The doors were closed but never locked then. The church had an inviolable status, and Tom Joyce the sacristan had finally conceded to Father Coffey's misguided or enlightened policy of never turning the key (and not telling Father Tom). Sin has no opening or closing hours, was Father Coffey's chilling dictum. To have any chance of a fair fight, neither should the mother church.

Because of a switched-on feeling and a May-time rapture, because of that same helpless longing to make the plot come out right that would accompany me through all my days, see me into and out of all the unscripted tumult, joys and mistakes that constitute a lived life, I stopped at the chemist's door.

When you're three inches off the ground, you don't see the potholes. I rapped on the door with the confident knuckles of a nuncio. Ryan's dog lifted his head to see if there was going to be singing.

I had no speech prepared. I had a shining. That would do for a starter, the rest would follow.

Inside the darkened shop a lamp came. The Yale lock turned and the door opened.

Doctor Troy looked at me. He was a man of few expressions. He had maybe five, all of which were cousins, and all of which involved moustache and eyebrows. His eyes had more weariness in them than any I had seen. They were deep and small and still, as though they were less for looking out than looking in, what he saw outside being swiftly accommodated into the general and ever-expanding category called humanity. Holding the door open, his eyes were saying *You?* and his moustache was saying it too, or something worse. Doctor Troy didn't move. Like Sophie earlier, he kept the door ajar and I had the second sensation of a Rubicon.

'Miss Mooney told me to call.'

'Miss Mooney?'

'Mrs Gaffney. She told me to.'

The moustache said something back to that. It wasn't repeatable. The doctor was likely revisiting his last sighting of me, slinking away after the evening with his daughter, adding this to the idiot who dived head-first off the Captain's Ladder, the three-day tramper at the gates, and the poor dimwit who tried to catch an electric pole, and he was caught between a sponge of pity and punching me in the face.

'She asked you to call?'

'Yes.'

'When?'

'Last time I called.'

'You're...?'

'A friend.'

He didn't move. His eyes didn't leave mine. He used one of the other expressions, in which his tongue pressed one side of his cheek. Then he held open the door.

'Thank you.'

He locked the door behind us and we went through the shop and at the doorway into the sitting room he said, 'She's up here.'

Doctor Troy was standing at the bottom of the stairs in the grey suit and waistcoat, revealing no more than he did any other time, but changing the air all the same. I looked at him. He gave nothing back but a dolorous gravity, and I went past him up the stairs, with each step aware of the weight of dread.

The door into the bedroom he'd left open. Annie was sitting in the bed, lying back against the pillows, her hands flat on the bedspread and her hair combed out long. From pain, her eyes were glistening. The same parentheses of the wince-smile came around her mouth when she saw me and I knew what I hadn't realised I'd known all along.

'You're not to tell him,' she said.

39

I went into the church that night. I don't mind admitting it. Desperation makes up its own rules, and I had been in a like place before.

After my mother fell the last time, she lived between chair and bed. She didn't complain. The fact that she didn't made it worse, because her suffering was clear and cruel, and I couldn't reconcile it. She lost her spirit-level, the world became unbalanced. If she stood up she felt she was falling down. She described the alarm of it, but without upset, it was just what was happening to her, and she thought if she didn't stand for a time the world would straighten up. Bernadette and Saint Teresa of Ávila were the prayer cards Mother Acquin sent and they were by the bed.

The tremors that came in my mother's hands she hid by a tactic of rosary beads. She picked them off the bedspread and twisted them in her fingers while I told her about my school day. Her teacup she didn't pick up until I'd left the bedroom. One day I came in and she was sleeping, and half under her pillow I found the pages. They were a white pad from my father's office, and on page after page was my mother's signature. Only it wasn't hers. Her handwriting was drunk, the letters toppling on to and into each other. Each time she wrote it her signature was less recognisable to herself. She had tried with different pens, tried with two hands, one holding the other, she had tried each letter separately, with infinite slowness in the dead of the winter afternoon, tried with all she had to keep her identity upright, but her signature kept falling over and by the last attempts it was the writing of a bird. She was too embarrassed by it to say anything, and I didn't say anything, and my father didn't say anything.

But soon enough the shake of her hands was betrayed by buttons. She couldn't dress herself. There was a day when my father and I brought her down the stairs between us to take her to a specialist in town. Her body felt disassembled. It felt as though only the worsted stuff of her dress kept her parts together. Her head went back. There was a day too when her words started buckling, and when she heard them she looked puzzled, as though to say *Who was speaking like that?* And when it happened again, she looked down at the space where the words had come out as though to see the mangled shape of them and figure out what it was she was doing wrong.

And so, gradually then, I understood that the systems of my mother were shutting down one after the other. She was going into a still and silent place, and only her eyes were the same. They had a wet look and watered from the corners and sometimes I dabbed them, and sometimes I didn't want to draw attention and pretended my mother's face was not softly weeping while I sat beside her.

In the same way the illness had come, I believed it could go. Mystery is in everything. What I did then I think any boy with a dying mother would have done, I negotiated with God. I started praying all the prayers I knew. When they made no difference, I looked up other ones, as though there was a combination I needed to crack. I'd pray them at night and in the morning look in on my mother before going to school to see if there was a change. In case the distance between heaven and earth was great and it took the prayers time to get there and time for the blessing to arrive, I'd check when I came home too.

One day, sitting beside my mother, her eyes softly weeping, I realised it was going to take more than prayers.

'I know you can hear me, Mam.'

Her eyes were a pale blue-green and they bore a look of acceptance I never saw again in this world. She was *in there*, was the thing that struck you. She was inside the prison of her body, and she was thinking and feeling and had no way left to get any of it out but for the steady watering of her eyes. And there was no way for me to help her.

There may be sons who would have been better able to bear it than me. My life has had many sufferings, but none equal to that.

'I'm going to become a priest,' I said.

She closed her eyes. Just closed them for a second or two, then opened them again. But it was enough. I felt the distance between heaven and earth was maybe not so far, my promise was heard, and my mother's suffering would come to an end.

I wasn't finished the first year in the seminary when she died.

———

I went into St Cecelia's that night not to pray that Annie Mooney would recover. I knew she would not, and Doctor Troy knew it and she knew it too. I went because grief has to find a home, has to find a place to settle, or the dark wings will overwhelm you and you will fall down in the road. I went into St Cecelia's because when you come face-to-face with suffering you have to negotiate.

I lit all the candles there were on the tabular metalwork before the statue of Saint Francis. I hadn't the coins for them, but I had another ten-shilling note from Ganga for the Mars and I posted that there, then I knelt into the pew furthest from the altar and looked up.

'It's me,' I said.

40

In time, Sophie Troy left Faha to go into medicine, and by a roundabout route, first becoming a nurse, after thirteen years she eventually qualified as a doctor in England, and soon after went to Africa and married a French medic she met there, and that's where I lost track of her.

Ronnie, I had a good few conversations with, she was the easiest person I ever met to talk to, and we went to the sea a few times and once took the train together, and I loved what I would call the soul of her, which was gentle and wise and kind and forgiving, and I'm not sure I ever met anyone as honest or good. But she had no love for me and couldn't pretend she had. She took care of the doctor when his mind started straying, and she cared for him in the falling-down house until he died and all of seven parishes came to the funeral, and to have something to live on she sold the house after that, and went to the city, but I was gone from Faha by then, and didn't see her again.

———

In the days following, still bright and blue and with no sign yet of the clouds returning, I called to the chemist's to see Annie Mooney. Because the people of Faha were used to having to invent a way to live, they got around the fact that their chemist was indisposed by a three-part solution. Mrs Queally did stand-in to keep the general customers served, and when she was unavailable an honesty tab operated for self-service, and once a day when he came to check on the patient, Doctor Troy filled the prescriptions himself and left them ready for pick-up. Annie was not bedbound the whole time. Whether from medicaments or defiance, she'd rally and dress herself and appear stiffly in the sitting room or in the shop and when her health was enquired about she'd smile the gentle half-wince and say she was just getting over it. Faha was not told the extent of it. The only people who knew were the doctor and Father Coffey and, by unaccountable good or bad fortune, me. Annie was one of those people who believe in signs, she told Father Coffey when he asked why I was there. He had the grace not to argue against something older than Christ, recalled the sacristan telling him all the candles in the church had been lit, and turned the blazoned cheeks towards me to see evidence of signpost. I didn't understand it, but neither did I argue against it. An unsaid understand-ing, born out of being in the company of suffering, meant the three of us, doctor, priest and me, were in a conspiracy of silence. Cancer was not a word in such common usage as now. People had a complaint, and then a worrying complaint, and then a bad one and then a very bad one, going around the naming as if to take from it some of its power, but there was still a seemingly inevitable declension in it. Annie had been to the hospital and had the tests that told her what she already knew. She had chosen not to stay in one of the places of care but to return to her own house in Faha to die.

The nature of her illness was subtle and ubiquitous. She had knives of pain in her back, now in her hips, now in all the joints of her. She had tumbling twists of a fawn nausea that came from nowhere and were signalled by her putting her hand on her stomach as though to still what was happening or hold there what seemed against her will to be rolling away. Her appetite was gone to someone else. She only realised it was teatime when I said it, and once, in a funereal humour, said, 'I can't remember, is it feed or starve the dying?' She laughed the soft laugh she had and her eyes, I've already spoken about her eyes, I can't make you see them, they looked at you and you felt seen. I know that sounds foolish, it's not.

And what was I doing there those days? The truth is, I wasn't sure, only that I needed to be. We all have our own reasons, most of which are subterranean, for wanting to try and do something. I didn't compute or calculate it. I just left the house in the mid-morning and walked to Faha, the electric vans and the crews hurtling past me in their conqueror's dust and the cows letting on to the fringe of their oblivion the knowledge their watering holes were dry. To Mrs Queally I had the licence of near or paused priest. She thought of me as Father Coffey's stand-in the same way she was for Mrs Gaffney and didn't question when I passed through the shop and up the stairs. The first time, Annie instantly erased my awkwardness by a benign look and the kindest sentence: 'I'm glad you came.'

Why that should be was harder to say. Some ends can be joined obscurely is the closest I can get.

I made tea, I made toast, of which she ate a bird's portion. I helped her move from the bed to the chair when, with an unfairness God must answer for, the bones of her ached from doing nothing. Sometimes she could walk, sometimes she couldn't. By the third day we had evolved the rules of engagement, when, with a single nod, she would let me help, and when she wouldn't. By the end of the first week, the rules proved written on water and she nodded more often, becoming aware that an endless humility was what was required of us in the last act. At those moments, getting my arm around the thinness of her, feeling, say, the cool quick-to-crease crêpe of her skin, trying to get close enough for my body to provide support, at the same time as trying not to make obvious her doll's helplessness, it seemed to me that in those moments in the long-windowed rooms above the chemist's in Church Street, Faha, we were in the naked heart of one of the fundaments of humanity.

By the parallel genius that underlies the caring profession, the indignities, awkwardness and embarrassments of physical failure were made easier for her because I was a stranger.

I answered Annie's questions about the day outside, about where the electricity crews were, and about myself, which last made dawn on me that it's only when someone asks you about yourself that you exist in the fourth dimension of a story. In none of this do I wish to pretend that I was any more assistance to her than anyone else might have been. I know I wasn't. I know I was each day singed some more by the terrible knowledge that I could not truly help her, that she was dying in the same slow way most people die, minute by minute and day by day.

Soon enough of course, Faha knew it, and Doady and Ganga knew it, and soon enough after that, I suppose, Christy did. I didn't tell him, but he was about in the parish enough and by that time the news was in the air. One evening after supper in the garden he asked Doady if it was true and she confirmed and confounded the situation in the same breath.

'It is, ask Noe sure, he calls to see her most days.'

His look would defeat the Dutch masters. He said no more until we were out of the townland on the bicycles on the crepuscular hunt for music. He introduced it using the short form: 'Annie?'

'Yes.'

A hill announced itself and we dismounted, the clicking of the bicycles and Christy's breathy recovery the only sounds. There was no moon, the rumbled dark of the country thereabouts like the abandoned blankets of a giant. The electricity was imminent but not yet switched on, the farmhouses and all human presence erased by the night.

'You didn't tell me?'

'She said not to.'

I knew that hurt him. I knew he was too big-hearted a man not to be pierced by that, but he showed it only by a small movement in his mouth and a palming of his beard, because he wanted to get to something more important.

'How ill is she?'

'Doctor Troy says she hasn't long.' His look said that wasn't possible and so I added, 'She's dying.'

The moment you say the words out loud they become real. Until then, you can think them, you can understand the medical fact, be clear and honest and rational, but because of a benevolent crimp in our nature, some part of you is still holding on to the possibility of hope. Some part of you is informed by the knowledge that the unlikely history of all of us everywhere has given birth to the single truth: *You never know.* But when you say *She's dying* out loud the words become a thing hard and cold and beyond negotiation, and it knocked down the walls of Christy's personality and he stopped on the road and I stopped beside him, and then, as though the air was going out of both tyres, he led the bike over to the ditch and laid it there and leaned against the bit of a broken wall. I pulled over beside him.

We stayed quiet and small in the immensity of dark.
And that, as they say, was that night.

———————

The days after that, Christy was drawn into himself. He lost some of the life of him, and for a time I thought it was going out of him at the same rate as it was going out of Annie. He knew I was continuing to visit her, but he asked nothing of me. Still, I felt a responsibility of bridges, to join both sides. I knew if I asked Annie if he could visit she'd say absolutely not. Despite the ravages that were apparent in her in the early morning, she hadn't lost her woman's right to choose how she looked to the world and retained a preserved dignity that made visitors unwelcome. 'What a fright I am,' she'd say, not with an exclamation mark, but with mixed awe and appal and the surprised smile of being an eyewitness to yourself. She'd pull the cuffs of her cardigan down over the thinness of her wrists to hide their reminders from herself. No, I knew she wouldn't want Christy to come, and so I didn't press her.

When I wasn't at the chemist's I was playing the fiddle in the garden to an audience of cuckoos. They had come again from Africa, a return so welcomed by the old people that it wasn't until I grew to this age that I fully understood it: it was the signal you had survived another winter. In the song of the cuckoo was embedded the simple joy of existence and because the bird was unseen and the song's two notes travelling from treetops it had the air of nature's telegraph. 'Great year for cuckoos' was Mick Finch's catchphrase, his surname lending him the authority of a cousin.

If, a year earlier, you had foretold a spring and summer of unparalleled sunshine, people would have told you they'd give their right arm for it. (Tim Kelly would have given you a small child.) But, because of a flaw in creation, even paradise became monotonous, and soon enough the heatwave had outworn its novelty. A new strand of Saharan complaint came to the parish, and in Clohessy's Mary Mulvey offered the Lord a suggestion to improve on His work, 'He should take the sunshine away for a few days to those that needs it, then bring it back again.'

As part of his pastoral duties, Father Coffey visited Annie a few times each week. She had been a regular Mass-goer same as everyone else, but she kept her religion in a tight box and made clear she didn't want any praying over her. There were to be no visits from the Legion, no rosaries, no holy candles. 'People die, I'm dying' was her précis of a philosophy of life factual and finite, and to be fair to him Father Coffey didn't try any funny business to come around her. He'd make his visit – 'How are we today, Annie?' 'Still dying, Father, how are you?' – and sit and have tea and biscuits, backhanding the crumbs off his trouser leg, and tell her about other parishioners he was calling on and that way keep her up-to-date on the illnesses going around, most of which were long-standing and with which she was familiar from the custom of the shop. Keeping her up-to-date was his version of saying *You're still among us*, and she got that I think, and listened, and sometimes when one of those sudden sleeps of medication or exhaustion would overtake her, he'd pause the update and wait, and when she'd return with a start he'd carry on without comment and in that be a testament to the Christian.

He didn't question me about myself or interrogate the state of my soul. I hadn't appeared again at his altar-rails. But, from his time in the parish so far, Father Coffey had taken a wisdom that wasn't in too many priests then, which was: leave things be.

Doctor Troy of course called every day. He looked at me as though I were an armchair in the wrong room. I would move out when he came in, and after, when he was leaving, he'd pass me the same look in the hallway. He had the fierce all-knowing all-judging eye of God in the Old Testament. A policy of keeping his patients' confidences behind his moustache gave him a frosty demeanour. I didn't mind. I appreciated that he was monitoring Annie closely and, to be honest, I was frightened, frightened when she took a turn, when her head went back into a precipitous sleep or when the pain outmanoeuvred the roadblocks of pills and it was two hours before she was due the reinforcements.

Sometimes there were rallies. I would call and Annie would be sitting up in a silver-grey cardigan and looking as though on pony and trap she had arrived at one of those vistas of grandeur plentiful in Kerry. There was a lightness in her, and at first it was puzzling because of the pain of yesterday. She saw my confusion, but said even pain must sometime take a rest, and recited the dictum of Felix Pilkington, 'Life is a comedy, with sad bits.' If you saw her then you'd fall into the trap of thinking a cure was coming. She'd ask you to pull back the net curtains to let all of the day inside.

From a perceived shortage of fresh air, no window in Faha was closed in that Spanish season, but when you drew aside the curtain it seemed you let in not only the air but a continental sunshine too, and you would not have been surprised if it had been ordered by prescription.

On one such day, Annie slipped away from pain. When I ascended the stairs, she was tidying her things. She wanted everything in order when McCarthy came to carry her to the mortuary, she said. Together then we emptied presses, chests of drawers. With a general's discernment, she would conquer by division, what to the dump, and what to Mrs Queally, who was Faha's artery to the charities in town.

And maybe because of this, because of the nature of time and its war with memory, because, as I know now, as you get towards the end you revisit the beginning, one day Annie Mooney finished going through her clothes, put her two hands on the support of the table, and said the thing I never thought she would.

'Tell me about him.'

41

I can't say I knew what would happen next. By a crossed wire in our brains it's only after a thing happens that you realise you knew it was going to. In this life, *I-could-see-that-coming* and *I-couldn't-see-that-coming* both amount to the same thing, because in neither case did you make a difference. What happened next, I didn't make happen. By no means direct or indirect did I suggest it. I was resolved to my station of visitor, house-caller, tea and toast maker, press emptier, and took a jigsaw solace in fitting in in that small way.

I told Annie about Christy. I told her about his arrival in my grandparents' house, about the work he was doing with the memorial, about our evening cycles seeking Junior Crehan, and also about Christy's singing outside her window.

'I remember,' she said.

'We were watching the curtain to see if it moved.'

She didn't say she was standing just inside it in her night-dress. She didn't say it had sent the heart in her skip to be serenaded by a street-singing out of storybooks. But she said it with her look. Then a realisation came to her.

'You've told him.'

'I had to.'

She winced a wince-smile and a ripple crossed her eyes.

'I'm sorry.'

'It's all right. He's your friend.'

I told her he asked about her. But she didn't stick to convention and enquire what he said, and at no point did I break the rules of our engagement by asking if he could come see her. There was a line there, I didn't approach it. Whenever I finished speaking about him, Annie didn't pass comment. She listened all right. She took it all in, but it felt the way it does when you know you're reading the last pages of a long book and you just need these final bits to complete the picture.

And that came about at my grandparents' a few evenings later.

A draughts tournament was underway out in the garden sometime between the sun going down and the velvet bats appearing. Ganga had a bottomless passion for the game. He played fast and found a confounding comfort in the reoccurrence of old games' mistakes, which he recognised a moment after he had made them. *Janey.* He had two kings to Christy's one and in the endgame the draughtboard had escaped its linear dimensions to become a fluid thing of backwards and forwards chasing that might have continued until forever but for the pulsing of the telephone.

Officially, Doady wasn't interested in the tournament, but she took an overseer's position and watched her husband's playing over a metronomic knitting that no longer required looking. When the phone rang she finished her line and put down the needles. In those days, time still retained elasticity and so you didn't run to the phone. It would ring until you got there. It was news from Kerry or a message for one of the neighbours. The house operated as a poste restante where word could be left, there was a jotter with irreducible pencil stub on the ledge beside the phone, and Doady had evolved a left-handed habit of dabbing the lead on her tongue in preparation to note the news even as her right one picked up the receiver.

It turned out she didn't need to write down anything. Outside, in the clement California of that evening we heard her *Hello?* and a louder *Hello?* her voice going into and down the line as if towards the caller, and then her *Yes* and *That's right* and then she had put down the receiver on the ledge leaving the line open and vulnerable as an infant on its back and come outside with the flutter-pulse that accompanies all events of the heart not just in old age and said to Christy, 'It's for you.'

Three heads turned.

Doady replied to the silent questions with a small back jerk of her head. Then, as though he had the whole of the next chapter, as though it arrived entire in the depths of his eyes, Christy rose from the game and went inside.

To those who hadn't the whole picture, Doady gave the primer: 'It's Mrs Gaffney.'

The evening cocked an ear then, maybe six ears, the air between the black-and-white of the draughtboard and the front door pulled taut to let the talk travel out along it. It was a lopsided exchange, but from Christy's first hard swallow and hesitant *This is Christy* to his near-whispered *Goodnight* nearly two hours later the other side could be imagined and the picture coloured in without going too far outside the margins.

Annie Mooney's first proper conversation with Christy in fifty years began with a blunt declaration: *I don't want to speak about me.* She wanted no acknowledgement of her illness. What she asked instead was for him to pick up the thread where their lives came apart and tell her where he went the day of their wedding.

348

His first words to her were the ones he had been holding in the barrel of his chest for so long they came out in a brine of sorrow:

'Please forgive me.'

Hearing that in the garden, the lenses of Doady's glasses flashed, two discs of the darkening night sky trapped in them, as yet no stars. She had the split reaction of all who come upon an instance of naked confession, not to listen, and to listen harder, and resolved this by picking up her knitting and craning her head back at the same time. Ganga seemed not to be listening at all but hummed a low 'Oh Susanna' and carried on playing the chase of the two kings after the one, playing both sides and still not winning in a game that had arrived in a place of constant motion and stasis both.

Aware of the audience in the falling dark, Christy lowered the receiver and bent his head to it, so he resembled nothing so much as a man speaking to his heart.

'We are too old for tragedy,' Annie said. 'And there is nothing to forgive.'

(Mrs Prendergast on the exchange in the post office had the best vantage and the truest version. She had a telephonist's intuition and a perfect knowledge of the timbre of secrecy in the human register. In the first three words of any conversation coming over the wire she could tell whether this was one worth listening to. She knew the music of yearning in a human voice, and with the headset on had developed a blind woman's sensitivity for sound, could listen into and along the wires, and did so now with her eyes closed and all other lines disconnected, leaving behind her body to go elsewhere through her ears, half a century before it would be commonplace. Mrs Prendergast heard it all. And after, she adhered to the strict privacies of the postman's code and told no one, until she did. Some stories are too good not to be told, was an alibi in Faha. She told it to her sister in Dublin, judging near three hundred miles a safe distance to let the cat out of the bag, but misjudging the legs of a story which started its return journey that same evening when her sister told a friend visiting from the story-bog of the Bog of Allen, Mrs Prendergast not only misjudging the cunning of the cat but the fleas of invention it would pick up along the way back. When, two weeks later, Mary O Donahue leaned into the counter to tell Mrs Prendergast in loud whispers what you wouldn't believe about that electric man above in Crowe's – Christy had been in prison in Mexico, he had seen the alligators sunning themselves on sandy banks and been seduced by bare-chested beauties with black hair and blue tattoos, been in thrall to the valentine bottom of a shopkeeper's wife, had gunpoint or was it knifepoint encounters and was rumoured wanted in three jurisdictions for *I wouldn't like to repeat* – Mrs Prendergast had to resist incrimination by giving the authorised version.)

The night fell and the bats came out and Doady started a rosary at a low volume the Virgin Mary wouldn't mind just this once. At Ganga's feet, Joe sometime snortled, part-sniff part-chortle, in the deep dreams of dogs, but otherwise there was no sound.

As I think I've said, at that time, telephone calls were short, so we kept expecting this one to end. The fact that it didn't already signalled the monumental. The rosary came and went. There was a litany in backup if need be. Doady took up the knitting and knitted some more in the dark, and, with the limits of the board blurred, Ganga kept moving the kings, one-time seeing a huff that didn't exist and another jumping his own piece and declaring victory until he remembered he was white.

When at last Christy hung up and emerged out the front door, he had the unshelled shyness of all who've encountered the naked heart. He had no idea what to say but needn't have worried because the old people had lived long enough to know how to circumvent embarrassment.

'My bed is calling,' Doady said, pressing down on her knees to alert them she was going to stand up after such a long sitting. She threw a hook of a look at Ganga. He was familiar with it and rubbed a quick rub on the back of his neck and stood, acknowledging the genius of Christy's game by telling him, even in absentia, 'You won.'

'I think I'll walk a while,' Christy said.

He went across the yard and out the gate that couldn't close and down the road in the direction of Considine's, what of his way he could see, hard to say, because there was no moon and he took no lamp, the red tip of his cigarette the only beacon.

When I called to Annie the next day she showed herself a follower of the Fahaean way by saying nothing about what was uppermost. There was no noticeable change in her well-being, by which I mean none I noticed. I knew she knew that I knew, and so on, but we put that knowledge back on the tree and made like the innocent. She was still in the throes of her tidying up and clearing out, and that occupied her until exhaustion came and she had to sit in an armchair. She fell asleep the way children do, as though a switch had been thrown. But she woke the way the old do, with a start, and the momentary puzzlement that she had been taken away without her say-so.

Christy, when he came home in the early evening, kept their lovers' pact of saying nothing. And when the telephone rang that evening he got up ahead of Doady and went to answer it and Ganga chose a soft hopeful 'O now!' from his compendium and let that stand in for all commentary.

This time he didn't have to say *This is Christy* and she didn't have to say *I don't want to talk about myself* because he already knew the way ahead, which was the way of the storyteller, and, as though all day he had kept his finger in the pages, he was able to resume where he had left off when the previous night she had interrupted his account of himself by the elder's admission *I think I fell asleep for a bit there.*

He spoke the same way he had the night before, with his head bent and the words crossing his heart. Here, now, in Annie Mooney, he found the audience I had failed to be for him. Through the shrewdness of age or lover's inspiration, he had already surmised that the way to prolong their reconnection was to invest the telling with vivid details, some of which, when he went to reach for them in memory, were not there, and he had to resort to a politician's ploy of inventing the truth on the spot. As though under the influence of our cycling sojourns along corkscrew bends and crooked boreens, he let the story go down side roads, diversions of no fixed purpose other than the contrary one of going a different way, and soon found he could talk for half an hour and be only a half an hour further along the tale of his life.

Sometimes, by resorting to tricks of flashback, he could end up before where he started.

Now, even Shakespeare needed the agent of applause, and his storytelling would have soon foundered if it were not for the small sounds of encouragement that came down the line from Annie. Her breath was at his ear. Christy listened to it and for it and when it held with attentiveness or sighed like a river or when she laughed the involuntary laugh of surprise at the turn the account had taken, these were lifeblood to the teller and on them the tale grew. That night he kept on until he realised she was asleep and he said her name softly *Annie?*

And then a little louder. And, when she didn't respond, he kept the line open and waited for her nap to pass, listening to the sea's tide of her breath in soft collapse sighing, and when Mrs Prendergast risked tarnishing the patina of her professionalism by coming on to ask, 'Is this call completed?' he said, 'No, thank you,' and she clicked off at the other of the three ends, and the click woke Annie and she said, 'Where were we?'

After the second call, we knew there would be a third. Human beings, after all, are quite simple, and a pleasure found is a pleasure to be repeated. On the third call, I think it was, Christy made his only misstep, and asked: 'Will I come there, to tell you in person?'

Annie's reply had such breathtaking frankness that it would pass into Faha lore and become a byword for woman's acuity and clear-headedness in the face of death.

'Let's not see each other until we are in the next place.'

By that same third call, in order not to be prisoners in the garden, but still not intrude, Ganga and Doady had improvised a code of behaviour that meant Doady could go to check on the fire, could carry in some of the ware, or go fetch her pipe, doing so with eyes but not ears averted and so catching gimlet phrases, *the captain said, 'There is no hope'* or *the snow to my waist* or *the sight of her, in her shift*, which she reported back without comment as she lit up or started on the next ball of wool. Ganga would sometimes go back the road to Bat, and sometimes I took up the fiddle and played, throwing up a perforated screen of music between us and the ruptured pair, consternating Doady a parcel because she couldn't confess to eavesdropping and say *Whist, I can't hear.*

I discovered the tunes made it as far as the village, when, the following day, Annie said: 'You play well.' It was her only reference to the phone calls, and she was the first person outside of the house to hear me play. It had the effect of all praise, it made flourish. I knew I was not good, mind, but I was better than the night before, and better the night after, and knew that sometimes when he had talked himself out on to a peninsula and had no idea where to go next, Christy held up the receiver to the open window and let me be accompaniment.

Some nights the calls were long, some short.

'I have to go now. Goodnight.'

At the end of none did Annie drop the breadcrumb trail and say, 'I will call you tomorrow.' Tomorrow was a presumption she was too clear-sighted to make.

After each call Christy was unable to be still. Some nights we took to the bicycles and went off wordless and full, past the pubs we usually stopped at until breathlessness and the weight of feeling meant we could no further. We went in for just the one and sat in the corner, hoping, by local miracle, Junior Crehan might appear. He didn't. Sometimes there was music, and much of it fine, but Christy was folded up in himself, knowing, as I did, that he was falling in love with Annie Mooney all over again.

42

One day after the next, the sun went through a wardrobe of pale skies. The miraculous blue, that had lost the name of miracle, was gradually screened behind a series of luminous veils. They were made of cloud, but not called cloud in Faha, because clouds there were the colour of hammered horseshoes and old bruises and these were joined in one continuous stretch without variants. The sky was almost white. It will burn off, was the common verdict. *We might get a drop of rain, and wouldn't that be all right too?*

The sunscreen was welcome. The days were still warm and humid, and still defeated definition among a population who could find no better description than *It's terrible close.* The closeness was both a pressing down from above, and a nearness that was felt but could not be explained in words. It was just *close.*

Annie did not call every night. Because there was no arrangement, no agreement that the call would be resumed the following night at such and such a time, each evening had the same suspended feel while we all waited and played distracted draughts to the vespers of birdsong. The call usually came around eight in the evening, but by female prerogative eight could be nine, could be ten.

The first night she didn't call, Doady secretly went in to check the line was working and wound the winder to get Mrs Prendergast (who was also waiting), and when she came on the line, Doady gave the not only lame but crippled excuse, 'I thought I heard it ringing.'

We sat and waited and said nothing but the same thought went like a needle and thread through each of our minds, *Is Annie all right?*

The following day I went to check. Doctor Troy was with her and Father Coffey was standing hot-faced at the top of the stairs.

'We need to pray for her,' he said.

I was grateful then to have the prayers in me. There have been times throughout my life when I've felt the same, that because of my childhood and education the prayers were things available to me, and I suppose there are few lives that don't encounter moments when all that is available is drawn down and clung to. We stood on the landing both of us. We didn't talk or face each other, but, in a kind of silent accord, we prayed.

When Doctor Troy came out he said, 'Don't tire her.'

We went into the room and Annie upturned our expectations by a gentle smile. 'My gentlemen callers,' she said. 'Will one of you make the tea?'

She was a remarkable woman, and, like all remarkable people, became more so the more you knew her.

'Tomorrow, bring your fiddle,' she said.

She made no reference to why she hadn't telephoned the night before, and I didn't ask.

After I left her I walked down to Avalon and Ronnie opened the door and brought me in for tea. We talked a good two hours on the weed checkerboard that had once been a patio. I wanted to lay my head against her breast. I wanted the world to stop awhile. Neither happened, but when I walked back down the avenue later I felt the workings of a balm.

That evening the telephone pulsed again and Christy fairly ran to it.

'And then…?'

'And then I went to Morocco,' Christy said, not missing the beat, and picking up from where he had left off, in the same way one tune bled into another in *seisiúns* and formed one continuous music, or, as he would become in the fable of this time, the Fahaean Scheherazade.

Inside the front window, he carried on with the telling, and outside in the garden Ganga and Doady and I breathed a little easier. I don't mind admitting that for a time I fell prey to magical thinking, whereby Christy could keep Annie Mooney alive by story, that as long as he was telling and she was listening she wouldn't die, and his account would stretch not only time but reality and keep forever at bay the moment that followed this one.

———

On one of the days around then a car drove into the yard and Harry Rushe landed. He was touring the district ahead of the switch-on. The parish was wired up now and ready and the crews had moved on. Christy was due to leave. Whether for professional or personal reasons, because the Board didn't like to let any household through its fingers, or because he was the kind of man who crossed all his t's, Rushe had run his finger down the column of Faha names that had turned into customers and tapped twice on the NC, Not Connected, against my grandfather's. He recalled his last visit to the house and a small vexation blew up along his gumline. He pressed it with his tongue. It worsened. He felt defied. He put on his hat and went to his car.

The debate between my grandparents as to why Ganga refused to take the electricity never happened. Doady knew her husband too well. She knew which things she could argue, and which she couldn't. She could berate him for all manner of inconsistencies: 'What kind of man puts the knives in with the forks? The spoons, I could find them anywhere!' But this was a fray without casualties. The electricity, she could tell, was not for arguing. Wives have to be wiser than their husbands. She didn't need to say anything to Ganga. She had lived with him so long she could look at his face in profile and read all that was in his head. She knew that it was not backwardness that made him reject the electricity, there were few men who would enjoy the wonders of it more. It was fear of what world they would be hurtled into the moment a switch was flicked. My grandmother understood. She understood the tightrope balance they had sustained for nearly half a century, a topsy-turvy way of living they had made up on the model of their own parents' and grandparents', which had survived the rearing of a dozen tearaway sons in four rooms in a drowned place on the far margin of the world, where belts could be tightened or loosened as needs be, and without anyone's say-so but your own. What Doady knew, without saying a word, was that, within the one-foot-after-the-other confines of that tightrope, they were free.

That she didn't bring up the question of the electricity with my grandfather was an act of love, and marriage.

'Boss at home?' was Rushe's greeting.

I put down the fiddle. Rushe had a deep-fried look, ginger and crispy. He took a planted stance in front of the low fire. He didn't take off his hat. The turf sent a few tongues of smoke towards the draught of him. There were two empty cans of peas sitting in the embers, an egg in each of them. Doady came in from the milking parlour, her hands pressing in a cloth.

'Boss around?'

'He's up the back.'

'I'll get him,' I said.

She offered the courtesies, going for the kettle.

'I won't have tea,' the last thing I heard.

I found Ganga up in the back meadow. He could be in that field, just standing and watching it, at any time, and you couldn't say exactly what he was doing, and if you asked maybe he wouldn't have been able to say, but the sight of him out there alone had a kind of sustenance in it and has remained with me as one of the certain good things in this life.

'Rushe is here,' I told him.

He smiled his round smile.

'Rushe, he wants to see you. He's in the house.'

When we came into the kitchen Rushe was still planted full-square in the same spot. Doady had had to invent a behaviour for a visitor who wouldn't take tea. It was plumping unplump cushions, including the dead one of *Old Moore's Almanac*. She needn't have bothered. Rushe was not for sitting.

'You decided to go against common sense,' was his opener. He pressed his tongue against the gumboil. For an engineer, he had exceptional narrowness of mind, or his focus was so sharp it only saw the one thing straight ahead all the time. At this moment that thing was my grandfather, who was also a gumboil.

Ganga's expression didn't change. It was the same round, open, hopeless hopeful look that had nothing in it but kindness and wonder. 'O now!' he said and bent to scratch Joe's head.

And the moment he said it, the way a light comes on, and shows you clearly the thing you knew was there all along, I realised he was losing his hearing.

When Rushe asked, 'Have ye considered what ye'll be missing?' and Ganga made no reply at all, I realised he had lost it. I looked to my grandmother, and knew at once that she knew, and that the deafness fell inside the pact of them, and it was all I could do not to be overwhelmed by the presence of love.

'We have,' Doady said. 'We're not taking it.'

Rushe had something in him that needed letting off. That's what I thought later. It was not so much that he saw an opponent in my grandfather, but the pressure of rolling out the network and dealing with every kind of unforeseeable delay, doltish and contrary, human and operational, had built up a head of steam that was all but visible hissing past the hairs in his ears.

'Ye'll be in darkness,' he said. The bad timing of the beautiful weather weakened the power of this. He resettled his stance square as a boxer. 'Ye'll be left behind. The rest of the world will move on. Not you. Your neighbours will have it. You won't. You'll be in nothing but hardship and loneliness.' He turned his look from Ganga to Doady. 'Once we leave we won't be coming back.' His eyes were grey stones, there was nothing giving in them.

To cover for her husband's silence, with a Kerrywoman's forthrightness, Doady said, 'We'll go our own way.'

Rushe scrunched up his face to show what the State thought of the individual. To signal a change in tack he pushed the rim of his hat up off the sweatband of his forehead.

'It's not because of the words we exchanged last time?' he asked Ganga. 'It's not against me that you're deciding?'

Ganga was listening hard with his eyes and looked to Doady. It *was* partly against Rushe, and the manner of his interrogation of me, I thought, a thought that made me complicit, and to break the moment I said, 'Will I make tea?'

'I haven't time for tea,' Rushe shot out and heard himself and regretted, it seemed, the persona he had to play, and he probed with his tongue and twisted his shoe a little back and over as though there was a butt smouldering underfoot. And then, because he couldn't abide inconclusion, because of a genuine fear he had overplayed his hand and because in that kitchen we were swaying on a rope bridge between the past and the future, he made his last case succinctly.

'Lookit,' he said. 'In a simple switch on the wall is the end of darkness. Is the end of cold. In a simple switch that could go right there –' he pointed to the same place Purtill had '– right there, the power to end all hardship. Think of it,' he said, looking directly at my grandmother. 'In one switch, all the cures for loneliness.'

Delivered in diamond absolutes, it was an invincible argument. Doady blinked at the brilliance of it. Briefly she wore the look of a woman who had spent twenty years trying to get through another day. She was pressing the swelling of her fingers. She wasn't looking at Ganga. For a moment she couldn't, for a moment the world was unbearable. Two hens came to the door and jerked their heads in twin jerks to attest whether it was safe to come in or not.

Then Ganga, who had heard little that was exact of what had been said, but had already developed a deaf man's intuition for the gist, smacked his hands together, and, turning his round beaming face on us, defeated all arguments by an unassailable conclusion:

'Aren't we happy as we are?'

43

Annie Mooney died in her sleep, Doctor Troy said. The last voice she heard in this world was Christy's. Christy had sat on the sūgán chair Doady had set beside the window for his calls and told her of the morning he woke with the realisation he wanted to be forgiven. Annie had begun to tell him again it wasn't required on her part, but all she managed was *You don't* and let the rest be silence because she found her breath short and knew a story should never be checked. He had told her all the failures of his life had been failures of love. He told her of the compulsion in him to seek out those he had wronged or slighted or ill-judged, those he had harmed through thoughtlessness. He told her he had found some and not others, and when he couldn't find someone he tried to make amends through a stranger. He delivered all this with a light touch, laughing a soft laugh every so often at the comedy of himself and the things a man can think up. Doady and I would hear the laugh come out the window and the open front door and experience the inner *ah-ha* of parents eavesdropping on their son's courtship and believing things were going well. Christy had talked that night for the prescribed two hours with two intermissions when Annie's breathing told him the medications had overwhelmed her. At those times he paused and held the receiver out in his right hand, looking at and into it, as though he could see down the line and see the flesh of her hand on the other end, and see her sitting propped there on the armchair with seven cushions that did not defeat the pain in her back and in her bones, her silver hair combed out, and her eyes wetly shining.

When Annie said, '*And?*' he came out of that dreaming and service resumed. He told his coming back to Ireland and travelling to Kenmare and on to Sneem and what it had felt to be in those places again where there was the strange human pleasure in painful memory. He talked of the streets that were familiar to her, and his making enquiries in the shops there, and when he did, they were young again, and he was a young man in corduroy britches asking about her in Hillary's and her heart was fluttering in the upstairs bedroom of her parents' house when her sister Mina told her. He talked them back to the beginning. He talked them back to where the story had taken a turn.

And this time it didn't. He came in the church in a tweed suit heavy with rain. The shoes of him were squeaking, leaking on the tiles, his forehead gleaming like he was a candle.

'Because there you were,' he said. 'There you were.'

Doady and I heard him say that twice. And after that he said nothing at all.

I have to go now, he told us later, was the last thing she said to him.

Mrs Prendergast called in the morning to let us know the doctor had been and found her. She was in the chair by the phone.

The funeral was enormous. It was one of those funerals when it seems that everyone in seven parishes has put down whatever they were doing to be there. I hadn't much knowledge of country funerals then, but when you came into Faha that morning and saw the gathering, the church overflowing, extra seats and benches of all sorts out the churchyard, the doors of the houses across the way open and people standing and sitting on every surface in the vicinity, the thing that sat in your throat was your heart and the thing you felt I can't do justice to, but it was *We are all part of this* and my participation, however small, felt humbling.

Christy was composed. He was a man who could constantly surprise you and his reaction to Annie's death was not an obvious grief. He had a gift for accepting life, and that included death. That was the thing I was too young to understand. He sat with Ganga and Doady and me in a privileged place Father Coffey had secured for us near the altar. By that time everyone in the parish already knew the fable of the phone calls, and in the absence of family members and close relations, his was the hand that was shaken in condolence. Doctor Troy acknowledged my loss by a tightening of his moustache and a firm press of my fingers. His eyes said *This is the world.* The trinity of Sophie and Charlie and Ronnie was there, each in their own variant of magnificence. They each held my hand lightly a moment and were gone, as was true of their place in my life.

The undertaker, McCarthy, who had a professional expertise for getting the behind-the-scenes story on the deceased, offered Christy a place as pall-bearer, and he took it. Tom Joyce tolling the bell, we all went out behind the coffin into the white screened light of that daytime and paused outside the chemist's shop, standing to attention in Annie's absence, but feeling the presence of her everywhere. Then down the crooked slope of Church Street to the graveyard by the river. The avenue had grown narrower in time as more graves were needed, and, by the necessity of being within earshot of the final prayers, the throng came in over ancient graves, some trying to keep inside the kerbing, and some not so much, until soon the cemetery entire was Faha's most populous place.

Father Coffey did duty for Father Tom whose chest was at him. The sight of him in his white vestments and purple stole against the green fields and running river was something out of earlier times. His voice cracked calling out the prayers, and when I looked over the sea of heads I could see Doady and Ganga, Bat Considine, Mrs Moore, Master Quinn, Mrs Prendergast, Mrs Queally, Mrs Reidy, Mona Ryan squinting, Mary Falsey upright, Matthew Leary kneeling on his grandfather's grave, the Cotters, the Keanes, the Breens, the Blakes, the Hehirs, Heaney the hackney, Greavy the guard, The German, Bubs and Roo, any number of Kelly and Clancy children, Sheila Sullivan dabbing her dribbling son, Mrs Sexton and her hat, the Devitts, Davitts and Dooleys, Murrihys and McInerneys, just outside the gate Mick Madigan, and feel something cracked in them all.

After the prayers, there was a cupped moment. Heads were still bowed. The sunlight was veiled but radiant still, and in that country graveyard it seemed was one of the fundaments of existence, a spirit of community. It sat there, in some part not assuaging but making liveable the harrowing knowledge of *I will not see that person in this life again.*

In a moment, the fringes of the crowd would fray. The shops and the pubs would reopen. Tractors would start up, horses and cars be untethered from the yards at Clohessy's and Bourke's.

But first, there was a raised note in Christy's voice.

It took a second for those who couldn't see the graveside, who were on the point of turning away, to turn back when they understood a man was singing. He sang as he had before, shut-eyed, head back and arms down. He sang the same song he had sung outside her window in the night. He sang it as if no one was listening but her. And all of Faha felt the same. In the face of the raw feeling, through a perfect stillness people made themselves invisible. Christy sang all the verses. He sang as though he was sending the song after her, as though the air and words of it could escape the confines of time and space and soon enough reach the next place where she was gone.

When he finished there was not a sound but for the original ones of river and air.

He and I went that evening on the bicycles as before. We heard music, but we did not hear Junior Crehan.

'I'll be leaving soon,' Christy said.

It felt like a blow you knew was coming but knowing hadn't lessened it.

'I want to thank you,' he said, and patted his breast for the matches.

'There's nothing to thank me for.' I struck the match.

'There is, though. So, thank you.'

We listened to three players. They were two old men and one woman of indeterminate age who played the concertina. They had a natural expertise that made it seem the music wasn't a thing learned. They had no ownership of it either. The tunes were in the air thereabouts. They were theirs only in the same way the fields and the rushes and the rain were.

They were of that place and had both the poverties and richness of it. And perhaps because of the complex of emotions I was feeling that evening, and because none of them could find their way into words, the more the musicians played the more it struck me that Irish music was a language of its own, accommodating expression of ecstasy and rapture and lightness and fun as well as sadness and darkness and loss, and that in its rhythms and repetitions was the trace history of humanity thereabouts, going round and round.

Which, in some ways I suppose, is what I'm trying to do here.

My grandparents never took the electricity. They didn't act as though there was a lack. They carried on as they were, which is the prayer of most people. They lived in that house until they were carried out of it, one after the other. Because the twelve sons in the corners of the world couldn't reach a verdict, the house was left to itself. The thatch started sagging in two places like consternated eyebrows, brambles overtook the potato ridges and came up the garden, and soon enough in under the front door. Soon, you couldn't see the house from the road. Soon, too, the bits of hedging Doady had stuck into the ditch to camouflage the broken Milk of Magnesia bottles grew to twelve feet and fell over and grew along the ground then, marrying thorn bushes and nettles and making of the whole a miry jungle. When the roof fell in the crows that were in the chimney came down to see the songbirds sitting in Ganga's chair eating *Old Moore's* and that way becoming eternal. When grown a man, one of the Kellys took out the kitchen flagstones for a cabin he was making. He took out the stone lintel over the fireplace after, and a year later came back for half the gable when he needed good building stones for a wall.

In time, as with all modest places of few votes, Government would be looking the other way when its policies closed Faha's post office, barracks, primary school, surgery, chemist, and lastly the pubs.

In time, the windmills would be coming. *Gairdín na scoile* and *Páirc na mónaigh* would be bulldozed to straighten the bends in the road to let the turbines pass. Any trees in the way would be taken down. Two- and three-hundred-year-old stone walls would be pushed aside, the councillors, who had never been there, adjudging them in the way of the future.

By that time, my grandparents' house would be another of those tumbledown triangles of mossy masonry you see everywhere in the western countryside, the life that was in them once all but escaping imagining.

———

Christy left the way he had arrived, without fanfare. I felt the loss of him even before he had gone. Which is, I suppose, as good as any a description of love.

I asked him where he would go.

'I have a brother a monk in France. I haven't seen him since I was sixteen.' The chamois face of him crinkled. 'I've a lot more to do before I meet Himself.'

Of all the things I wanted to say to him, I managed none. I gave him the box of matches, I seem to remember. But possibly that didn't happen. As I think I've said, there are some memories you can't lean on. You sense the railings of them but you don't reach out a hand.

He paid Doady the rest of the week and tried to pay her for the rest of the month, but she wouldn't have it. For two weeks she didn't find where he hid the money until Mrs Moore was dusting the willow-patterns. We didn't know he'd cleared the phone bill either. After he was gone, we started hearing stories of the things he'd been doing around the parish. Little by little they would leak out. He was above with Conefrey's one day when Kevin had a mare foaling. He was with Michael Dooley doing the barrow in the bog. He was with Breda and Mary and Eileen Donnellan the time all three were hunting their brother's missing calf. He was cooking daily dinners for Mrs Blackall, from whom he had bought his wedding suit when she had a shop in Kenmare. In his afterlife he grew radiant. What was true and not true hard to distinguish, because in Faha people had an insatiable craving to be part of a good story.

I missed him. I've already said that. I'll say it again. I missed him as much as you can another human being. The night after he left I found the musketeer's shirt under my pillow, with a pencilled note. *Good luck on the hunt for J. C.*

———

I stayed on with Doady and Ganga that summer, trying to figure out where the loose wire of my life could lead. At no point did either of them ask me my intention. Nor did Father Coffey the times he found me in the back pew where my prayer was always the same. *It's me.*

That summer there was a *fleadh* in Miltown and a general gathering of musicians from all corners of Ireland and many come home from elsewhere too. They came like a caravan out of olden times, came on foot and by thumb, by car and van and bus and train, by bicycle and horse and car, carrying their instruments and setting up in every nook and cranny of every pub and house they could find, so that when

I arrived the only problem was where to go first. You heard the music escaping out the windows and the front doors. The horses in the street were listening to it. You went in someone's door in the mid-morning and there were eight musicians of all ages playing on stools, cigarettes smoking and more on a saucer served, the woman of the house unperturbed by a kitchen commandeered in jig-time. They may have been playing since the night before, or the day before, their number growing and diminishing in clock-less time, the only consistency the continuing of the tunes, the glasses, cups, mugs, bottles that lived on every flat surface and never had time to be washed. The players played for each other, listening to and looking at each other's playing, as though all were relations distant and close at the same time, and when I was in their company loneliness was banished.

The second day I went there I brought the fiddle. I didn't come home that night. I may have the night after, but maybe not. Somewhere in Miltown that time, I heard Peggy Healy, Tom McCarthy, Solus Lillis, Patrick Healy, I saw Dan Furey dancing, I heard Micko Dick Murphy playing tin whistle on the bar of a bicycle being carried into town. I heard Cissie and Manus and Josie and Patsy and Sonny, I saw a buck set danced by a crowd come down with Michael Downes from Cloonlaheen on the shores of Doolough, and one evening in a public house out the road by the place called The Hand, I heard a thin man in a dark suit, with an easy, open expression and swept-back hair, playing 'The Mist-Covered Mountains' and that man was Junior Crehan.

O now!

A bird in a tree had brought the tune to him, he said. He played 'The Sheep in the Boat' and other jigs and after he played the hornpipe 'Caisleán an Óir'. The rest I can't be sure of. There was 'The Connaughtman's Rambles' and 'Father O'Flynn' maybe. He was neither showy nor august, but he had the authority of tradition in him and the sense of that place. The feeling of it can't be captured. I kept turning to look at Christy, because we'd done it, we'd found him, and I wanted to see the joy I knew would be in his face.

It was there, even though he wasn't.

Listening to Junior play, a key turned in me and a door opened, just not the one I expected. I knew I could never be a player like that, I lacked that skill and belonging, but knew too that music and story would be part of what I would be.

When Doady said she'd had another letter from Mother Acquin, I told her to write back that I'd heard from my mother and would take it from here myself.

I came and went from Faha the next few years, living the haphazard made-up life of those following their heart. I took the fiddle with me into the wave of the culture just starting to rise at that time. Each time I came back I thought to stay longer, and each time thought I would be back soon.

When I came to America it was to be for a short time, I would be back in Faha before long, but by dint of life and circumstance before long grew longer and Faha further, and going back cannot be done now. It is not a question of time or distance or money or the coming-apart bicycle of an old man's health. It is not because I have fallen three times now and know what lies ahead. The truth is, like all places in the past, it cannot be found any longer. There is no way to get there, except this way. And I am reconciled to that. You live long enough you understand prayers can be answered on a different frequency than the one you were listening for. We all have to find a story to live by and live inside, or we couldn't endure the certainty of suffering. That's how it seems to me.

And so, because, at the end, we all go back to the beginning, because of the enduring example of Christy telling his story down the line to Annie, because after more than sixty years my mind is back in that place among those people from whom I took the lesson of how to be a fully alive human being, I will carry on here, carry on through the electric pulses of this machine to tell the one story we all have, the one we've lived.

44

The 8th of June is the day recorded in the annals above in Dublin for when the parish of Faha was switched on. It says no more than that. It lists all the townlands in the Rural Electrification Scheme and the dates they were connected to the national grid. The last place connected was in 1977.

In Faha, in the week leading up to the switch-on, there was the general commotion that accompanies all one-off ceremonial occasions in small places, the official and unofficial committees, the drawing-up of the guest list, the redrawing of it when the argument was won that political bias should play no part, the seating plan (where political bias could, and did, play), the flowers, the banners, the music, all of which was informed by the consensus on one abiding principle: that Faha do it better than Boola. There would be all the components of the annual village parade, except this time it would not be moving. In the hierarchy of invitations, one had been sent to the Bishop, in whose palace the electricity had been burning for decades, another to the Deputy whose constituents were still hoping to lay eyes on him. The councillors, the nuns, and the priests of other parishes were on Mrs Queally's list.

Knowing well the inner nature of its customers, their sense of history and deep appreciation of any attention from

Dublin, the electricity company promoted the idea that each village mark the moment of connection by a function. The switch-on could have happened at any moment once the wiring was completed, but, with a modern genius for publicity, the Board said they would send a photographer to record the event for posterity, and a cardboard poster. They announced the noon of June 8th as the birthday of electricity in the parish and Rushe sent word to the Master, as Head of Committee, that it would happen in Church Street at the transformer on the pole outside St Cecelia's.

Around this pole of Mr Salovarra from Finland gathered the aura of history. On the days of the lead-up the seating was set out on the slope of the churchyard, facing away from the church. (Father Coffey regretted the symbolism and what it foretold for modern times, but what-to-do?) Those without the privilege of seats could set up opposite in the constitutional places along the walls and windowsills. Strings of triangular flags of blue and gold were strung from the upstairs windows across the street. They were venerable and rain-washed from years of drowned football finals and parades and were bluer and more golden – *saffron*, Felix Pilkington said – than anyone recalled when Tom the sacristan and two of the Kellys hung them in criss-crossed archways beneath a luminous sky. Tipping its cap to modern times, Faha's first, and only, ban on traffic for the day was announced from the altar by Father Coffey. (It was not so much to the few car drivers he was speaking, but to Micko King in the Men's Aisle, who had an outside farm on the other side of the village and was wont to drive his frisky, free-dunging herd through the streets and down the footpaths, the buildings on both sides having a funnel effect and compensating for his lack of drovers.)

All the usual small emergencies arose and were resolved after a Fahaean fashion. There was a hectic day of fierce carpentering when Seamus Nash finally arrived to put up the stage, and another to take it down a level when it was adjudged a hangman's scaffold. There was a motion put forward by the Faha Players that to give the pole the authority of centre stage it should be painted, but the problem of whether to buy the paint in Clohessy's or Bourke's would require a Solomon, and Master Quinn postponed the vote.

Aware that a noontime switch-on in June would lack the theatre of one in winter, the company sent Moylan's van, loaded with electrical machines and any amount of cable, to hook them up. Moylan was in his element. He came the day before to test out the stage. It was better than a country kitchen and allowed for his more expansive gestures. If he had the robe he could have played the Messiah.

When the day finally came, I wasn't sure Doady and Ganga would want to go. Theirs was one of the few houses in the parish not taking the electricity, and I took the shallow view that they would want to turn their backs on the excitement of others. I supposed Ganga would find the bog needed him and Doady disappear into the milking parlour or to one of the many jobs around the house that always had an air of the imperative. After Rushe had left there had been no further debate as far as I knew. There were no arguments, no self-pity on Doady's part, and no regrets. The remarkableness of the old people was without measure. That's a fact. So, I shouldn't have been surprised when, the night of June 7th, Doady put the amateur curlers in.

The next day, at eleven o'clock, New Time, we set out by horse and car to go and see the future. The road into the village was already alive. To allow the children to be eyewitnesses to history, the Master had closed the school. (It was a gesture of grace that outlived him, for in sixty years' time, there were still old men in the parish who could recall the day, being in around the stage and watching Moylan, and running home after to wait impatiently for the dark to fall so they could flick down the pip.) On the roads there were children running, there were whole families moving, bicycles, cars with ten in them, some doing shuttle journeys to pick up some more. On the outskirts of the village, Quinlavin's forge operated as the no-go point and the field next to it a general corral.

As I've said, the fine weather had become so customary as to go unremarked, but the energy of that noontime was doubled by the warmth, and the liveliness of the crowd wore the hall-marks of an outlawed crossroads dance. No one wore a coat. Because of the solemnity of history and respect for engineering, men kept their suit jackets on and endured a lathering sweat. In Mick Liverpool's black-and-white photographs of that day you can't see the sunburn and the freckles of the heatwave, but you can the general glowing, and the smiling pride. They are some of the only surviving photographs of the parish entire, as if it were the last day of community and after this people would stay in their homes among the comforts of an electric solitude.

Half an hour to noon, Church Street was thronged. The shops stayed open, the pubs had forgotten to close. The Bishop, whose stomach had been brutalised from attending switch-ons at parishes east, sent his apologies and a bespoke blessing. One of the councillors papered over the Deputy's failure to appear by a knowing look, a lean-in and the soft-voiced catch-all of 'Matters of State'. Faha didn't mind. The people had lived too long within the wound of neglect to feel the fresh slight. Rushe was there, and Moylan was just off the stage, which was occupied by an unlit standing lamp with no shade, the bare bulb like an exposed eye, a washing machine, a toaster, and an iron on an ironing board. Equally exciting were the cables that came up to and across the stage. (*Isn't there a fine nest of 'em?*)

Another signal of future times, when exactly it was noon was for once not at the discretion of the Church. Rushe had a wristwatch, and he was the one who would give the word. He hadn't the personality for the pantomime. He had a get-in-and-get-out manner and was unsuited to the role of ceremonial general. When Doady and Ganga and I came within sight of the stage, he was waiting for Father Tom to stop talking to his parishioners and take up his position next to the washing machine.

My grandfather had a bottomless love for Faha, and although he himself wasn't taking the electricity he couldn't stop beaming at the marvel of it come to his own parish. 'O now!'

The current of course was already there, and had been for some days, just not switched on. But the theatre was that, at the signal, Rushe would raise and then lower his arm, and at that moment the electricity for Faha would be turned on in the capital at the other side of the country, and in a first demonstration of the actual speed of light, instantly, the light in the standing lamp would come on.

Because of his affinity for dramatics, to get around the glary quality of the day, Moylan had recourse to a magician's know-how and secured a black card to hold up behind the bulb once it lit.

As befitting his seniority, Father Tom was to give the Bishop's blessing. Father Coffey would be standing alongside with three priests from neighbouring parishes and one back from Africa. But when Rushe came and told him it was nearly noon, Father Tom played a round of Church versus State and said the holy-water bottle was empty. Father Tom was an old-time operator and enjoyed the look in Rushe's face. He'd enjoy it again with his tea and Marietta biscuits later with Mrs Prendergast. He himself had the wisdom to know that the thing that came between intention and its execution was life, and that in a place half a century behind the world another ten minutes would be no catastrophe. (The wisdom ran out there because he sent one of the Kellys for the holy water. I don't know which one, at that age they all had the same tadpole face, but whichever it was, he defied all calculations of time and distance and didn't come back, and still didn't, finding a fresh wrong way to do a thing, and Moylan had to announce the hold-up to the crowd but assure them that Dublin was on standby.) It all added to the open-air theatre. Every seat was filled, every vantage point taken. Bourke had outdone Clohessy in ceremonial touches by flying the tricolour, and while waiting for Kelly, children started saluting under it and running away, another coming to it and saluting and running away in turn.

When Kelly came back with his trainee-devil's look and the holy-water bottle was finally loaded, Master Quinn gave a nod to Father Tom who stood to signal his own noontime. He was large and slow with a largeness and slowness decreed fitting, and the hush that fell over the crowd put a glimmer in his eye as he realised that mankind had still failed to kill off Christianity.

The moment Father Tom stood, the crowd pressed forward as one. The people performed the same miracle they did each Sunday in St Cecelia's by moving into a space where there was none.

At an up-nod from Rushe, Moylan was off. 'Reverend Fathers and Sisters, ladies and gentlemen...' He wore the best of his two-toned shoes and spoke as if in an amphitheatre to multitudes. You'd pay money to see him. He said the same things he said in other parishes, which were the same obvious and portentous things you could make up yourself, but the reality of what was about to happen before our eyes lent them gravity.

I looked at my grandfather looking up at the stage. He couldn't hear what was being said, but his face was full of happiness. Doady was holding on to his arm against the jostle of those younger, the suns of her glasses flashing. I don't think I could have loved them more.

And it did not matter that all of this would pass, that's what occurred to me. It didn't matter this time and place would be gone, that these feelings would go to the place of all feelings once pure and complete. It didn't matter that Sophie and Charlie and Ronnie Troy would slip out of my life, and Christy and Annie Mooney, and then Ganga and Doady, that all of them would be gone but be like remembered music or the amassed richness of a lived life. Because at that moment I understood that this in miniature was the world, a connective of human feeling, for the most part by far pulsing with the dream of the betterment of the other, and in this was an invisible current that, despite faults and breakdowns, was all the time being restored and switched back on and was running not because of past or future times but because, all times since beginning and to the end, the signal was still on, still pulsing, and still trying to love.

Father Tom threw the holy water at the pole and said the Bishop's blessing. Harry Rushe held his short arm in the air.

He held it long enough for some to think the twentieth century might not come.

Then he chopped it down through air, and the light bulb in front of the church came on.

There was a gasp. And then ripples of applause that sounded like a tide coming in across stones.

Quickly then, the crowd turned from the church to go inside the shops to see if the electricity had crossed the street. The festivities were curtailed by human curiosity, because soon enough people were hurrying to their own houses. Faha emptied quicker than it filled.

My grandparents, of course, were in no such hurry. By the time Ganga and Doady and I came out to Thomas and the car, Church Street behind us was deserted, the tricolour and the banner flags just starting to flap with the first whisperings of a coming breeze.

We went, unhurried, at one-horse speed, out of the village.

Somewhere just past Considine's I lifted my face. I held out my palm.

It had started raining.

Acknowledgements

It seems to me that everything you read and everyone you meet that inspires or moves you contributes in some way to the book you are writing, so a list here would be as long as the book itself. But among the many books that have gone into this one, I would like to acknowledge *The Quiet Revolution: The Electrification of Rural Ireland* by Michael Shiel, a book my father gave me, and Barry Taylor's superb *Music in a Breeze of Wind: Traditional Dance Music in West Clare 1870–1970*, which I borrowed from Martin Keane, for three years. This novel was written in Kiltumper in the company of the extraordinary music of The Gloaming.

Once again, I am enormously grateful to Caroline Michel, and all the team at Peters, Fraser & Dunlop. To Michael Fishwick and all at Bloomsbury in London, to Lea Beresford and all at Bloomsbury USA, my sincere thanks.

To Deirdre and Joseph, who continue to be the light in every day.

And lastly, to Christine Breen, the beginning and end of everything.

A Note on the Author

Niall Williams was born in Dublin in 1958. He is the author of the Man Booker-longlisted *History of the Rain* and eight other novels including *Four Letters of Love*, set to be a major motion picture. He lives in Kiltumper in County Clare, with his wife, Christine.

niallwilliams.com

A Note on the Type

The text of this book is set Adobe Garamond. It is one of several versions of Garamond based on the designs of Claude Garamond. It is thought that Garamond based his font on Bembo, cut in 1495 by Francesco Griffo in collaboration with the Italian printer Aldus Manutius. Garamond types were first used in books printed in Paris around 1532. Many of the present-day versions of this type are based on the *Typi Academiae* of Jean Jannon cut in Sedan in 1615.

Claude Garamond was born in Paris in 1480. He learned how to cut type from his father and by the age of fifteen he was able to fashion steel punches the size of a pica with great precision. At the age of sixty he was commissioned by King Francis I to design a Greek alphabet, and for this he was given the honourable title of royal type founder. He died in 1561.